CITY OF REFUGE

Also by Tom Piazza

Why New Orleans Matters

My Cold War

Blues and Trouble

Understanding Jazz

True Adventures with the King of Bluegrass

Blues Up and Down: Jazz in Our Time

The Guide to Classic Recorded Jazz

Setting the Tempo (editor)

CITY OF REFUGE

a novel

TOM PIAZZA

HARPER

An Imprint of HarperCollins*Publishers*

www.harpercollins.com

CITY OF REFUGE. Copyright © 2008 by Tom Piazza. All rights reserved. Printed in the United States of America. No part of this book may be used or reproduced in any manner whatsoever without written permission except in the case of brief quotations embodied in critical articles and reviews. For information, address HarperCollins Publishers, 10 East 53rd Street, New York, NY 10022.

HarperCollins books may be purchased for educational, business, or sales promotional use. For information, please write: Special Markets Department, HarperCollins Publishers, 10 East 53rd Street, New York, NY 10022.

Designed by William Ruoto

Library of Congress Cataloging-in-Publication Data

Piazza, Tom.
    City of refuge : a novel / Tom Piazza. — 1st ed.
     p. cm.
    ISBN: 978-0-06-123861-1
    1. Disaster victims—Fiction.   2. Hurricane Katrina, 2005—Social aspects—Fiction.   3. New Orleans (La.)—Fiction.   I. Title.

PS3566.I23C57   2008
813'.54—dc22   2008013673

08   09   10   11   12   ID/RRD   10   9   8   7   6   5   4   3

For Mary

With gratitude: Cal Morgan, Amy Williams, Mary Howell, and Lillian Piazza. For precious time and space: Yaddo, the MacDowell Colony, the Virginia Center for the Creative Arts, Jean Howell, David Mayberry, Leslie Gerber, and John and Carrie Brown. And in memory of Norman Mailer and Harold Cavallero.

"Can you live without the willow tree? Well, no, you can't. The willow tree is you. The pain on the mattress there—that dreadful pain—that's you."

—JOHN STEINBECK, *The Grapes of Wrath*

"Pilate saith unto him, What is truth?"

—JOHN 18:38

I

Parade coming. Could be any Sunday, just about, especially in the fall. People on the steps of shotgun houses, shoulder to shoulder on the sidewalk, watching everyone passing by, ice chest just inside the door full of beer and wine coolers and lemonade, people all out on the grassy neutral ground cooking up food—SJ, too, with his converted oil drum. That's their place, across from Shawnetta's house, where they stake out when they steak out. Hot dogs, too, for the kids, burgers.

Lucy up on the second step, drinking that wine cooler she likes, shaking her hips in time to the band in the distance, salt-and-pepper pincurls plastered flat to her forehead, waving to friends, high-spirited, "Hey baby." Shawnetta right up there next to her wearing her new lime-green matching top and bottom, shaking it in time.

"Hey SJ," Lucy shouts, loud and raucous, trying to get his attention, but he's across the street, across that river of shouting, talking humanity and of course he doesn't hear and she waves a couple of times and Bootsy sees her from his beach chair over in the little area they roped off and she's going to point to SJ when someone bumps into her and almost knocks her off her place and she says, "What the fuck you bumping into people?" and Shawnetta says something to her that makes her laugh and the anger is gone as quickly as it arose, and that was Lucy—mean and evil one moment, but then gone just as quick.

Always a few white folks mixed in, threading through, making their way along, old hippie-looking types with weathered faces, or youngsters wearing military fatigues and dreadlocks and what SJ calls a pocketful of metal in their face; they don't bother anybody and nobody bothers them. You wouldn't see many down where she and SJ live, on the other side of the other side of the tracks, unless they were driving down to Caffin Avenue to take a picture of Fats Domino's house.

Now along come something you don't see every day, a sweet-looking white boy in his late thirties probably, wearing nice-looking, respectful clothes, leading a little blond girl can't be more than seven by the hand. Pointing at things and bending down talking to her.

Lucy on the steps laughing at something and notices this nice white boy looking up at her, smiling, and the little girl, too. "Hey white folks," she hollers at them, raucous and unsmiling, holding up her bottle of wine cooler. The man laughs at this and says a hearty "Hi," and the little girl—listen at this—says plain as water, "Hey black folks!" with this big smile on her face. Lucy and Shawnetta, both startled, laugh and laugh at this, and Shawnetta says to the man "You need you something to drink? What about something for your girl?"

"Sure," the man says, and tells the girl to say thank you. Shawnetta opens the door and bends down to the cooler and Lucy tells her, "Give him a Crystal Mist. You ever had Crystal Mist, white folks?"

"Nope! But I'm looking forward to trying it . . ." Before he finishes his sentence Lucy has turned away and is telling Shawnetta to get the little girl one of the lemonades.

"You like lemonade, baby?" she says, bending down to the little girl, who looks back up right in Lucy's eyes and nods a big, exaggerated nod, and Lucy says, "Good. Everybody like lemonade." She opens one of the cans of lemonade and hands it down to the girl. Then Shawnetta passes her the bottle of Crystal Mist, which Lucy hands to the man, saying "Welcome to the ghetto!" He holds his bottle out to click, and Lucy does, then she notices the little girl doing the same thing and clicks

with the girl. The man takes a swig and raises his eyebrows and says, "Wow."

"Yeah, it's good, baby," Lucy says. "Y'all having a good time?"

"We always do."

"Good. Y'all be careful."

And the man takes the cue to head along, and the little girl says "Thank you" one more time but the nice woman's attention has already turned elsewhere, and the girl walks off with her father down Galvez Street through the crowd, to find Mommy at the corner of Canal and wait for the band to come.

1

Deep mid-August in the New Orleans heat. Not even much traffic a block away on North Claiborne, a Saturday afternoon, and the sound of SJ's hammer going in the stupefying thick air. SJ was almost finished framing the new shed he was building in his backyard. Wiring and Sheetrocking would be for after Labor Day. Way off in the distance, past the Industrial Canal and the reaches of the Upper Ninth Ward and the Bywater, the skyscrapers of downtown and the iridescent blister of the Superdome roof lay naked under the brilliant sun.

Out front, SJ's truck and his van sat in the curved cement driveway he had laid in front of his house (he had moved the structure back seven feet to make room for that driveway), with the magnetic sign on the door—New Breed Carpentry and Repair, and his phone number. It had been cheaper than getting it stenciled on the door itself, and it worked fine, he got calls off of it. He had, however, painted his own name in script on the front fender, the way the taxi drivers did, for an extra touch of distinction. Most of his work came from out in New Orleans East, a sprawling area of new houses and curving, landscaped streets in the subdivisions, reclaimed from swampland in the 1970s, where he could certainly have moved, if money were the only question and he had wanted to leave the Lower Ninth, which he didn't.

SJ's father had built his own house in a vacant lot on North Miro Street, five blocks away, when he came back from World War II, with two-by-fours and weatherboard and nails that he salvaged from all around and saved up by his mama's house. He pulled the nails out of scrap wood, carefully, or found them on the ground, and sometimes even straightened them if they could be straightened, one nail at a time. He kept them in what his mother called put-up jars, sorted roughly by size and thickness and purpose. SJ had kept that old house, although his father was dead and gone, and he rented it out to a widow lady. Sometimes when he wanted to get off by himself he would walk those five blocks to the old house and sit on the side steps and think.

He hammered some finishing nails into a line across the bottom of a small French cornice. He was trying something different with this shed, which he had seen in one of the books his daughter, Camille, sent him from North Carolina, something a little more decorative in a different way, not just utilitarian. His thin, ribbed undershirt, with thin straps over his shoulder, was soaked through with sweat, which glistened on his shaved head, shoulders and upper arms. Around his neck on a thin chain hung a St. Christopher medal. In his mid-fifties, SJ was still a powerful, compact man. He loved to build things, to work with his hands, and he loved to cook, especially outside, and he liked to read. After Rosetta, his wife, had died of an aortic aneurism six years earlier, he had read less and built more.

He would finish the line he was working on and then stop for the day and get some food going. He would go out to find Wesley later if he could; he had left his nephew to finish up a part of the job the day before and Wesley had left the tools sitting outside and SJ had come out in the morning to find them slick with overnight wet. He had wiped them down and put them in the oven to sweat them out, but he didn't understand that carelessness at all. His nephew was a smart young man, nineteen years old and teetering on the edge of something anyone in the Lower Nine knew all too well. Lately he had been riding around at night on these motorcycles where you had to hunch way over, weaving in and out of stopped traffic. Where he got the money for the bike SJ didn't know and Lucy, SJ's sister, would not say. At least, SJ thought, they had the bikes to work on. Working with your hands kept you focused on the real world. Still, you could hit a pothole on of those bikes and end up in a wheelchair for life.

Two weeks earlier the police arrested Wesley for beating on his girlfriend. SJ had drilled into his nephew many times the importance of surviving the encounter with police when you had one. Wesley had a quick mouth and a mannish attitude, but he had done allright, at least he hadn't gotten the police mad, and SJ got the call from the jail at 3:30 in the morning and SJ and Lucy had to go down and get him out on bond and later on SJ had demanded an accounting from his nephew.

"Uncle J she slap me and I didn't hit her. I'm not lying." They were sitting in SJ's living room, the sky just getting light outside. Wesley had on jeans with the crotch halfway down to his knees, and an oversize T-shirt hanging out, and he had taken off his Raiders cap at his uncle's request. His reddish skin seemed to be breaking out, and his hair was uneven and untended. "Then she slap me again and called me a pussy. What I'm supposed to do?"

"Walk out the room, nephew. You already paying for another man's baby. How she going to respect you? You need to find a woman who gonna watch your back and not put a knife in it. It doesn't matter how good that pussy is, you got to stay alive."

Wesley looked up at his uncle then, sly smile, the charming look, "It is good, Uncle J."

SJ allowed himself a small laugh. He knew as well as anyone. He remembered one of the old blues records his father liked to play, something about *"Some people say she's no good, but she's allright with me."*

"Well," SJ said, "don't be beating on no woman, nephew."

"But it's like you have to or her girlfriends be talking about how she play you."

"Why you care what they say?"

Wesley shook his head, looked at the floor. And anyway SJ knew the answer. You care because you are young, and that is your world, and most of your understanding of who you are comes from how other people act toward you. That is the whole thing until you get the ground under your own feet. Some of them found it in the military. Young men had to prove themselves. They could do it in healthy ways or unhealthy ways. The range of options had a lot to do with where you were born and what color your skin was. That was an old story.

SJ had gone through his own foolishness back in the day, the mid-seventies, after he came back from the army, drinking and gambling, rolling dice, which was what he had liked. Wearing the old Shaft pimp clothes for a while, and staying out and acting foolish and getting into arguments and coming home drunk—the street wasn't as bad then as it was today, but you could still get cut or shot very easily. And one day he awoke at noon, and Rosetta had packed two suitcases full of clothes and was dressed to leave. SJ jumped up and immediately started to fall over, dizzy from the night before, and he had to take a knee on the floor before he could get up and say, "What is this?"

Rosetta was calm as could be. She told him quietly that he worked very hard for his money and had a right to do with it as he pleased. She didn't want to stand in the way if this was how he wanted to spend his money and his life; he had worked very hard and she would not stand in his way; she loved him too much. She would always love him and wish him the best . . . and she was zipping up one of the suitcases as she said this, and each profession of love felt like a slap in the face and made a panic rise in him.

If she had told him to stop what he was doing he could have started hollering about how it was his money and he would do what the goddamn hell he pleased with it, but she had covered all that before he said a word and now there was nothing to holler about, nothing to grab on to. Half an hour later he was promising that he would not gamble a dime again and drink neither, and he had kept those promises. Well, in fact he liked to taste a beer every now and again on a hot day, during a cookout or a second line, or on a rare occasion after a workday, especially if he had company working. But not two beers, not ever.

He was no choir boy, though. SJ knew how to take care of himself, and how to take care of his family, and one needed to know that. He didn't make a show of it or act tough. When he went out he carried his father's old straight razor in his right sock, and a derringer in his pocket. There was a saying: "Lower Nine, don't mind dyin' . . ." But SJ did mind dying, or at least dying over nothing. If it came down to it he would rather see the other fellow die. Yes he would.

Around front, SJ set his carpenter's apron down in the bed of his pickup and went into his van to straighten some things he had left in disarray earlier. The inside of the van was a portable workshop, and SJ always had his tools in order before he ate dinner, unless he was going to work later on in the night. He still kept his nails sorted in jars, the way his father had. He loved this time of day in the summer, six-thirty or so, when in some other time of the year it would be dark already, people walking and bicycling by. The heat didn't bother him. Across the way Bootsy and his wife and sister-in-law always sitting out in front talking and laughing, and the sweet-olive tree by Mrs. Gray's fence next door throwing off all that scent. A woman named Sylvia who lived two blocks down toward the canal passed by, wearing a dark green crotcheted hat and pushing a grocery cart, and said, "Allright," with that slow New Orleans drawl, and SJ looked over at her and smiled and said, "Allright. Joe finish that siding?"

"He'll get it."

"I know that's right." Finished with the van, he went around to put some of his materials inside the steel lockbox that sat behind the cab of his pickup and lock it down. A young man with a long T-shirt and dreadlocks walked by, throwing a gum wrapper on the ground, and smiled at SJ and said, "Allriiight." SJ nodded briefly back at him and said, "Allright" in a short rhythm, without being rude but without any invitation to more closeness. The speech patterns in certain New Orleans neighborhoods approach the complexity of Chinese in the shades of meaning that can be extracted from the tiniest gradations of inflection and timing. Sometimes these gradations can mean the difference between life and death. SJ recognized this young man as one of the group that Wesley had been spending too much time around, and SJ's "Allright" conveyed: "I see you, I recognize you, I have no reason to be rude to you or more than basically polite, either; I am secure where I am, and I will be watching you as you continue down the street," which SJ did.

He loved living in the Lower Ninth Ward. Its rhythm was his rhythm, despite the danger, the violence. It was their place; it belonged to the people in the Ninth Ward and they knew it and they managed as they could, and they were proud to have made lives there. No one had ever promised them, of all people, that life was going to be easy or without daily struggle, and there, at least, they took pride that it was their own struggle. And, unlike in some other parts of town, there weren't a lot of people from outside coming through to bother them. SJ had built part of it, just like his father and grandfather, and it had made him who and what he was, and it had made his parents and almost everyone he knew.

People elsewhere didn't understand it. He had family in Texas, just outside Houston, whom he liked visiting; they lived in a subdivision where only half the lots had been developed, and the lawns were struggling where they even existed, but each house had some land around it, even beyond the large yard, and his cousin Aaron was able to keep goats and chickens and they had a horse to ride, too. They always barbecued outside when SJ visited, sitting around in the dusty evening, often with Mexican accordion music floating across from a few houses away. Nobody bothered anybody.

"Look here," Aaron would say to SJ, "why you want to go back up in there and worry about you gonna get shot some night?"

"Why am I going to get shot?" SJ replied, sipping at his one beer and enjoying the breeze on his face.

"They don't have to even mean to shoot you," Aaron's wife, Dot, said.

"They don't have to mean it," Aaron repeated. "That's right. Get hit with a stray shot. You move out here get you two or three acres, ain't nobody bother you. Get that boy out of that bad, too."

Wesley was their best argument, SJ knew, no doubt. But it wasn't just Wesley; it wasn't that simple. He would have to move Lucy, too, and then what would happen with Daddy's house, and Lucy's house, and his own house—the shelves and the cabinets and wainscoting and molding and trim, the wide pine floors? And the workshop out back that he had worked on for two years, all the wiring he had laid in . . . People who didn't build things themselves thought everything was interchangeable. But you didn't just get up and leave the place you had fought to build.

"It's not the same thing," SJ said.

"Why it's not?"

"If they told you you could live in China and have a big house and a big yard and pay less money, would you do it?"

"They got plasma TV?"

They laughed about it, but that was more or less the signal to drop the subject until the next visit, and their talk turned to the

NCAA finals. Aaron's own son went to Grambling and had been to New Orleans twice for the Bayou Classic, and the stories that got back to Aaron had confirmed his sense of New Orleans as a place for freaks, period.

Finished outside, now, SJ locked up the truck and the van and walked up the three steps into his wood-frame house, a shotgun double that he had altered into a single-family arrangement. The rooms were small and the ceilings low, but everything had been done well, not like some of the cheap work he had seen out in the East, or the careless renovations he saw Uptown, where the landlords milked all that Tulane student rent money out of their decaying housing stock. Six years ago, after Rosetta died, he had put a camelback upstairs on it—two rooms you reached by a stair that went up from the side of the living room, and he slept in the left-hand one. You didn't have to worry about building variances so much in the Lower Nine since they weren't too serious about checking, and even if they did it was an inexpensive proposition to cut through any red tape—and it was a roomy, good house. Often Lucy stayed over in Camille's old bedroom, downstairs on the left side. It was just as Camille had left it; she had stayed there on visits home from NC State.

He walked inside, ready for a shower, and in the living room he found Lucy, sitting on the couch, asleep. His older sister, Lucy, with her head down, chin on her collarbone, snoring, her black T-shirt riding up on her stomach and her pants unbuttoned, and they had slid open enough so that over her drawers he could see the top of the scar from the Charity Hospital C-section that had brought Wesley into the world. Her pincurls were plastered down on her forehead and the sides of her head like the swirls in a rum cake. Her skin was dark and dry and in places almost blue-black, the color of gun metal. She had diabetes she didn't take care of, and she had heart trouble and she drank too much and she had been an on-again, off-again user of combustible cocaine products. And in fact the nice white social worker lady had questioned in strong terms whether Wesley might not be better off placed in foster care, but the fact was, above all else, that Lucy truly loved Wesley and the boy knew it and it was the closest, most stable relationship in his life. SJ loved Lucy, too; almost everybody did. She could get drunk and act foolish, but it came out of a generosity of spirit.

SJ took a long look at her, sleeping there, her head resting against her collarbone. Then he bent down and touched her gently and said, "Wake up. Wake up, sister. Let's eat something."

2

Craig Donaldson finished a cup of lemon ice, which he had carried across Carrollton Avenue from Brocato's to the *Gumbo* offices in the midday heat, and he was just about to call the music editor to check some last-minute changes when his cell phone rang. He pulled it out of his pocket, checked the number first—it was Alice—and flipped it open, saying "yeah" in his cut-through-the-preliminaries voice. An intern passed and looked at him questioningly; Craig held up one finger and turned slightly away.

Alice was upset, and it took a moment for her to quiet down; when she did it turned out that their daughter Annie had gotten called into the principal's office, in this first week of school, for using a bad word.

"Craig, is it too much to ask that my seven-year-old daughter grow up without calling people 'motherfuckers' and dancing like a hooker?"

"Alice," Craig began, trying to suppress the adrenaline rush of annoyance he invariably experienced when he heard this sound in Alice's voice, "*our* daughter is not 'growing up calling people "motherfuckers."'" She picked up something bad and we'll talk to her and explain to her why it's bad. This isn't the end of the world. We can deal with this. Where are you now?"

"I'm at Boucher, sitting on a bench."

"Do you need me to come there?"

Pause. "No." Then, "Craig, I need you to take this situation seriously and not just blow it off . . ."

"I'm not blowing it off. I'm just saying that I don't think this is some insurmountable thing. This is what parents deal with . . ."

"Oh . . . right . . ."

Breathing through his nose, he went on, ". . . and also we're closing the issue and I'm about to go into a meeting so I'm a little stressed. If you need me to come there, I will. If you don't need me there I'll talk to Annie when I get home, and our daughter, who is very smart and a good person, will understand. And I—we—will talk to her for as long as it takes for her to understand."

"Fine," Alice said, and the connection ended.

Craig flipped his phone shut, stepped into his office, closed the door and sat down at his desk to let his heart slow a little. The cell phone rang again almost immediately. This was a pattern; without looking, he flipped it open and said, "Alice . . ."

"Don't forget to pick up the cake at Gambino's."

Craig searched his memory . . .

"For Malcolm's party tomorrow . . . ?" Alice said.

Right, Craig thought. Of course. "I'm on it. Thanks for the reminder."

"You're welcome," she said. She was quiet for a moment. "I love you."

"I love you, too."

After he closed the phone he felt an immediate easing of his heart rate. He hated arguing with Alice. Even before they had to deal with the "Is-New-Orleans-The-Best-Place-To-Raise-Our-Children?" argument—for that matter even before they moved to New Orleans from Ann Arbor and had nothing worse to worry about than what kind of olive oil to buy at Zingerman's—when they differed on certain issues they became not just strangers but enemies. For the duration of the argument, she hated him in an impersonal way, as if he represented all the forces of entropy in the world. And he knew to his shame that for those minutes when they were in the middle of it and couldn't find their way out, he hated her, too. And he hated hating her. The couples therapist had helped some. They probably owed her a debt for that final "I love you," for example.

It was strange to him that the things she seemed to get such a kick out of when they were still in graduate school in Michigan—his enthusiasm for New Orleans music, his acquaintance with all the secret handshakes and lore and iconography of the city's labyrinthine culture, gained during his many visits, and the way that on their trips there he could lead her through what seemed a glorious and dangerous underworld full of music and food and sex—became the things about him that seemed most threatening to her and, of course, to their children.

His office was a shrine to all that lore and iconography. Behind his desk chair hung a framed 8-x-10 photo of Fats Domino, signed to Craig by the Fat Man himself. The walls were festooned with ancient album covers, photos, posters for club appearances by New Orleans rhythm and blues legends, an old 78 record on the King Zulu label, menus from favorite neighborhood restaurants, the jacket of a 10-inch Woody Guthrie LP on Folkways, which was a souvenir of his old folky days in Ann Arbor, and a photo of Craig with the pianist and singer Dr. John, taken backstage at the New Orleans Jazz and Heritage Festival the year after they moved to town. Nobody had ever had more of a crush on New Orleans than Craig Donaldson, and in these last years he had lived it out to the hilt. As the editor of *Gumbo*, he knew everything that was going on in the city; he was invited to everything and he knew everybody. The only problem was that Alice didn't like it there anymore.

Partly it had to do with her difficulty in finding her own identity in the city. It was, after all, Craig's place; it had been his before they moved there, and ever since he had bounced from doing little music reviews for magazines and occasional stringer work for the Associated Press to being the editor of *Gumbo*, she had come to feel, on bad days, like a caboose on his train. She missed painting and teaching, although she and Craig had agreed that she would spend these years as a full-time mother. But partly, Craig realized with increasing gloom, her restlessness had to do with facts about the city with which it was difficult to argue. Friends had been robbed at knifepoint; others had had their houses burglarized or cars stolen or vandalized; there was fear involved in walking the streets at night even in their quiet neighborhood, the public schools were overwhelmingly lousy, the infrastructure was decaying . . . The things that in some lights contributed to the city's charm of Otherness had changed their nature, for Alice at least, when at some unremarked-upon but irreversible point they had stopped being Other. Craig had come as close to going native as an outsider could get in nine years of living there, or so he thought. Alice, on the other hand, clung to her Otherness as if her life depended on it.

Craig's desk phone rang; it was Scott, who was putting together the literary supplement. Shyla Bruno was doing a review of Philip Roth's newest book, and Craig said, "You going with 'Goodbye, Portnoy' for the head?"

"No—listen to this—Allen came up with 'The Gripes of Roth.'"

Craig waited a moment and then issued one of his patented, arch, stagey chuckles. "Bingo," he said.

"You want to go with that?"

"We're there."

That evening Craig pulled their 1999 Toyota up in front of their house on Cypress Street under the big oak tree Craig loved. Their house was nestled in a small neighborhood tucked between Carrollton Avenue and Broadway all the way uptown, just past the Tulane campus and Audubon Park, the opposite end of the city from the French Quarter, a leafy suburb where the old families used to go in the summer to escape the heat and pestilence of downtown.

Their block was shaded by ancient oak trees whose roots buckled the sidewalks in front of charming, unassuming houses occupied by a mix of working people, lawyers, musicians, and teachers. Largely because of Boucher School, one of the few really good public schools in the city, the area was popular with families, black and white, generally upper middle class, who stayed involved in the school. Maple Street, with its shops and its bookstore and its little restaurants and shoe repair and dry cleaners, was five blocks away, an easy walk on a nice day. Oak Street, more rough and tumble but with the same mix of services uptown of Carrollton, would take you out to the Mississippi River levee over the railroad tracks, and along the River Road into Jefferson Parish toward the far reaches of Airline Highway and Jefferson Highway, with their seedy hotels and flea markets.

Craig pulled the round, heavy, caramel-iced doberge cake for Malcolm out of the backseat and brought it surreptitiously to their next-door neighbors' for safe keeping until Malcolm's birthday party the next night. When Craig arrived home Alice was preparing dinner, Malcolm was in his booster chair, squirming, and Annie was playing by herself in the dining room. He experienced the small but distinct sense of vertigo that would occasionally visit him on viewing the Evening Tableau as he walked in, the feeling that he had stepped into a television show written by someone else after being awakened from a deep sleep and with no time for rehearsal. The feeling always burned off quickly, especially when he got to spend time alone with Annie. Alice turned to face Craig as he approached to give her a hug. He said, "I'm sorry for earlier."

Her mouth tightened involuntarily for a second, then her expression eased and she said, "Me too."

Relieved, Craig said, "I'll go talk to Annie." Alice nodded and turned back to the stove.

For Craig, his daughter was everything good in the world, a summary of all tenderness and vulnerability. Malcolm was an alien to him much of the time, a small organic robot of pure animus that could have come from Alpha Centauri for all Craig saw himself in him. But in Annie he saw his own self as a child—lonely, creative, his parents headed for divorce. She was interested in things, and she loved New Orleans. He took her out to parades way back in the neighborhoods; he wanted her to feel comfortable around all kinds of people, in all kinds of environments. He wanted her to grow up loving life, and especially this city, to embrace, and not fear, its peculiar riches.

And yet he saw a sadness in her that seemed somehow to have been passed down genetically, a melancholy as characteristic of him as his hair color or his chin, a kind of habitual mourning that the world could never live up to its best moments. And yet also such a willingness to meet the world halfway, such ability to pass the time with deep concentration, those dark rings under her eyes, which broke his heart. Fragile, almost translucent skin—she had been slightly premature. On the rare occasions when she needed to be reprimanded she would be hurt for days if she thought the scolding unjust. Alice tended to be short with her, and impatient, and Craig was Mr. Fun, or he tried to be. Sometimes it seemed to Craig that Annie was a prisoner in childhood, serving out her sentence as patiently as she could, but her incarceration would scar her for life. In any case he approached the prospect of disciplining her carefully, trying not to track the mud of any other set of issues into the conversation. He especially did not want to hand down to Annie the legacy of a broken home life.

Craig went to where she was making something with construction paper at the dining room table. Her involvement was absolute. "Hey," he said, "what's that?"

"It's houses," she said; she didn't look up.

"Hey, Annie. You know I love you, right?" She nodded, without looking up. "You know Mommy loves you, right?" After a moment, another nod, slighter. "Do you want to tell me what happened?" Annie shook her head no. "Annie—look at me." Annie looked up at her father and her eyes, large under normal circumstances, were slightly magnified by a film of tears. "This is going to be fine. It is fine. We love you and we know you are a good girl and I want to talk to you so that you know why this happened."

The phone had been ringing and now Alice poked her head around the corner, and said, "It's Bobby."

"I'll call him back," Craig said, without taking his eyes off of Annie.

"Annie," Alice said, "let's clean up; we need to get the table cleared off so we can set it for dinner."

"It's a real bad word," Craig said. "You don't want to be saying things like that. And just because someone else says it doesn't mean it's okay. But you know that, right?"

"I know." She had started scooping her paper and scissors and tape and crayons off the table, everything together like a greedy poker player raking in her chips, into her plastic box.

"Give me a hug."

After a moment's delay she turned and ferociously hugged Craig around the neck. Then she let go and put the lid on her box and carried it to the corner of the living room where it belonged.

In bed later, in her long cotton nightgown, Alice read through her catalogs. J.Crew, The Territory Ahead, Crate & Barrel, L.L.Bean, Winter Silks, J.Jill, Williams-Sonoma. It was Alice's habit to read before they went to sleep—she couldn't calm down otherwise, she said—and it had been a speed bump in their intimate life for years.

Craig had given up arguing about it. Once he had shown her an article in one of her own women's magazines that named reading in bed one of the top-five "stoppers" to a healthy sex life. All it did was get her mad.

Now, in bed, Craig watched a Seinfeld rerun, wondering how he could get Alice's attention without starting a fight. She pored over the catalogs as if each page contained potentially crucial information about their future, occasionally dog-earing a page. Catalogs with dog-eared pages, which were about half of them, went onto a small mountain of catalogs next to her side of the bed, never to be looked at again. She looked lovely to Craig, in a virginal, Midwestern kind of way, in her nightgown with its modest neckline and her light brown hair with blond highlights (she must have just gotten those done this week) cut jawline-length, and she wore reading glasses that, he always thought, gave her a slightly severe, sexy-librarian look.

He repositioned himself so that he was hiding behind the catalog, down by her knees, and he reached up with one finger and pulled the top of the catalog back toward him enough to see her eyes shift from the page to his eyes. They were poised, noncommittally, between amusement and annoyance for a pivoting moment, and Craig said, "Hey there," archly—the wrong approach.

"Hey there," Alice said, flatly, flipping the catalog back up into position.

Craig reached up again with his finger, this time sliding it under the catalog and pulling it up so that he could peek at her from underneath.

"Craig," she said, angrily, slapping the catalog down a little harder than she had intended to. She thought of how she wanted to be approached by him—straightforwardly, without all these passive-aggressive games. "If you want something why can't you just ask for it?"

"Maybe I don't want to have to 'ask' my wife if she'll make love to me," Craig shot back, without losing a moment. "Maybe I don't want to have to climb over a fucking catalog to make her notice me."

Alice was quiet for a moment because she was so angry she didn't know what to do or say.

"I mean," Craig went on, knowing that he should drop it right there, "just write me a script if there is a way I have to say it."

"I don't want to have to write you a script," she spat.

"No, you just want me to say what you want me to say in the way you want me to say it, without having to tell me."

"No—I want you to act like a man instead of like a little boy who doesn't know how to get what he wants."

"Fine. Maybe I can order 'what I want' from a catalog." Lame, he thought, but . . . whatever. He turned toward the TV. As Craig did this, Alice let her catalog fall forward onto her lap and stared straight ahead for a moment, a sign to Craig that she might be getting ready to get out of bed and go downstairs to read and maybe even sleep on the couch. And since being left alone in bed would be intolerable to him, he preemptively got up himself, put on his slippers and walked around the bed to the door. He would go to his study for half an hour or so. As he passed he saw out of the corner of his eye that she was still staring straight ahead. He walked out of the room.

Twenty minutes later he opened the door to their dark bedroom; the lights were off, the TV off. He padded quietly around the bed to his side, took off his slippers and slid under the covers next to Alice. She had been asleep, but she stirred slightly as he got into bed. She lay there with her eyes closed, and Craig tried to think whether to say anything or just to go to sleep.

"Are you okay," she said, half-asleep, eyes still closed.

Craig, suddenly grateful beyond measure for the overture, the excuse to drop the guns and swords, said, "Yeah." Then, not wanting it to sound curt, wanting to keep the door open, he added, "I'm really sorry."

"I hate fighting," she said. She shifted again.

"I do, too," he said, and he found that hot tears were coming out of his eyes. When he sniffed reflexively, Alice heard it and reached up to touch his face, felt the wetness, wiped it away, said, "Oh . . ." and brought his face down to kiss her. Craig slid his hand along her warm waist and felt Alice's hand go up behind his head, and they drew closer together, embracing and kissing, and for the first time in two months, or was it three?, he pulled the bottom of her night-gown up and touched her with his middle three fingers and heard her familiar soft groan, and they made love quickly and quietly, and afterward as Craig lay on top of Alice, spent and satisfied, swimming in a warm salt lake in the dark, floating, Alice looked up at the ceiling and cried tears of her own, silently. When Craig noticed them and asked, alarmed, what was wrong, she shook her head and said, "I'm just tired and this was a hard day." She patted him on the back. "That was nice, making love," she lied. They kissed a little more, then she got up and went into the bathroom to wash; Craig rolled to his side and went to sleep, and Alice came back to bed and quietly turned on her reading light.

3

Every year as August wanes and the new school year looms, New Orleans can expect to see at least one or two storms. They are as much a part of the calendar as Thanksgiving or Easter. Many people who can leave town do so, driving to Baton Rouge, or Lafayette, or Jackson, or Houston, just in case the weather does enough damage to pull down the electrical grid for a couple of days. Many others choose to stay.

The Winn-Dixie on Tchoupitoulas Street and the Sav-A-Center on Carrollton and the old Schwegmann's on Elysian Fields, all the Walgreens and the Rite-Aids and the little corner stores everywhere sell out of gallon jugs of water, and three-gallon jugs of water, and twenty-four-packs of half-liter bottles, and they sell out of flashlights and candles and batteries of all sizes for the flashlights and the radios. If it looks really bad, the Home Depot and Lowe's and every small lumber yard and hardware store will sell out of plywood for covering windows, and during the day before landfall you will hear hammers going in neighborhoods that are to some degree quieter than usual because half the people have gone.

Friends call friends to see if they are staying in town. The old-timers miss Nash Roberts, the fatherly WWL weatherman who always seemed to have a better sense of a storm's direction than the slick new weathermen with their computers. People know, in principle, what is possible with a hurricane—the flooding, the tidal surge, the wind damage, the power failures. But they had lived through Betsy, or they had stayed by their cousin for Camille, or Ivan, or Georges, and they had come through allright. Maybe they had to replace a window, or some roof shingles, or they sat with no electricity for a couple days, cooked with sterno and ate by candlelight and had block parties on the street with the beers they had stockpiled in their coolers. New Orleanians knew how to turn deprivation into an asset; they had the best gallows humor going, they danced at funerals, they insisted on prevailing. They had heard it all before, and most of the time it turned out to be a false alarm. The regular challenge made them defiant. Especially in the working-class neighborhoods. The poorer the neighborhood and the harder people had to fight to stand their ground through the years, the less likely they were to jump ship and head for higher ground, even if they had the means to do so.

Evacuating was expensive. It cost money for gas, money for hotel rooms. Those who had family had a leg up, but if you didn't have the cousin in Baton Rouge or Brookhaven or McComb or Holly Springs, it was a hotel, and it was expensive, not just the hotel but eating out every meal. And lucky to find a room, because everybody else was trying to squeeze into the same hotels. The traffic was horrible. If you had children, or aged parents, preparing them for the several-days' trip under unpleasant circumstances was no fun, especially when it was a false alarm time and again. What if you run out of Pampers? What if you run out of Depends? What if Mama Stel goes to the bathroom in the backseat again while you're stuck in traffic on I-10 for eight hours? And what about the pets? You just going to leave them leashed in the backyard to fend for themselves? You have to bring the pets. Never had a carrier for them, and the hotels don't want a bunch of dogs barking and cats peeing in their rooms. Then you get wherever you're going, and after a day or two when the storm passes you have to pack everybody up again and make the drive back, sitting in traffic. Maybe you had to miss a couple days' work, besides, and your boss doesn't like that and hires someone who doesn't leave town every time the wind blows. Wasn't a mandatory evacuation.

That's if you have a car in the first place. If you depend on the bus, which is most of working-class New Orleans, then it isn't even a question, unless maybe your nephew comes by, or your daughter, and insists on taking you out of town in his or her car. A way of dealing with it, an attitude, begins to set after a while. You don't really want to be the only family in your neighborhood evacuating all the time; that smells funny. Especially if it's a neighborhood where people watch and notice things and wait for a house to be vacant for a couple of days, a house with a nice TV or sound system, since generally the people who have the money to leave have the money for things that might be valuable at resale. So you stay and stick it out, and then you tell stories about it, and that becomes part of the texture of life, too. Someone with no stories to share is suspect. You prepare as well as you can, and you ride it out.

In neighborhoods where people expect to be comfortable all the time, where they are used to having services and attention, the prospect of being without those services and that comfort and attention, without electricity and a steady flow of electronic information, without refrigeration and air-conditioning, is not a badge of honor. The badge of honor is being able to ride above the discomfort, arranging things so that you and your family are not sweating it out in the grease pit with everyone else. Who can blame them? If you could get out of 100-degree heat and spoiled food and no lights for a few days, why not? The boss usually understands; hell, the boss has left town himself, and shut the business down prudently. The question is not usually whether to evacuate, but where.

Storms are a regular feature of late summer and fall, but they have to compete for attention with all the other regular features—

the children starting school and needing help with their homework, the social aid and pleasure clubs planning their annual fall parades (getting outfits made, hiring cars and bands, arranging for police permits), the uptown Mardi Gras Krewes starting to plan their winter balls and debutante events, the Mardi Gras Indians resuming Sunday night practice at neighborhood bars all over the city.

Other modern American cities have their holidays, their First Night celebrations and film festivals, but they are contained, and discrete. They happen, then they are over. In New Orleans, on the other hand, geography and time, food, music, holidays, modes of dress and ways of speaking, are part of an integrated fabric. People dress in certain ways for certain events, and certain foods are eaten on certain days, and neighborhood is connected to neighborhood by parades that traverse the length and breadth of the city, accompanied by music that everyone knows and, in most cases, dances to. On Labor Day the Black Men of Labor will start their parade at Sweet Lorraine's on St. Claude Avenue and wind their way, dancing, through the streets, with their patterned umbrellas, followed and surrounded by hundreds of people from all over town. On Sunday Miss Johnson and her mother are dressing in white for services at the AME Zion church, and Lionel Batiste will go to Indian practice (on Mardi Gras his suit will be purple and this week he is sewing a beaded patch that Little Boo, who lost a leg in Vietnam, drew for him—an eagle with a rabbit in its claws), and Bill and Ellen are going to the Cajun dance at Tipitina's up on Napoleon and Tchoupitoulas, and the Scene Boosters are having their parade, and that's how you know it's Sunday. Monday is red beans and rice, at home or at some neighborhood restaurant—the Camellia Grill or Mandina's or Family Tree or Dunbar's or Liuzza's, maybe with smoked sausage on the side. On Thursday you go to zydeco night at Rock 'N Bowl, or Kermit Ruffins at Vaughan's or Ellis Marsalis at Snug Harbor. Friday night is an end-of-the-week drink with friends at the

Napoleon House or Junior's or the Saturn Bar or Madigan's or Finn McCool's, and Saturday night is Saturday night all over the world. And if it's any other night you could go to Brigtsen's or Herbsaint if you have the money, or Upperline or Clancy's or the St. Charles Tavern, or the Acme Oyster House or Henry's Soul Spot or Crescent City Steaks or Frankie & Johnny's or Casamento's or Pascal's Manale, and you know that street, or you don't know the street but it has a smell and a rhythm and a personality, and getting there is part of the experience, and you form a map in your heart of all the places that make you so happy, and there are always other people there being happy, too. No matter what you may be dealing with in life, you can still enjoy a bowl of gumbo or some shrimp creole, can't you? Of course you can.

And Bobby stay by his mama house on Soniat Street down the other side of Magazine and we live up Back O'Town Gert Town Pigeon Town and every Sunday we go by Chantrell house after church and did you remember to pick up the chicken at Popeye's? And Father purchased that house on State Street from Grandfather for one dollar; he attended Tulane, as did the three generations before him. Or he went to LSU, or Loyola, or Xavier, Jesuit or Newman or Holy Cross or Ben Franklin or St. Aug or Warren Easton, and he worked for Hibernia Bank or the Sewerage and Water Board, or Fidelity Homestead or the Post Office or Avondale or he washed dishes at some joint in the Quarter.

And when Brother Joe or Ray or Cool Pop goes on to glory we can carry him through those same streets where he rambled and rolled, and we can have a little taste in his honor, as he so often did in others' honor. And the band will play "Old Rugged Cross," and everyone will follow the pallbearers as they carry the casket along that pavement one halting step at a time, slowly at first, guided by the bass drum, with the trumpets wailing out the melody and the clarinets answering in liquid streamers of descant, and then, at the signal, the drum tattoo and, like Christmas-tree lights switched on, the mourners jump and the street explodes in sliding, turning, prancing, strutting steps, men and women alone or in fleeting partnership, and maybe you are there with a bandanna wrapped around your head as you pull up the cuffs of your pants to execute a particularly intricate set of crisscross steps up on the sidewalk, up on the porch, up on the light pole, up on the car, and that song and that sound and that rhythm seeps into everyone's knowledge of that street, and those houses, and of life and death and space and time itself.

And in September it's school and in October it's the Jolly Bunch anniversary and November it's Thanksgiving and the Fairgrounds open and December it's Christmas and January it's getting ready for Mardi Gras and February it's parades and Mardi Gras, and in March you catch your breath, and then it's St. Joseph's Day and then Jazz Fest and then school-letting-out time and then it is the hot months and things get slower and thicker and oppressively hot, and usually in August or September you will have to deal with one or two storms.

Nobody in the Williams family had ever evacuated for a hurricane.

On Thursday evening Lucy leaned against the kitchen counter at SJ's house, a half-finished can of cold Colt 45 in her hand, regarding the weatherman on the TV with antagonism. Across the room, SJ shook cornmeal from a bag onto three folded paper towels; on the stove oil was heating in a skillet, and in the sink a one-pound plastic bag of chicken tenders slumped against itself. Between the two windows over the sink hung a small crucifix, supporting a dry and faded bow of palm frond still left up from Palm Sunday.

"That motherfucker better stay in Florida," Lucy said, draining the can. "I'm supposed to start working over at the Hair Stop." She set the can down on the counter. "Jaynell tell me I can help her with the braiding."

"When she told you that?" SJ said. "You didn't tell me."

"Last week. She called and asked could I come and help her out."

"Is she still doing the dinners?"

"Yeah, but that don't pay nothing."

Lucy, like many others, pieced together a living for herself by keeping expenses low and weaving thin filaments of income into a web that could support her even when one or two of those filaments dropped out. On the first of each month she got a regular disability check from Social Security. She had worked for her friend Jaynell when Jaynell was serving plate suppers at her shotgun on Dorgenois, and she worked washing and folding at the Spin-N-Clean on Law Street, and she had worked in the booth at the parking lot all the way on Elysian Fields by the river until they put her on overnight the same week one of the other cashiers got held up twice. She waited tables for a year at the Coffee Pot in the French Quarter, and she had been a chambermaid at the Maison de Ville but had gotten fired for drinking on the job, just one little beer. She didn't have to pay rent because they owned the house, and her income was too low for taxes and Medicaid paid for the medications that SJ insisted she get and which she never took.

She walked to the refrigerator to get another beer, stopping to look at the photos attached to the door with magnets. Two different studio portraits of her niece Camille in graduation robes—one from high school and one from North Carolina State. Camille's senior prom picture with the corsage on her wrist next to that boy who got killed; one of Wesley from three or four years earlier in a football uniform, kneeling on one knee and holding a football upright on the other, looking proudly at the camera; a sepia-toned photo of their father in his World War II uniform, which they had had copied from the curled, brittle original they found in a box in the old house after he had died; a color snapshot from the early 1980s of their father and mother together at the anniversary party they had at the catering hall on Franklin Street; and a square black-and-white photo of SJ and Lucy standing shoulder to shoulder, they must have been maybe seven and eight, in front of the old house on Lizardi Street— SJ frowning, squinting, into the sun, and Lucy with a giant grin on her face, wearing a little blouse with a big tulip their mama had sewed onto the front. Lucy opened the refrigerator door and pulled out another Colt 45.

"Camille look so pretty in that picture," she said, opening the can. "Samuel, why you don't find a woman? You need you a woman's touch. Put some flowers around."

"Feel free, sister," SJ said, rinsing the raw strips of chicken under the tap. "Anytime you want to bring some flowers is allright." He flicked a small wad of the cornmeal into the oil to see if it was hot enough yet.

"You know what I'm saying, Samuel," she said, watching the weatherman with his bad toupee gesturing at a swirl of clouds on the radar screen. "They need Nash Roberts back on," she said. "Where he went?"

"I imagine he retired." SJ stopped what he was doing at the sink and walked over, drying his hands on a dish towel, to watch the weatherman with Lucy. Footage from Florida—trees down, a million people without power. "They saying it's headed to the Gulf?"

Lucy grunted, and SJ watched the images carefully. When the commercial came on he went back to making dinner and said, "Have you talked with Wesley?"

"I haven't seen him for two days. When y'all had that fight?"

"That was Monday."

"Well however many days that was."

That previous Monday night Wesley had shown up for dinner after disappearing for two days—he knew he had left his uncle's tools sitting out and that SJ would be angry. SJ and Lucy were in the kitchen just as they were now; the sound of footsteps had come from the front of the house, and then Wesley walked into the room, wearing blue cut-off sweatpants, high-top sneakers, an oversized white T-shirt hanging down to his thighs and a baseball cap, backward.

Lucy set her beer down on the counter without letting go of it and put out her free arm for him. "Baby boy," she said, with a slight mock grandeur that meant she was on her way to getting drunk.

"Where Luther at?" Wesley said, walking to his mother and hugging her briefly. He looked around the kitchen, restless, looked at the TV for a moment, went to the bowl of grapes on the counter.

"He in Boutte," Lucy said. "You forgotten about that?"

"Take your hat off," SJ said.

Wesley took off the cap, ran his hand through his chaotic hair quickly and said, "Sorry Unca J," shot a mischievous smile at his mother, who gave him a little smile back, and pulled some grapes off their stems to eat. "You still mad at me about the tools Unca J?"

SJ took a moment to breathe evenly before saying, "What do you think?"

"I think Unca J mad at me about the tools." Wesley ate another handful of grapes.

"Then why do you need me to tell you something you already know?"

"I meant to put them away, Unca J. I finished the cornice and I saw what time it was and I had to go. I was going to come back later."

"Sister," SJ said, "can you get the dishes out the icebox."

Lucy retrieved two plastic bowls, one with chopped onions and one with chopped bell peppers, and set them on the counter where SJ had arranged several large cloves of garlic.

"You like that bike you've been riding?" SJ said.

"Unca J, I didn't . . ."

"Be quiet. If you loaned me that bike to go get you something at the store and I went and got it for you and then left the keys in the bike sitting out at the curb, how that make you feel?"

Wesley looked down at the floor; Lucy watched the baseball game on the television.

"How that make you feel?"

Wesley looked up at his uncle, then looked away, frustrated and angry that he was being backed into a corner.

"How many times I'm going to have to ask you this question?"

"It was a hammer and an apron and some nails. How much that can cost?"

"Two hammers and a wedge, but it's not about that. It's about are you paying attention to what you doing. And I didn't hear nobody say 'I'm sorry.' I heard 'I meant to do this' and 'I meant to do that.'"

Wesley turned and walked out of the kitchen and had not been back since.

Now, on Thursday evening, SJ and Lucy brought their plates into the dining room to a big cypress table their grandfather had made that could seat ten people if it had to, and they joined hands as they always did, and bowed their heads, and SJ said, "Father, we thank you for the food you place on our table, and for us being here together. We pray that you keep us and those we love safe from harm and hunger. And we want to pray for Wesley, too, that he will come back unharmed and that we will be a whole family again. Amen."

Lucy said "Amen" along with SJ as she reached for the sweet potatoes. "You kept that short, SJ," Lucy said. "Daddy say thank you for so many things by the time he finished the food be cold."

They sat silently, eating. SJ loved his house, with its waist-high wainscoting in the dining room, rescued from the old Tranchina's

Restaurant he and his daddy had demolished. The wide plank floors
in the living room were varnished seat planks from high school
bleachers from the West Bank. SJ had done all the work himself,
treated the wood, replaced all the joists under the living room floor.
On the wall, a painting of two swans that Rosetta's sister Vonetta
had made; she had had a scholarship to an art school somewhere and
had died of a brain tumor when she was nineteen. That was a long
time ago.

"Samuel," she said, "why you think you never got married
again?"

"No particular reason," he answered, pouring some root beer
into his glass from the bottle on the table.

"But it seem like you never even go out or nothing."

"What about Melva?"

"That bitch was no good for you, Samuel. That not what I'm
talking about. I seen her last week out on the corner, you know what
I'm saying; she look like . . ."

SJ put up his hand and said, "I don't really want to hear about
that, Loot. I don't necessarily want to hear about it." It had been
a brief relationship, five years in the past, but despite the woman's
bad behavior SJ saw no reason to take pleasure in a catalog of her
misfortunes. The relationship hadn't made him especially anxious to
try romance again. He had felt old impulses aroused that he didn't
need to be dealing with. One night he actually found himself walking to Junior's with a .38 in his waistband looking for a man he knew
Melva had spent some time with, and luckily right up by Tennessee
Street saw himself almost as if from above, like a voice saying to
him, Are you going back to that? Is that what you want? And he had
turned around and walked back to his house and wept in frustration
and loneliness. But after that things were over with Melva, and he
didn't bother about it anymore.

"What about Leeshawn, Samuel?"

SJ wished his sister would stop the line of questioning. "She more like a cousin. Or used to be. Anyway I can't see her without I see a teenager, and she lives in Los Angeles." Actually, he remembered, she had moved back to Houston after her marriage failed. Didn't matter.

"She ain't no teenager no more for a long time, SJ. She allright and she like you."

"I don't see you with nobody, Loot," he said, deflecting the question. "Why you don't make time for a man?"

"I don't need nobody, Samuel. It allright at a distance. I get involved, it like my shit fall apart instantly. Like you carrying a grocery bag and the bottom fell out. Cans rolling all up and down the street—cabbages and shit . . ."

In the distance they heard a familiar sound, a blunt tut-tut-tut. They got quiet for a moment to see if there was anything else coming. Although all manner of gunfire was common, you always stopped to listen where it might be coming from. SJ said, "That sound like it by Holy Cross."

Another moment and Lucy said, "Look here, you heard about Joseph back in jail again?"

"Joseph from the East?"

"No, Samuel, Joseph you used to call Squatty."

"I am surprised to hear he's still alive."

"You want to hear about a dumb motherfucker? He taken some lady's purse uptown, and then he taken the bank card and use it and forgot he needed the secret number, right? So the machine keep the card and he starts tripping and calls the service number on the machine complaining about he can't get the card out. On his own goddamn cell phone, Samuel."

"That's how they found him?"

"No; police saw the nigger at the bank machine in the wrong neighborhood and decided to see what was he doing and he just run, left Shontay sitting right there in the car with the motor running."

"They arrested her, too?"

"No, they let her go."

This made SJ think of Wesley again, and he remembered the Saints tickets. One of SJ's customers had given him two tickets to the next night's New Orleans Saints game at the Superdome. The Saints, the great Lost Cause of their city. SJ wasn't that much of a football fan and he had been assuming he would give the tickets either to Bootsy or to Roland from his crew. It occurred to him now that they might be an incentive for Wesley to show his face again, and he mentioned this to Lucy. He knew that Lucy often knew how to get in touch with her son even if she didn't let on to SJ.

"I'll let him know if I talk with him, Samuel." SJ knew also that his nephew played football on Sunday mornings at Joe Brown Park, and he asked Lucy if Wesley would be there on Sunday. "One thing Wesley don't never miss is football," she replied.

How much anger was a man supposed to carry around?

On his knees, by his bed, one hand over his eyes. The nightly wrestle, the quarrel, the accounting demanded.

Lucy's questioning had unsettled him. His own daughter, Camille, would tell him he needed to find someone to keep him company, cook for him, soften and brighten his days. But he was used to doing for himself—cooking, laundry, cleaning . . . It was an echo of the discipline of the army, the one good thing about the army. Introducing someone else into the equation at this point was more than he could manage. And when he had dated a woman he couldn't escape feeling that he was being unfaithful to Rosetta. He kept her pictures around, her vases and little things, fetish objects. He could not accept her death. Everyone said you had to accept God's will, but in SJ's heart he accepted nothing. Accepting things as a fact of life was different from accepting them in your heart.

The injustice of her being taken from the world weighed in his heart like an anchor. He had taken care of her as she wasted away. She never cared for expensive clothes or fine jewelry; she was without envy of others. The other women in the neighborhood turned to her instinctively for advice, even women ten years older than she was. She had a fine, long neck that he liked to kiss, and when she got sick he used to brush her hair. No amount of "It's God's will," and "She's gone to a better place, SJ" from her friends and from Father Moreau could make it all right. Nothing could redeem it for him. The only thing that helped, at all, was working with his hands—building, making. He managed himself and his business, but something had gone out of life for him, perhaps permanently. Functioning in the face of any injustice disfigures you. If it kills you or drives you crazy, you are disfigured, and if you can contain it and channel it and work around it, you are still disfigured.

He tried to concentrate, on his knees, listening for a voice out there, somewhere, as if he were standing on a beach at night. Where was justice? His own father, a man who had raised children, built houses from the ground up, flew supply planes during World War II, facing that condescension from the baby-fat white boys half his age in their chino slacks and Oxford shirts from Perlis. They would call him "Uncle," with their unwarranted familiarity. "How 'bout that overhang, there, Uncle? You're going to fix that right?" Then afterward, "Good, Uncle," clapping him on the shoulder and SJ could read his father's expression behind the mask. His father never gave them the "yassuh" treatment; he kept his dignity, smoked his Nat Sherman shorties, dressed well and never let himself forget who brought the meat to the table. But it was because he knew his own worth that the injustice of it burned so.

Work had been his father's way of insisting on being in the world. SJ had inherited that, along with a faculty for it, a love for the tangible and the tactile, the fact of something being there afterward.

The pride in getting something right, knowing your tools, having a firm grasp of principles. This was what had rescued him from the chaos of his own nature, and it was what he had to pass along to Wesley, but it came through with an urgency that made Wesley want to run away, stake out his own territory, escape the life of steely deflection of injustice, duty, responsibility, find a place of flexibility and possibility.

SJ saw that and it only made him press his points home harder and more insistently, and he knew it drove his nephew farther away—even though Wesley had that same faculty, could fix things, seemed to know instinctively how machinery worked, could take apart clocks and radios, motors, put them back together. Aside from Camille, Wesley was what he had right now of a future, and he saw Wesley straining against that same realization that he himself had strained against as a young man. Wesley didn't want to end up like SJ, living alone, running a tight ship, priding himself on his discipline, the ability to maintain a nonnegotiable pride in oneself and one's ability, and to contain the anger that, no matter how well contained, was still without redress, the chronic undervaluing of men like his father and women like his mother, which ate away at him, at his veins and his muscle, his blood pressure, dragged at his heart and constricted his veins. Wesley wanted freedom but he didn't know where to find it.

SJ had found it, for a minute, in the army. The army had given him mixed gifts. A pride in his physical abilities, in his will and his stamina, exposure to people from other parts of the country and the world. It had also left him with a permanent shame for some things that he had seen and one thing he had participated in and which he had never, ever, discussed with anyone, not even Rosetta, and never would. But it left a residue, a stain that dried and stiffened into a distrust of human possibility, and a deep mistrust of a God who could look down on such a scene and do nothing. Ultimately, it turned into a shame at existing in the first place, chronic, like arthritis. The steely armature of the code of brothers, the conviction that they were absolved by their circumstances for their misdeeds . . . Even with those who bought into the code completely, the conviction went only so deep and concealed a molten center that could explode without warning. All those men who snapped at some unpredictable stroke of the clock and took their mad moment on a roof someplace and left a few people dead, or howling on the sidewalk, clutching their leg, then turned the carbine on themselves . . . How many of them had shared those same brotherly experiences in Vietnam? The anger stayed with him now, thirty years later, watching the tough talkers who had never seen war themselves, mama's boys dressing up in uniforms they had done nothing, themselves, to honor, sending soldiers off to yet another place they didn't understand, on a mission with no intelligible goals . . .

Breathe, SJ.

Rosetta had saved him; he could very easily have ended up like a lot of others. She had given him years of family and stability, raising Camille, going to the school plays, cooking dinner for friends in the neighborhood and family, Christmas, holidays. Decorating the house, dyeing Easter eggs, putting up pictures, and photographs, fabric flowers, little vases that she loved. He still had Lucy, and Wesley, and Bootsy across the street, North Derbigny, his street, their street, and the life of his neighborhood, where almost all of them had lived for decades. Neighbors for whom he had done light carpentry work for free, older ladies and men to whom he gave money now and again, the corners where you could remember your father walking, or playing as a boy with a friend who might still even live there, a senior citizen, now, like yourself . . . That continuity stepped in to fill the cracks at times when it seemed like nothing made any sense. You had a place, a role to fill, a sense of being part of something bigger than yourself, a community.

SJ didn't participate the way he used to. When he was young he used to like to get out there behind the parades and do that second-line, dance with his podnuhs, slide his cap to the side, what they called acey-deuce, jump in with Leon or Joe, get the counterrhythms going, the little sleight of hand with the feet, the head doing one thing and the shoulders another and the hips—integrated, and part of the larger flow, stopping to hug your aunt-tee up on her steps; it didn't matter if it was an anniversary or a funeral. People from other places mistook it for carefree happiness, but it was not that at all. It was joy at connecting the world of the spirit with the physical world, the Word made flesh (and bone and muscle and sound), a sacrament without a sacrifice. Not that they necessarily would have thought of it in those terms, unless they were like Mr. Perrilliat with all his books, a little old berry-black man who talked like a professor and was rumored to have gone to Howard University decades earlier and worked maintenance at the Criminal Court, where the lawyers called him Mose and tipped him five bucks at Christmas . . .

SJ didn't jump into the parades anymore. He would hook up the big oil drum he had converted into a grill and barbecue on the neutral ground during a parade, and he would be the center of all the family and friends, and neighbors in beach chairs joking, eating, being themselves while he cooked up the pork chops and the hot sausage, and hot dogs for the kids, and that was enough for him. What was it that kept him out of the parades and the dancing in the street? What was he holding tight on to in his heart? Once in a great while, if the mood was just right and he was feeling good, he might do one of his old-time moves from back in the day, ankles bucking in, hips shaking in syncopated time as he expressionlessly turned some meat with a long fork, and maybe Lucy or Shawnetta or Bootsy would holler something at him and he would crack up laughing. And all around him all that defiant laughter and defiant grace that kept them all alive.

Before he got up off his knees, he asked again to be shown the way, if there was a way, and he prayed for Lucy. SJ knew she wasn't taking her blood pressure pills and diabetes pills; he knew because once when he had carried her back to her house from a drunk he had checked in the medicine cabinet and the three month-old prescription bottles were in there, full and untouched. His guess was that God, if He existed, must have felt about humanity somewhat the way SJ felt about Lucy. Maybe God had problems of His own. Maybe the creation, as grand as it was, had something flawed in it, something He hadn't gotten quite right. All that work, all that love and beauty, and still the warpage in the mechanism. People prayed for His compassion and understanding, but maybe mankind had to have compassion for God, too.

Talk like that drew strange looks, and SJ knew to keep those particular thoughts to himself most of the time. The only exception was sometimes, on visits to Texas, when he and Aaron's wife, Dot, would argue about it. SJ would push her to the point of exasperation while Aaron sat back and laughed.

"That is the most ignorant thing I ever heard about," she would say, frowning at him across the table in their kitchen. "How can you talk about the Creator of Heaven and Earth struggle like a man? You talking about God. Do you understand? He created everything . . ."

"That mean He created good and evil, right?"

"Oh shit," Aaron said. "Here we go."

"The Devil create the trouble of this world, SJ. And you have a choice to make. Don't matter if you want . . ."

"If God created everything he created the Devil, right?"

"And the Devil had pride within him and that's why he fell. Because he wanted to put his own will up against God, just like you doing."

SJ would chuckle at this, along with Aaron, but Dot maintained her stern look. "You trying to understand God's motive and if you could understand that you would be God."

"Let me ask you something, Dot. Why he made Abraham to almost kill his own son?"

Dot looked at him incredulously; the answer was not just obvious but so obvious that the question itself was suspect. "Why do you even ask something like that? You read the same Bible I read, SJ. He was testing Abraham's faith . . ."

"Now, see . . ." SJ said, smiling, "you talking like you know his motive."

"I'm saying what the Bible says," she almost shouted. "I'm not making up no science fiction."

"The Bible says that God and the Devil hang out together. They bet on how bad the Devil can mess over Job before he turn his back."

"I don't want to hear no more." Dot started to walk out of the room, turned and stepped back. "You need to think about one thing. Life is suffering, and God have His reasons. Whether they make sense to you don't make no different. But at the far end there is a reckoning. God send everyone their own portion of suffering. It's not about if God love you you don't suffer. The Savior said it easier for a camel to go through the eye of a needle—Praise God—than for a rich man to enter the kingdom of God. Jesus don't lie . . ."

Dot and Aaron. SJ took hold of the bed now and rose up slowly onto his feet as he did every other night, having wrestled his questions to a draw, and got himself ready to go to sleep in the one-hundred-year-old bed that had belonged to his grandparents.

Five blocks away, Lucy on the couch reaches out to Wesley's picture and turns it so she can look at it. Television remote across the room but she is where she was. Was where she is. She helped him buy that bike and now that's what he did nights. The Crystal Mist sound just like fruit but with the wine tang. Taste she means. With that mustache thought he look so grown up. She missed out on that when he turned sixteen; SJ and her supposed to take him to the Piccadilly Cafeteria but she didn't make it that time. She bought him that watch that the strap broke. Remember your mama, she said, crying. I know it don't look that way but I love you. That one time he drove her to the emergency room. But how he drive her without they own a car. That time he got her the big comb for Mother's Day said Goody on it. That was in her dresser.

"Wesley," she slurred out.

Big comb said Goody; back when he was small enough he'd push his head under her arm and rest there with she on the couch but he grown now, say I love you mama. I love you. I love you baby boy. Don't never think you too old. My boy drove me . . . someplace. Not on the bike though. No, no. I love you mama he say. Where Wesley?

He tells himself he is not looking for Chantrell but of course he is. Bent over the hand grips, T-shirt flapping halfway up by his rib cage in the backdraft, up and down the hot night streets alone, under the dark, leafy oak trees, or on the broad avenues under streetlights. Speed was its own reason.

Feelings suck you under; compassion is an undertow and you ward it off with money and watches and cars and sunglasses and clothes, and that made you different from who? Some are truly hard and some are weak, and some are taking some time in the land of hard and will use what they learn later in a constructive way, and some will end up on the greasy asphalt behind the Winn-Dixie at three in the morning and maybe even still there at dawn, the spreading puddle around their head like an obscene misshapen wine-colored halo no longer spreading, drying around the edges, with their pants around their thighs after they slid down and they tripped and the two others caught up with him and laughed at his pleading for mercy and shot him twice in the head and then ran off. And even those two, if things go right and they end up in court, still trying to play defiant but taken out of their feedback chamber of friends and images, and then in jail, long hours to think, end up realizing that they made an error.

Wesley right on the edge. Staying by Roland in Gentilly off Broad behind the Fairgrounds. Flirting around the edges of it, getting the taste, trying it on. What it feels like to slap a woman. Or standing squarely, hands crossed in front of you, staring eye to eye with another young man, as if in a mirror, to see who blinks. Slumped on the couch, staring into the cell phone with the game, or the messages. The difference, if it was going to make a difference, was that he had a family; he knew what a home life looked like and he had seen how it worked. He was trying to find a place in a world where there weren't a lot of second chances.

Wesley loved and looked up to SJ, but he needed to get away from him, too. The discipline and ethic of hard work that had been a lifesaver for his uncle was suffocating to him. Not even that he didn't believe his uncle was right—maybe because he believed his uncle was right. It didn't matter—it was the completeness of the worldview, the emotional urgency of his uncle's concern and anxiety, his sense of rightness, the sense that what had worked for him worked, had come across to him, that made him feel that he needed to get out from under.

Unlike many, he had the images of another way, but they hurt, too. Pictures taken by SJ during his time as an amateur photographer (his darkroom was long in disuse; he no longer saw the point after Rosetta died, except for the corny pictures that Wesley chafed at now); he could remember himself in a short-sleeve white shirt and bow tie with that exaggerated smile he used to put on for the camera when he was six and seven and eight, or out in Texas riding that pony he wanted to take home. Or in the kitchen at his birthday party, with Lucy looming over him, a paper hat on her head and the light from the birthday candles making her look spooky. He could outrun all of that; the bike was a speedboat cutting through the water, a long touchdown run. Home hurt, and look what the world outside said was of value. Things and more things. No mercy for losers, voted off the island, off the stage, off the show. The camera always on you and when it was off who cared about you anymore? Don't look back, Wesley.

4

The next morning, Friday, Craig awoke with a warm fizz of hopeful-
ness in his brain and body, left Alice sleeping in bed and went downstairs to put on coffee. The previous night's lovemaking had seemed
to him a moment of real touching and caring that he—*they*—had
been missing badly. As long as they could get to that, he thought—
that arc between them, the contact—they had something to build
on, there was a way forward.

Early sunlight came into the kitchen through the backyard trees.
He turned on the morning television automatically—traffic reports,
headlines, weather. The storm they had been watching had moved
into the Gulf; there would be a couple of school closings, nothing
big. They'd monitor it during the day and if it looked like a potential problem they could leave the next day or Sunday, go to Oxford,
Mississippi, as they had in years past, make a little vacation out of it.
Outside, the morning was bright and rich with color.

He counted out spoonfuls of coffee into the filter basket,
looking out the kitchen window onto the brick patio, which was
ruptured in places by the knuckles of roots from the grizzled oak
tree that shaded their cookouts and cocktail parties. Some days he
couldn't get over the faint smell the oaks gave off as they dried in
the morning sun when he walked out the front door to pick up

the *Times-Picayune* in its plastic sheath, or the feeling of warmth he got coming back inside and greeting the Big Ugly Lamp that sat on the mail table in the front hall like some decadent Statue of Liberty, welcoming visitors.

The Big Ugly Lamp was the first thing they had bought for the house after moving to New Orleans, at the Jefferson Flea Market. Its saddle-stitched shade hovered obscenely over a massive base, a kind of bloated cement cruller that looked as if it had been finished in blue stucco then dotted with gold highlights on its wimpled surface, a twisted pastiche of Jean Arp and LeRoy Neiman. They had seen it and had both started giggling at it simultaneously. "That poor lamp," Alice said. They examined it, and Craig said, gravely, "It'll never survive on its own." Buying it was a vote for generosity of spirit, a talismanic embrace of the limits of taste. "Here we are in New Orleans," the lamp had said for them both. Everything is part of the parade; everything gets to dance.

In the past few months the Big Ugly Lamp had served mainly to remind Craig how rarely he and Alice found themselves on the same page anymore about gestures like that. But on this morning it seemed a harbinger of possible rebirth. Everything Craig saw made him happy—the primitive and "outsider" art on the living room and dining room walls, the children's toys in their boxes at the ends of the room, the huge redwood picnic table that served as their dining room set, the laundry stacked up behind the partly open louvered doors to the laundry alcove, Annie's and Malcolm's watercolors on the refrigerator door, in this, the first house he had owned. Instead of feeling like an unprepared extra in someone else's television show, he felt himself right in the center of where he wanted to be.

To his surprise, he heard little bare feet approaching, quickly, around the corner of the kitchen wall, and then Annie herself followed the sound in, running, in her pajamas, breathlessly saying, "*Daddy . . . Daddy . . . when are we . . .*"

With an air of mock seriousness, Craig held up his hand and said, "I'm sorry . . . I think we're forgetting something?"

Annie stopped short, squeezed her lips together trying not to laugh.

"Can we say, 'Good morning, Daddy'?" Craig said, a caricature of officiousness.

"Good morning, Daddy," Annie repeated, dutifully.

"'How are you this morning, Daddy?'"

"Daddy, stop it!" Annie said. "Do I have to wrap my present for Malcolm now?"

"Shhh," Craig said, "not too loud, okay? Let's have breakfast and get dressed first. If you don't get it wrapped now you'll have time after school. How come you're up so early?"

"I heard you brush your teeth and I'm excited about Malcolm's birthday."

She climbed up on the maple veneer bar stools they had around the counter island and he set out her cereal bowl. His heart was flattened with joy and love, as it always was, seeing her sitting there eating her cereal, with her blond hair falling across her forehead, with its pale bluish veins visible under her skin. They lived a block from school, so there was less of a rush to get Annie pulled together for her day than there might otherwise have been, and Craig let himself feel simple pleasure in watching his daughter eat her cereal in the warm kitchen in the warm house he had provided, in the city he loved.

As Annie brought her bowl to the sink to rinse, her mother walked into the room, dressed already and moving with a deliberate, businesslike rhythm. Craig's heart fell slightly; in his mind some gauzy oasis of morning lounging, leisurely romance after the kids were out the door for the day, unrealistic given their logistics to begin with, evaporated. He tried to send her a little smile, edged over to kiss her as she poured out her cereal, but her attention was on the television, where they were back to talking about the storm; they were monitoring its movements, it had lost strength over Florida but was reforming "nicely" over the Gulf.

"Oh, good," she said. "We're going to have to evacuate again."

"No we're not," Craig said. "It's hundreds of miles away and it will pull east the way they always do." On the screen, the disingenuously concerned expressions on the broadcasters' faces slid quickly into equally disingenuous hearty cordiality for a segment on a local chef.

After several minutes, Annie went upstairs to finish getting herself dressed, and Craig took the moment to ask Alice if anything was wrong. Expressionlessly, she replied that they needed to talk. "What's wrong?" Craig repeated. Alice shook her head, looking, to Craig, as if she were about to cry. "I'll call in late," Craig said.

He deputized Scott, the managing editor, to proof the final pages, then got Annie in gear to head out and walked her the block and a half to school, while Alice drove Malcolm over to their friends Chris and Lisa's for a playdate with their two-year-old, Bonnie.

Forty-five minutes later Craig and Alice sat down across from each other in two living room chairs. Craig looked at her seriously. They had learned some things from therapy. One was to never interrupt. Another was to not raise your voice. Another was to closely monitor your own facial expressions for annoyance, exasperation, etc. Things could arc quickly out of control in accelerating, centrifugal curves; chain reactions in which the way the other person spoke or looked, matters of tone and inflection, became the topic of argument rather than the supposed actual topic. They both realized that that was the sure road to dissolution. But managing a conversation despite all the stored-up anger and frustration was not easy.

Craig waited for Alice to begin speaking, since she had called for the talk; this was the unspoken rule. For all that he was hurt and frustrated by what he thought of as Alice's distancing, Craig was never unmindful of her intelligence, her strength, her total commitment to the children. He wasn't sure what the problem was this morning, but he felt the glow and fizz slipping away, and reflexively, as if to try and hold on to it, just as she was about to speak he said, "Okay, wait, can I say one thing really fast? I wanted to say that last night made me really happy. I felt like we found a place that we hadn't visited in a while, and I felt like it brought us closer together, and I am really happy for that."

Alice nodded thoughtfully, pressed her lips together and looked him in the eyes. The remark made her furious. Craig had a way of framing their conversations, a kind of presentational aspect, as if he were reading a proclamation, that drove her crazy. Plus he had violated the unspoken etiquette of their conversations by speaking first when she had been the one asking to have a talk, which she read as a way of him discharging his anxiety about what she had to say by taking some kind of control, and it really pissed her off. Not to mention the obliviousness about the night before. So instead of the conciliatory, helpful approach she had envisioned, she spoke more sharply than she meant to.

"I was happy we were able to get past our fight," she began. "I do think that is important . . ."

Craig had noticed a pattern in the previous couple of years: they would get close, make love, then, inevitably, the next day she would be distant, even hostile. His provisional theory was that she had a chronic fear of closeness. She was happy to let down her emotional defenses, but then she got angry at being vulnerable. Still, he couldn't help taking it personally, and, trying to deliver the line as a joke, he said, "I take it you're saying that the sex wasn't too great."

Incredulous, Alice said, "Would it be possible even for a minute for me to finish what I have to say without it being interpreted— wrongly in this case—and summed up by you?"

"I'm sorry," Craig said. "I shouldn't have interrupted. And it was a stupid thing to say."

She was quiet for a moment, and then, showing that she had

been awake during their couples therapy sessions, too, she said, "Thank you," and they were back on track. A year and a half earlier they would have gone all the way down that rabbit hole, arguing about how they argued, increasingly angry with each other.

"I want us to have a serious discussion about what we are doing with our lives," she went on. "I don't like having to evacuate my house a couple times a year, take my children out of school, leave and not know what will be left of my house when I get back . . ."

"*Our* house," Craig offered, firmly.

"Dammit," Alice said, "can I finish my sentences without having them corrected or edited by you?"

"Not if you are going to write me out of the script."

It took a moment, but she went on, with a harder edge in her voice now. "I don't like getting called into school because *our* daughter is using words like 'motherfucker.' And I don't like worrying whether I am going to make it alive from *our* car to *our* house when I come home after dark. I don't like hearing about *our* friends being held up and wondering when it is *our* turn. And above all, Craig, I don't like not even being able to voice these concerns to *my* husband without getting into a fight every time."

"Where would you like to live, Alice?"

"You know . . ." she said, leaving the sentence dangling, pressing her lips together and looking out the window. She shook her head. "That's not even the point."

"Then—listen to me, Alice, please—I need to know what the point is. This is our life. I have a really good job here that provides for us and our children. We have a house that we love. Our daughter is in a great school, a block away from our house, along with the children of our neighbors, whom we also like and have a community with. We have friends all over the city, great food, music when we want to hear it, and our children are exposed to other children from all kinds of backgrounds. Yes, the city has a lot of crime, but so do most cities . . ."

"Not like this."

Craig stopped speaking, with his eyebrows raised, and after a moment Alice said, "I'm sorry."

Craig went on. "Yes, we have to evacuate occasionally, but it doesn't take all that much, we have a nice two-day vacation in Oxford, and then we're back. We have a life here. I'm trying to figure out what it is you really want, realistically. We've had this conversation at least a dozen times . . ."

"A dozen?"

". . . and I never know where it leaves us," Craig went on, letting the interruption pass. "We've had good times here, haven't we?"

"Of course," Alice said after a brief hesitation. "We . . ."

"Then—bottom line, then I'm finished—I need to know what it is you want, what you really want. Otherwise this is just like picking at a scab. If we're going to be here I want to be here."

They sat there, practically knee-to-knee, and the thing that was really at issue, the unnameable thing that neither of them could see clearly or focus on because it was too big and too close and too nameless, rotated above their heads like a mirrored ball over an empty dance floor. The argument was never really about logistics but about each one's desire for the other to feel what they felt. How had they gotten so dug into their positions?

Alice looked at Craig evenly and seriously and said, "I want you to acknowledge that this is a scary, backward, inconvenient place to live, and that we are putting our children at risk by living here."

"So—bottom line—you want to move. Right? Where do you want to live? That's what I asked you before."

"I'll repeat what I said, Craig: What I want is for you to acknowledge . . ."

"Right, right—that New Orleans is a horrible place and we should go back to Ann Arbor."

"No," she almost screamed. What she wanted was for him to

acknowledge that her fears had some basis in the reality of the situation. At least that way, if they were going to stay, they could face the fears together, instead of her feelings being negated because there was no immediate practical solution. She wanted them to be on the same page; that in itself would have relieved much of the pressure that fueled her anger.

That is what she thought, when she could think quietly about it, although there was another element, harder to admit. She was, at heart, jangled by the city. It was garish, loud, full of abrupt and, to her, inharmonious contrasts. Yes, it was fun to visit, fun as a spice, as a side dish. But as she had gotten older she found herself, to her surprise, wanting something closer to what she had never wanted for herself growing up. Muted colors, tasteful room arrangements, recognizable social and cultural activities with literate, educated friends . . . All the things she had grown up wanting to escape, the overtones of class anxiety that drove her crazy in her parents, she was discovering to her own intense discomfort were embedded in her. And in her hopes for Annie and Malcolm. She wished that Craig could have shouldered some of that desire, let it rest less completely on her shoulders. She had married someone who reflected her need to distance herself from her upbringing, and now because of that she had been left alone to defend the part of her that was still stuck back there with those values.

And for Craig's part, Alice had been the person who completed his adventure, the perfect companion to his love for the city and the life that he had sought out for himself. Alice had been the one who combed the newspaper looking for new restaurants to try out, and who bought the guide books and found romantic bed-and-breakfast getaways in plantation houses half an hour out of town. Craig had found nothing less than himself in New Orleans, and then he had found Alice, and the picture of his life seemed complete. And now part of that picture was shifting out of recognition, for reasons he didn't understand, and the loss was stabbing him in the heart. He wished that she could at least have admitted a sense of loss for her youthful embrace of the city; that might have let them share the experience more. But instead he felt as if she were, simply, attacking this place and the life that they had loved and shared together. As if she had become a different person.

They both felt the sense of loss. And as they sat there, some angle, some look caught unguarded, some ghost of memory passed over them because at almost the same moment they both began to speak, then they both chuckled at the collision. Craig let Alice speak first.

"Can we please have a conversation—not now, but sometime—about other options? Just talking about it at least will feel like I'm not . . . I don't know—trapped in someone else's movie."

Craig breathed from his stomach. "Why don't we plan a meeting. Let's set a time and a time limit, and agree that whatever we are thinking about will get an airing."

They took each others' hands, looked in each others' eyes.

"Can we go have fun now?" Alice said with a crooked, almost apologetic smile.

"Are we okay?" Craig said. "Do we need to talk some more?"

"No," Alice said. "We're okay. Thank you."

Holding her gaze, Craig said, "Thank you."

The conversations were necessary, and exhausting. They ended them feeling closer, feeling relieved; it did not escape their notice that a fundamental difference had been left unresolved, but at least they could go on with their day.

That Friday afternoon, Craig opened the backyard shed and dragged out the big, high wooden table that they used only for crawfish boils, spread it with layers of overlapping newspaper which he secured to the legs with duct tape. Then he got out their six tiki lamps on poles and drove them into the ground at strategic points around the yard. He hung strings of small paper lanterns from tree to tree to drain-pipe. Alice was in charge of picking up some of the food; guests would be bringing other dishes potluck style. Around two o'clock Craig went to *Gumbo* for an hour and a half to oversee a few last-minute changes in the issue that was closing. And, at Alice's urging, he called the Lamplighter Hotel in Oxford, Mississippi, and made reservations for three nights starting the next night, just in case the storm started heading for New Orleans and they decided to evacu-ate. There was an escalating amount of talk on television and radio during the day about the storm's possible path.

Around five o'clock Doug Worth brought over his crawfish rig, a fifteen-gallon pot with a cage that fit snugly within it and would contain the crawfish, which were lowered, live and writhing, into water that was heated to boiling by a low portable gas stove. They set it up in the dirt driveway around the side of the house. Doug, raised in Mid-City, was a New Orleans institution. Thin, short, with long blond hair and mutton-chop sideburns, always dressed in a plaid Western shirt, he was the lead guitarist and singer for The Combus-tibles (he also played in spinoff bands like Desire Street, the Cres-cents, The Goombahs, Candy and the Canes . . .), one of the great bar bands in the history of New Orleans. They could play anything, it often seemed, as long as the song had been recorded before 1970. Their specialty was obscure New Orleans rhythm and blues, things that felt new because nobody knew them but specialists, like "Loud Mouth Annie" by Big Boy Myles, or "Every Time I Hear That Mel-low Saxophone" by Roy Montrell. The Combustibles had a stand-ing gig at Rock 'N Bowl on Carrollton Avenue every other Friday, a bowling alley where the band set up on the mezzanine level while people bowled away next to them, and danced in front of them, and they played at high school proms, corner bars and restaurant openings, debutante balls and biker parties. They had a dedicated local following and they put out records every two years or so on their own label, Making Groceries, which the drummer's wife sold at a table during their gigs. Doug was an unofficial music historian, who could tell you anything about Guitar Slim or Lazy Lester or Barbara George or Dave Bartholomew or Smiley Lewis.

Doug lived with his wife, Connie, two blocks from Craig and Alice and was the most popular father of all the kids in their tight group in that neighborhood. Since he didn't have a regular day job, he had a degree of surplus energy for toting his own two kids and their playmates around the block on his old Union Pacific train service cart—down Plum Street to the corner of Burdette to the snowball stand, then back along tree-shaded Willow Street. Every other Saturday he would get out his guitar and invite all the kids and their parents for an informal sing-along in his backyard, where he would lead them in "There's a Hole in the Bottom of the Sea," or "The Green Grass Grows All Around," or "John Jacob Jingleheimer Schmidt." Sometimes the other members of the Combustibles would drop in and help out. He had a way of bobbing his head when he spoke to people and looking up at their face from underneath; he would come up to someone as if he had a great secret and, looking around, put his hand to their ear, draw near and whisper "I'm going to get another beer." Back when Craig was still new in town he had interviewed Doug for *Gumbo*, and Doug had said, "Man, sometimes I feel like I'm just a hologram, like I'm here because there's all this great music and food. Like all I want to do is just express that stuff, you know?" Craig loved the image—a person who was entirely a function of the community around him. Craig and Doug were warm neighborhood friends, not late-night secret sharers, but Doug represented to Craig a lot of things he thought he might have liked to be had the road curved differently and he had been a musician instead of an editor.

As the time approached for the party, Doug left to go out to Metairie and pick up two sacks of crawfish. The guests started arriving around six p.m., setting down presents inside on the picnic table and beer and wine on the kitchen counter where Alice was still chopping ingredients for salsa. Mike and Jane brought over the birthday cake. Craig's best friend Bobby and his girlfriend Jen arrived. The two ad sales reps from *Gumbo* came together. Arthur Borofsky, *Gumbo's* publisher, arrived, with a large and elaborately wrapped gift. The guests made their way out into the backyard under the big tree, Christmas lights were strung up over the big wooden table, and around the fence several hooked strings of lights in the shape of red chili peppers. Scott, the managing editor, arrived; Chris and Lisa from down the block with their daughter Bonnie and their five-year-old Nick, Fred and Tanya with Walker and Justine and Jenny. Craig had hooked up the speakers in the backyard and had his iTunes run of Huey Piano Smith and the Clowns doing all their New Orleans hits like "Rockin' Pneumonia" and "Don't You Know, Jockamo" and "Well, I'll Be John Brown," which the kids loved because of all the funny voices the singers used. Eventually the house and yard were filled with forty adults, maybe more, and at least twenty-five kids, half of them prekindergarten. Some of the men gathered around the television in the living room to watch that night's preseason Saints game against Baltimore.

Craig ran around attending to details, small emergencies, transport of food and emptying of garbage bags. Few things made him happier than this, having his friends in his house, with the music he loved playing and his children happy with other children, Derek standing in the kitchen joking with Chris. The men were wearing Hawaiian shirts or other relaxed clothes, and shorts, and the children drew with crayons and Magic Markers on big sheets of butcher paper on the picnic table in the dining room. Later they would clear it off for the birthday cake and all of that. *"You got me rockin' when I ought to be rollin',"* Craig sang along with The Clowns, icing down a six-pack of beer someone had brought. *"Don't you just know it? . . ."* Ben, the cook from Siesta Restaurant, leaned over and whispered a quick joke in Craig's ear, and he was gone before Craig could straighten up and answer.

When he was able to take a break, Craig stepped outside and found Bobby, Jen and Doug, standing in a cluster. Doug had put on giant rubber Halloween monster feet. (Someone pointed at them and said, "Where'd you get those?" And Bobby said, "Those are his own feet.")

"So are we going to see Rickles in Biloxi or what?" Craig opened with. The comedian was coming to one of the Gulf Coast casinos in late September, and Craig was going to use his *Gumbo* credentials to try and get a break on some tickets.

"Absolutely," Bobby said. "Let's get a limo." This was light irony; they were a scruffy-looking gang in shorts and Hawaiian shirts; Bobby and Doug both wore two-day beards.

"Hey, I'm in for fifty bucks." Craig said.

Someone nearby mentioned something about the storm in the Gulf and they all involuntarily listened for a moment; someone else in the other group said they had heard on the news that it was veering east and was supposed to hit around Biloxi. That's what the storms always seemed to do. There, or somewhere around Pensacola.

"I'm sick of these fucking hurricanes," Jen said, with her hand halfway down the back of Bobby's jeans. "It's like sex with Bobby. They make a lot of noise and act like they're going to blow the walls out and then they go someplace else and leave you sitting there just kind of damp and let down." Craig raised his eyebrows and laughed in shock, while Bobby stood there with a look of amusement, unflappable.

"Listen to this," Doug said. "Sam Fucking Butera is going to be at Rock 'N Bowl."

"No way," Craig said.

"That's what John Blancher told me. Some time in October. Hey—Olivia . . ." Doug said, his attention caught by one of his children leading three other kids in a run through the backyard, "no running, baby." She listened, and slowed down.

"With the Witnesses?" Craig asked.

"Can't have Sam Butera without the Witnesses."

"If a Butera plays without a Witness," Bobby said, "does he make a sound?"

"Does he get any reviews?" Jen said.

"Does he get union scale?" Doug said. "What," he said over his shoulder. "Okay . . ." turning back to the group, he said, "Time to drop the bugs. Call and ask Blancher if you don't believe me." He walked away toward where the pot was boiling, next to the mesh sacks full of trapped, struggling crawfish.

"I thought Sam Butera was dead," Bobby said. He pulled out a pocket notebook and a pen and made himself a note.

Craig had met Bobby on his first visit to the city, at the Maple Leaf Bar on Oak Street, during Jazzfest. Craig was waiting for a beer at the bar in back, and he noticed a man roughly his age, dressed in a Hawaiian shirt and shorts, standing nearby, also waiting for a beer. He was short and chunky, with sandy hair and round steel-rimmed glasses, and his face was set in an expression of ongoing amusement. He got his beer, noticed Craig looking at him, pointed to the beer and said, "Got a problem with this?"

Even though the sentence could have been taken as confrontational, the fellow had one eyebrow raised, archly, and Craig understood it as a lampoon of the kind of sudden weirdness one might encounter in most bars. Poker-faced, Craig answered, "Maybe I do."

The fellow laughed, turned away and surveyed the room.

Since the guy seemed in no hurry to continue speaking, Craig began to introduce himself. Before he could get two words out the fellow said, "Chicago?"

Impressed, Craig said, "Minneapolis, actually. That's pretty good."

"First time, right?"

Now Craig couldn't help registering his surprise, as well as a mild irritation. "What, is it written all over me?"

"Basically." The guy looked down pointedly at Craig's feet, which were clad in penny loafers and no socks.

Craig looked down, too, and said, "What's wrong with that?"

"Nothing," the guy said. "You play pool?"

As Craig racked up the balls a short, dark-haired woman with black plastic-framed glasses from the 1950s and a ponytail appeared and spoke to the other fellow, whose name was Bobby. Indicating Craig, Bobby said to her, "He's from Minneapolis."

"Who gives a fuck?" she said, staring at Craig unsmilingly. Craig laughed out loud.

"He's allright," she said, frowning. "How long is it going to take you to destroy him at pool?"

"Five minutes, maybe less," Bobby said, cheerfully.

"Hurry up," she said. "This band is giving me a headache."

They didn't talk about much personal that first night; just music they had seen at the Fairgrounds, checking each other out. Craig gleaned a few things about Bobby and the woman, whose name was Jen. Bobby had grown up in New Orleans in Mid-City, went to Catholic school and then Loyola, wrote articles about music here and there. Jen came back half an hour later and insisted on leaving.

"You here for the week?" Bobby asked Craig. "Come by—we're having a crawfish boil tomorrow. It's by Coliseum Square. You got wheels? You know where that is?"

"I can find it."

"You know where Race Street is?"

"I can find it."

Shaking his head, Bobby wrote down the address and phone

number on a napkin. "Call me when you get lost and I'll talk you in. It'll be the house with the Sugar Boy records playing."

"You know about Sugar Boy?" Craig said.

Bobby frowned, affronted. "My uncle had a bar on Rampart Street . . ." he began.

"Oh fuck, here we go," Jen said. "Don't get him started on Uncle Snake. Come on; let's go home and screw."

Smiling and shrugging at Craig, Bobby let Jen drag him away.

The next night, Craig found his way to Bobby's backyard, full of people standing around laughing and talking under Christmas lights strung from tree to tree. Jen walked immediately up to him and said, "I'm glad you lost the loafers. Bobby's inside slicing something in the kitchen. I don't cook because I don't want to be a slave to some fat fuck who spends his days in an office and then expects me to be his whore when he gets home. You got a problem with that?"

"I could make it my problem," Craig answered.

"*Rumble!*" she yelled, turning only one or two heads. "The kitchen door is over there." She left his side, heading for a group of people in the far corner of the yard. That night Craig met half a dozen of the people who were still his closest friends, including Doug. Through Bobby, Craig had been able to step into the aquifer of New Orleans life—not just the music and streets and restaurants, but the home life—Bobby's mom, who lived in Mid-City just off of Orleans Avenue near City Park, loved to cook big Italian meals and invite Bobby's friends. Craig spent his first New Orleans Thanksgiving at Bobby's mom's house.

They had shared half a house in Mid-City themselves for a year before Craig went back to Ann Arbor to finish grad school; later, Bobby's house became the place where Craig and Alice would stay on trips down. Bobby pieced together a living writing about music for small local publications, *Wavelength* and *OffBeat* and *Cultural Vistas*. Craig always told his friend that he should try and expand to write for national magazines, but Bobby didn't seem particularly interested; he was a creature of New Orleans, bred and born. There had been a moment after they had known each other for a couple of years when Craig raised the question one too many times, and Bobby's reaction let him know that he shouldn't bring it up again. Behind the exchange lurked the fact that Bobby was a native New Orleanian and Craig, no matter how much he loved the city, was not. He let it drop and never picked it up again.

They went with Jen and Alice to Oktoberfest at Deutsches Haus on Galvez Street and ate knockwurst and sauerkraut and laughed for hours, danced the chicken dance to the oom-pah band. Alice and Jen, slightly cool to one another at first, discovered that they shared a guilty taste for Neil Diamond, and one night Craig and Bobby listened in horror as their partners sang the entire lyric to "Brother Love's Traveling Salvation Show" outside the Maple Leaf. They danced to Snooks Eaglin or the Radiators at Tipitina's, went to second lines on Sundays in Central City. Alice had always loved it, and Craig knew he would marry her and have children with her. She was, he thought, like him; they both came from outside the culture but knew how precious it was, and how rare, what an opportunity it offered to enjoy life. They would find themselves simultaneously turning to look at each other in the middle of a meal, or listening to music, as if they had read each others' minds; they would lock eyes and then as if by mutual agreement continue on with what they were doing. It was on one of those delicious and heartbreaking nights, when things seemed to be at the peak of what they could be (and the sweetness was sharpened with the tenderest melancholy, always somehow present, that this moment would not last forever), that Annie was conceived.

Now, years later, at his son's third birthday party, on yet another sweet, humid night (he could almost believe, after all these years, that they would never end), Craig took a deep breath and looked around. Through the groups of people he saw Annie across the yard, dancing—jumping up and down in place, really—with her friend Natasha from Boucher. What a beautiful evening, he thought. Even after nine years living in the city, he could still be stopped in his tracks by the smell of a sweet olive tree. It weighed on his heart that Alice wanted to move. She would try and act as if all it took was talking about it, but he knew she was tired of it. How could he trade this warmth and happiness for some yuppie party, he thought, in God knew where. Minneapolis. Which was a great city, with lots of smart, literate folks . . . But so earnest, in their Polartec fleeces . . . He had tried to describe it to friends up in the Midwest; some of them got it, some of them didn't. The magnolia trees and the oak trees under the heavy liquid air, the smell of crawfish boil floating toward him and the flowering trees, surrounded by other people who also got it, loved it . . .

His eye came to rest on Bobby, who gave him a seraphic smile and said, "Bummer, huh?"

"You know, I still can't fucking believe it sometimes."

They stood there in silent appreciation for a few moments, in the dimming light of the waning summer evening. Inside occasional group hollers, like bursts of confetti from a cannon—the guys watching the Saints . . .

Craig and Bobby both noticed Arthur Borofsky looking their way. Borofsky was a character out of a comic opera—portly, flamboyantly mustachioed, given to baroque, grandiloquent speech. He was younger than he looked, a strange parvenu in a Panama hat. Even after six years of working for him, Craig felt uneasy around Borofsky. He regarded Craig as a fellow sophisticated outsider in a province full of charming eccentrics, and it made Craig intensely uncomfortable. Craig felt toward him, on bad days, as a character in some gothic tale might feel toward his doppelgänger, some bird of ill-omen with an attitude of disturbing familiarity . . . Borofsky was standing with a man in his mid-thirties, about five-seven, with neatly cropped hair, wearing a yellow Lacoste shirt and pressed khaki shorts, brand-new Top-Siders and no socks, sunglasses hanging from around his neck on a pair of Croakies.

"Who's that with Emil Jannings?" Craig said.

"Never saw him," Bobby said. "Looks sort of like you did when you got to town."

Craig took a step back from his friend, frowning and laughing with wounded pride. "Ouch," he said.

"Check the shoes," Bobby said. "Uh-oh."

Borofsky was walking the fellow in their direction. From about ten feet away he held out his hand grandly and said, "I believe you should meet these two gentlemen. This is your host and the editor of the award-winning lifestyle magazine *Gumbo*, Craig Donaldson."

"Chuck Bridges," the stranger said, looking Craig directly in the eye and putting his hand out to shake. He repeated "Chuck Bridges" to Bobby, and said, "I didn't catch your name . . . ?"

"Bobby Tervalon."

Borofsky said, "He's too modest to say it, but he means he is THE Bobby Tervalon, music critic extraordinaire. A gentleman and a scholar." The presentation of clichés in full regalia was a specialty of Borofsky's.

"Hey, what about me?" Craig said, joking with the boss.

"I have already enumerated your many sterling qualities to Chuck. Chuck is here doing some very important and even, I might say, visionary real estate development work. You all will profit from knowing one another." Borofsky held out his hands as if giving a blessing to them, then drifted off.

After a moment, Bobby pointed to the newcomer's feet and said, "Are those Docksiders?"

Slightly confused for a moment, the man named Chuck followed the line of Bobby's finger down to his feet. They both saw him register what Bobby meant, then the man looked up at Bobby and said, "Top-Siders."

They carried on some labored small talk. Chuck was from Houston, but he was staying in Metairie for now, fixing up a few properties in the area, getting ready to flip them. Craig listened with a clenched annoyance; another outsider who didn't really get the place, coming in to figure out a way to exploit it, instead of honoring and enjoying it. The real estate market had been booming in the past two years—good news for Craig and Alice, of course, but also a sign of increased interest from wealthy people who wanted investments or second homes in town. Chuck said he was, in fact, getting ready to "flip" a property on nearby Lowerline Street . . . He pulled out a business card case and handed them each a card. "You guys live in this area?"

"This is my house," Craig said.

"Great block," Chuck Bridges said, expressionlessly. "You're a block from Boucher School. Thinking of selling?"

The question was so abrupt and tactless that Craig couldn't tell immediately whether it was a joke, which it was not. "A lot of people are looking to sell right now," Chuck Bridges went on. "It's a good time to do it. Properties right in this area have gone up about fifty percent in the last three years. I think they're still undervalued. We've flipped four in the past five months."

"Well," Craig said, "we don't think of it as a 'property'; we think of it as a home, and my wife and I and our children are happy here."

Unoffended by the tone of Craig's response, and with the same healthy and vacant expression on his face, the man said, "Keep my card and call if I can ever be of any help. Are you in the area?" he asked Bobby.

"Me? No; my wife and I live in the old Blue Plate Mayonnaise condos." Craig looked at his friend; there was no such place.

Chuck Bridges looked into the distance, riffling through a mental card file and coming up empty. "They haven't developed that yet," he said, frowning ever so slightly.

"The one in St. Gabriel," Bobby said, helpfully.

This was the location of a women's prison. Bobby was laying it on thick for the guy.

"Oh," Chuck Bridges said. "Didn't know about that one." Turning to Craig, he said, "Nice meeting you. Let me know if you're thinking about selling."

"Sure thing," Craig said as the guy walked away. When he seemed safely out of earshot, Craig said, "Who the fuck invited him?"

"He seems to have taken quite a shine to you."

"I'm serious. I want to know if this is going to be some kind of infestation. It's like finding the first ant in your kitchen. Now I can't have a crawfish boil without getting hit on by real estate speculators? My fucking 'property . . .' Is that how they talk in Houston?"

"Hey," Bobby said. "Houston's all right. Arnett Cobb's from Houston."

"The Blue Plate Mayonnaise condos in St. Gabriel . . ." Craig said.

"They're extremely undervalued," Bobby said. He squared himself and looked at his friend. "Got under your skin, huh? Everything okay?"

Craig let out a big sigh, looked around the yard. "I had a pretty upsetting talk with Alice today."

"You want to talk about it?"

"Not especially. Same old thing."

There was a general movement toward the driveway, and Doug walked past them, toward the kitchen, saying "Bugs are up" as he passed. Then he stopped himself, took a step backward and whispered something in Bobby's ear, walked off again. At Craig's raised eyebrow, Bobby said, "Another beer."

"Annie," Craig called to his daughter, "Let's go eat some crawfish."

In the driveway the high wooden table, with its several layers of newspaper, now supported a giant mound of steaming, dark orange crawfish. Nine guests were already gathered around, squeezing the highly seasoned meat out of the tails, sucking the juice out of the rest of the carcass and then going immediately for another, washing them down with beer and also eating the potatoes and corn on the cob that had been boiled along with the crawfish. It was one of the most ingrained communal rituals in New Orleans, everyone eating from the same horn of plenty, facing one another and talking, talking, talking as they ate, about music they had seen, city politics, the Saints game, which was still going inside, making jokes, making plans, making good-natured trouble. People came and went from the table, but the table was always encircled by people.

Craig went inside to get a stool for Annie, who was holding their spot. When he brought it she got up and started in; at seven, she was an old hand at the process. Craig stood behind her, reaching around her to grab the reddish prizes, once in a while grabbing one that Annie had claimed as her own, enjoying her protests. He loved that Annie took such pleasure in this ritual, threw herself into it so completely. Alice came over, too.

"Where's Malcolm?" he asked.

"He's inside playing with Franz and Sherri."

"How great is this?" Craig said to his wife.

Her mouth full, she gave her husband the thumbs-up.

"Daddy," Annie said, "why do they call them mudbugs if they don't have any wings?"

"What kind of question is that?" Craig said, teasing. "Ants don't have wings, and they're bugs."

"I'm serious," she said, in a whining voice.

"I am, too," he said. "I'll bet you more bugs crawl than fly."

"What about flies?"

"What about spiders?"

The others at the table began to chime in. "Centipedes."

"Cicadas."

"Locusts."

One guy, a dishwasher up at Jacques-Imo's restaurant and a friend of Doug's, volunteered "nutria," a rodentlike animal native to Louisiana, and was jeered down by everyone.

"What about beetles?"

"What about caterpillars?" Craig said.

"Caterpillars turn into butterflies!" Annie said triumphantly. She started giggling.

"Alice," Craig said, "can you help us here? Annie and I are having a disagreement over whether more bugs crawl or fly."

From the other side of the table, Alice, who had been listening, said, "What about gnats?"

"What are gnats?" Annie said.

"They're little tiny bugs you can hardly see," Craig said. "You see them more up north than in New Orleans."

"There are plenty of gnats in New Orleans," Alice said. "Fleas, too."

This was a reference to a problem they had had with their late indoor-outdoor cat Mr. Bill. Alice had wanted him to be an indoor cat because it was so easy to pick up fleas in the hot weather. Craig argued that the cat needed to be outdoors to let off steam. He prevailed, but the fleas Mr. Bill occasionally brought in would inevitably be the topic of some small barb from Alice, along the lines of (with a false breeziness), "Oh, look at that. Another flea." Craig took a swig of beer to wash away the unpleasant association.

"A cockroach!" Annie said.

"Cockroaches spend more time crawling than flying," Craig said.

"No, Daddy—there's a cockroach!"

It was crawling up one of the table legs, unusual because the two-

or three-inch-long insect pariahs tended to avoid groups of people. Craig reached over and flicked it off with his finger and it flew a few feet to the side of the house next door.

"Yay!" Annie said. "It flew!" She laughed and pointed at Craig, and Alice joined in the laughter; it was, undeniably, a point for the other side, and Craig said, "All right, you win. For now. Later I'm going on the Internet and get a list of all the crawling bugs."

"Flying bugs!" Annie said.

Around 9:30 or so the party, full of children as it was, began to fray and unravel; people began drifting home, and Craig began to get a jump on bagging up some trash. At one point he found Alice outside in the backyard; he walked up to her and tried to kiss her but she drew up her shoulders and said, "Not here."

"What's wrong?" he said.

"I'm just not comfortable with that, around people."

"Come on!" Craig said. "It's a crawfish boil . . ."

"Can you just give me a little space for a minute," she said, looking up at him. For a moment Craig wasn't sure whether she was going to cry. He walked off, with his warm mood bruised.

Carrying some plates back into the kitchen, he ran into Chuck Bridges, the real estate guy, who was eating a sandwich. "Didn't get enough bugs, Chuck?"

Chuck looked at him a little vacantly. "Bugs?"

"Crawfish."

"Oh," he said, good-naturedly, and waved his free hand. "Too much trouble for too little meat. I'll take a ham sandwich any day."

Eventually, the rest of the guests left; Doug took the crawfish rig back to his house and Craig and Alice cleaned up the yard and the kitchen. On the late news the storm was a big item, along with the Saints' 21–6 loss to Baltimore. They discussed what they should do about the hurricane. It was a huge storm, and apparently getting bigger, but it did appear to be turning east, toward the Florida panhandle or Mississippi. Still, with a storm that large, even a near miss could create problems that would make it worth leaving the city for a couple of days. At Alice's urging, Craig called their hotel in Oxford and double-checked their reservations for the next three nights—Saturday, Sunday and Monday. They would check first thing in the morning, and if the storm hadn't started to dissipate, or if it changed directions, they would pack up and head for Oxford.

Craig left the tiki lamps up in the backyard, jammed garbage bags full of newspaper, crawfish husks, used lemons, corncobs and paper towels, tied them shut and dragged them to the curb, gathered beer bottles and put them in the recycling box, while Alice got the kids to bed and washed dishes and wiped down the kitchen counters. Then they and their neighbors and most of the rest of the city went to sleep.

5

Overnight, the National Weather Service revised its projections for the storm's path. The high-pressure system that the meteorologists thought would continue to push the storm eastward did not hold, and the storm, which had drawn strength steadily from unusually warm waters in the Gulf of Mexico, began once more to angle north by northwest, toward New Orleans. The projections had it hitting late Sunday night or early Monday morning, although there was still, conceivably, time for it to change its course again. The weather report usually offered a cone of possibility, an angled path within which the storm would likely travel. On Saturday morning, New Orleans was again in the middle of it.

By the time Craig was up and making coffee the early news shows were full of grim talk about the storm, now a Category 4 hurricane named Katrina. The Weather Service ranked hurricanes in categories, according to the strength of their winds, with Category 1 having winds below 95 mph, and Category 5 winds over 155, certain to cause widespread catastrophic damage. Anything ranked Category 3 or higher was considered to be extremely dangerous. The city was being evacuated.

Leaving was still technically voluntary, but the police and state troopers were setting up contraflow, in which the interstate highways leading into and out of New Orleans were all turned into outbound routes. Ordinarily, given the news, Craig and Alice would have been packed up and nearly ready to leave, somewhat insulated from worry by the fact that the storms always seemed to miss the city and nothing bad had ever happened to their house or their immediate neighborhood. Still, they would leave to avoid the inconvenience and discomfort of a possible electrical failure; they would arrive at the Lamplighter in Oxford, get settled, wake up in the sunny, familiar-feeling hotel room and walk down to the courthouse square and eat breakfast, run into other New Orleans evacuees, go to the book shop, visit William Faulkner's house, eat at the fun restaurants and head home after the danger had passed. Craig actually looked forward to the break.

But on this Saturday morning Malcolm woke up vomiting and running a 102-degree fever. Alarmed, Alice called Dr. Bernard, who was out of town for the weekend according to the answering service, which took their number and said that the doctor would be checking his messages. Malcolm clearly could not travel until his fever lowered and he stopped vomiting. Alice gave him liquids and tried to get him to keep some Tylenol down, and she sat with him in his bedroom, stroking his hair and comforting him, occasionally wiping his forehead with a cool, damp cloth.

Friends called throughout the morning to see where Craig and Alice were headed. Craig's sister Debra phoned from Seattle to make sure that they were leaving town. Arthur Borofsky called, from Natchez, to urge Craig to leave as soon as possible. Doug Worth checked in to see if they needed anything; Connie and the two children were headed to Hammond, but Doug was going to stick around to keep watch over his house. Bobby and Jen were packing up to stay with friends in Baton Rouge, a fact that felt ominous to Craig since Bobby never left for hurricanes.

The morning news shifted further into disaster mode with each quarter hour. Satellite images of the swirling white cloud mass, which seemed to cover the entire Gulf of Mexico, flashed constantly on the television, with regular updates on its gathering strength. Across New Orleans people who rarely if ever evacuated were packing up to ride out the storm elsewhere, as if driven by reports of an invading army approaching. Everyone knew that the traffic during evacuations could get apocalyptic as a storm approached. Everyone knew someone who had spent ten hours making the ordinarily one-hour drive to Baton Rouge during the evacuation for Hurricane Ivan the year before, or else they themselves had done it. Many left earlier than usual in an attempt to beat the traffic, while others waited until the last minute, hoping that the storm would miss and they would be spared the horrible trip.

While Alice took care of Malcolm, Craig handled the tasks he and Alice would otherwise have shared—the familiar stowing of valuables, the placing of plastic garbage bags over furniture near windows—they had it down to a routine, as they did the restoring of order and normalcy quickly when they returned. He got Annie's breakfast ready for her, and then he gave her a few little tasks to do to keep her busy—carrying some laundry upstairs, emptying wastebaskets from the bedrooms. Craig went room by room through the house, forcing himself to breathe and remember that the storms always turned out to be false alarms. Packing was something they did to be responsible in case the worst should happen, but it would be all right.

Just before noon Craig took a break and stopped into the kids' bedroom, where Malcolm was propped up in bed with Alice reading to him.

Alice looked up at Craig from the book in her lap and said, "How's it going?"

"It's going fine," he said, looking down at his son. "The question is how's it going in here. You okay, Big Chief? He walked over to the bed and crouched down, smiling at his unsmiling son. He put the back of his hand against the boy's forehead, which was very warm.

"We just got some Fructalite down," Alice said, looking at Malcolm, "and a Tylenol and we're going to see how it goes, right Malcolm?"

The boy nodded weakly.

It always touched Craig, and made him faintly jealous, to see how tenderly Alice acted with Malcolm. She had more patience with him than she did with Annie, who was generally much more agreeable. She certainly had more patience with him than Craig did. Craig had little intuitive feeling for what his son was feeling or thinking, the way he did with Annie. In Malcolm, furious energy and stubbornness alternated with interludes of passivity and what Craig had learned in therapy to call regressive behavior—wanting to be carried, wanting to be fed. On the one occasion when Craig had used that phrase in reference to Malcolm Alice looked at him as if he was out of his mind. "Regressive behavior?" she said, almost laughing in Craig's face. "He's two years old." Craig had answered that Annie hadn't acted that way when she was two, but the point stuck. The truth was that the passivity reminded Craig uncomfortably of a side of himself. In any case on this morning the boy was unquestionably sick, and Alice's tenderest, most nurturing side came out, as it always did, and Craig was grateful.

To Alice, Craig said, "Would you like me to put together some lunch for you? It's noon."

"I'm okay," Alice said, smiling up at him gamely. Craig leaned down toward her and they kissed. "Can you get Annie's lunch, though?"

"I'm on it," Craig said. To Malcolm he said, "You're going to be okay, Big Man. You want anything from downstairs? You want me to bring up Thomas the Tank Engine?"

"No thank you," the boy said, an unusual locution for him, and said so simply; Craig felt a pang of tenderness for his brave son. "Well allright. You just let me know and I'll bring it up."

"Thanks sweetie," Alice said to him, opening Malcolm's book again as Craig went downstairs to make lunch for Annie.

After lunch, with the house more or less prepared for them to leave, Craig drove to the *Gumbo* offices in Mid-City to look around and make sure things were battened down. The traffic was heavy along Carrollton Avenue, but once he got past the interstate underpass by Tulane Avenue it abruptly lightened. The *Gumbo* parking lot was empty and Craig pulled up by the front door of the low, single-story building. He opened the door with his key and punched in the code on the security system; the reception area was dark, but enough light came in through the drawn blinds that he could see. He closed the door behind him and walked through the reception area to the main hall, where he walked past the empty cubicles and offices. The halls of the office were quiet.

In his own office, Craig turned on the small table lamp next to the couch, and his desk lamp, then he shut the door. He sat behind his desk to think if there were anything he absolutely needed to do or to have with him. The offices were located in a solid, modern, low building built almost like a bunker, so it wasn't going to blow away. He reasoned that everything was probably as safe there as it would be anywhere. The windows were double-thick and insulated, to keep the air-conditioning bills low. He looked around at his autographed photo of Fats Domino, at a poster on the back of his office door for the production of *Streamers* in which he and Alice had met, in school. His CDs, books written by friends and strangers, his own files containing everything he had written and copies of every issue of *Gumbo* that he had edited—283 of them, as of the previous week.

Nothing ever happened, he reminded himself. The odds were way against it. But there was a different tone this time in the news

reports. He pulled out his top right desk drawer and took a Benevol from the bottle he kept in there, a mild tranquilizer that he
liked to tell his music pals acted as a sort of Dolby system, cutting
out just the unpleasant highest frequencies. He got some water out
of his own private cooler (the one little luxury he had half-jokingly
insisted on in negotiations with Borofsky) and took the Benevol.
He sat at his desk and closed his eyes and breathed deeply, slowly,
several times, from his stomach. It will be all right, he said to himself.

Where would he be if this were all gone? All this life had been
a kind of exoskeleton, or scaffolding, inside which he had assembled enough of a self to keep the operation working. His self was
invested in the city, in its rituals; he read meaning into it and it
returned the favor by endowing him with a set of coordinates, a
loose confederation of attitudes, and a community of others who
operated under the same constellation. It was not a constellation
of meaning he'd been born into; it was a refuge he'd found, a world
that worked in a way he needed the world to work, a safe harbor to
get away from something in himself for which he lacked a name,
some emptiness, some longing, some intimation that perhaps he
did not really even exist . . . But what if it wasn't here anymore?
Where, exactly would he be? Where was he? There had to be some
kind of point to it all . . .

This was a bad way of thinking. He was supposed to be calming
himself down and not driving himself crazy with unanswerable questions. Keep breathing deeply, he thought. Center yourself.

Useless. After a minute or so he opened his eyes, stood up,
turned off the lights and lingered in the doorway of his office to take
one more look around. He thought if there were anything he wanted
to take with him just in case, then he decided to take nothing, as a
gesture of faith. Maybe if he acted as if everything was going to be
fine, it would be.

• • •

SJ walked four blocks toward the Industrial Canal from his house to where they had closed off part of Tennessee Street for Little T's birthday party. The neighborhood was lively with Saturday activity, slightly quieter because some had left, but most of the Lower Nine had stayed put. Hammers were going here and there, people putting plywood up over windows, but it seemed generally like a regulation Saturday. There hadn't even been a question about whether to go ahead with the block party.

That morning, SJ had driven all around the neighborhood, looking for Wesley—across Reynes Street, past the park, and down North Tonti past Forstall, right again on Andry. He knew that one of his nephew's best friends lived over on North Miro, and also the girl's cousin was on Lizardi, and SJ had decided to invest forty minutes or so driving around to see if he could catch a glimpse of Wesley or find someone to ask. He was concerned especially to find out if his nephew was aware of the coming storm and prepared. And, too, he wanted Wesley's help preparing his house and Lucy's house. Looking for Wesley, frustrated by his nephew's disappearance, SJ was balanced between anger and worry. The two emotions often came packaged together for him.

SJ had most of what he needed stockpiled at home—plywood, fitted with special hooks, batteries, candles, radio, water. SJ didn't work on Saturdays; he kept the day set aside for himself, usually to pursue the various projects he had going around his own house. This Saturday wouldn't be much different, aside from helping some neighbors board up their houses. He stopped into Happy Shop to buy some gum, a small store run by a Vietnamese family, located on North Claiborne. Some people in the neighborhood had an antagonistic attitude toward the Nguyens, who ran the place, especially some of his fellow veterans, but SJ was always friendly to them.

Now SJ could smell the grills going a block away. On this afternoon he wore a white ribbed light cotton sweater, a small gold cross on a chain around his neck outside the sweater, a beige cap and a pair of beige pleated slacks. He cut a figure in the neighborhood, liked looking good when he went out. An elder statesman, but still young enough to take care of himself and others. It was a hot, sunny afternoon, and he walked past the houses with pleasure, the familiar houses, wooden shotgun houses, brick houses, cinder blocks, but mostly classic wooden shotguns. Most—even the poorest—had some little decoration, touches of individual sensibility, a hand-carved sign over the door reading THE JOHNSON's, or a fanciful flower grotto set inside a truck tire, or a couch outside on the porch. It was home, this neighborhood. One man, whose name SJ never could remember, was grilling something on a little hibachi in his driveway and called out to SJ "Ready in five if you hungry, J." He passed the house of a man everyone knew only as Mr. Joe and saw the chickens the man kept in his yard behind his waist-high hurricane fence. Up on the corner of Tennessee Street and North Derbigny he waved to two women he knew, who were sitting out on some steps as he approached.

"I was saying to Jawanda," one of the two, named Delois, said, without preamble, "I always like seeing you because you pulled together." She smiled up at SJ from under a bright yellow, crotcheted hat. She was missing her two bottom front teeth.

"Look like *GQ*," the other one, Jawanda, said. She wore a tight-fitting black top and her hair was in curlers.

He leaned on the iron railing on the steps going up to their small porch, where they had a cooler out.

"How is Marvin coming along?" SJ asked.

"See, that's what I'm talking about," Jawanda said, taking a big slug off her beer.

"He supposed to be rotated out," Delois said, "but now I don't know. They got him on extra rotations."

"That's what I'm talking about."

"See, that ain't right. When your time up is supposed to be *up*. Reserves ain't supposed to be but one goddamn weekend a month. And Marvin on his third rotation straight through."

SJ lifted his cap with one hand, ran the other over his smooth scalp and replaced the cap. "They trying to fight a war like there's no war going on. They need to put in the draft again."

"What good the draft gonna do, J?" Delois said. "They just need to get out of that motherfucker . . ."

A man in his fifties walked up to their little group, wearing an oversized black T-shirt with the words GHETTO CASH on it over a picture of a gun. "Allright," he said, and SJ put out his hand to the man, who took it in an old-fashioned soul handshake, forearms at right angles and thumbs pointed upward. The man had graying hair and a goatee and eyes that slanted downward slightly at the sides, giving him a look somewhere between laughing and crying. He and SJ had been in Vietnam at the same time.

"Shan-DRA," Delois yelled to someone in the distance. "Tell Tee-Bo get out that street."

"What the draft does," SJ said, "is if everyone had to send they son or daughter over wouldn't be no more war in Iraq."

"Yeah, you right about that," the man, whose name was Alfred, said.

"How's your mama?" SJ said. "She doing allright?"

"The diabetes got on her," Alfred said, "and they amputated her leg. She in a wheelchair. But she allright. She steady getting stronger. When she start hollering about she want her hair done I'll know she allright."

"Are you going to move her for the storm?"

The man shrugged. "She won't go. She stubborn. Don't want to leave the house."

"Where Lucy at?" Jawanda said.

"I don't know," SJ said. "She'll probably come by later. Lucy's on her own clock."

"I know that's right."

Down the block children played in an inflatable house filled with brightly colored plastic balls. At the far end was a platform with a couple of turntables, and some of the neighborhood young men were playing hip-hop over the speakers. Up and down the street people had their own little hibachis and grills going.

"You got your house boarded?" SJ asked the woman named Delois.

"What I'm protecting, J? I can't be lifting that wood, take it up, put it down once twice a month. Ain't nothing ever happen anyway. What they say about this one."

"Mayor said on TV this one going to be big," Jawanda said. "They telling people get out. Oliver Thomas was walking around here early talking about get out of town."

"That all C.Y.A.," Delois said. "They really thought something gonna happen they make it mandatory and have buses lined up all on Claiborne. Shit. You can't get up and run every time somebody say Boo . . . You don't hear nobody talking about evacuation plan, meet here, do this. They just covering they ass for the white folks and the insurance. Plus my check coming on Thursday; I ain't about to leave."

"I'll come by tomorrow and put up some wood," SJ said.

"No, SJ," Delois said. "I ain't want to sit around in the dark listening at the wind. I want to be able to get out if I got to get out." SJ looked around him, and he remembered an image from when he was barely in his teens, of the streets flooded during Hurricane Betsy, and helping his father pull his mother and Lucy in a dinghy they had gotten from somewhere.

"Well . . ." SJ said, straightening up, brushing off the side of his slacks, "you call me, let me know if you want me to come over and board you up, hear?"

"Thank you baby," Delois said, reaching her arms out and hugging SJ.

"I'm-a walk over and see what they got at the truck."

"Hey SJ, that's good. They got Italian sausage cooking there by Charles."

Alfred took his foot off the ladies' steps and said, "Y'all see Tina, I'm just down here."

"Allright, baby."

The two men walked off to get some food. They never talked about the army at all, or even brought it up. They talked some about the sad Saints game the night before, but mostly they just walked along enjoying being there. The street was full of life; groups of girls stood talking and eyeing groups of boys who pretended not to be eyeing them back, or who communicated with them by pantomime and facial expression until the girls turned away, giggling or with expressions of exaggerated nonchalance and even dismissal. Older people sat out on steps, leaned on railings, talking to one another or just watching the activity in the street. They knew the story behind the story of everyone on that street. They had seen neighborhood adults turn into the old people who sat behind their walkers; they had seen their friends' and cousins' babies turn into these young men and women, had seen the young men and women in band uniforms and cars, in graduation robes and caskets.

SJ and his friend stopped and got hot sausage at one of the grills, and while he was waiting SJ noticed Wesley, down toward the end of the block, talking to a couple of other young men by the turntables. Behind the turntable platform he could see a couple of the motorbikes they rode around on.

When they had finished eating, SJ said goodbye to his friend and walked down to where his nephew was. Wesley and another young man were talking, shoulder to shoulder, conspiratorially, Wesley looking from under his brows at the other young man as SJ approached. Then Wesley acknowledged his uncle with his eyes and a short head bob, finished whatever it was he was saying to the other young man, and as SJ walked up to them Wesley turned and gave his uncle a quick one-arm hug, a sign of affection, but delivered in a self-assertive manner of which SJ took note.

"This my Uncle J," Wesley said to his friend, a smiling young man with very dark skin wearing a white T-shirt with one of the ubiquitous airbrushed legends on it in lurid pink and black script, this one reading R.I.P. BOONIE—SUNRISE SEPTEMBER 18, 1988—SUNSET JUNE 3, 2005—NEVER FORGET YOU deployed around a silk-screened photo of a young man, smiling, a gold cap shining on his front tooth, holding his hand up with two fingers sticking out at angles . . . They had the T-shirts made up to memorialize friends, brothers, cousins, classmates who went down usually from some violence.

"I didn't catch your name," SJ said.

The young man laughed for no particular reason, as if SJ had made a joke, and said, "I'm Tyrell. My mama Minnie."

"You Minnie's son?" SJ said, genuinely surprised. He had not seen this young man for years. He hadn't seen Minnie for a couple of years either, for that matter. "Where you been hiding?"

"Oh, I been out of town for a couple year." Saying this, he smiled, almost boyishly, embarrassed, because it probably meant prison.

"But you back now," SJ said.

"Yes, sir," Tyrell said.

"Your mama all right?"

"She all right," Tyrell said. "She stay in San Antonio by her cousin." He turned over his shoulder at something someone said, laughed, turned back to SJ. For a fleeting moment SJ saw the eleven-year-old he had known, peeking out from that hardening face with the two gold caps on the front teeth. There was that mixture in his manner, SJ thought, the childhood that never got a chance to come to a natural close, and the guardedness, the mask, that they all developed now.

"I'm going to talk to Wesley for a minute," SJ said.

"Allright," Tyrell said, slapping Wesley's fingers with his own, giving a little twist and then snapping at the end. "SQUEET!" he said in parting, in a high voice, and Wesley laughed as he turned to talk to his uncle.

"I can use some help boarding up your mama's house tomorrow morning. You can come by my house." He did not ask where Wesley had been. That would have implied that that place, whatever it was, was more important than where he, SJ, was.

"Okay Uncle J."

"Around ten, mid-morning. We'll take the truck and do your mama's and then do mine. If the storm hits, come stay by my house."

"Where Mama going to stay at?"

"With me. We got the second floor."

"I'm-a stay by Mama's make sure nobody loot it."

SJ considered this for a moment. Wesley was looking over his shoulder at where the young men were.

"You got everything you need over there? You got you water, batteries?"

"I'll get 'em tomorrow from you Uncle J."

"You sure?" SJ was watching his nephew, noticing the distraction, no way to be sure what it was about.

"Yeah," Wesley said. Then, focusing back on his uncle, meeting his eyes, he said, "Don't worry, Unca J; I be allright."

They looked at each other, gaze to gaze. Then SJ said, "Allright. Tomorrow morning, hear?"

"I'll be there."

"I shouldn't have turned on the news," Alice said. She had taken a break around two o'clock to eat a quick sandwich; the mayor was on TV urging everyone to leave the city as quickly as possible, saying, "This is the one we feared." Now they knew they would have to leave the city no matter what kind of shape Malcolm was in. He seemed to be feeling somewhat better, but he was still sick. Under any circumstances he would do better out of New Orleans if the city was going to be without power for several days.

It was late Saturday afternoon; the storm was predicted to hit late Sunday night or early Monday morning. They discussed the question at some length and decided that they would prepare everything and leave at dawn the next morning. Late as it was, and with the traffic as heavy as it doubtless was, they could easily end up stuck for hours in the dark on unfamiliar roads. Craig called the motel in Oxford and was told that he couldn't cancel only that night's reservation; the hotel was anticipating too many people. The only thing to do was to pay for all three nights' reservations, eat the charge for that night, but at least they would have a room when they got to Oxford the next afternoon.

While Alice started getting dinner ready, Craig went upstairs to his study. He wrapped a plastic bag around his Association of Alternative Newsweeklies award, a clear resin cube with his name and *Gumbo* embossed on it, and put it in the closet at the top of the stairs. Into that closet he also moved his parents' wedding picture ("You want this thing?" his mother had asked him, cavalierly, as she was cleaning out one of her various apartments years before), and some other framed photos from his desk. On his office floor, a cheap oriental rug that had been his since boyhood. His father had given it to him for a birthday, with no explanation, a strange present to give an eleven-year-old, but Craig had come to find its dark brown and black and ivory sawtooth optical-illusion pattern absorbing and comforting, and he had taken the rug with him to college and then journalism school. His poor father. Craig rolled up the rug tightly, to protect it, and placed it on end in the far corner of the closet.

Then he noticed the book Annie had made for his last birth-day—construction paper stapled together with photos pasted into it of musicians, cut out from magazines, and on the front, drawn in Magic Marker, a line drawing recognizable as a trumpet. He also placed this in the closet and began looking around his office, anxiety blowing up in him like a sudden squall. He took a break to get another Benevol.

Downstairs, Craig heard Annie telling Alice, "Mommy, I think I have a stomachache, too." Alice, frazzled and worried herself, sized up her daughter, said, "Stop it. No you don't. Drink this," and poured her half an inch of scotch in a juice glass, telling Annie to drink it down in one shot and get into bed.

Around nine o'clock that evening, crawling out of his skin with restlessness and anxiety, Craig decided to take a run down to the French Quarter and go to Rosie's to see who was still around. There was always something going on in the Quarter, and Craig felt as if he could use a boost. Alice was okay; they had their place, the kids were stable, and it was okay for him to head down for an hour or so.

Rosie's On Decatur was a no-frills bar frequented by the city's journalists and criminal lawyers, news cameramen and housepainters, a combination gossip hive, pressure valve and sandbox much like the no-frills journalist bars you can find anywhere in the U.S., with some significant modifications, including the giant moose head over the bar mirror that ran almost the length of the room's right side, its antlers festooned with Mardi Gras beads, the twinkling Christmas lights encircling a coffin that hung suspended from the ceiling over everyone's heads, the video poker machine right next to the pinball machine in the back, and the jukebox full of New Orleans music. It had the usual framed book jackets on the walls, to which nobody paid attention, and it had two TVs going, one on ESPN and one on a news channel, usually CNN. Craig liked to stop into Rosie's at least once a week. If you skipped for too long you weren't up to date on the latest scandals and gossip. Craig was not a bar type of guy in his heart, but he liked the gossip, he liked seeing people; showing up there was almost a professional obligation.

Rosie's front wall opened onto the Decatur Street sidewalk through a window that functioned as an open-air bar behind which denizens could sit with their drinks and look out on people as they passed, offering their commentary. It was always occupied. Craig walked in and surveyed the handful of people at the three raised tables on the left, silhouetted against the gaming machines in the back. A little quiet, but the room felt reassuringly ordinary. As he looked around he heard a familiar voice lacerate the air in angular Balkan cadences.

"Craik! Sit down and haf a drink. Whatever you are looking for you will not find it. You are gettink morose."

Serge Mikulic was as much a fixture at Rosie's as the moose head over the bar. His twice-weekly column in the *Times-Picayune* came at local questions from his own peculiar sound and experience as an émigré from Serbia. "Growing up in a corrupt pestilential backwater has given me invaluable insight into other corrupt pestilential backwaters," he once famously remarked. "I was made for New Orleans." Serge also taught journalism at the University of New Orleans, but no one would guess it to see him sitting at Rosie's bar chain-smoking, arguing, with his peculiar sardonic superiority, with the various politicos and fellow journalists at the bar and, on the rare occasions when there was no one present to argue with, arguing with the television commentators on the news shows, or the coaches and commentators on the sports shows. Serge Mikulic turned attendance at Rosie's into an art form.

"Where's Dave?" Craig asked as he pulled out a bar stool and sat. Dave was Serge's best friend and constant foil at Rosie's, a news cameraman for WYAT-TV and Vietnam vet.

"He's throwink his money away on video poker. Now he has a system which will make him rich. I asked him to advance me enough for another scotch."

"I'll have an Abita," Craig said to the much-pierced bartender. When she went to get the beer Craig said, "She new?"

"She's been fillink in for Martine this week. She's afraid of magnets." Serge took a long pull on his drink as Craig paid for his beer. They clicked bottle to glass and as Craig took his first long swallow Dave walked over. Serge regarded him balefully.

"Where's my next scotch?" Serge said.

"It's in the poker machine."

Dave approached the bar, leaning against it with the palms of his hands and doing pushups against it. "Hey Meena . . ."

"He thinks he is going to haf sex with the bartender," Serge said to Craig. "He is under a misapprehension."

"So, Serge, what do you think about the noise bill?" Craig asked, referring to one of the perennial efforts on the part of some French Quarter residents to ban music from the streets.

"It doesn't matter because Hurricane Katrina is goink to come to town and reorganize city government for us."

"You think it's coming?" Craig said, trying to sound more amused than alarmed.

"No question."

"Are you going to leave?"

"Can a cypress tree leave a swamp? I am a live oak in a swamp of scotch. I am like termites who die if you cut off their water source . . ."

"Man, why don't you shut up," Dave said, coming over with his drink.

"He is frustrated because the bartender has repulsed his middle-aged efforts."

"You should have seen him the other night," Dave said. "Some guy who works at a Radio Shack on the West Bank came in and started talking about how forty years ago he had heard Clay Shaw plotting the Kennedy assassination. Serge calls him a retrograde fellow traveler and starts ranting about conspiracy theories and how if the guy had grown up in Transylvania or someplace he would really know about government conspiracy."

"I wanted to see how steady he was on his feet. I am afraid I offended him slightly."

"Just slightly," Dave said. "Hey I liked the piece you wrote on Irma Thomas."

"Thanks," Craig said.

"Fuckink prick," Serge said, vehemently. He was looking up at the television over the pass-through to the street, which was the one that always had the news or political shows on it. Craig and Dave followed Serge's gaze up to it, where an interview was in progress with Bobby Wise, the radio talk-show host. He had been in the news lately for some remarks he had made on immigration and border patrols, advocating a shoot-on-sight rule along the entire Mexican border.

"That son of a bitch," Serge went on. "He said the other day 'Why should we let them come here and work for minimum wage when we can pay them sixty cents an hour if they stay home?' Look at them— it's a fuckink love fest. No wonder—it's Fox . . . Bartender . . ."

The bartender came over and Serge said, "Put the channel back on CNN. What is Fox News doing on there?"

"That's what was on when I turned it on, Serge," she said, grabbing the remote and searching for CNN.

"It's channel twenty-nine," he said, disgustedly. After she had changed it and walked away to serve another customer, Serge said, "Fuckink replacement bartender."

"Hey," Dave said. "I have a date with her next Tuesday."

"That is science fiction," Serge said, looking at Craig. "So aren't you evacuating for the comink cataclysm?"

"You mean the hurricane?" Craig said. "We're leaving tomorrow."

"Good luck with the traffic," Dave said, looking up at the TV. "Serge called Nash Roberts at home. In Mississippi. Called him out of retirement."

"Are you writing a column about it?"

"No," Serge said. "I just wanted to see where God, in the person of Nash Roberts, thought I would be most likely to witness the apocalypse with my own eyes," Serge said.

"Even Nash Roberts can't predict a storm's path this far in advance," Dave said.

"Wait and see," Serge said.

Another half hour went by amid the banter, the familiar mode, and toward the end of it Craig noticed a foaming feeling in his stomach, a carbonation of fear, or dislocation, like what he had felt earlier at the *Gumbo* office, as if he were looking at all this normalcy and familiarity from outside, from somewhere in the future, after it had all been wiped away. It came up unbidden, like a sudden and overwhelming wind. Craig told himself to relax, that they had been through this many times. Somehow, the familiarity of these surroundings was upsetting him. He waited for the feeling to pass, and when it didn't he took his leave. As Craig said goodbye to his friends and walked toward the door, Serge called after him, "See you downriver."

6

Even before daylight on Sunday morning the traffic had thickened
and slowed to a crawl along the roads leading out of the city. The
hurricane was headed directly for New Orleans, and at the last
minute, now, even people who had never before evacuated finally
packed bags, threw blankets and bottled water in their car, or their
neighbors' car, or their brother's, along with one or two toys for the
kids, their medicines, their pets, all grabbed in an escalating urgency,
along with last-minute things that struck them—either heirlooms
(*Oh, get the wedding album . . . take the wedding album . . .*) or
odd choices that crossed their field of vision at some final moment
and were suddenly irradiated with meaning—that old lamp that had
sat for decades on their mother's nightstand, or a favorite picture
from the wall—and started out of town, faintly dazed with a sense
that this might in fact represent the end of everything they had ever
worked for, or taken for granted, heading toward some undefined
future. Countless copies of that day's *Times-Picayune* sat unsold all
over town, with the headline KATRINA TAKES AIM.

Some headed northeast, across the water toward Slidell and on
to eastern Mississippi and Alabama. Others headed north across the
Lake Pontchartrain Causeway to Mandeville and Covington, or out
Interstate 10 to Laplace and then north through Manchac toward

Hammond and McComb, up toward Jackson. And many more than that were bound straight west on I-10, toward Baton Rouge, or Lafayette, and then north to Shreveport or straight west through the long stretches of eastern Texas and finally to Houston, or up to Dallas. They had a hotel reservation, or they had a brother or a second cousin or an old college roommate somewhere where they could stay for a night, or a few nights if they needed to.

New Orleans is surrounded by water. The Mississippi River forms the crescent-shaped southern border, where the city's highest ground rises to meet the levees along the cuticle-shaped riverbank. To the east of the city is Lake Borgne, and to the north is Lake Pontchartrain, a 630-square-mile brackish lake. Off to the west is swampland that had been partially tamed decades before; pilings had been sunk into the mud and the lake bottom, and causeways had been built heading north, northeast and west, and bridges had been built across the Mississippi River to the suburbs of Gretna and Marrero and Terrytown on the Westbank.

The city proper forms a kind of shallow bowl, half of which sits technically below sea level. Most of New Orleans would flood even in a heavy rain if it were not drained by a network of pumps, built nearly a hundred years ago, that suck the water out of the city's subterranean drainage system and push it into canals at 17th Street and London Avenue, and into the Industrial Canal that divides the Upper and Lower Ninth Wards. The water level in these canals is higher than street level in many places alongside neighborhoods like Lakeview and Gentilly, and it is held back by levees, built decades ago by the United States Army Corps of Engineers. Residents near these levees had been alarmed, for years, by evidence of seeping water around the giant earthen banks, with no identifiable source. In other places, concrete walls, which had been driven down into the humped levees and extended up above them to hold back the water in the canals, had buckled slightly and shifted out of line, like teeth in need of straightening. The residents' alarm had caused some investigation, which had concluded that there were structural problems with the levees and the flood walls, which bore further investigation and, most likely, extensive and expensive repair. The reports were made, and nothing ever happened. By Sunday morning, most of the city's population was trying to get out of the cracked bowl ahead of the hurricane.

Police and state troopers had blocked off most roads leading into the city, and they routed traffic on the interstates so that all lanes were pointed outbound. This helped to a degree, but all it takes is for one badly serviced car to break down and block a lane, and traffic slows sharply. If another breaks down a bit farther on, it will cause a monumental snarl. People who are rattled, distracted, scared and in a hurry often do not drive well, and even minor accidents slow traffic for hours.

By eight o'clock Sunday morning, an apparently endless river of traffic crawled along Interstate 10 westbound under a withering sun, toward Baton Rouge and Lafayette and Texas. Cars inched along at ten miles per hour, and five miles an hour, past the shopping malls and chain stores of suburban Metairie and Kenner, all of them locked and shuttered now in advance of the storm. In Kenner, an accident blocked a lane of traffic, and cars merged, inched in, slowly, haltingly, squeezed into already engorged lanes, past the airport, which would shut down operations at five p.m., and into the causeway above the swampy area set aside for a spillway should the Mississippi River threaten to rise dangerously high. Police cars parked at angles, their red and blue lights flashing; occasionally one would zoom along the fire lane, siren hooting and burping, toward some invisible emergency. Across the long swamp between there and Boutte and Laplace and farther on toward Gonzales and Baton Rouge, the two eastbound lanes on the raised concrete roadway had been converted into westbound lanes as well, and in all lanes people sat at their steering wheels, or in passenger seats, staring straight ahead, grateful when they could move forward twenty feet without stopping.

Those who kept their radios on were bombarded by exhortation:

"If you have not yet left the city we have one word for you: Leave. *You can come back and rebuild later."*

"That's right, Jerry. This is a Category Five storm, it's not just a puddle-jumper to ride out by candlelight. We're looking at these images right now on the screen and you just can't believe the size of this thing."

"We're going to go now to Andrea, who's in our storm center . . ."

. . . and its audience sat at a standstill, staring into the distance past the heat vibrating above the hoods of their cars, waiting to move another ten feet away from home, away, out, gone.

It was nine-thirty before the Donaldsons had thrown the last pillow in the backseat and found the one toy that Malcolm wanted to take, which they could not locate anywhere, and obsessively doublechecked on the refrigerator and the lights and the other appliances. Finally, packed with pillows and water and blankets and towels, and everyone's special bag and clothes and toiletries, they set out through their neighborhood's eerily silent streets, rounding the corner onto Willow, and up to Carrollton, where they made a right turn and headed for the interstate.

Craig knew that they would hit terrible traffic. He assumed it would take them close to half an hour to get out of the city. Oxford was usually a six-hour drive; figuring an extra two or three hours, maybe they would pull in around seven that evening . . . Once they were out of the New Orleans bowl he could relax. They had hotel reservations; they would be all right. He had taken one Benevol to steady himself, but he had tanked up on coffee as well, to stay alert and focused.

In the backseat Annie and Malcolm sat in an unusual silence
as they drove past the familiar houses and street signs—Jeannette,
Spruce, Hickory, Panola—along Carrollton, which was almost
empty of other vehicles, deserted feeling under the beautiful shelter-
ing oak trees. Alice, next to him, was silent as well, and Craig fought
to keep a hovering panic at bay. They clipped along, away from
the river and toward the interstate, past the familiar restaurants and
stores, but as soon as they passed Claiborne Avenue traffic began to
back up from the entrance to I-10, still a mile or so away. A double
line of cars, vans, trucks, and SUVs fed slowly past the fast-food
places and the Pep Boys store and Xavier University, and into the
overloaded evacuation route.

Alice had tried putting in a cell phone call to her mother, but
she had difficulty getting through. After two attempts she gave up
and sat silently as well. Craig drove with his foot on the brake: roll
for ten feet; stop. Roll for seven feet; stop. Stopped, stopped, roll for
ten feet, stop . . . the traffic was slowing to a near standstill as they
approached Five Happiness, the Chinese restaurant where they liked
to eat on Friday nights, just past Pep Boys.

As he nursed the car along a few feet at a time, Craig felt claustro-
phobia entering him, stealthily, like a force of commandos in black,
spreading out down the unlit backstreets of his body, his stomach,
his chest, his legs. His clothes felt intolerably tight along his shoulders, his ankles. He realized that he would lose it if he had to sit in
the long line just to get on the westbound interstate. The prospect
was equivalent to contemplating a slow death by suffocation. His
forehead and chest were wet with sweat. He considered taking another Benevol, but that would have made driving hazardous.

"We can't do this," Craig said. "We'll never get out of the city
this way."

"Craig," Alice said, "we just have to deal with it at this point."

"Why are we stopped?" Annie said.

"There's just a lot of traffic, honey," Alice said.

Craig ran through the possibilities in his mind. He knew that if the traffic was this bad on Carrollton it would be impossible on the interstate. His plan had been to take the interstate west to where I-55 peeled off heading north toward Mississippi. That was beginning to seem like a bad idea. The rains at the leading edge of the storm were probably no more than a few hours away. Airline Highway, with its traffic lights, would likely be just as bad as, or worse than, the interstate. He could head out Carrollton, make a left at Canal and snake around the cemeteries and out Metairie Road, but they would still have to deal with the interstate. The Earhart Expressway would be the same story, eventually. The interstate was the bottleneck.

He decided to head for the Lake Pontchartrain Causeway. That led from the western suburb of Metairie straight north across the lake to Mandeville. If they could drive out Carrollton, and then Wisner, all the way to the lake, then cut across on some of the smaller streets and hit Causeway just north of I-10, they would at least bypass the westbound mess on the interstate. It would be better to be moving slowly on backstreets than to be stuck at a standstill on the highway. Once they were across the lake and out of the New Orleans bowl, they could make their way west to I-55 either on Route 190 or I-12 and continue north into Mississippi. The main thing was to get out of the bowl as quickly as possible; after that they could consider their options.

"We can't do this," he repeated. "It's going to take us two hours just to get on the interstate." Rolling his window down, Craig gestured to the car on his left that he wanted to maneuver out of the line, and started nosing out to the left. Alice noticed and said, "What are you doing? We can't get out of line . . ."

The car let him in, and Craig yelled "Thank you!" to the driver, pulled in front of her almost perpendicularly and, with a deep breath, swerved into the left lane, around all the cars merging right for the interstate entrance. From the backseat Malcolm's voice said "Stop it!" and Craig could hear Annie trying to shush him.

More emphatically than she intended, Alice said, "What are you doing? How are we supposed to get out of town?"

Craig swung the car crazily to the curb, across Carrollton from Thrift City, and brought them to a lurching halt. His hands were shaking on the steering wheel. "I am going to get us out of here," he said, struggling to keep his voice steady. "I want us to get out of here as badly as you do. But I can't do anything if you won't let me do it without yelling at me." He felt tears coming and he ordered them back.

They all four sat there, suspended for a long moment, silent and alert, and then, looking carefully in the side-view mirror, Craig pulled the car out onto the road and headed up Carrollton through deserted Mid-City, flying along at 50 mph with no problem, passing Banks Street, Canal Street, Venezia, Brocato's, the *Gumbo* offices— the streets all so quiet. They passed City Park and the New Orleans Museum of Art behind its long avenue of oaks and then drove out along Bayou St. John all the way to Robert E. Lee, where Craig allowed himself a small sense of satisfaction; they had clipped off a portion, at least, of the impossible traffic by doing this.

At Robert E. Lee they turned west, with the neighborhood called Lakeview to their left, and made their way past Bucktown through the traffic that was slowing and thickening once again, with cars heading for the Lake Pontchartrain Causeway. They crossed the bridge over the 17th Street Canal that separated Orleans Parish from Jefferson Parish, where the traffic now started to constrict and halt again, making its way through construction lanes, and snaking through residential streets en route to Causeway. By picking his way through the backstreets, Craig got them almost to the Bonnabel Canal, eventually turning left and coming to West Esplanade, and a glacial crawl, once again.

It took another thirty-five minutes to drive the half mile from the Bonnabel Canal along West Esplanade to Causeway, and the line of cars crawling north across the lake. That was an hour and a half for a trip that usually took fifteen minutes. At that rate they would get to Oxford, Craig calculated, at dinner time the next day. But of course the traffic wouldn't stay this bad all the way to Oxford.

Once he knew there were no other, better options and they were committed to the plan, Craig relaxed a little and was able to try lightening things up a little. "Okay," he said. "How are we doing?" Annie was in the backseat playing some kind of little game with Malcolm. Without looking up, she said "Fine." He looked at Alice to see if they were friends again yet, and she stared straight ahead out the front window.

"Once we get across the lake," he said, "we can hit 190 or I-12 and take that west to I-55."

She nodded. After a few moments Craig turned on the radio, switched it to AM looking for a news station, and pulled in an amped-up announcer who was saying, *". . . Hurricane Katrina, now a monster* Category Five *storm. The folks at the National Weather Service tell us that you'd rather live through a nuclear attack than a* Category Five *hurricane. So if you are out there, batten down the hatches, secure what you can, but get to someplace on high ground, away from the shore. We are hearing predictions of a tidal surge of up to twenty-five feet along the Gulf Coast, so you need to find a place now. As we say, this is* the big one . . ."

Craig and Alice both reached for the knob at the same time; Craig got there first and turned it off. For the kids' benefit, he said, "They say that every time. Hey, who wants to go to the bookstore in Oxford?"

"I do!" Annie said.

"Good!" Craig said. "We're there. And we'll have breakfast at Proud Larry's."

"Yay!"

Craig pulled out his cell phone and tried Bobby's number, got a "circuits busy" message, hit "end" and then immediately hit redial and the phone started ringing. After a ring and a half, Bobby's voice came through the phone, saying, "Ranger Rick."

"Where you at, Daddy-o?"

"Living the high life at Pam and Mike's in Baton Rouge. Where you at?"

"We're doing the big slog trying to get to the causeway. It took us like an hour and a half and we're just past Bucktown."

"Shit. Where are you going? Oxford?"

"That's the plan."

"Wait a second; Jen wants to say something to you."

This was good. As long as Craig had the lifeline to his friends, he knew he could maintain. The shallow banter was the signal that things were still normal. He glanced quickly at Alice, who was looking out the side window, in her own world.

"Hey," said Jen's voice, cocky, challenging. "Sorry we're gonna miss our weekly fuckfest."

"So Bobby knows about that?"

"He's been videotaping them from the closet."

Craig let himself laugh at this; he needed it. He laughed at it more than it deserved.

"Listen," she said, "if it's really bad come stay in Baton Rouge. Seriously. We checked with Pam and Mike and they have an extra bedroom."

"That's great," Craig said. "Thanks. Let's hope we don't need to be gone that long."

"Right, but I'm just saying . . . What . . . ?" she pulled the phone away and Craig heard Bobby's voice saying something and then Jen laughing. "Bobby says we would have to cut out the Sunday-afternoon 'appointments' though."

"No deal," Craig said.

"How's Alice?"

"She's fine. You want to talk to her?"

"Put her on for a second."

Craig handed the phone to Alice and continued the slow, stop-and-barely-go progress driving. Now that the phone wasn't in his ear he looked out the windshield at the sky, which was overcast. There was no breeze, apparently. Not quite an hour later, just before noon, they had moved the next half mile it took to put their front wheels on the causeway that would take them across Lake Pontchartrain and out of New Orleans.

Wesley never showed up at SJ's house that morning. SJ thought to take a break from securing his house to go to Joe Brown park and see if he could find Wesley playing his Sunday-morning football game, but there wasn't enough time.

As the exodus went on, those who had stayed in the city prepared, knowing that they were in for a long night at the least. The block was a little quieter than usual, but it was never crazy on a Sunday morning to begin with. SJ drove to Lucy's house on Tennessee Street to put up plywood. He let himself in the front door, assuming that his sister would still be asleep in her back room. To his surprise, he heard movement from the rear of the house, the kitchen, and he walked in, announcing himself in advance so as not to scare her. She was standing at the stove in a housedress, wearing a hairnet and pushing some scrambled eggs around in a skillet with a spatula.

"Samuel, hand me that Crystal sauce from over by the toaster," she said, as if in greeting. "There's more if you want me to put you on some."

Wordlessly, SJ handed his sister the small bottle and walked to the refrigerator to pull out the egg carton.

"I know you wondering, Samuel," Lucy said. "Wesley by his friend's house in Gentilly. He didn't want to tell you, but I'll tell you. So you don't need to be worrying. I think he worried about this other boy Chantrell been seeing and just trying to stay back some, see what's happening."

"Why didn't he tell me himself?" SJ said, feeling the anger rising. "Why did he have to tell me he would help me this morning, be at your house, and then he's someplace else?"

Lucy stood at the stove, quiet for a moment, poking at the eggs with the spatula, thinking. "You set a hard example sometime, SJ."

"What is that supposed to mean?" SJ said.

Now Lucy looked at him, frowning. "I mean you got a way that you go that you think is right." She paused and looked at him.

"What's wrong with that? Somebody got to keep things to-gether."

"Sometimes shit can be too damn together. Like it don't give anybody any room to . . . to make a mistake or nothing. That boy look up to you—who the fuck else he got to look up to Samuel?"

"Then why does he . . ."

"Don't talk now," she said. "Ain't a motherfuckin' answer for everything. He doesn't want to look bad, you understand? To you, I'm saying. He don't want to look bad to you. We adults, or trying to be . . ."

"Better be," SJ offered.

". . . and we know when you try and avoid some shit it catch up with you. Wesley still finding that out. It not like he making mistakes out of trying to fuck over somebody, Samuel. He don't know if he can be who he thinks he supposed to be. Or who you want him to be. Fuck," she said, turning the gas burner off quickly and scraping at the eggs, which were smoking in the pan. "Forgot I was cooking." She eyed the eggs. "They be all right."

SJ sat quietly, knew his sister was telling the truth. "I knew something was going on. Is this boy threatening him?"

"I don't think is a threat exactly," she said. "Get out a couple of plates and knife and fork. I think it just something he'd rather not deal with."

They got the food into the plates and Lucy set the skillet back on the stove and came back to the small kitchen table and started to eat with her younger brother. As he sat eating, SJ realized that it was one of the rare times that Lucy actually felt to him like the older sister she was. She was thoughtful and present, and he realized that it was, odd as it seemed, a relief to hear her talking to him in the way she had.

They didn't talk about the question anymore; SJ got the plywood up and Lucy said she would come over in the late afternoon. She wanted to wrap up some things and stash them in closets. When he left he stood out front, looking around, looked at the Industrial Canal levee two blocks away, looked at the neighborhood full of people going about their business. And for just a fleeting minute he had the thought that it might be a good thing that Wesley wasn't staying there. Then he headed back to his house.

Bootsy came over from across the street and they dragged the large sheets of plywood around front from SJ's backyard shed, along with his roofers' ladder. Each window had a special technique for attaching the plywood, depending on how the window was exposed to potential winds and flying objects. A few sheets had been stolen from the back of his truck earlier that year, so he had enough to cover only the most necessary windows. The ones on the side facing downtown and the canal he left open because that side was protected somewhat by Mrs. Gray's house. They put up the specially fitted ones on the lee side on the second-floor camelback, with hooks that could be disengaged from inside.

Then they went to Bootsy's and secured his place as well as they could; it was a less complicated job, as it was only one story, low to the ground. When they were finished with Bootsy's they looked in on Mrs. Gray, who was being picked up in an hour or two by her son, who would take her to the home of some cousins in Laplace. SJ assured her he'd keep an eye on her place. They made a few more rounds and then around one o'clock stopped into Happy Shop over on North Claiborne to get a sandwich. Minh, the owner, was outside, hammering up wood.

"Close at noon," he said, over his shoulder, at their approach, meaning the store was closed. Then, seeing who it was, he nodded twice to himself, and climbed down, saying, "Mista Jay, you leave?"

"Nothing to leave for, Minh. Can we get a sandwich?"

Shaking his head, Minh preceded them into the darkened store, muttering to himself in Vietnamese. "All we got ham sandwich rye bread. Cooler shut down."

"Put some mustard on mine, Minh," Bootsy said. "Brown mustard if you got it. Where you stay at for the storm?"

"Only French yellow mustard. We stay cousin Westbank," Minh said.

When they had their sandwiches, Minh said he would put it on account, he had to hurry, and SJ and Bootsy thanked him and walked down the street together, enjoying their sandwiches.

"I love a goddamn ham sandwich, J," Bootsy said. "Only thing I like better be a liver cheese sandwich, and a Big Shot pineapple soda. I wish they had the brown mustard though."

They walked along, slowly, the occasional car passing on North Claiborne. They talked some about the Saints game Friday night, about this and that.

"Lucy staying by you?" Bootsy asked.

"Yes," SJ said. "I put up wood by her house earlier."

"Man, you were here for Betsy?"

"I rescued people in a boat with my daddy."

"Mmmh," Bootsy said. "We was in Kenner. Of course, being significantly"—he took pains to articulate the word despite the sandwich still in his mouth—"younger than you, I have less memory of those days." There was a two-year age difference in Bootsy's favor, which was a reliable source of pleasure for Bootsy when things got slow.

Poker-faced, nodding slightly, SJ replied, "And it is impressive how you managed to put on so much more weight than I have in such a limited time."

"Look here, I still got my hair."

"Gray as it is."

They walked along North Claiborne, laughing occasionally, until they had finished the sandwiches and thrown the wrapping paper away in a garbage can at the corner of Reynes Street. They walked the neighborhood streets, through all the memories, which did not need to be spoken of because they were in them. The day was starting to cloud over just a bit.

Around three in the afternoon Lucy came over to SJ's house and they watched the television some. SJ made calls to his crew members and a few other people to make sure they were okay, told them to come by his house if they lost electricity. Around six o'clock SJ fried up some fish and he and Lucy got ready for the weather to roll in.

It took the Donaldsons ten hours to reach Jackson, Mississippi, ordinarily less than a three-hour drive and less than half the way to Oxford. Cars broke down along the Lake Pontchartrain Causeway every half mile, it seemed, and traffic would need to merge and squeeze into one lane or another to get around them. At one point, traffic stopped completely for twenty-five minutes. Midway through the four-hour ride across the lake toward Mandeville, with all the stopping and going, Malcolm threw up in the backseat. The vomit smelled of soured milk and rotten vegetables, and the smell filled the car and Craig began to retch but fought the reflex back. They crawled along, when they were able to move, at five to ten miles an hour in the bilious heat, with all the windows open, Alice and Craig arguing about what to do. Alice reached back to clean Malcolm's face and hands with some of the wet wipes she had brought, but they were no match for the magnitude of the problem. Craig refused to pull over, saying that the cops needed the breakdown lane clear to get past and handle the accidents and breakdowns, and besides, what were they going to do, just wipe out the seat and leave the wipes out there in a pile on the road? They needed to get across the lake, and he would not stop.

When they finally made it across the causeway and put their front tires on solid ground again, they stopped along with hundreds of other evacuees at the first service station and waited on line for twenty minutes to use the clogged, fouled toilets. The attendant had given up refilling the paper towel dispenser and had left a few dozen banded bunches of paper towels there, many of which, used, littered the floor like piles of soggy leaves around the overflowing wastebaskets; you had to kick them aside to walk to the one toilet or one urinal in the men's room. Craig tore open one of the paper bands and took three handfuls of the fresh ones, wet half of those with water from the faucet, and did his best to clean the backseat and get Malcolm clean. He got a couple of long looks as he came out of the restroom with all the towels, and he had been on the verge of asking one man what the fuck he was staring at, but he resisted the impulse.

After half an hour they headed out again, and it was clear before long that they would not be spending that night in Oxford. The smaller roads they had to take through Mandeville and Covington to get eventually to I-55 were squeezed to stoppage like capillaries by edema, circulation choked, apoplexy on the near horizon. The Donaldsons spent hours in stopped traffic on small tree-shaded roads, single file, and then in go-five-feet-and-then-stop traffic, and then go-twenty-feet-and-then-stop traffic, and then traffic halted completely for ten minutes because of a car with a dead radiator blocking both lanes, then only one lane, and finally on I-55 north of McComb the traffic a steady twenty-five miles an hour until another accident halted things completely for twenty minutes.

Pine barrens of Louisiana and southern Mississippi for hours, nothing to be seen but the endless line of red taillights stretching off into the afternoon as the light slowly drained from the sky. Craig and Alice agreed that they would not try for Oxford and would spend the night in Jackson, assuming they could find a place to stay. Oxford was another three hours past Jackson, even with no traffic, and they had no steam left; they were exhausted.

At 7:30 p.m., ten hours after they had set out, the Donaldsons followed the curve of I-55 into Jackson, took the first exit possible, and drove around Jackson's streets for fifteen minutes, twenty minutes, until they hit an arterial road that they followed north, hoping and praying to find some kind of small hotel that had been over- looked in the rush. Finally they topped a rise in the road and, from a distance, saw a sight that almost made them weep with gratitude, the bright lights of the Best Host Inn, nationwide beacon of comfort from coast to coast, with its familiar logo in pulsing neon out front, power, solidity, warmth, light . . .

"What do we do if there are no rooms?" Craig said, thinking out loud.

"We can't keep going," Alice said. "We have to find something." Both the kids were asleep under the blanket in the backseat. It took five minutes to follow a long, slow line of cars into the parking lot. Neither Craig nor Alice said anything; obviously the chances were overwhelming that the place was full. Stopping the car would wake the kids up, but there was no real choice.

Craig pulled the car over behind a dozen other parked cars; the lot itself appeared to be filled, and there were cars parked on the grass by a gated area that he took to be the pool. He got out and told Alice he would go inside to check out the situation, and she could stay there with the kids.

A crowd filled the lobby, but to his surprise there was almost nobody lined up at the desk.

Craig approached a tall, pleasant-looking clerk who gave him a commiserative look and, before Craig even reached the desk, said, "You know what I'm going to say, right?"

"We'll take anything," Craig said.

The clerk, pointed over behind Craig, toward the large, lodge-like lobby which Craig, zoned out, hadn't even glanced at, and Craig followed the direction of the finger and saw, to his disbelief, the entire lobby spread with blankets, people on couches, on the floor, televisions going. From behind him, Craig heard the clerk say, "Every place in town is the same story."

Craig stared at the scene, sick in his stomach. A moment later he turned back to the clerk, who was holding up a finger, telling another newcomer to wait for a moment. "I have two small children. What do I do?"

The tall clerk's face softened a little, helplessness wrinkling the corners of his eyes. "We can put you down by the pool," he said. "That's the best I can offer you at this point."

"The pool?"

"We have an indoor pool on the lower level. There are beach loungers down there; we can give you blankets and pillows. I wish we could do more. Or you can try and find a space on the floor in the lobby." To another new person he said, "We're full up; sorry." Then to Craig, "Let me know what you want to do."

"Every place is like this?"

"Yes sir," the clerk said, his tone already contracting slightly at Craig's vacillating and the pressure of more arrivals.

"Okay," Craig said. "What do I need to do?"

"Just go on down and pick a spot and then come back up and we'll give you some bedclothes."

"Should I pay you now . . . ?"

The clerk waved his hand dismissively. "We're not going to charge you to sleep in a beach chair at the pool."

A man who had approached the desk asked, "Does anyplace around here have any room?"

Craig headed back out to the car and told Alice what the story was. "I guess we can just leave the car here; people are parked all over the place."

"We can't sleep in the pool, for God's sake," Alice said. "Where are we going to change clothes? How can we sleep . . ."

"Alice, look . . ." He took the standard deep breath. "There are people all over the lobby sleeping. All the rooms are sold out, and there are no rooms anywhere nearby. What do you want to do? Should we keep driving? I can't do it. I say we just get it, claim our little place, make it an adventure"—Annie rustled in the backseat, waking up—"and make the best of it and then God willing we head back tomorrow. Or we head to Oxford tomorrow. We've got the room up there." Alice finally agreed, and they moved inside.

On the televisions in the wood-paneled living room of the lobby, images of the storm filled the screens in lurid color, with voices of urgent report, miles per hour, looking like a direct hit, radius equal to, water temperature, landfall estimated at, evacuations have been ordered for, storm surge as high as; this would go on all night as the country watched one of the largest storms in recorded history head straight for New Orleans. Unremarked in any of the reports were the dozens of places along the levee system that had been designed improperly, built improperly, and around which water had been seeping for years like blood from diseased gums. But it was all beyond anyone's control now.

7

SJ fell asleep on the couch just as the sky began to lighten. The wind had started to rise as the sun went down the night before, and it had kept rising. The sound went from a whistling to something deeper, a groaning sound as if you were pulling a rope through a hole in a piece of sheet metal. This groaning started and stopped unpredictably, leaving only the whistling behind it. Odd moments of near-calm were ruptured by abrupt shrieks of wind. Lucy sat on the green upholstered chair in the living room; she could have slept in Camille's room, but she didn't want to be alone.

SJ left the lights on so that he would know exactly when the power went off, which happened around one a.m. He was stocked with flashlights and batteries and candles if they were necessary. Somewhere around two in the morning, with the wind very high, he heard a loud, vibrating sound coming from the back of the house, off the kitchen; he made his way quickly to the back with his flashlight beam, slipped the dead bolt and opened the door and saw through the lashing rain that the rear gutter had come detached at one end and was waving around. Something large came flying through the beam and smashed into the old shed on the left side of the yard. He closed the door again and threw the bolt and something smacked into the side of the house with the sound of a door slamming, then there was a kind of clacketing sound like he remembered from putting baseball cards in his bicycle spokes when he was a kid, then that stopped.

He knew there would be roof damage; the question was how much. He followed his flashlight beam up the stairs and looked in the rooms, sealed like tombs to the raging outdoors, the howling and groaning outside contrasted with a creepy stillness within. Two rooms; nothing apparently amiss. He walked back downstairs and spent the rest of the night prowling the house this way.

He was on the couch with his flashlight in his hand at his side, he had fallen asleep, when something shook him. He sat up, still asleep in the gray morning light, but buffeted by something profound, like thunder he thought at first. As he listened, sleep draining from his head like water from a sieve, trying to determine its shape, a second pounding, shaking roar exploded and the house shook again.

Now he was awake, and he knew what had happened, knew before he saw it. He ran to the front door and opened it to see a car rushing by, upside down on top of a foaming river of sticks and debris. A moment of free-fall in his mind before he slammed the door and reflexively started for the back of the house. Three steps and water was swirling around his feet, dragging at the cuffs of his trousers; he stepped higher, idiotically trying to keep his feet dry, when he realized he didn't know where Lucy was. He hollered her name out, as loudly as he could, heard something break behind him and turned to see one of Rosetta's vases fall off a pedestal and smash on a table, and as he watched the broken crater of the vase scoot across the room on the water the window on the right side of the house exploded—the image he had was of someone throwing up—it spewed inward, glass, sash and blinds, the foaming water following it into his house, and he turned and ran for the stairs, with the water up to his knees, yelling for Lucy, who had appeared in the door of the rear bathroom and seemed to be frozen in place. She was staring down at the water, and SJ went to her, the water now to his thighs, and took her by the wrist and when she didn't move, said, calmly as he could, "We'll be allright upstairs," and she started following him and they made the stairs, the water now at their waists, and climbed, and by the fifth step they were out of the water, and he told her with his hand on her back to keep going, and he didn't look back either. As long as the house doesn't go, he kept thinking; as long as the house doesn't go. He couldn't feel the house shifting at all, but it was hard to tell with the wind shaking it. The upstairs bedroom was pitch dark and stifling hot. He felt for and found the flashlight he had laid on the dresser, and with it he located the matches and a candle, which he lit, concentrating on keeping his hand steady. He got Lucy settled and sat with her; they said a prayer together and she said it with her lips shaking. After she had stopped shaking, he got up and retrieved one of the gallon water jugs he had laid in upstairs along with some food for a couple of days, and pulled the plastic cap off of it and poured some into one of the glasses he had put up there and handed it to Lucy. She drank it.

"I didn't think we'd never use those supplies," SJ said, trying to keep his voice as even as possible. "But that's what Daddy always said, have a second floor and put food and water up there."

"I know that; Daddy said that," Lucy said. "Daddy said that. Have you some water for three days." SJ drank some, too. The radio was downstairs, useless now, even though he had batteries. He hadn't thought to have a radio up in the room. When he was sure that Lucy was at least stable, he went to the stairs to try and see where the water was.

The surface of the water was up to within two feet of the downstairs ceiling, and an unbroken river seemed to swirl from his living room out to the street. The façade of his house had been pulled off by the water. The seven feet he'd moved the house back from the sidewalk might have been the reason the house was still standing at all; the rush of water had been deflected by just enough. Then he thought about his van, and the truck. He sat still for a minute on the top stair, trying to breathe slowly, trying to gauge whether the water was still rising, and how quickly. It seemed to have slowed. He went back to check on Lucy.

Lucy seemed to be hyperventilating and SJ sat with her in the wobbly candlelight and told her to look at him, which she did, and he said, "We are going to be allright. The worst is over. We are going to be allright."

She looked into his eyes, and nodded her head and said, "Where Wesley at?"

"Wesley is allright. He's in Gentilly by his friend. Wesley allright. Do you hear me?"

She nodded, exaggeratedly, and then she began sobbing in his arms, shaking, and SJ held his older sister in his arms, and after no more than a few seconds, she said, "I be allright, SJ. I will be allright. But stay with me, don't leave me here."

"Nobody going nowhere," he said. "Nobody going nowhere."

8

Craig woke up slowly, feeling as if he had had no rest at all, as if he were on a hospital gurney in a tank . . . some kind of tank . . . he drifted . . . then, suddenly, all awake, his heart pounding, he sat up, almost losing his balance out of the narrow, plastic-banded chaise lounge where he had spent the night, in the humid chlorine funk of the swimming pool room. Alice's chaise was empty, as was Malcolm's; Annie was dead asleep in hers.

A sharp pain shot down through Craig's shoulder blade; inhaling made the pain wow up. Your regulation sleep-in-the-wrong-position muscle freak-out. He stood up carefully. Around the cement floor that surrounded the rectangular pool were maybe fifteen other families in various attitudes of sleep. His watch said 8:30. The journalist in him felt as he did on the morning after a big and heated election, the itch to get the results. He wanted some coffee badly, and even worse he wanted to see the news, find out what had happened with the storm. But he couldn't leave Annie there. He debated whether to awaken her.

"I'm awake, Daddy."

Startled, he looked down at Annie, who was in exactly the same position as before, eyes closed, and wondered if it could have been someone else's child talking. He kept looking at her, then he looked around the immediate area. He was tired.

"Here, Daddy."

He looked back at Annie, quickly, and she seemed, again, un-moved, except for a smile that she was trying to hide, before she broke up in giggles.

"You little fibber," Craig said, bending down and tickling her. That was another thing he loved about his daughter: She joked, he thought, like a New Orleanian. Now she squealed at the tickling and Craig noticed someone nearby shift in their sleep and open their eyes, and Craig quickly stopped and said, "Shhhh . . ." to his daughter.

He sat down on the chaise next to her. "Did you get any sleep?" he whispered to her.

"Yes. I was scared for a while but then I went to sleep. Malcolm went to sleep right away."

"Malcolm can sleep through anything except a normal night."

"Where's Mommy?"

"I don't know. You want to go find her?"

Annie nodded and sat up and they started off to the exit, but Craig stopped, looking back at their stuff. "I don't think anyone's going to bother our stuff, do you?"

Looking back at their little camp, Annie shrugged. Craig went back and retrieved his cell phone; Alice had apparently taken her Big Bag . . . They could go. Everybody there was in the same situation.

Upstairs they found Alice standing in a group of people watching one of several TVs positioned throughout the lobby, where the news was being reported live from New Orleans and the Gulf Coast.

"Where's Malcolm?" Craig said.

Alice pointed to the couch right behind her, where Malcolm was totally immersed in a small truck that he was driving into an abyss between two cushions. "It missed New Orleans," Alice said. "At the last minute it jogged east."

"What?" Craig said. "It missed the city completely?"

"Not completely," Alice said. "But it was weaker than they thought it would be, and it went off to the east."

All around the lobby people—black and white, young and old—ambled around, drinking coffee and eating doughnuts, or lolled, asleep, in sleeping bags on the floor and on couches. Around the televisions, denser groups of people sat, surfacing from sleep, hopeful that the storm had in fact, like so many others, missed the city.

On the television a reporter in a yellow poncho with the hood up was reporting from a side street in the blowing wind; the screen showed serial images of downed trees, glass windows blown out of a hotel, a traffic light that had come off its wire and was sitting, broken, in the middle of a street, looked like around Howard Avenue, Craig guessed. The reporter was saying, "This is still a very dangerous storm; anyone listening needs to stay inside to avoid getting hit by flying debris. It is not safe outside yet. As I was saying, here is the view down Canal Street, we have a number of trees over and broken windows, and it's just a mess out here. So stay inside, but, again, it does seem as if New Orleans has dodged the bullet once more, as Hurricane Katrina heads off to the northeast . . ."

Craig and Alice put their arms around each other and stood there for a long moment, watching.

"Can we go home?" Annie said.

"Not just yet," Craig told her. "We need to make sure it's all clear and then see what's happening with the traffic."

"They have a buffet over there," Alice said.

"I could use some coffee. Did Malcolm eat?"

"Yes, but he'll have to eat again before we start back. I'll start packing up."

"Let's give it a little while before we start back," Craig said. "We should see what's happening with the electricity."

"I can't spend another night on that chaise lounge," she said.

"Well, it doesn't look as if you'll have to."

They stood there together for a moment, looking blankly at the television images. "I can't keep doing this every month," Alice said. "This is crazy."

Craig was about to say "It's not 'every month'," about to step on the rapidly moving walkway that led to one of their entrenched arguments, but he stopped himself. He was too tired, and too close to the edge, and he knew Alice was, too. So, instead, he said, "Let's get through this and we can talk about it when we get back, right?"

Alice pressed her lips together, nodded, looked up at him, right in his eyes, for a long moment. "I love you," she said.

Craig frowned, smiled at her, said, "Really?"

"Yes." She put her arms around him and hugged him with her head on his chest, and they stayed that way for what were, for Craig, several long, blessed moments during which all the pain of the world disappeared.

Craig got himself a cup of coffee and got some cereal for Annie, and then he and Annie went out for a walk to look around. The sky was gray and mottled—the outer edge of the hurricane as it made its way north—but they walked out, holding hands, through the parking lot and down the hill on the sidewalk to the intersection. Craig treasured these moments when he could get away with Annie. Alice tended to make her nervous and quiet, but when they were alone she asked Craig questions about everything, and shared her own developing inner life with him. Now, walking, she asked if New Orleans was still going to be there when they got back, and Craig assured her that New Orleans would still be there and would always be there.

"I want to always live in New Orleans," Annie said, and Craig heard the words with a happiness that, even as he held on to them, he knew wasn't quite right. It was his love of New Orleans he was hearing reflected, and that he needed to hear reflected, not hers, not exactly. He knew that putting the weight of his own needs on her would do her no good in the long run. But for right then, after the upset of the past couple of days, he would let this be their I-Love-New-Orleans club. He needed it.

Then she asked him what made hurricanes happen, and Craig struggled briefly to retrieve enough information in his mind to fashion a coherent answer that could satisfy her as they walked part of the way up another block. But by that time the first few drops of rain had started falling. It began as barely perceptible needle-pricks of drizzle, and then those began to be interspersed with drops that felt fat and round like grapes, and Craig knew that the sky was about to open up. They ran back to the motel, getting pretty well soaked in the last fifty feet. They stopped under the canopy and watched it coming down in sheets, with a sound like frying bacon.

"Wow," Craig said, "we just made it."

"Yeah."

"Let's go see what Mommy's doing."

They found Alice back in the pool area, gathering their stuff. Annie went off to grab Malcolm and walk him around the pool. "Maybe we ought to sit tight and see what the storm is doing before we give up the space."

Alice looked up at him. "I'm not staying in this pool another night," she said. "I don't care if we have to sit in traffic for another ten hours."

"Listen to what I'm saying," he said. "It's not just the traffic. If we head back now we'll be driving through the storm. Look what it's doing outside. We need to wait until it passes."

"Fine. I'll pack up the car and we'll leave after the storm passes."

"The roads might not be passable. There might be flooding."

"*Craig,*" she said, exasperated.

"Fine," he said. "Pack up the car." He walked away.

Craig got himself a bagel with peanut butter from the buffet. He walked over to a group of people who had gathered to watch the news coverage from New Orleans on one of the four or five TVs. It was somewhere around ten a.m., and people were crowded onto the three couches near the TV, and another ten stood around. A newscaster, his face eerily lit against a darkling, chaotic background that turned out to be the Superdome, was saying that parts of the roof were blowing off the building and it was raining in on the people who had taken shelter there. One short white woman with a definite New Orleans accent standing next to Craig said, to no one in particular, "The power went out on 'em."

Craig said, "It looks like they have lights, though."

The short woman looked at him, half-smiling. "Dat's the backup generators, dawlin'. We'll see how long dat last."

A heavyset African-American man in a blue and red polo shirt, standing on the other side of Craig, said, "The power is out in the whole city it looks like."

That, Craig knew, was more or less to be expected after a storm of that size. Outside the sky was dark, but they were inside, they were warm, they had the television going, there was food. They were okay for a while. Craig knew that he wouldn't relax until he knew just how bad the damage was. It did sound as if the city had escaped the worst once again. If the power was in fact out and the storm was still going, they were certainly not going back to the city that night. Alice was reading *Sense and Sensibility* on a couch, with Annie next to her drawing in a sketchbook and Malcolm on his knees looking over the back of the couch at someone, making faces.

Restless, Craig walked out front under the motel canopy. People smoked and looked out at the rain and the abnormally dark sky, punching numbers in on cell phones; once in a while someone would come running up to the shelter with a jacket over his head, looking around, smiling. Craig pulled out his cell phone to call Bobby. His first try yielded nothing; on his second he got an "All circuits are busy; please try your call again later" message. He waited for five seconds, tried it again, same thing. He flipped the phone shut, looked around. He noticed the heavyset African-American man from inside, closing his own phone and shaking his head, looking over at him.

"Yours, too?" Craig said.

"I think they are all down," the man said.

Craig asked the man if he was from New Orleans, and the man said he was.

"So are we," Craig said. "What part of town?"

"Gentilly," the man said. "Up off Mirabeau." Craig knew the area as a middle-class black neighborhood of tidy, almost suburban homes.

"Oh yeah," Craig said. "Are you going back tonight?"

The man looked at him as if to see whether he was joking. "I don't think any of us is going back in tonight. They have to send in tree crews, electric. It's going to be a few days." The man chuckled.

Craig checked his watch; it was just after eleven. Maybe it was subliminally noticing a line of cars backed up by the light at the corner, their headlight beams cutting through the driving rain, maybe it was something else, but on an impulse, an intuition, Craig felt for his car keys in his pocket, moved to the edge of the canopy, gauged the distance to his car and, taking a deep breath, made a run for it, got in soaked, and drove it to the gas station on the corner, waited for five minutes in a line of three cars and then filled up the Toyota with gasoline. Later, when the power went down in Jackson and the gas pumps couldn't pump, he would look back on that, at least, as one good decision he had made.

Back in the motel, Craig noticed something slightly different in the tempo of things, a different deployment of people somehow, some difference in the distribution of people, and then he saw Alice gesturing to him across the long lobby from one of the couches where she was gathered with a large group, watching the television.

Something was wrong; he could tell that by the looks on people's faces.

As he arrived, one of the reporters, on the street in what appeared to be the central business district, a deserted side street, was speaking into the camera, saying, "As we said a few moments ago, we don't know where this water is coming from. One city official told us they thought it might be a broken water main, but we now have word, just in, a report of a possible breach in a levee along Lake Pontchartrain that might be connected in some way to this water. These reports are very preliminary, though, Regina, and of course we'll keep you up to date as we find out more."

9

Wesley awoke from a fitful sleep on his friend Roland's couch; his T-shirt was wet with sweat, and the lights, which had been on when he fell asleep, were off, along with the air-conditioning and the rest of the power. His cell phone said it was 10:09 in the morning. Outside, rain was spitting and splattering against the windows. Trees blowing.

He got up, walked to the door of Roland's bedroom, where his friend was asleep, mouth open, holding desperately onto a pillow, a comforter tangled around his bare legs. Wesley walked into the darkened kitchen, opened the refrigerator, which was still cool inside, felt for the carton of milk, opened it, smelled it, and drank greedily from it. They were still there. One more hurricane.

Back in the living room he retrieved his cell phone and walked out onto the screen porch. He wanted to call over to SJ's house and check on them, but he knew his uncle would be angry with him for not showing up to help the previous morning, and also for not staying by his mama's house overnight as he had said he would.

He had been staying at Roland's most nights for the past two weeks. There was another young man in the Lower Nine who had gone out a couple of times with Chantrell, and Wesley had heard that the young man, whose name was Elias, had been talking about fucking Wesley up because he had hit Chantrell. Wesley didn't take the talk completely seriously, but anyway he also liked to be off on his own sometime instead of just at his mama's house. He and Roland delivered pizzas for Café Roma four nights a week; they liked to ride the bikes, talk bikes, just chill together, watch a movie, play PlayStation. Roland also had a widescreen plasma they liked to watch movies on. Roland's uncle, who owned the house, wasn't around much.

Wesley tried Chantrell's number and got an "all circuits busy" message. Then he called his friend Ray-Ray and got the same thing. He stood looking out absently at LaHarpe Street, waiting for his head to clear from sleep. The street in front of Roland's house had flooded a bit at the edges, nothing special in a heavy rain. They had put the motorbikes in the shed in back, the way they always did, to keep them out of sight. He debated about going to get them and putting them on the porch, but the bikes would be too visible on the porch and the rain seemed to be slacking off. He figured they were safest where they were for right then at least.

He went back inside but it was dark and there was nothing to do with all the power off.

Restless. He tried the cell phone again; no luck. Then he thought to try Roland's phone, which had no dial tone when he picked up. His own cell said it was just about ten-thirty. He found his jeans on the leather chair where he had left them folded, a habit he'd learned from his Uncle SJ, snapped them open and pulled them on leg by leg over his boxer shorts. He uncrumpled his white socks and got them on, then his sneakers. He grabbed his keys and money from the coffee table and headed out to look around. He would let Roland sleep a while.

Wesley made his way in the light rain and wind to the end of the block, turned left and then cut across a short street and came out on the corner of Broad a block from where Bayou Road made its diagonal cut, headed for the Fairgrounds. He crossed Broad, which was empty of cars. Across the middle of the street, a gigantic piece of twisted metal that looked like part of a store awning, and a garbage can rolling back and forth in the middle of the street like a severed head. The traffic lights were out. The dogleg of Bayou Road merged into Gentilly Boulevard, the street and sidewalks full of downed branches, leaves and debris, wood, shingles, glass thick on the ground, gnarled lengths of gutter. One house seemed to have had its roof torn off, and a little bit past it Wesley saw the roof, fractured and sitting on edge, between the house and the one next to it. Two men stood looking at it. A few people were out on their porches.

As he made the curve onto Gentilly Boulevard, Wesley saw a disturbing vista in the distance, as if a mirror had been laid over the street reflecting the wide, dark canopy of oak trees so that the same image was reflected upside down. It was disorienting. For a few blocks in front of him there was only a little water on the sides of the boulevard, by the curbs, but six or seven blocks down, water covered the narrow grass median strip in the middle of the road and made the glassy illusion.

He headed for a grocery store two blocks down, thinking to see if there was anything to eat. A few people were carrying groceries out of the store's dark interior and putting them into an SUV that sat at the curb in water up to the middle of its hub caps. Wesley recognized one of them as Roland's cousin, a slightly older fellow named Lonnie. Lonnie acknowledged him briefly as he passed carrying a bag of groceries.

"Where Roland?" Lonnie said.

"He sleeping back at the house," Wesley said.

Lonnie looked very disturbed. "He still asleep?"

"Yeah," Wesley said.

"The canal broke," Lonnie said. "They had a break up by Mirabeau. That's where all this water come from. We got to get out of here."

Wesley said, "Where you heard that?"

"Kwa-ME," Lonnie shouted into the store, ignoring Wesley's question. He stepped up into the store and left Wesley on the sidewalk. The water in the distance seemed to have crawled nearer, but it was hard to be sure. Lonnie came out of the store at a trot, dashing past Wesley. "You going to come with me or not?"

Wesley's first thought was to get to his uncle's house and make sure his Mama was okay. He climbed into the Explorer without knowing where Lonnie meant to go. "We got to get Roland," Lonnie said. "When we get to the house, run inside and get him. Not walk, you hear?"

"You can bring me down Claiborne to my uncle house?"

Lonnie looked at Wesley as if there were something wrong with him, and didn't answer. Halfway back to Roland's house the water looked too deep for the Explorer to continue straight to their destination.

"I can't get through here," Lonnie said. "Meet me on Esplanade by the red statue. You know the statue?" Esplanade Avenue was laid along a slight rise, the highest ground in the area.

"Yeah."

"Meet me there."

Wesley got out of the car as Lonnie turned and the Explorer cut a wake through the shin-deep water, and he ran, high-stepping, through the water for a block and a half the rest of the way to Roland's house. He let himself in, dripping water across the living room all the way to Roland's bedroom, where he saw only Roland's empty bed.

Wesley hollered out his friend's name, dashed into all the rooms of the house, but his friend was gone, no question about it. When he was absolutely sure, he started for the front door at a run, then he remembered their bikes. He turned around, ran back through the kitchen and opened the back door and saw that the yard was a lake, the water knee-deep against the shed. The bikes had to be flooded, he knew, if they were even still there. But he opened the door anyway and ran across the yard, opened the shed door enough, hard against the water, to see the bikes there, in water to the tops of the wheel rims. He got back into the house dripping water all over, looked around, made sure that he had his cell phone, and headed out to meet Lonnie.

Outside, now that the rain had all but stopped, neighborhood people were out on their porches, talking to one another across the street. The water had reached the second step on most houses, and the residents assumed, knowing nothing of the levee breaks yet, that it was from the heavy rain. Wesley made his way carefully through the water, which was just above his knees. As he waded, he again tried SJ's number and Lucy's number and now had no luck at all, not even a circuits-busy. Nothing. He replaced the cell phone in its faux-leather holster on his belt, thought about the water, then removed the phone from his belt and rigged it so that it would hang from the neck of his T-shirt. The streets were uneven and sometimes the water got deeper, sometimes shallower.

On North Dorgenois, a block and a half from Esplanade, he saw an old lady across the street, in water up to her chest, holding on to an iron railing leading up to a shotgun house. She was looking down with a frown on her face; her wispy gray hair was pinned up and her yellow housedress ballooned around her in the water. She appeared frozen in place. Wesley called to her, asking if she were allright. The old woman looked slowly up at him, smiled slightly around her eyes, then turned back down to regard the water again with a frown.

Torn, the thought of Lonnie waiting pressing on him, the urgency to check in with Lucy and SJ, but still this woman wasn't moving, and Wesley waded across the street, careful not to lose his footing, until he was by the old lady on the other sidewalk. Again she looked up at him slowly with that smile, and said, "I was just going out to make groceries; I had the money in my pocket . . ."

Wesley could tell that the woman was disoriented; he asked where she lived and she said "I stay by my daughter's house." Then he asked where she was going, and she looked him in the eye, puzzled slightly by the question, it seemed and, frowning slightly and laughing at the same time, her eyes clearing, she said, "I don't know."

"This ain't your house?" he said.

"No . . ." she said, looking back down at the water.

"Listen," Wesley said, "it's a flood from the canal. I'm going to carry you to Esplanade. You allright with that?"

Her eyebrows went up slightly in mild wonderment and she shrugged, saying, "I guess that's allright . . ."

Wesley took a deep breath, set himself as well as he could, and then he slid his right arm under her arm and around her back, crouched down, closed his eyes as his head neared the water, feeling for the back of her knees; he found them, slid his left arm under them and with a sweep lifted her and stood full up, then began carrying the woman toward Esplanade. It was only after he had done it that he realized that he had submerged his cell phone as well. "Where did all this water come from?" she asked, almost amusedly.

At Esplanade he was able to set her down on the ground. She was barefoot. He was unclear at that moment which way the statue was. Half a block down on Esplanade, the winking, twitching blue lights of a patrol car, and two officers, one white and one black, standing by it.

Wesley told the old woman to wait where she was and he took off at a trot through the leaves and around the branches, one of them huge, that covered and crossed the wide, shaded avenue, to where the two police were, along with two patrol cars, one with its lights on. They took no apparent notice of his approach. The largest of the officers, the white one, leaned against one of the cars and a black officer with a shaved head leaned against another. They didn't seem particularly concerned about anything.

"Excuse me," Wesley said, remembering, as he always did, SJ's injunction to be polite to police. "Where the big statue at?"

"You mean that statue?" the white officer said, turning only partially toward Wesley and tilting his head as if to point behind Wesley. Wesley turned around and saw the statue, right there at the place where Esplanade and Bayou Road forked in two. He could not see Lonnie's Explorer. The officer was saying something to the black officer about overtime. Wesley saw no sign of Lonnie.

"Did you see anybody around here in a green Explorer, like he waiting for somebody?"

Now the white officer turned his head again toward Wesley. "Nobody supposed to drive through here."

Looking around for Lonnie's Explorer, Wesley said, "There's a old lady down here got trapped in the water and I carried her but she need help."

"Everybody got to go to the Superdome," the officer said.

Absently, and feeling a slight panic rising in his stomach for no reason he could identify quickly, Wesley looked around and said, "I got to find Lonnie and Roland."

"Sorry," the big white officer said sarcastically. "I don't know where Lonnie and Roland went." That seemed to be the end of discussion as far as he was concerned.

Now the black officer spoke up and said, "There are buses down at Claiborne shuttling people to the Superdome. You can pick up one there."

Wesley looked back up Esplanade toward where he had left the woman, whom he could no longer see.

"That old lady can't make it to Claiborne walking."

"This ain't a limousine service," the big officer said.

The black cop gave his partner a stony look, stepped toward Wesley and led him a few steps away.

"Where is the woman?" the officer said.

"She's down on the corner, but now I don't see her."

"I'll get down to her or send someone to look for her in a few minutes. Is the rest of your family safe?"

"I don't know. I was supposed to meet Lonnie and Roland. Lonnie said a canal broke by Mirabeau."

The officer frowned slightly. "We haven't heard anything about a Mirabeau break. We heard the Industrial Canal broke into the Lower Ninth, maybe that's what they were talking about."

Wesley looked at the officer. "What?" he said. "Why you said that?"

"There was a levee break. The whole Lower Nine is under water."

"Why you said that?" Wesley repeated, hearing himself almost yelling at a police officer, but he was sliding suddenly down a steep incline with nothing to grab on to. "Where my Mama?" he said, hearing the hysteria in his own voice as if at a distance.

Regarding the young man evenly and cautiously, the officer said in a steady voice, "Be cool, little brother. Your mama live in the Lower Nine?"

Wesley was breathing hard and rapidly, looking at the officer, looking around in a panic. The beefy large white officer was walking over now, with his right hand on the gun in his holster, and the black officer waved his partner back with a look of annoyance.

"Listen at what I'm saying," the black officer said. "Your mama all right. They had buses to get the people out. They taking everybody to the Superdome. She allright. You need to get to the Superdome and you will find her there."

Wesley's heart pounded against the inside of his chest, and he thought he was going to throw up. A storm of firing neurons in his mind pushed and pulled at him: Lonnie was not where he was supposed to be; these police didn't know where the water was coming from; he should have stayed with his Mama and Uncle J; he lied to his uncle; maybe his Mama was drowned. He had started shaking, looking up and down the street. "I got to go home."

"Go down to Claiborne," the officer was telling him, in a steady voice. "Don't bother going down to the Nine; they got the buses down there bringing everybody to the Superdome. You hear me? That's where they going to be."

Wesley nodded his head jerkily, looking up and down the street. His teeth were chattering. "I got to find my Mama and Unca J."

"You allright if you get to Claiborne."

Wesley started running down Esplanade toward Claiborne Avenue. Two blocks into the run he remembered the old woman, but there was nothing he could do about her now. He had done what he could do. He kept going, running when he could, toward Claiborne. A block and a half past Galvez Street there was water again, stretching off as far as he could see.

1 0

Through the morning they huddled in the sweltering dark. Outside, the wind howled like a madman in chains. For three hours Lucy and SJ sat, holding hands much of the time. When something hit the house with a sudden violence, Lucy's hand would tighten on SJ's. The light of the candles wobbled and threw shadows on the walls and the plywood covering the windows, as brother and sister waited for their new world to be revealed.

The room was a capsized rowboat, under which they breathed the few remaining minutes of the illusion that this might all somehow be a passing nightmare. The dresser with the lace runner that Rosetta had bought just after their wedding, Rosetta's small jewelry box, her combs—all of it where she had left it, just as she had left it; he had never had the heart or the desire to remove any of it. Perfume bottles. On the wall, flickering in the candlelight, the old framed print from their father's house, of the man and woman in the field bowing their heads for the evening church bells. This was the armature that SJ had left in place for the years since she had died, around which he had constructed a careful life for himself, and tried to provide a continuity for Lucy, Camille, and Wesley.

By ten a.m. the winds had noticeably lessened, and by eleven the worst of it was clearly over. The temperature in the bedroom had risen steadily; it was now above 100 degrees, and humid as a green-house. They could hear the water lapping under the bedroom floor; from outside they heard distant voices hollering. Lucy was breathing heavily. "Samuel," she said. "There going to be snakes in that water. What if the snakes come up in the house?"

"Snakes won't come inside a house," SJ lied.

"SJ, I got to go. Where I'm supposed to go, SJ?"

"Sister," he said, "just take a flashlight and go into the bath-room."

"I ain't got to do nothing but pee," she said, still holding on to his hand.

"You need me to walk you over there?"

"I'll be allright, SJ." She stood up, let go of his hand reluctantly and took one of the flashlights, switching it on and walking out of the room, past the landing. SJ heard her stop for a moment before she reached the bathroom. When he heard no more, he called out, "Sister?" He waited another moment and then got up quickly and walked to the landing where Lucy stood looking down at the dis-turbed water eddying three steps down from where she was, replac-ing what had been the living room. The legs of the couch poked up out of the water, floating like a potato in a soup, curtains floating like weeds . . .

"Nothing we can do about that right now, sister," he said. "We are upstairs, we dry . . ."—he spoke to her calmly, as she stared down at the water—"If the house ain't washed away yet it ain't gonna wash away. We are safe for right now. You hear me, Loot?"

She nodded.

"Go on do your business. We going to be all right. They'll send out rescue today certain, soon as the wind cuts out. We'll pick up the pieces later. Come on."

"Yeah," she said, walking into the bathroom. SJ went back into the other room without looking downstairs again. His heart beat rapidly against his ribs, or so it felt; the air was poisonously hot. He sat on the edge of the bed in the wobbly candlelight.

When Lucy came back into the room SJ stood and said, "Come on sister and help me with this."

He walked to the window on the eastern side, raised the bottom part and felt with his fingers to where he had put the toggle hooks on the bottom of the plywood. He unhooked them, first one side, and then the other, and, with the bottom edge free, he pushed it out slightly so that he could see down the side of the house. The sight jolted him even though he had anticipated it; instead of the eighteen-foot drop to the ground between his house and George's next door, there was water below the window, maybe five feet down. For a moment of vertigo he almost considered not finishing the job; he didn't want to see what was out there. But he grabbed a chair from the desk, brought it to the window, stood on it and pulled down the top inner window six inches, then reached in with his fingers to feel for the upper left toggle hook.

"Be careful, Samuel," Lucy said. "Careful you don't fall out."

SJ pushed slightly against the weight of the plywood to unhook the toggle, and—*there*—there went the toggle on the left side, and the plywood swung down to the right and the daylight slammed into the room from the triangle of window visible above and below the skewed, dangling plywood, and there, outside, was their new world.

They were in a lake, roofs like the tops of submerged turtle shells, bunched together at angles to one another. The view kicked the mind like a boot kicking an anthill; once-coordinated functions in the brain suddenly aswarm with inscrutable and uncoordinated urgency, trying to piece sense back together. Treetops against their own reflections with water rippling around the branch tips, a slight current moving away toward the east. A voice hollering in the distance. Another.

$\bullet\ \bullet\ \bullet$

When the worst of the immediate shock had stabilized, SJ went to remove the wood from the bedroom's front window, which gave onto the pitched slant of the peaked roof of the front part of the original one-story house. He put on a pair of old sneakers, then raised the bottom part of the inside window and climbed out, steadying himself and sitting for a moment on the windowsill. To his immediate left the roof slanted up at a thirty-degree angle, maybe four feet to its peak. He had built the camelback so it sat down not quite directly on the floor of what had been the attic, and the roof peak rose up between the windows on the left and right side. Down the slant of the roof to his right, he could see the gutters perhaps two feet above the surface of the muddy-looking water. Half the shingles on the roof had been torn away, down to the tar paper.

He wanted to get to the peak of the front roof and look toward downtown and the canal and see what he could see. The houses that had not been smashed into matchsticks had obviously been pushed or floated off their piers and shifted so that they sat diagonally, or were pushed up against other houses. The damage seemed to even out a little the farther it got from the canal. All through the water floated knots and clots of smashed wood, the remains of other houses; the front grille of a car bobbed like a fish with its nose sticking out of the water. Easily two thirds of the houses on North Derbigny Street were gone. Forty yards away he saw someone halfway out an attic window.

"Hey down there," SJ called out. "Are you allright?"

The man was answering, but SJ caught only a couple of the man's words.

SJ took several deliberate steps up, crabwise, crouching, to the peak of the roof, which he grabbed with his hands and looked over toward the Industrial Canal, where what looked like a long, shallow waterfall spilled water steadily into the lake that had been the Lower Ninth Ward. Off in the distance he could see the buildings of downtown.

He counted the tops of eight houses visible between his house and the Canal. All the rest was water choked with occasional tree branches breaking the surface; the houses had been destroyed or submerged, smashed into the floating piles of weatherboard and two by fours and automobiles that undulated in the water for as far as he could see. A block away water bubbling and churning from a submerged, ruptured gas line. Below him, amid a cataract of smashed weatherboard, face-down in the water, a man, unmoving; his white T-shirt had ridden up his back almost all the way to his shoulders. A black dog swam by. Not twenty feet away, the sole of a sneaker stuck out of the water, held up by an ankle attached to an invisible leg, waving slightly, probably snagged on something below the surface . . .

SJ closed his eyes. He held on to the roof ridge and kept his eyes closed for some seconds. Then a rising in his stomach, and he vomited down the side of his roof, once, and twice. Breathed through his nose. Then he spit after it, to clear his mouth, took in three deep breaths, which made him slightly light-headed, recovered.

"Samuel?"

"I'm allright," he said to his sister.

He edged slowly backward from the front of the house toward where the peak he straddled abutted the face of the camelback. He took hold of a vertical steel pipe, a plumbing vent that he had installed himself, bolted to the main stud with heavy-gauge U clamps in three places. He pulled against the pipe, and it was solid; there was enough room behind it to slip something, which was what he had wanted to know. If they needed to get down they could tie a rope around it, if he could find a rope upstairs.

Back inside, SJ rinsed his mouth with water from one of the water bottles he had stashed. Lucy sat on the bed looking stunned and vacant. "Pack you a bag for when the rescue comes," SJ said. He tried his cell phone, which was dead, then he walked across the landing to the other upstairs room, a combination storage room and office for his business. A tree had taken out part of the rear corner of the roof. He tried the land line extension he'd put in, but it was dead, too. He grabbed his old faux-leather-bound personal business phone book off the desk, quit the room and closed the door behind him.

SJ got several pairs of socks and underwear out of the dresser and put them in his small green army duffel, along with two pair of slacks and two shirts. From the top dresser drawer he retrieved a gold piece and a watch that had belonged to his father, both of which he wrapped in a handkerchief. Rummaging, he found a brown cardboard folder with an embossed logo for the Cavalier Club in Houston. He opened it and saw a color photo taken at a table in a nightclub—he and Rosetta, must have been the late 1970s. She wore a dark green dress with what she called spaghetti straps on the shoulder. He remembered that dress. He still had the big mustache at the time. He took a long look at the photo. Then he folded it shut again and put it back in the drawer.

Lucy had two main things on her mind, the first being Wesley. He had told her that he was staying by his friend Roland's house, but her phone wasn't working either so she couldn't call him. After they got rescued she would go and try to find him up to that playground where he played basketball sometimes by the Fairgrounds. There would be people who would know where he was, anyway. Lucy was also without money, and worried about how she was going to get her monthly disability check, since it didn't look like there was going to be any house to deliver it to and it was supposed to come on Thursday. But she knew the lady at the Social Security office up off of Franklin Avenue, she used to help Jaynell do her hair. Name of Mrs. Ferdinand. She would call her after they got someplace and she could help her track down the money. She wasn't worried too much about where she was going to stay. If she had the money she could find a place to stay. But the first thing she needed to do was find Wesley.

Neither of them had any idea of what was going on in the rest of the city. They had no idea that New Orleans East, where so much of SJ's business was, had also flooded, miles of houses and town houses and condos occupied mostly by the black middle class, soaked and ruined, and beyond it St. Bernard Parish, full of working-class and middle-class white people, and descendants of Islenos from the Cape Verde Islands, fishermen and oil-rig workers and dock- and ship workers, all gone—the levees had failed up and down the line and drowned Chalmette and all the rest of St. Bernard in water and oil from catastrophic spills, the water up nearly to the top of the Wal-Mart off of Judge Perez Drive.

And they couldn't have known that the levees had failed along the canals that stretched into the heart of the city from Lake Pontchartrain, as well. They didn't know that both the design and construction of the levees had been flawed, misreckoned by the United States Army Corps of Engineers, so that badly designed flood walls had not been driven deeply enough into levees made of soil that was too soft and unstable to support them in the first place. For years, the upper-class white folks who lived in Lakeview regularly saw water seeping through the levees and the flood walls along the 17th Street Canal, and the middle-class white and black folks who lived in Gentilly reported the same along the London Avenue Canal; both of those neighborhoods were now in the process of being obliterated by catastrophic breaches in those levees, which would go on to flood eighty percent of the city of New Orleans before the water level in the city became even with that of Lake Pontchartrain.

And they very likely did not know that this exact scenario had been predicted in detail a year before Hurricane Katrina in a computer simulation dubbed "Hurricane Pam," conducted by Louisiana

State University, nor that the study's conclusions and recommendations had been shrugged off by most of the officials who should have been listening, nor that the federal funding to implement the study's recommendations was cut off by President George W. Bush, who needed the money for other things. And so they couldn't have known exactly how despicable a lie it was when the president told the news media later that week that nobody could have predicted the levee breaks.

Two hours had gone by and no rescue teams had arrived, nothing except one or two helicopters that passed over. SJ had spent the better part of an hour on the front roof, made a sign from the top of a box in the storage room and Magic Marker: "TWO OF US HERE."

Now he looked down at the dark and oily water, where clumps of fire ants floated here and there, drifting, and he tried to think what a next step could be. He had looked, scanning, off to the left and right, toward the front of the house, the back of the house, he had done this at least a few dozen times over the last two hours, before noticing the small boat, a dinghy—unmistakable—maybe thirty yards off from the rear corner of his house. It appeared to him like an optical illusion popping into focus, it suddenly bespoke itself out of all the detail, in the middle of one of the ubiquitous floating islands of smashed wood and tree limbs. Many people in the neighborhood kept boats, which they could put in their pickups and drive ten minutes and go out into Lake Pontchartrain. Immediately it became the most important thing conceivable for SJ to retrieve it. There was no way to do this but to swim for it.

SJ climbed in the window, pulled both sheets off his bed and tied them end to end with a double knot. He wet the knot with water from one of their bottles so that it would hold better. Then he carried the long sheet to the front window and, stooping under, carried the sheet out with him, stepping carefully up to the roof ridge and straddling it with his back to the street, facing the plumbing vent pipe that he had checked earlier. He looped one end of the sheet around the pipe and pulled it back to himself, enough so that he could make a good tight double knot in it. Then he let the rest of the two tied sheets hang down—they were plenty long enough to reach the edge of the roof and help him get into and out of the water.

SJ climbed back inside and stripped down to his boxer shorts.

Lucy had been watching wordlessly. Now she said, "Samuel, what are you going to do? You're not going away and leave me?"

SJ told her about the rowboat, and that the sooner they got themselves to safety the better off they would be. "Make sure you got your bag packed. Pack you a bag with some things you need, Loot," he said. "Get you a couple water bottles, some underwear, your medicine, some kind of change of clothes, allright, and be ready."

"I did that already Samuel," she said. "You ain't going off the roof?"

He said, "No other way to do it." She stared at him as he turned away and headed for the window.

Out on the roof, barefoot and naked except for his shorts, SJ took hold of the long, knotted sheet and tested it several times with increasing weight to make sure that it would hold if he used it to hoist himself back out of the water when he returned. Then, holding on to it, taut all the way to the pipe, he crouched and duck-walked his way backward, squatting, letting himself hand-over-hand down the length of the sheet, to the edge of the roof. There he crouched and peered down into the water, which had risen to within a foot of the gutters. What made him most nervous about this expedition was the inability to know what was under the water's surface—floating debris, fences, glass windows lodged upright—the one thing SJ could not do was get a long gash in his leg from a rusty car bumper as he swam, his foot catching on something . . .

He shook his head, looked up at the clear sky, breathed. You prepare as well as you can, and then once you are prepared you stop worrying and you act. He scanned the surface of the filthy, mirrored water, reflecting trees, house gables, the sky, followed its surface down to where he imagined Caffin Avenue was. Then he turned and lowered himself to his stomach on the shingles, with his legs dangling out over the water—he would have to get clear of the gutter. He let the long end of the sheet drop into the water, and, slowly, he lowered his legs so that he was jackknifed around the gutter with his legs in the water, feeling with his feet for any debris. Then, with a push, he let himself fall backward into the warmish soup with the side of his camelback looming above him and Lucy looking down from the side window.

Stay shallow, he thought. The best thing for him would be to swim with a breaststroke rather than plunging arm strokes that might inadvertently strike something; he would try and keep his entire body as close to the surface as possible. Move like a tadpole.

Turning onto his stomach, he began swimming toward where he knew the dinghy was. Five strokes and shallow kicks and he came to what appeared to be the floor of a porch with part of a screen attached, sticking up at a crazy angle out of the water. He pushed against it and swam around, careful of the wavy, serrated edge of the ripped screen. A few more strokes and he was up against the edge of a logjam of smashed wood, mostly weatherboard but also some elements he could clearly identify as window sashes, jammed up with a waterlogged down comforter and what looked like a dresser drawer, clothes floating. The whole mess formed a cataract maybe fifteen feet wide.

SJ made his way carefully to the right along the edge of the mess, watching for nails in the wood, the side of his camelback towering on his right and shadowing the water. He knew there was the spiky top edge of a hurricane fence somewhere beneath him; if the fence was five feet high and the water was about twelve feet deep, judging by the level it had reached on his house, he had plenty of room. He pushed the twisted comforter out of his way to get past it but it was caught on the edge of something, it was out of whack, and, looking across two feet of water at the flowered-patterned comforter he was pushing he realized that a person was tangled in it. He was pushing against a person's close-cropped hair, a brown head, the body underneath it motionless and floating upright in the water like a buoy.

SJ yelled out—reflexively, without thinking, startled, shocked, backstroked to get away from the body.

"SJ. What's wrong? You allright?" Lucy above him, in the window.

"Go on inside, Lucy, get packed. Leave me do this." He willed himself to keep his mouth quiet, his body taut, nerves screeching, shivering in the water. He said to himself sternly that he knew he would find this. Go to the boat. Worry later. Go around it and go to the boat.

Giving the comforter a wide berth, he swam along the edge of his house until it opened out into the area where his backyard would have been. Both sheds were gone, or underwater. Somehow a car had gotten back there and was floating. The boat was thirty yards over to the left, as he had estimated it, in another cataract of smashed wood.

Seven or eight long strokes, floating as close to the surface as he could, and he was at the island of debris where he believed the dinghy to be. Carefully, he pushed himself to the right along the edge of the spiky wood, being careful about the nails he saw, twisted and dangerous, sticking out from the flotsam. He could see the edge of the dinghy rising above the wood perhaps two feet above the surface of the water. The problem would be how to get into the boat, and how to propel it. He had provisionally decided that a piece of light-weight weatherboard would be the most likely choice for a paddle. But getting the dinghy all the way back to his roof by swimming and pushing it would be tough. Maybe he could push it ahead and then swim after it. It would get jammed up with all the other junk. How about first getting to the boat, Williams.

Pushing the floating garbage carefully out of his way was unpredictable since it wasn't all on the surface. SJ found that pulling at it was more effective than pushing, which only pushed him away. By pulling apart tangled pieces of wood he tended to pull himself in toward the center of the tangle. This was slow work, and the pieces had been threaded together, nails catching on other pieces, sometimes four and five ragged-edged slats almost woven together, interlocking with other pieces, with rough, splintered edges that pushed against SJ's arms and legs and back. Under the surface he could feel his legs bumping up against objects. As much as possible he tried to keep his legs drawn up; he did not want to get a puncture from a rusty nail, although he realized that was almost inevitable.

It took twenty minutes for him to reach the side of the dinghy, which he grabbed on to with both hands, resting from the exertion. The metal boat was painted light green. It had a large dent in the side but it seemed otherwise sound. How to get into the boat was the question. There was an oak tree not too far away with limbs low over the water's surface, and he pushed against the side of the boat, trying to push it toward the tree. He would place one hand against the side of the boat and shove it through the smashed wood and floating debris. He had no leverage, though, and the progress was minimal. At one point he felt a longish flat surface under his feet, which could have been the roof of a car, or a refrigerator, something metal, and he used it to brace his feet and push the boat; this helped free the boat from the huge tangle in which it had been trapped, and he headed now for the tree by pushing the boat just enough, and then swimming after it.

In five minutes, SJ had moved the dinghy adjacent to one of the oak tree's limbs. Carefully he positioned the boat just to one side of the limb, then, reckoning the distance up to the limb as well as he could, SJ lunged up out of the water and grabbed on to the limb with one hand, but his hand slid off with some loose bark and he felt his palm go raw. He fell back into the water, water in his nose and eyes, and a sharp pain in his foot. Steady, Williams, he thought. He knew that was inevitable at some point. Back to the top, shook his head, blew the water out of his nose and tried it again. This time he got a hold of the limb and hoisted his other hand up so that he had hold of the limb just over his head, hanging from it the way he used to hang underneath the diving board when he was a kid, at the one public pool that was open to "colored" people . . . In pulling his other hand up, however, his belly had inadvertently pushed the dinghy, which started wandering off. Quickly SJ pulled himself up and—his stomach muscles were still strong—got one leg out of the water and snagged the edge of the dinghy with his heel, pulled it back into position, and, pushing the edge of the boat down, into the water almost and pulling the dinghy under his body, he was able to get himself over and into the boat's cradling metal interior, wobbling side to side in the water.

The abrupt change of perspective took a moment's adjustment. He gave a quick look around and the dinghy seemed fine. About three inches of water in the bottom, maybe it had been under a shed that had finally blown away, maybe it had been upside down and rolled. It did not matter. He checked his foot, which appeared to be all right, to his surprise.

Over the edge, now, SJ reached his hand to paddle toward the clot of wood to find a slat of weatherboard to use as an oar. He rejected the first two before finding a section about four inches wide and three feet long; the weatherboard felt solid, and it had a place where he could work it with his hands with no nails. Lucy was watching from the window of the house, and he waved at her as he started back.

SJ pulled the dinghy as close to the side of his roof as he could get it. From his perch on the seat of the dinghy he saw chests of clothes floating, sneakers, plastic water jugs. SJ knew very well what was necessary, which was to cauterize some faculty of speculation that had anything to do with emotion or empathy and concentrate on necessary action. This was another gift from the army. That was the only way to get through. The bill would come later, and it would be steep in proportion to the material you did not think about initially. But it was the only bargain available.

At the edge of his roof—the water seemed to have risen by some inches during his expedition—he took hold of the end of the sheet that he had left dangling into the water and looped it through the eyelet bolted to the front of the dinghy, tied a half-hitch to secure the boat and then, grabbing hold of the sheet as high as he could, stood carefully, pulling the boat under the eaves, got one foot up on the roof over the gutter and pulled against the sheet to hoist himself up.

His plan was to get Lucy, and anyone else he could get along the way, to the Claiborne Avenue bridge. It went over the canal, and he considered it to be the most likely staging area for any rescue efforts. In any case, it, and the St. Claude Bridge, were the highest structures around. Neither he nor anyone else had any idea of the extent of the flooding, but he reasoned that if the Upper Nine was allright across the canal, rescue buses would be there waiting to take people to shelters. Surely everyone knew by now about the Lower Nine flood. He could drop her off and use the boat to rescue as many as he could before his hands gave out.

Lucy had the shopping bag that she had packed earlier. "I feel like I need to take something else, Samuel," she said to him as he put on dry underwear, trousers, and shirt, and then a sweatshirt on top of that.

He was shivering. "It so hot, why I'm shaking like this?" He said this out loud and realized he didn't need to be saying anything that might make Lucy worry. There was a slight distortion, a bleed out the edges of his sense of timing, and he recognized this as a symptom of shock, and one that he could not afford. A slight crazy which would not under any conditions be admitted, thank you; dismissed. Ha ha ha ha. Willing himself to change the subject back to her remark, he said, "Like what you think you missing?"

"I don't know," she said. "I'm glad you allright, Samuel." He turned and saw that she was standing in the same place she had been, weeping.

"Okay, Loot," he said, stepping over to her and embracing his sister. "It's going to be okay. We will find our way through. Why you don't take this here." He let go of her and went to the dresser and picked up the small painted plastic statuette of St. Christopher that had belonged to Rosetta. He looked at it closely; some paint had come off the shoulder and baby Jesus' halo had cracked in the middle, but he was the patron saint of travelers. "Here."

"This belong to Rosetta?"

"She want you to have it," he said.

"Allright," she said, and placed the statuette inside the shopping bag, on top of the clothes.

"We need to set out," he said.

"You ain't bringing a bag with you?" Lucy said.

"I need to save space in the boat. Listen to me," he said, at the expression of fear in her eyes. "I'm going to get you someplace safe, I won't leave you till you safe. But then I have to help get people. People trapped, doesn't look like nobody doing nothing about rescue."

"Don't leave me someplace alone, Samuel."

"You're not going to be alone. You going to be all right. I won't leave you till I know that and you know that."

She nodded.

"Come on, Loot."

11

All over the city, people started walking. They carried duffel bags and backpacks and suitcases; they dragged plastic coolers and red wagons and pushed shopping carts full of whatever they could salvage. They waded through knee-deep or waist-deep water from their submerged front steps to their flooded car, or they came out of their dry house onto their unflooded street to find their car buried under a collapsed tree. More than a quarter of a million people had evacuated New Orleans; those left in the city had radically disconnected experiences one from another; communications had failed completely—phone lines and cell phone connections, all down—and the citizens walked around feeling their way as if blindfolded, pitched forward into a radically altered moment-to-moment continuity of which it was impossible to make reliable sense. Everyone began to improvise using whatever information or tools they were able to get. People streamed out into the streets, blinking, setting out for the unknown, as if on some perverted version of Mardi Gras, in which all bets were off and anything could happen.

On Monday, although nobody knew it yet, the water had only just begun to rise; it would keep rising until that Thursday, from more than a dozen breaks in the levee system, which let water gush and roll in from Lake Pontchartrain to fill up the bowl of New Orleans. On Monday, in many areas, you could still walk outside in the early afternoon and think that you had made it through once again, toughed it out one more time and emerged victorious into the eerie calm, the walk through the quiet, dripping, leaf-strewn streets with the downed power lines and enormous tree limbs blocking the way, walking around in the silence, inspecting the destruction, knowing it would be cleaned up again within a few days. And then, late that day, or the next, the surprise at the water making its way up the street like the tide coming in on the shallows, the leading edge filling the holes in the streets with eddying water, advancing perhaps a foot every twenty seconds, and fifteen minutes later the whole block flooded to the tops of the curbs, then the bottom step up to your house, and then farther and higher, depending upon how far you were from the break that was sending all that water, and how high the land in your neighborhood was.

Some went to sleep in a dry neighborhood Monday night and awoke on Tuesday to find their living room under five feet of water. Caught unaware, many of those left alive looked out their windows upon a totally altered landscape. Others—postal workers, teachers, retirees, amputees, grandmothers and mothers and war veterans—paddled to stay afloat in their living rooms, their heads two feet from the ceiling, holding on to their floating furniture, in the darkened, dank interior, the restless bobbling sound of the water lapping at their walls, their curtains billowing underwater like seaweed, the pictures still hanging, submerged, on the wall, toys floating next to their head, and maybe their cat with its eyes wide and its claws dug into the side of the floating, upended sofa. Some people made it out to the roof; some hung on until rescue boats came, and some never did make it out at all.

After the rasping and shrieking wind, the objects slamming into houses, now the silence, the absence of all the subliminal sounds that ordinarily populated the landscape. Streets empty of cars, trees empty of birds, all air-conditioning units still, no radios, no televisions, everything still except for car alarms that had been triggered, and house alarms, spooling out idiotically under the midday sun . . . Later there would be helicopters passing over, and rescue boats, then, again, long stretches of silence. The people who were trapped in their attics, or on their roofs, had no idea of the scope of what had happened, nor, for that matter, did people who were able to be out and around.

Around the country, by contrast, those watching the scene unfold on television were immersed in constant information. Terse, professionally concerned announcers conveyed the barely credible facts, directed the traffic of information and speculation, introduced the color reporting, the on-the-spot interviews. CNN, FOX, the gravely serious anchors, the familiar faces—Anderson Cooper, Brian Williams, Nancy Grace, Larry King—the harried, urgent-sounding correspondents, increasingly disbelieving as the scope of what had happened was revealed in images that shifted rapidly from one place to another, point of view bouncing from one to another like pinballs pinging, everything bathed in the incessant double message of the media—urgency and detachment, emergency and control, constant feed and ever-increasing hunger. The media emitted a processed discontinuity, whereas the people in New Orleans experienced an unprocessed continuity, a broken narrative in which they were forced to either sink or, somehow, swim.

But from outside it was the greatest live, real-time spectacle since the attacks of September 11, 2001, or perhaps the O. J. Simpson trial. An epic story, unfolding in real time, does not come along all that often, and when it does the fascination of it is absolute. Like white blood cells streaming toward an infection, broadcasters, print journalists, photographers, bloggers, flooded into New Orleans and began pumping out information, filtered and unfiltered. The news media's attempts to piece together birds' nests of sense and coherence out of the twigs and scraps and shards of disconnected information was itself a drama.

• • •

Until the power went out in Jackson, Craig and Alice watched the televised news along with everyone else in the lobby of the Best Host Inn. The roof of the designated "shelter of last resort," the New Orleans Superdome, where twenty thousand people had gone for shelter, had started tearing off from the wind, and rain was coming in. Cameras showed people getting up and moving haltingly down their rows of molded plastic seats, falling raindrops shining in the camera lights, moving to a dry corner of the Dome, people who had camped on the Astroturf taking their bedrolls and walking to a position under what remained of the roof. Because the people in other parts of New Orleans had no idea of this, a steady stream of people seeking refuge continued to arrive there from homes that were flooding in Gentilly, in Broadmoor, in the Upper Ninth Ward, Central City and elsewhere. But viewers in the rest of the country on Monday did not yet know the extent of the flooding.

From the news reports on Monday, Craig and Alice knew they were not going back to New Orleans that night, and perhaps not for several days. They agreed that they should move on to Oxford, where the hotel had kept their reservation for them, which they found out in one call from an office phone that one of the desk people let them use. Late Monday afternoon they headed out for the three-hour drive to Oxford.

After Jackson, Oxford was an almost miraculous oasis of comfort. The sidewalks of the courthouse square were swarming that Monday night with evacuees from New Orleans and the Mississippi Gulf Coast. Early that evening it still looked, from out of town, as if most of New Orleans might have escaped the worst, although everyone knew by then that the towns along the Gulf Coast—Bay St. Louis, Gulfport, Biloxi, Pass Christian—had been hit by powerful winds and a tidal surge that had wiped out hundreds of beautiful homes along the shore, along with the stores, and the casinos, and the causeway connecting the towns. So the crowd lacked the usual transitory nervous elation that is a by-product of having evaded disaster, the gaiety, fueled by the knowledge that your home would be there when you got back, that there would be a little cleanup to do, but that life would be going on as usual. Instead, for the Gulf Coast evacuees, there was a somber quality, as if they had gathered for a wake. And by the end of the evening, things began to turn ominous in the news from New Orleans as well.

The breaches in the levees were now widely reported, and they were more numerous, bigger, and more widespread than had been apparent earlier in the day, and it was clear that the city was beginning to fill with water from Lake Pontchartrain. Efforts were under way to stanch the breaches with giant sandbags dropped from Coast Guard helicopters, especially at the 17th Street Canal, which threatened to flood many of the most populous and historic parts of the city. More than one commentator observed with some wonder that the president of the United States was still on vacation at his Texas ranch, and wondered aloud why he had not cut short his siesta, given the magnitude of what had happened.

The storm itself had been devastating, but the truly crippling disaster for the city was the flooding, and it quickly became apparent that that aspect had been a man-made disaster. As the news of the levee breaches began to sink in, announcers began to make comments to the effect that large parts of New Orleans might end up being uninhabitable for the foreseeable future. On Tuesday morning at their hotel in Oxford, Craig and Alice began the process of making calls, like tens of thousands of others, to figure out a place where they might stay for a little bit longer, to use as a base until they could get back to the city.

Their family network, such as it was, was scattered across the upper Midwest. Craig's father was dead and his mother lived in a tiny apartment in Minneapolis, so there was no help there. Craig initially lobbied for heading back down to Baton Rouge, but the city had been swamped with evacuees, and their friends Pam and Mike's house was already filled with Bobby and Jen and, now, another couple. They definitely did not have room for four more people there. The last alternative was Alice's parents.

Craig braced himself for Alice's call. A lot of the tense side of her personality came straight from her mother. Her parents lived just outside of Birmingham, Michigan, although they said they were from Birmingham proper; their social anxiety was palpable and constant. The first time Craig had visited there with Alice, her father had driven them to dinner by a circuitous route that, Alice later admitted to Craig, was almost three times as long as a much more direct and perfectly pleasant ride just because it went through a more affluent area. Visits home tended to draw out Alice's worst anxieties. The tension between her and her mother, who had grown up very modestly in Ypsilanti and had married a not-spectacularly-successful lawyer with his own class hang-ups, was heavy enough to sink a boat.

Alice made the call. Her mother's first words were that she never understood why Alice would want to live down there in the first place. When Alice indicated they would likely need a place to stay for a while, she hemmed and hawed, saying, "Well . . . these are such tight quarters . . ." ("Tight quarters?" Craig said after the call. "They have five bedrooms." At that, Alice quickly became defensive and said, "Well, they just got the Akita, and they are redoing one of the rooms; it's not like they live in a mansion," and Craig kicked himself mentally for not remembering that, no matter how much Alice complained, she would find a way to explain or rationalize her mother's responses if he joined in.)

Her mother suggested that Alice call Uncle Gus, her father's older half-brother, who lived outside Chicago. He and his wife, Jean, lived in a gritty old Czech/Polish suburb west of the city, and Alice's mother said she thought they had a whole new room that they had just redone. After her mother gave her Uncle Gus's phone number, Alice's father got on the phone and said, "Hi, princess. Thought you'd get a kick out of hearing that John Leland finally shook down the settlement money on that Harvey case I told you about last time you were up here. Is Craig keeping you warm?"

Stupefied, Alice said, "Dad . . . Are you aware of what's going on down here? Have you looked at a TV set? We don't even know if we have a house left."

"Yes, dear, I do in fact watch the news, and I would like you to keep in mind that the rest of the world has not stopped existing. Of course we have been worried about you. I just thought you might like a little relief and a reminder that life goes on. My advice is to loosen up just a tad, dear."

When Alice got off the phone she was almost shaking with rage.

1 2

Midday on Tuesday, and SJ probably should have taken a break. Using the strip of weatherboard for an oar, he paddled the dinghy down what had once been Reynes Street.

Silence. Or not silence but an alteration in the aural wallpaper—the usual distant cars, radios, air conditioners, replaced by a dense, barely translucent stillness, punctuated only by discrete signs of action—a voice, in the distance, or a boat motor, the occasional ratcheting helicopter overhead or, twice that day in two different locations, a bubbling churning that was more felt than heard, churning, boiling water caused by a ruptured gas pipe under the thick surface. One careless match or cigarette flicked away and the oil and gasoline that drifted and spread here and there in dark multicolor on the water would ignite and those gas bubbles would become geysers of flame.

This, now, was New Orleans.

He had put on his old army-issue green fatigue all-weather hat to keep the sun off, but the heat and exertion were extreme, and the water in his jug was gone. Through the morning he had paddled around the lake that had been his neighborhood all his life, finding people, helping them into his dinghy, carefully, carefully, and depositing them back at the Claiborne Bridge, where the word was that trucks were coming on the other side of the canal, or buses. Across Claiborne Avenue in the Holy Cross neighborhood, the destruction was less complete; many of the houses had at least stayed in place, although most of the single-story dwellings were flooded to the roofline.

He had done the same the previous afternoon after dropping Lucy off, until finally, exhausted, he had gone back to his house to get some sleep. Today, Tuesday, there were more boats—motorboats, rowboats, neighborhood people like himself, outsiders, some police and marshals, and the first helicopters. All of them were busy nonstop. Some of them appeared to be kids, or hunters—red-faced Cajun boys in duck-hunting outfits, who had gotten there God knew how. As they passed SJ pointed them toward places where he knew people to be stuck. His hands were getting badly blistered and raw, but he didn't stop.

The farther he got from the actual levee break, the more people there were to rescue. In some areas, the water was up only to porch level. Twice he encountered old couples, in their seventies, sitting with suitcases, dressed nicely and waiting for the buses they had been told would come to get them in case of emergency. Those he picked up SJ would ask if they had their ID and necessary medicines. Those he passed when his boat was full waved weakly and smiled, maybe nodded. They had learned patience and endurance over a lifetime, along with gratitude for any small sign of progress, any tiny ray of light through the dark.

Late in the morning another dinghy had approached him, rowed by two young men in white tank tops and blue jeans cut off at the calf, bright boxers bunched over their waistbands, and one of them called out, "Mista J . . ."

As the boat approached, SJ saw that it was Tyrell, the young man he had seen after so many years on Saturday at the block party, with Wesley. The young man had a vague smile on his face, a stunned expression overall. "We been steady picking up people Mista J."

"Is your family allright," SJ asked. "Your mama?"

"She didn't make it, Mista J," the young man said, smiling slightly, and frowning simultaneously, looking SJ in the face. "She didn't make it." Smiling slightly more now, and his eyes suddenly larger with tears. "We going to see about Danny cousin over by Holy Cross. Your house okay, Mista J?" The other young man was not paying attention, looking around, scanning.

SJ hardly knew how to answer. He was able to do no more than shake his head.

Tyrell smiled again, and shrugged—the dissociation, which would become one of the most common facts of human interaction in days to come—and the two young men headed off to their fates, and SJ continued looking for people.

Inside himself, SJ was locked down as well as he could be. He was needed, as long as his hands held up on the oar and he didn't overheat. Piecing together what all this meant was for later. He had shifted into a mode of pure action, and he knew from experience that he would pay for it eventually. He still, for example, had dreams involving a baby he had seen in a village after an action during his time in Vietnam, facedown with its back open like a geode, seething with maggots. Seeing it, he had felt himself starting to go, to lose his grip, and he forced himself to push it down, put it away; there was no alternative at that time to his being able to function. But the image did not disappear merely for being submerged, any more than what was under these flood waters had stopped existing just because it was hidden.

After the first two people he saw floating facedown, he had wrapped up the part of himself that would react, the way you would tape up a sprained ankle so you could walk on it. He was needed. But spreading like a bruise under that tight bandage were all the questions he could not yet face directly, the facts that could not be carried, the meaning of the extinguished lives floating like garbage, discarded, unneeded. And why had this flooding happened, what had caused the levee break that had trapped and drowned people in the homes they had acquired through a lifetime of work and struggle?

As the day wore on, former Specialist Four Williams wondered where the military was—the Marines, the Army, Airborne—there was nobody, except for some Coast Guard helicopters. No sign of transport at the overpass where he had been dropping people off. The levee had broken at dawn the previous morning. Here it was the middle of the next day, T plus 30 at least, and they had had no reinforcements, no help, he meant . . . He had lived through Hurricane Betsy, but this was something else. Hurricane Betsy was something to get through. This was the end of something. For many people he passed, it had already meant the end of everything.

He probably should have and would have taken a rest under ordinary circumstances. But the degree and the extent of the need around him was overwhelming, and he kept on as long as he could, through the long, nameless reaches of the afternoon. Around six p.m., after dropping two women off at the bridge, he found himself about to get out of the dinghy and lie down on the asphalt roadway as it rose on its incline out of the floodwaters. And he knew then that he needed to stop, and he paddled back to his house with what was left of his energy, secured the dinghy fore and aft as well as he could to the gutter, and hauled himself up by the sheet, barely able to, out of the dinghy and onto his roof.

For a moment he looked down and thought about trying to pull the dinghy up out of the water and onto the roof somehow; he was afraid that it might be stolen while he was asleep. But it was hard to pull even a lightweight boat up out of the water, and he was as tired as he had ever been in his life. He made sure the boat was secure one more time, then he dragged himself inside, through the window.

Night. Tired as he was, he had trouble getting to sleep. Voices in the distance reflected oddly off of water, sounded closer than they were, sometimes almost as if they were in the room with him. Shouts, weeping, even low, monosyllabic conversations. The day's images had been too strong to leave at the door and too relentless, and all that machinery was hard to shut down. Past and present mingled, and the future was all over with. He lay on his bed because he was physically exhausted, but it was better when he was moving. When he lay still it all seemed to swarm around his head like bees because there was nothing to shoo it away.

He could do no more that day. His hands were shot, but then his entire body was shot, arms, back, shoulders, legs. He lay throbbing in a darkness he had not known for thirty-five years, since patrols in the jungle. Somewhere well after dark a wailing started—impossible to tell where or how far away—a woman's voice, weeping, sobbing, saying indistinct words. The sound spoke of pain that would not heal, a scar that would bleed without ceasing. He lay on his sheets wet with sweat, in a darkness beyond darkness, and the weeping didn't stop, and it was unendurable to hear.

Finally SJ sat up, stood slowly, blindly and, crouching, felt his way to the rear window, which was open for what little breeze was available. He shouted, "Where are you?"

Weeping stopped.

Again he spoke into the dark: "Are you allright?" A moment later, he wondered if he had in fact spoken the words.

The voice in the dark began weeping again, then SJ heard it say, "No . . . *No* . . . oh no . . ." and the sound could not be escaped and it demanded an accounting of an absent God. What do you do, SJ? Jump out of a dark window into an invisible lake full of sharp edges some invisible distance below, swim who knew where in the dark . . . ? Of course not. Of course not. He turned back in the direction of the bed, tripping but not falling over a chair. He found the bed with his searching hands, felt along it to the right place and sat down, tried to breathe deliberately, and finally lay down again and fell into a fitful sleep that gave him no rest.

Glaring wobbling light awakened him, morning yes, reflected light on ceiling from the jittery water, voices in the distance, sleep draining out of him . . . The ratcheting sound was a helicopter, undeniably—but how? Then this was home again, and everything came back quickly. He sat up in the impossible heat. This was Wednesday; shouting. Helicopter blades fade. His whole self hurt.

He put one leg then another over the side of the bed, stood, steadied himself, stood. Pounding heart suddenly; ran to the front window to look and the boat was gone.

He pulled on his shorts and climbed out onto the sloped roof once he was sure he had his balance, scooted down crabwise to see if the boat had perhaps just come undone at one end and drifted to one side. Voices in the distance; a motorboat maybe five blocks away. No dinghy; the shredded end of one line hung down where someone had cut it loose with a knife. Would he have even been able to use it; hands so sore. And then something caught his eye in peripheral vision, noticed down and to the left, and he looked, focused, and there were two of them floating facedown. One was naked, its bottom presented to the sky for care that would not be forthcoming, and the other with a diaper unfastened at one hip, floating loose, filth spilling out of it, an umbilicus of shit, bumping up against the gutter, lazily, like any other garbage in the water, two brown babies out there just like any other garbage, and SJ started shaking, his whole body, as if in the worst of fever, muscles contracting, squeezing his bones as if to crack them; he shook, racked with spasms, even when he tried to look away, and he didn't stop even after the motorboat with the two policemen came and helped him off the roof.

13

They took him to the Convention Center, eventually, a large, modern complex just uptown from the French Quarter and backed up against the river; it had been opened the day before, Tuesday, to warehouse the overflow of people who were no longer being allowed into the Superdome.

All day Sunday and Monday and Tuesday citizens streamed toward the Superdome from around the city. The Superdome was a product of the mid-1970s, designed for football games, concerts and other epic indoor events. It had concentric stacked, ringed halls, concession stands, box seats and sky boxes and media rooms, and it was a center point of civic pride, certainly among the business leaders, and certainly to the fans who loved the New Orleans Saints with a tragic love, since the Saints traditionally made a weak showing. It sat in the middle of what was called the Central Business District, much of which had been constructed on the bulldozed site of one of the roughest areas of the city in the early years of the twentieth century, an area where the legendary Buddy Bolden had played jazz in the Eagle Tavern and Louis Armstrong was born to a prostitute in Jane Alley. All that was gone now, replaced by parking lots and skyscrapers and hotels, and in the middle of it, the Superdome. The Superdome had been designated the shelter of last resort in case of a major hurricane, as well, stocked with food and water adequate for a day or two of city-wide inconvenience until basic services could be reestablished.

Beginning Sunday, most of those who stayed in the city walked there and stood on line for hours to gain entry. Once inside, they camped in seats, they camped in hallways, and in the upper-level seats, and on the Astroturf where the New Orleans Saints had played the previous Friday night. The atmosphere on Sunday was tense, as it always is before a large storm, but it also contained an undercurrent of festivity; New Orleanians knew what to do with interruptions of business as usual, and few of them really believed in their heart of hearts that after all the false alarms this could really be as bad as the worst projections had it.

On Monday morning, large parts of the roof blew off in the astonishing wind. When the storm had passed and electricity was out, more people came, and as the flooding filled the city even more came, wading through the water in the surrounding streets, and by late Monday the facility was overwhelmed; when the crowd edged toward 30,000, on Tuesday, the authorities, in disarray themselves and worried about a complete breakdown of order, began routing people to the Convention Center, which had no provisions at all—no water, no food, no toilet paper, no medical personnel. Inside, the Convention Center was impossibly hot, airless and dark; its cavernous exhibition rooms and dark halls served primarily as a giant bathroom where people squatted in corners and then cleaned up as well as they could.

Hundreds preferred to camp on the sidewalks in front as the long and incomprehensible days of that week went by—Tuesday, Wednesday, Thursday, Friday—and no help arrived. Afternoons melted into sundown, then the long night amid the moans and curses and weeping of everyone around you, then sunrise again and still no food, and no information, no news, no visit from any representative of a coordinated authority to give you the comfort of what to expect or the sense that anyone even knew you were there or cared, in the brutal, stunning heat, as people suffered all around, and you wondered how long you could last after your blood pressure medicine ran out, or your insulin, or your oxygen . . .

Everything was on overload, and what would be the use of trying to construct a sequential story when, as one day went by, and then another, and another, time itself was perverted, turned into a garbage dump under the hot blue sky. The drawers had been pulled out of every dresser and the contents dumped on the floor; every narrative was twisted and mocked, torn out of any context and flung down next to the grandmother of someone else's narrative; elderly people in open-backed hospital gowns, ripped out of their own story and set down with their IVs in wheelchairs in the middle of the street, hungry, deposited by someone who left to save themselves, not even wished good luck, madness dragging at the cuffs of your pants, dragging like devils in the pit, hissing at you, beckoning, the palsy in that old lady's face, the old man with a plaid short-sleeve shirt and a green suitcase. You can't construct a sequential narrative; the parts don't fit together; characters are in the wrong place; Prince Hamlet plays the sitar on a cooler full of body parts, Santa Claus has lice, Rosa Parks is having a heart attack on the curb and Mister Rogers blows Paul Robeson for a cigarette and the Andrews Sisters and the Supremes lift their skirts in a darkened corner and hope for the best. Oh yes, they have lice, too. What are they trying to tell us? Why have they all been placed together in this narrative? What do they all have in common? If the Depression didn't reveal it, or the Holocaust, or the photographs of Emmett Till, or Goya's Caprichos, why should these mismatched socks, this salvage, mean anything now? Why should it make any sense? Don't you know garbage when you see it? And, no, you can't leave, because your mother, your own mother—yes, her in the wheelchair, there, look at her, the one with the large stain under her, and the bedsores forming from being in her own fluids for a day and a half—is senile and frightened, and at least here there are other people around. And besides, if you could see far enough up in the sky, that little flashing sliver, that is Air Force One; the president of the United States is up there looking out the window at the pretty designs made by the water—*That's the Mississippi River? That sorta squiggle there?*—wondering what he is supposed to do and if he will have time for a nap and an hour with the video games before having to face the cameras again and say something to make it sound as if there is still a narrative in place.

If you are in it you don't see the news coverage, the anchorman, the commercials for Dodge trucks, any more than Job saw God and Satan make their wager at his expense. The mind cannot process all the disjunction, the endless din echoing in the Superdome halls and the sour itch in your clothes, the booming echoes overhead in the Dome, with its patch of sky visible, the intolerable hallways clogged with people sitting on the floor, waiting for the bathrooms, through the endless stretch of ruptured time, on lines that wind off into the gloomlight as if following the curve of the rings of hell, but a perverted inferno, set up by the guilty for the innocent. The mind goes on overload and only scraps adhere, like rags caught on sticks and flapping in the wind—a baby's bib, let's say, white with yellow piping around the edges and a Teddy bear printed on it, crumpled and left on the floor in the sweltering, darkened toilet stall, barely visible next to your foot, caked with feces among the paper towels and fouled underwear, amid which you squat over the bowl full to overflowing with a sickening stew, laced with blood, that made you retch to look at it, let alone to smell it, trying to position your legs so that you can add to its contents without touching what is already there, a shirt over your shoulder that you will use to clean yourself afterward and leave on the floor with the rest of it, and this is the shelter provided you, the emblem of the quality of thought and caring devoted to your fate, and you will remember that bib, it is your new flag, and where is the baby it had belonged to?

And, outside, the lines of people waiting to take your place once you are finished, or the rest of them camped out in the generator-lit halls dark as twilight, sprawled against the cinder-block walls next to water fountains that do not work, overweight women in tight blouses, frail old women in hairnets, uptown men trying to read by the dim light, children in their last disposable diaper, long since full, running a toy truck along the floor in fierce concentration among the bags and garbage, the heat like a poisonous liquid and the stink like a throbbing, deafening noise you can't escape, and more are camped two feet away, and even more past them, and on down the hall as it makes its curve into the hellish twilight gloom, or through the passageways that lead out into the stands and cantilever into the cerulean realms of the artificial sky, the great wounded vault of the Superdome, sleeping, feeding, staring into space, unaware of the flooding, the levee breaks, the Dome and the entire city and maybe the entire nation a ship without a pilot, battered and headed for disaster.

In the midst of it, with up and right and green and there and down and left and here and red jabbering incoherently, you did what you could until help arrived, whether you led a child by the hand through the ruined streets, or endured the blazing sidewalk heat in the crowd outside the Convention Center, or sat trapped in a wheelchair in your living room, abandoned by the nurse, as the water crept up around your ankles, and then your knees, praying, knowing that God never sent you nothing that you couldn't handle, so it must have been someone else sent all that water that rose mercilessly past your lips and nose (they found you later, out of your wheelchair, under your refrigerator, which had floated and come to rest on top of you), or squatted with hundreds of others in the red haze of afternoon amid the other garbage by the side of the empty interstate, waiting for a helicopter, or a bus, or a truck, waiting for passage up and out to some city of refuge waiting on a strange horizon.

II

1 4

They pulled in just after seven-thirty on Wednesday evening, the sky a deepening blue behind the silhouetted trees. They had exited the expressway west of the city and followed Uncle Gus's directions through a progressively aging exurban landscape, the rusting entrails of the nation, with Chicago itself little more than a muted glow against the darkened eastern sky. Initially they drove along the broad commercial strips, the shining neon arteries of chain restaurants and motels and auto equipment stores, then the directions took them through the older, two-story brick downtown areas of several towns, until they began to have to keep an eye out for Wabash Avenue, where they would make a left and go up the small hill, making another left on Saginaw, onto a street of close-together single-family homes built in the 1920s, most of them two-story wood-frame houses with an additional floor up top for a finished attic, and almost all with a wooden porch out front.

Craig had met Gus and Jean ten years before, at the wedding, and he had not seen them since. He remembered Gus as resembling his idea of a teamster, a short man with a lined face and a graying crew cut, wearing a rough gray herringbone jacket and a dark blue cloth tie. Jean didn't say much. Craig was unaccountably anxious, now, about arriving at their house for this indeterminate stay. Alice, at least, seemed relaxed; he could easily imagine what the emotional climate in the car would have been had they been about to stay with her parents in Michigan.

A driveway consisting of two pebbly parallel cement ribbons ran through the inclined alley along the right side of the house, but Craig parked on the street at curbside and sat for several long moments behind the wheel. Alice immediately set about getting Annie and Malcolm out of the car. After a minute, Craig pitched in, while also taking in what he could of the working-class neighborhood, and the house he was getting ready to enter for the first time.

Alice's Aunt Jean, a thin woman with short, steel-gray hair and wearing an apron, greeted them at the door, hugging Alice as they squeezed in through the front vestibule. Gus waited just inside the living room and shook Craig's hand as he entered. Craig noted the same crew cut, all gray now, plaid flannel shirt. The house smelled of cooking. Craig greeted Gus as "Mr. Brunner."

"Feel free to call me Uncle Gus," the older man said to Craig. "I've been called worse."

"We have been watching and praying for you," Jean said. "It's just terrible what happened to all those people." The small living room was snug with upholstered furniture, fringed lamps, wall-to-wall carpeting. At the far end, an old television set in an oversized maple console; facing it, a couch and a chair with an antique lace antimacassar.

Jean gave Craig a hug, too, and then turned a wide-eyed enthusiasm loose on Annie and Malcolm; Annie was polite but shy, and Malcolm showed Jean his Smurf pillow. "Which one of the Seven Dwarfs is that?" Aunt Jean said, bending down toward Malcolm. Craig watched Alice hug her uncle and say, "It's great to see you two." Gus hugged her back, and Jean said, "You must all be exhausted. You can just go right upstairs if you want; Gus'll get you settled. I have some boiled beef and cabbage in the kitchen; it's ready when you are." Looking at the kids, she stooped down slightly and said, "I'll bet you two are hungry." Annie nodded dutifully and Malcolm hugged the Smurf pillow.

Gus walked outside with Craig to help with the suitcases, and Craig felt around in his mind for a way to make conversation, anxious at the same time to get to a computer and see what he could find out about where the flood water was uptown. "How long have you lived in this house?" he managed to ask.

"Forty-five years next March," Gus said. "The house is right about eighty years old. Almost as old as me."

"You're not eighty," Craig said, stopping in his tracks, genuinely surprised.

"No, you're right; I'm not." The older man gave Craig a comradely clap on the shoulder. "Just wanted to see if you'd give me an argument." He hoisted one of the heavy suitcases out of the trunk.

Inside, Gus led his four guests up the stairs. "We've done a little remodeling since you've been here, Allie," Gus said. "It's a climb. Hope you're in shape, Craig!"

"Oh, don't worry about me!" Craig said, in what he hoped was a hearty voice. "I've been doing my aerobics." He wondered if the man knew what aerobics were.

They slogged up the carpeted stairs to the second floor, following the landing around to the left. The walls were hung with studio portraits of their two sons in college graduation robes, and smiling with their families. At the end of the second-floor landing, a table with a vase of cloth flowers. They made the turn and Gus led them up a narrower staircase to the newly finished attic where they were to stay. At the top of the stairs, Uncle Gus halted the caravan momentarily to feel for the light switch.

"Here she is," he said.

Craig followed his two children and his wife into the fluorescent-lit converted attic and stood beside them, taking it in. The room was the size of a large tent, with bright white, bare walls. Craig could stand upright in the middle of the room, where fluorescent light panels formed the flat apogee of the ceiling, but on either side of the panels the ceiling sloped sharply down toward the eaves, where Gus and Jean had put two small cots for the kids under the small dormers, one on either end of the room. The head of the grown-ups' bed was up against the bare wall opposite the door, a double bed with a light green chenille spread on it and a slight body-size depression in the middle. A small round wooden table next to it, supporting an empty green ceramic bud vase. The only light in the room seemed to be the overhead fluorescent panels.

"Bathroom's on the second floor; I forgot to tell you that," Uncle Gus said. "Over there you have your air unit," he said, pointing to a grill set into the wall.

After a moment or two, Alice said, "It's perfect, Uncle Gus."

"It's not home; I know that. I just hope you will make yourselves at home and stay as long as you like."

"Thank you so much," Alice said, putting her arms around the old man and, Craig could see from her back, starting to weep. Annie looked up at Craig with her eyebrows raised slightly, questioning, and Craig tried to pantomime that Mom was tired. He rubbed Alice's back as she hugged her uncle.

"We can't tell you what this means right now, Uncle Gus," Craig said.

"Oh, don't even think about it. We've all just been so worried for you. Jean's got some supper ready for you she just has to heat up; you come on down whenever you're ready."

Malcolm had started to fuss after seeing his mother crying, and Alice picked him up to comfort him. When Uncle Gus had gone back downstairs, Annie walked right over with her little pink-and white suitcase to the bed on the left, bounced down on it and said, "Daddy can I have this bed?"

"Sure, Annie, but let's ask Malcolm if that's all right. Malcolm, can Annie sleep in that bed?"

Malcolm, sleepy, in his mother's arms, nodded his head and then turned it away and lay it on Alice's shoulder. Alice looked at Craig and indicated that she wanted him to take Malcolm, which he did.

"I'm going to start setting up camp," she said.

Grateful for the fun-adventure overtones of the remark, Craig hefted Malcolm in his arms and brought him over to the other bed, saying, "Come on, Malcolm; let's see how your bunk is." Craig remarked to himself, as he had many times in the past, how strong Alice could be. Sometimes it meant shutting out some sensitivity. But when the chips were down, she could deal. As he carried his son to the other end of the room he cast his eye back to Annie, who was unpacking her clothes, like her mother.

"Where should I put my clothes, Mommy," she asked.

"We'll get that figured out in a minute, Annie Fanny."

Setting Malcolm down on the bed, Craig leaned to look out the small window under which the bed lay. Blocks and blocks of houses, lights coming on, against the dark blue evening sky, the pre-Depression beginnings of suburbia, when Chicago was rolling in money. How were they going to do this, he thought?

"Look, Malcolm," Craig said. "That's a pretty good view." His son lay on his back, waiting passively to be undressed for bed. Craig would not let himself think what a long and difficult period lay in front of them, and at the moment he didn't blame his son a bit for being tired and wanting to be taken care of. He bent down and kissed the boy and said, "You know I love you, and we are going to get through this." Malcolm put his arms around Craig's neck and hugged, and Craig was very, very grateful that they were all there together.

• • •

After they got situated, the four of them came downstairs and ate steaming plates of beef and cabbage, with horseradish—or Craig and Alice did; Annie and Malcolm both opted for peanut butter sandwiches—and watched the nonstop coverage on the small TV on the kitchen counter. They switched back and forth between CNN and Fox, as well as the networks. They watched the images from the Convention Center and the Superdome, the incompetence of the government agencies. Craig glimpsed Peanut, a waiter at the Camellia Grill, talking to one of the reporters, just a flash as he turned on the news, and he wondered about the other guys who worked the counter there and who always made a fuss over Annie and Malcolm when Craig or Alice brought them in—Marvin, Donald, Michael, Matt the cook, Darryl, Ray, Cool Pop, old Mr. Bat who had retired . . .

The only bright spot on television that evening was an hallucinatory moment that took them by surprise amid the nightmare scenes at the Superdome and the Convention Center. It was a crowded bar, apparently, and Craig watched in stunned amazement as the sardonically smiling face appeared, next to the woman reporter for CNN, who was saying, "Here at Rosie's on Decatur Street, you could almost think that nothing has changed in New Orleans. This, we believe, is the only bar in the city to have stayed open for the entire duration of Hurricane Katrina. The power is out, but Nicole is dispensing drinks by candlelight and we are talking to New Orleans *Times-Picayune* columnist Serge Mikulic. Mr. Mikulic . . ."

"Please call me Serge," he said, twinkling, charming.

"You seem to have a pretty merry crew here. Were you surprised to find Rosie's open?"

"No," Serge said. "Closing Rosie's would be like turnink off the lights on the Statue of Liberty. And anyway there has been a certain continuity, since we have not left Rosie's since the beginning of the apocalypse."

"Have you been here the entire time?" the reporter asked.

"What better place could one be?" Serge said. "In New Orleans we celebrate disaster; we drink and dance at funerals . . ."

From the background, a voice—clearly belonging to Serge's friend Dave—saying, "There's gonna be a lot of people lined up to drink and dance at yours," and Serge allowed himself to laugh at this. Craig felt like diving through the television screen to be there with them.

"Is this your funeral for New Orleans?" the reporter asked, idiotically.

Little lines formed around the corners of Serge's eyes, signaling an especially barbed response on the way, but before he could get it out he was interrupted by a commotion, what sounded like a clattering of hooves, and Serge turned, camera lights on the back of his head now, and through the open window onto Decatur Street they saw first one mule, then two more mules, trot by, halters on their heads, then another lone straggler, clop clop clop, heading toward Esplanade.

"They have cut loose the carriage mules. Look at that." Serge said. In the background, people in the bar rushed to the front window to look out at the street. Turning back to the puzzled reporter, Serge said, "The carriage mules from Jackson Square, apparently. It is the end of civilization as we know it." He held up his glass of scotch, toasting the camera, and said, "Cheers." And as the camera pulled back for the reporter's wrap-up, Craig could clearly see Dave sitting at the bar next to Serge. Serge and Dave at Rosie's! How bad could things be?

The mild, twisted exhilaration did not last long, as the coverage turned from that small island of gallows humor to the deluge of misery surrounding it. The water was still rising steadily in the city, although hard information about exactly where or how much was hard to find. The Coast Guard helicopters had so far been unable to stop the breach at the 17th Street Canal. The Superdome was in a shambles, and they had been sending people all afternoon to the Convention Center, where no provisions had been made at all. Television cameras cruised past hundreds of people sitting on the sidewalk outside the Convention Center, white and black, in wheelchairs, with IV tubes on stands next to them, all of them stunned, angry, afraid.

The interviews on the street were hard to watch. At one point a reporter spoke to a middle-aged black man wearing only a black T-shirt that said GHETTO CASH with a gun under it, holding a boy of about six by the hand, wandering the street. The cameraman asked where they were going, and the man said, "I don't know."

"In what part of town do you live?"

"We in the Ninth Ward," the man said, looking around as if hoping to see someone he knew. The boy stood next to him, frowning. "All we got is what's on our back. There's nothing left. My wife . . . My wife . . ." And the man broke down in tears, in front of the camera, and the newsman, plainly unsure what to do or say, said, "Is your wife all right?" The man shook his head and stood crying in front of the camera, holding his boy by the hand, and the newsman said, "Well . . . we will hope and pray that your wife will be all right . . ." Then he turned back to the camera with a grim expression, saying, "As you can see, Gina, there is no shortage of misery and confusion in New Orleans this evening, as residents await some word from the local authorities about where to go for help, food, or the most basic information. This is a chaotic and increasingly desperate scene here."

In that kitchen west of Chicago, and the living room, with its shut-in old folks' close smell, they watched the nonstop coverage, that night and for the following days. They relied on reflexes to help them establish order and coordinates for themselves. By phone, and via the Brunners' creaky dial-up computer Internet connection, they tried to track down friends. There was no way to have any idea of how the house had fared, the *Gumbo* offices, Boucher School.

In those first days it was all but impossible to get an accurate idea of where the floodwater was, or how deep it was, in most neighborhoods. The official word by Thursday was that eighty percent of the city was underwater. But what did "underwater" mean? Did it mean ten feet in the street? Did it mean two feet? What would happen to the water system? What would happen to the sewers? They found Internet addresses with satellite photos of the city and pored over them, trying to figure out how far the flooding had reached into which areas. When they had finally gotten in touch with a handful of friends, they shared sites, chat groups, blogs that offered information. Boucher set up an information clearinghouse for the parents and teachers.

Jean watched the news, shaking her head, repeating phrases like "those poor people." Gus's reaction was a little beefier. A Korean War veteran, a photo of him in uniform still hung in the living room. "Where the hell is the National Guard? They need to start laying down the law in there."

"They're all in Iraq," Alice said, and her uncle declined to respond.

Occasionally images of looters would flash across the screen, the same three or four brief clips, usually black males with their arms full, glancing sideways at the camera or, shirtless, up against a storefront being detained by police. Gus's anger at these images was palpable. "Now, I have to ask," he said, "isn't that just . . . animalistic? Don't those people have any sense of right and wrong at all?"

Craig took a deep breath. "Those people" could, of course, be read in a couple of different ways. "I think it's a little hard to tell," he said, "how many of them are taking things they need and how many are actually 'looting.'"

"Well, it's kind of hard to figure how anybody down there in that situation needs an armful of shirts and a TV . . . Look at that one there—they're laughing."

"Okay; hush up now Gus," Jean said, clearing the plates off the coffee table where they were watching.

"Well, I guess I'll just go and be quiet," Gus said, scowling at the television.

Alice started making phone calls the day after they arrived to see about getting Annie into school, since there would be no school in New Orleans for the fall semester, at least. Alice had a couple of college friends in the Chicago area. One, Stephanie, who was married to an architect and lived in Winnetka, told Alice about a Montessori school in Winnetka, which was too far away for Annie, but the Montessori network was banding together to try and provide space for displaced New Orleans children. Two phone calls put Alice in contact with a school less than ten minutes away, St. Lawrence Montessori, and she made an appointment to visit with Annie on Monday.

The principal, a tall, vigorous woman in her thirties with a mane of wavy red hair swept back and fastened with an elastic band, was appropriately solicitous about the fate of New Orleans and assured Alice that there would be a place at the school for Annie. They were offering a complete tuition waiver, in addition, for children displaced by Katrina. The building was bright and cheerful, on an oak-lined street; full of vivid construction-paper cut-outs, and books arrayed neatly on shelves underneath the classroom windows. The children looked smart and happy and well-cared-for on the playground, and Alice loved it. It reminded her of all the best of Boucher School, except that it was much smaller than Boucher. And it was private. They worked out the logistics easily, and Annie was scheduled to start school at the beginning of the next week.

When watching the televised news became too much, and when he began to feel badly about tying up the Brunners' land line, Craig walked around the neighborhood to burn off nervous energy and to take his mind, even if only for a few seconds at a time, off of what was happening to the life they had known. Up and down the alleys of Elkton Craig walked, subliminally astonished by the solidity of this neighborhood, the tiered fire escapes behind the houses, the garbage cans set out for the trucks on their dawn runs up and down the hidden arteries of the town. The walks grounded him somewhat, even if just in his own body, but they also took on an oddly distorted aura. The disjunction between what had happened to his own reality and the continuity in this new place created a strange and pervasive sense of unreality, a kind of paranoia, as if nothing he saw was what it appeared to be.

Craig knew he needed to get to work on something, although he wasn't sure just what. The Brunners had generously offered Craig the use of the dining room table as a desk, but he couldn't get Internet reception there on his laptop, and Aunt Jean couldn't resist talking to him as she went through, even if it was just to say that she wasn't going to talk to him. He needed some space to himself.

On Friday of that first week, Craig found a solution, half a mile away, in the gentrifying neighborhood everyone called OffWabash, a string of three blocks that had apparently been dipped in money and on which new, trendy-looking stores were growing like crystals among the old Czech grocery stores and dusty tailor shops. Women's clothing stores with inscrutable and vaguely South American or French-sounding names (La Bahía, Alizé . . .), a brilliantly lit fine stationery store right next to a Chinese laundry, a bookstore (Sister

Carrie's). Most important, he found a coffee shop called Brew Horizon, which had wireless Internet service and where he could set up, do e-mail and establish some kind of base.

Brew Horizon was eerily similar to every other independent coffee shop in gentrifying old neighborhoods around the country—the coffees listed in colored chalk on blackboards hanging on the walls under pressed-tin ceilings and expensive track lighting, large burlap bags of coffee beans here and there for effect, auxiliary items—coffee carafes, teapots, chai—for sale on shelves, art by an employee or a friend of an employee for sale on the walls, people lined up to give drink orders to tattooed baristas . . . The whole combination made him feel momentarily and unreasonably elated, as if it were the possible base for a new life, as Maple Street had been back in New Orleans, with its shops, and the Riverbend so close by with the levee, and the Camellia Grill. Predictably, the balloon of his elation began to deflate as soon as he thought of New Orleans.

But he knew to expect that, and Brew Horizon was exactly what he had been hoping to find. For several days, Craig felt as secure as one might feel in a weatherproof harness securely lashed to the side of a mountain in a snowstorm. He was able to get a start on whittling down a pile of unread e-mails that had grown by over three hundred in less than a week. They came from friends, family members, old schoolmates, people he had met once seven years ago, and no matter how quickly he answered them the number never seemed to shrink. Everybody wanted to know not just how he was, and the family, but how *it* was, what it was like to live through what he was living through, something to make it comprehensible on a human level. All of America, it seemed through the window of his laptop, was overwhelmed with awe at the scale of what had happened, and the suffering they were witnessing on television. Over a table halfway back, Craig sat, with his laptop plugged in, writing, answering e-mails, drinking coffee. He would go back to the house for lunch and to see Annie and Malcolm. Some days he would get a panini right there at B Hor, his new private nickname for the place, which he used in e-mails to friends and to Alice.

He also began making phone calls to generate some work. *Gumbo* had suspended publication for the indefinite future; the restaurants and other businesses whose advertising revenue underwrote the paper were closed; the offices were unusable, the staff was scattered across six states—and he would need to start making some money. And, too, he knew, he needed to keep himself from going crazy from the overwhelming sense of powerlessness. He wanted to make some kind of contribution. And he wanted to find a way to respond to what some public officials were saying. The Speaker of the U.S. House of Representatives, Dennis Hastert, a man with the face of a malevolent toad, if toads were pink and flabby, had said that large parts of New Orleans should be bulldozed, and that it didn't make sense to save it. Remarks like that made an aurora of heat and anger collect around Craig's head. He wanted to do something to answer.

Like Alice, Craig had several college friends in Chicago, one of whom was Peter Morehead, an editor at *CHI EYE*, one of Chicago's alternative newsweeklies. They had stayed in loose touch since college largely because they were both involved in the alt newsweekly business. According to Peter's office voice mail, he was out of town until Monday, September 5, and Craig left a message in the hopes that there might be some freelance editing or proofreading he could pick up, maybe even some kind of guest editorial. He called other friends, left messages, sent e-mails.

He and Alice bought Tracfones at a nearby Wal-Mart and set about trying to contact their New Orleans friends. Everyone he spoke to was in shock. He finally reached Bobby and Jen in Baton Rouge, and he managed to track down Doug Worth, who had joined Connie and their kids in Hammond. Doug told him that the floodwater had apparently not reached their immediate neighborhood, and this was important news. It meant that their house might be livable.

After the initial elation at finding a base during those first days of free-fall, Craig began to notice odd symptoms in himself of something he couldn't name at first. He had started to find the people who came into the café irritating, for no reason at all that he could tell, except that they looked happy. They looked as if they took their coffee shop and their safe, dry streets and houses for granted. As if this were the way things were. Also, after living in a place that was so multiracial, the rarity of black faces struck him as odd. He would look around at the housewives waiting on line for their four-dollar lattes, with their kids in strollers, talking to one another about all the stuff of day-to-day life, entitlement oozing out of their scrubbed pores all over the floor, and Craig would find himself thinking about the Café Rue de la Course on Oak Street, or maybe about Vaughan's or Little People's, or Shakespeare Park. Then he would start thinking about the people who lived around Shakespeare Park, and Kemp's Lounge, and all those little grocery stores, and that soul food place that used to be right on the corner of Washington and LaSalle that had the great macaroni and cheese that Bobby had shown him when he had only been in the city a month, and the other restaurant in the lady's living room that had the jukebox with all the gospel records on it, and the parades going up Washington, and he thought about the images he had seen the night before, and that morning, on television as he ate his dinner or ate his breakfast, and that his children had to see it and live through it, and anger began to coil around his heart like a snake, irrational anger at everyone around him who was going on as if life hadn't been interrupted, as if the greatest single forced migration in American history since the Dust Bowl hadn't just happened, as if their little arguments, their irritations and snits added up to even an ounce of shit . . .

His pulse at such moments was elevated, heart pumping and

breath coming hard, and when he would get the crucial moment of distance and take a slightly calmer breath, sometimes tears would come to his eyes. He knew what this was; he had heard about post-traumatic stress disorder for years in other contexts, and it didn't take a PhD to recognize it. When it would hit him he would get up and take a walk outside for a minute and clear his head if he could.

Privately, Craig called this the Weird Anger, in an effort to en-capsulate and reduce its power, but when it came it was almost over-whelming. There were other symptoms, such as the bouts of crying that came out of nowhere, triggered by almost nothing. Someone would ask him how his home was—using the word "home" and not "house"—and he would feel his stomach buckle and he would be unable to answer. If they said "house" he could usually get through the conversation. Or walking into a store and hearing Louis Arm-strong playing over the sound system and having to turn around and walk out, covering his eyes. Any display of empathy, even those that did not go past the surface, could reduce him to tears, and Alice reported the same thing. Even the most obvious tourist emblem—a drawing of jazz musicians playing in a gift shop, or even the French Market brand coffee, for example, that the Brunners had bought to make them feel at home, could immobilize them with instant and overwhelming grief. The memory of the tenderness, the generos-ity of spirit, that was in the air in New Orleans, the small things that everyone they knew seemed to appreciate, the appreciation for the fleeting hours and minutes, expressed in gratitude and dance and eating together . . . Anyone who indicated that they understood what the loss of that meant, or indicated even that they couldn't un-derstand, but that they sympathized, felt like a friend for life, and at the same time made palpable how much they had all lost. Or might have lost, since nobody was sure yet what parts of the city had been affected in what ways.

On Tuesday, a week after they had arrived in Chicago, Craig

was sitting at his table at Brew Horizon when his cell phone rang. He was trying to encapsulate and neutralize one of the Weird Anger attacks. This one had been triggered by a thin fellow in a yellow and black bicycle riding outfit, carrying his helmet and waiting on line with his own personal travel mug, which he obviously carried with him everywhere. He appeared to Craig to be very satisfied with his life—proud, very likely, of his solar panels and recycling bin, his virtuous light conservation policies at home—the type, Craig thought, who thinks cars should share the road with bicycles, who rides in traffic and gets righteously indignant when drivers don't treat him like another car. Didn't he understand that cars are large, and powerful, and that he existed only by their sufferance, that they could knock him over if they hit him? Didn't he understand how dangerous the world is? It was criminal, sang every nerve in Craig's body, to gauge the forces around you so lightly—someone needed to tell this fool—criminal to assume that there is a right order of things, that someone who has not been adequately socialized by your rules won't break through and crush your satisfied, healthy, enlightened ass up against a wall until blood comes out of your ears, smash your fucking bike to fucking pieces . . .

The phone rang again. Craig felt faintly nauseated, in need of a walk, but on the third ring he checked it, saw a local number he didn't recognize, and decided to answer.

"Yeah."

"Have I reached the Swiss Family Donaldson?" the voice said.

"Who is this?" Craig said.

"Ah, how quickly they forget old friends. Craig, It's Peter. Morehead."

"Peter!" Craig said. His friend from the *CHI EYE*, his old friend . . . vertigo in the stomach, the shift from the magnetic field of the Anger to this avatar of the Lost World, the Old World, of friendship and family and continuity . . . Peter . . . "How's it going? I'm sitting here in my new coffee shop in trendy OffWabash . . ." shifting into the familiar mode, the deflective cleverness mode, the old-friends mode . . .

"Well the question is how's it going for you? Is your house all-right? Bring me up to date."

Craig liked Peter's voice; it was a cultivated voice, yet a vernacular one, familiar yet without any unwarranted breaches of good manners. How was he supposed to give a measured, civilized answer to this direct question? He did the best he could to tell his friend what he knew, how he was, how Alice and the kids were, what he knew about their house and neighborhood. Like everyone, Peter wanted to know what Craig thought about the mayor of New Orleans, Ray Nagin, what he had heard about the various parts of town, about the reports of police looting and deserting, about Craig's job. Craig told him as much as he could, and even before he had a chance to ask Peter about whether there was any work at the *EYE*, Peter brought up the topic himself.

"Well," he said, as Craig spun out an extended cadenza about the evacuees and the potential political meaning of the diaspora that was under way, "before you waste any more of this insight in conversation with me, how would you like to write something for the *EYE* about it?"

"Seriously?"

"Well, yes, in fact. Let me tell you what we had in mind. I've already spoken about it with Lee Binner, our editor. We'd like you to think about doing a series for us on the storm, the diaspora. One a week, say fifteen hundred words each. Longer if you want. There are at least a couple thousand evacuees in the Chicago area right now, and there are sure to be more. We'd like to hear what they have to say, and we would like you, as at least a temporary transplant to Chicago yourself, to report on what the city is like over the course of, say, the next two months or so, more or less anything you want to do. And we'll pay you a thousand dollars a column. Not a princely sum, but maybe it will help a little."

After expecting at most to be offered an article or two, or some freelance copyediting work, Craig was overwhelmed. Craig had chafed at not having sufficient opportunity to do his own writing while at *Gumbo*. Borofsky kept him too busy editing nightlife supplements. This was almost too good to be true.

"Peter . . ." Craig stammered for a little equilibrium. "Are you serious?"

"Stop asking me that. We consider this a good opportunity for us. Okay?"

"Of course. I feel like I've been going crazy not being able to do anything . . . this is just . . . amazing."

"Well, don't go crazy. And let's have lunch once you have a clear day next week. Does that sound good?"

"It sounds better than anything I've ever heard in my life."

Peter chuckled and said, "We'll trim that out of the final version. I'm sure it's a bit of an overstatement. You always had a flair for the dramatic."

"Says the former secretary of Theater Arts." This was the college drama organization, to which they had both belonged.

"I'll start the paperwork going for your first check; I'm sure you can put it to good use. Do you think you can write the first one for us by Friday? Just sort of introducing yourself and letting the readers know how you got here?"

"Friday?" Craig said. "Sure. Sure I can do that."

"Good. If you can get that in I'll edit it over the weekend and we can get rolling."

After he got off the phone Craig closed up shop at Brew Horizon for the day and went back to tell Alice about this good luck.

• • •

•••

Craig titled his column "Down In The Flood," after the Bob Dylan song. Following Peter's suggestion, he wrote the first one about their evacuation and how they got to Chicago, and what they were struggling with in thinking about the future and the present and the past. It was a solid, lyrical column, which he wrote at Brew Horizon in two days. He could as easily have written five thousand words as the fifteen hundred he turned in. Peter did very little to it in the way of editing, published it and got him a check in the middle of his second week there. A thousand dollars a week was almost too good to be true, but Peter meant it, and Craig took Alice out to dinner with the first check when it came, while Gus and Jean babysat the kids.

1 5

Lucy awoke, heard breathing as if someone asleep next to her, sat up heart racing. Milky light gave a dim, bluish cast to an interior, a room. She had been dreaming about something that was already beyond retrieval, and she had no idea where she was. Obviously others in the room, sleeping.

"*Samuel*," she said in a stage whisper, propping herself up on her elbows, then quiet to see if an answer would come. There was a bunk above her; she was in a bunk bed. She looked down at her legs under the sheet; there she was.

By then she was remembering, and she didn't call her brother's name again. She lay back down on the thin mattress. After a few moments looking up at the bottom of the bunk above, she sat up again, carefully, legs over the side of the bed, still in her clothes from the night before, ran her hand over her face a couple of times. People sleeping in another bunk bed maybe six feet away, and in a cot set crossways by the small window that let in the day's first light. Heavy funk of bodies that had spent five or six days unwashed in the Superdome or the Convention Center, then on that bus, and the almost palpable heaviness of sleep filled the small space.

She stood up, slid on her shoes and walked to the door, opened it as quietly as she could, and stepped outside into the humid Missouri morning air. They hadn't been able to see much of the place the night before. Their bus had pulled in, near midnight, after long hours on interstates through Texas and Arkansas, and state roads, and then county roads, and finally on gravel and dirt, through a countryside hooded in darkness, dark farming country with no face, no landmarks. Under lights strung up on poles they were greeted by anxious-looking white folks who brought them into a low cinder-block hall, took their names and addresses, and assigned them places in cabins, where they set down whatever they had managed to bring with them and fell asleep.

Their destination was this place, Little River Camp, used for one week a year as a Bible study camp by Methodist youth, and for another two by ministers for annual retreats, a collection of twenty-eight small cinder-block cabins, a larger cinder-block dining hall and another cinder-block common building, all bare of anything but the hardware of beds and no-frills chairs. There was also a chapel building with pews, and two trailers that could serve as offices. It took up no more than four acres in the middle of miles of fields stretching off as far as you could see. They had ended up here by the merest chance, after being turned away from two facilities, one in Texas and one in Arkansas, that were full. The bus driver's cousin was a minister and he thought he had heard of this place and the driver had called him and the Red Cross was contacted. They told them to come on, and then ran around putting together the basics of bedding and hygiene and food on about ten hours' notice.

Lucy walked out of the tiny cabin, which was shaded by tall trees of a type she had never seen, and stood on the small, crumbling lozenge of cement in front of the door. In the distance someone walked deliberately across a stretch of gravel, probably one of the Red Cross. Other than that, nothing stirred. From one of the cabins in the distance she heard a baby crying.

She didn't want to go back inside, so she decided to take a little walk around, see if she could find a cigarette. She had no idea what time it was, couldn't remember what they had said about meals; they had said a lot of things very quickly, and not much of it stuck. Lucy walked across the sandy area in front of her row of cabins, toward the low building where they had taken their names the night before. It was hot already.

She came out into the gravel parking lot where they had gotten off the buses and looked past another row of cabins, across what seemed at first a great emptiness, planted with what looked like dead shrubbery. As she walked to the edge of the brownish field it came into focus for her, and she said the word to herself: "Cotton." She let herself look around, 360 degrees, and all she saw was cotton fields. That was the emptiness they had been driving through the night before. The camp was a small, tree-shaded island in the midst of it all.

The door of the low building was open, and there seemed to be some kind of activity going on inside, so she walked over and poked her head in.

"Oh!" a voice said, one of the white people in charge of the camp, a short lady with light brown hair, wearing a white polo shirt and khaki shorts. "We have a customer," she said merrily, walking over to Lucy. "Come in, come in! At least someone was listening last night when we gave out the mealtimes. How are you? Did you have a good sleep? You must be exhausted. My name is Shauna."

"Allright," Lucy said, nodding at the lady and putting out her hand to shake the hand the lady proffered. "I'm Lucy."

"The food is over there at that window. Just get you a plate on that table and head right on through. Doesn't look as if you'll have to fight the crowds!"

Lucy smiled politely and looked over to the serving window where a large white man in a yellow T-shirt stood. "I might eat in a while," she said. "I was hoping I could find a cigarette. You don't have no cigarettes here?"

"Oh no," the woman said, pursing her lips and putting a naughty sparkle in her eyes. "I'm not a smoker. I'll bet you Steve might let you have a cigarette. He's from the EMS, but I don't think he comes in until eight-thirty."

"Uh-huh," Lucy said. "Well thank you. I'm-a take a walk around. Y'all have phones?"

"We're working on getting them," the woman said, her tone contracting just a bit because of what she took to be Lucy's abruptness. "We should have some phones for you to use later on today."

"Okay," Lucy said, starting to walk off. "Thank you."

"Don't miss breakfast," the woman said, with some alarm. "We have a lot of food that's going to go to waste if people don't eat it. We stop serving at eight-thirty on the dot."

"What time it is now?"

The woman looked at her wristwatch and said, "It's ten after eight . . ."

"I'll be back," Lucy said. "Is that cotton?"

"Yep, it surely is," the woman said. "We're about a month away from harvest!"

"Allright," Lucy said, walking off. The woman frowned, puzzled, then turned to the man behind the serving window and shrugged.

Lucy was already making plans for what she needed to do. First and foremost was to figure out how to start finding Wesley. And SJ. And, second, she needed to know who the person was who could make her time at this place as smooth as possible. She needed some fresh clothes sooner than soon. With any luck she would not be there long. But however long it would be, she needed to hook things up. It looked to her more or less as if she was starting at zero.

Lucy Williams was nothing if not a survivor. She had barely started eleventh grade in 1966 before she quit school, pregnant with her first son, Albert, born severely handicapped. Albert had been the beneficiary of Lucy's extended family, which took him in and took up the slack and found a way and filled out the forms and called cousins and made sure he was clean and fed during those times when Lucy was out of control. But the boy had died when he was nine, from a respiratory ailment that came out of nowhere and killed him in two days.

Wesley had been a surprise for thirty-seven-year-old Lucy, an accident; his dyslexia and slight hyperactivity may or may not have been a result of the cocaine she had been smoking at the time and which had exaggerated the recklessness that resulted in his conception. Her decision to keep him was questioned by everyone except Lucy herself, who reasoned, to her friends, that the welfare money that his arrival would generate would be a help around the home. That's what she told her friends, but there was something else, harder to define, in the mix; she just had a feeling that this baby wanted to live. She kept him for good and bad reasons, both. One set or the other would be in the forefront, depending on how high she was.

After Wesley's birth she straightened out for a while; SJ had rehabbed the house on Tennessee Street for her and the baby, and she moved back to the Lower Nine in 1989 with her two-year-old, from a depressing apartment building off of Jackson Avenue. But the rocks and the bottles continued to be an undertow for her, and she would go in and out of that life, unpredictably. In recent years her weakness had been alcohol. She loved Wesley, and Wesley loved her. And yet there was a part of her that was separate from him and everybody else, that needed to be dissolved in drink or smoke, answerable to nobody, and that part had made her be absent for Wesley at important times.

Lucy was tough. She had an old-time habit of carrying a straight razor, and once in the middle of some partying that had gotten out of hand, serious freakishness in a house that all she could remember was somewhere around the Brown Derby on Washington Avenue, threesomes, trains, very depraved shit, which she did not go in for, and a guy named Joseph, who was always around on the fringes, came up to her where she was having a good time just being high on a couch. He had his pants off and he walked right up to her and pulled his drawers out over his thing and put it right up to her face. When she told him to get his thing the fuck out of her face he slapped her and grabbed the back of her head and tried to force her to take it in her mouth and she was not so high that she couldn't slide her razor out of her right pocket, flick it open and draw it, hard, across the back of his thigh just above his left knee. He howled, and with good reason, because she had nicked his femoral artery and blood was squirting out as he jumped backward, zip zip zip, and it sobered her up rather quickly and a friend of hers got her out of there and to the friend's house where Lucy stayed for a few days. The guy she cut survived, which was very lucky for him since you can bleed to death easily that way. Those were different times; everyone knew that Joseph was brutal and acted crazy and they figured he more or less got what he deserved.

Long years, making it however you could. Her salvation was that she also had this other world she could walk into. SJ and Rosetta, Camille, family dinners. She loved Rosetta deeply, as everyone did; there was in Rosetta not a trace of condescension toward Lucy, or superiority or judgment. Wesley had a second mother in Rosetta during those times when Lucy was unable to take care of him properly, and an older sister in Camille; they had bought his football uniform for him in high school, and had taken him on vacation with them once to Disney World. There were years when Lucy was healthy and present and they would have great Christmas celebrations at SJ's, where everyone joined in and Lucy could manage to get something for Wesley that he really wanted, and Uncle SJ and Rosetta would get him something good, too—a football, a bicycle, clothes. Camille was the one who would occasionally get her cousin a book or some music. They would all go to church.

Then there were other years when Lucy was out somewhere at the end of a long string, when she couldn't even get it together to buy him anything. One year it was a red plastic truck from the Dollar Store, still in its plastic on a cardboard back, with one corner slightly open, not even wrapped. Wesley always managed, with Rosetta's help, to get something for his mother. The boy was always so happy when his mother was there for the holidays, a smiling little boy in a short-sleeve white shirt with a red bow tie, his mouth always with that muscle tension as he smiled for the photos.

They decided to keep the kitchen window at Little River Camp open for an extra hour, since it was, after all, the first day, especially after Steve got there from the EMS and insisted they do so, although the Red Cross woman in charge, Betsy, was against the idea. "It immediately sends the wrong signals." Steve reminded her that these people had just spent three days on buses with no change of clothes, after being flooded out of their houses and in many cases sleeping on the side of a bridge or at the Convention Center. "We can cut them some slack," he said, laconically and pointedly.

Steve, a skinny twenty-three-year-old who looked like a skinny seventeen-year-old, was an unlikely seeming liaison for these hundred and thirty African-Americans from New Orleans. Unlike the others in his family, he had spent a little bit of time outside of the Missouri Bootheel, a tab of land in the southeast corner of the state that extended down into what might otherwise have been Arkansas. He had spent two years at Southeast Missouri State in Cape Girardeau, on the Mississippi River, north of Sikeston, so he had a slightly cosmopolitan aspect that was not immediately discernible to outsiders, nor was it particularly appreciated by the other members of his family. He wore a faded EMS T-shirt, shorts frayed along the bottoms and metal-rimmed glasses. His skin was so pale as to appear almost translucent, and the traces of a persistent adolescent acne inspired little faith, initially, in many of the evacuees.

But Lucy, standing outside, taking stock of things in the hazy morning, noticed the skinny kid walking from the dining hall to the office trailer, because three different Red Cross people approached him, one at a time, to confer about something, and afterward the skinny youngster would walk away, only to be stopped by another Red Cross. He, she assumed, was the man to talk to.

When he disappeared into the trailer, Lucy gave it about one minute and then walked over and knocked on the door. A voice said, "Come in."

Inside, the young man was kneeling on the floor behind a computer, connecting some wires. When he saw Lucy, he put down his screwdriver and stood up, pushing his glasses back up his nose.

"Hi," he said, friendly, but looking at her as if taking her measure quickly. "We're not quite open for business, yet."

The first thing she noticed was something fleeting and correct in the young man's presence. A mix of friendliness and reserve, unlike the kind of unwarranted familiarity she often encountered from people who looked like him.

"Allright," Lucy said. "I don't mean to bother you."

"No bother," he said. "We're just playing some catch-up ball here pretty fast. How can I help you?"

"You're Steve?"

"That's me. What's your name?"

"I'm Lucy." The young man had put out his hand, and Lucy shook it dutifully. "The lady said earlier you might have a cigarette?"

Steve laughed slightly, reached into the pocket of his shorts and pulled out a crumpled pack of Camels. "If that's all it is, I can help you out." He shook one up from the pack for her, which she took. "In fact, why don't you keep the pack."

"Then you don't have none."

"Yeah, but I can run and get more no problem. Go on and keep it. Actually let me bum one back from you and we can smoke together. I'm about due. We better stay inside or the RC will be all over us."

They lit up and stood there for a few moments, looking around the trailer, which was dark and smelled of mildew. Cockeyed, dusty blinds on the windows.

"You live here?" Lucy said.

"I live in Caruthersville. It's about half an hour from here."

"Where we?"

Steve tried to see in her face if this were a joke, and he saw that it was not. "They didn't tell you where you are?"

She shook her head. "I know we been in Texas and Arkansas on the bus, and somebody said Missouri, but, you know . . ."

"I can show you," he said, standing up and going to a duffel bag on the floor. "What part of New Orleans do you come from."

"We from the Lower Ninth Ward."

The man rummaged in the bag, pulled out an atlas. "Did you evacuate before the storm, or . . ."

"I was in the house when the water came," she said. "It come just like a tidal wave. SJ and I was on the second floor and it was just like you had a lake in your living room."

The young man sat on the edge of the table and looked at her, listening intently. He made no exaggerated show of shock or false solicitude; instead his expression deepened into concern and concentration, which confirmed for Lucy that this one was allright.

"They didn't tell you about none of this?" she said.

"I've been watching it on the news," he said. "But they didn't give us any information about who was coming here. They just said evacuees and gave us a head count. They said you made a couple of stops along the way." This was dry humor.

"We been on the bus three days," she said. "SJ dropped me off at the Claiborne Bridge and I walked over to the other side and these boys had like a, almost like a bulldozer or something, give me a ride and I walked the rest of the way to the Superdome, stayed there I don't even know how long. Three days, four. I don't really know. Then they had the buses and they took us to Houston first and they didn't have no room, then they took us to Hot Springs, and they didn't have no room. Now we here."

Steve listened, took another drag from his cigarette and stubbed it out in the unused sink of the trailer. Lucy liked the fact that he didn't seem in a hurry to talk at her. He listened. That in itself was unusual. White people, in her experience, either ignored her completely or they were very self-conscious. The more well-intentioned they were, the more self-conscious, usually. This one wasn't.

"Okay," he said. "Here; look."

He opened the atlas on the computer table and showed her the United States map. He moved his finger around the page for a second, found New Orleans and said, "Here's New Orleans." She looked over his shoulder, nodded. "Here's Houston. Here . . ." searched for a moment . . . "there it is . . . Here's Hot Springs."

Lucy nodded.

Looking at the map, Steve pointed and said, "Here is where you are now. There's the Mississippi River. There's Caruthersville. You're here, just over where it says Kennett."

Lucy peered at the map. Somewhere out in that map, she prayed, SJ and Wesley were safe, and until she knew otherwise she would believe it. But looking at the map made her feel a tilt of anxiety in her stomach.

"Is it gonna be phones here sometime we can call to our people?"

Steve didn't understand the question as it came out, and he asked her what she had said.

"We can make phone calls later?" she repeated.

Straightening up from the atlas and rubbing one of his eyes, Steve said, "Yep, you surely can. That's what they told us anyway."

"Y'all can hook us up finding our people," she said.

He nodded, pulling out the chair by the computer, a signal that he was ready to get back to work. "Once we get these computers wired in they have a bulletin board they established on the Internet to put people in touch with each other. I need to get this hooked up, actually."

"Oh, I'm sorry," Lucy said.

"No, no," the young man said. "If you come back later on, we can get you registered and start the ball rolling. Do you know if your family's safe?"

"I can't really say," she said. "But God make a way. My brother been through the Vietnam and losing his wife and his baby boy and he a survivor. Wesley, my son, he smart, too. I know they all right."

Once again the young man nodded and looked at her straight on. "Come back in a couple hours and see me. Knock on the door if you don't see me outside."

"Allright," Lucy said. "Thank you, hear?"

"It's what I'm here for," he said, kneeling back down behind the computer.

That morning, the first two vans came in with clothes from local churches. They set to work after breakfast putting up a tarpaulin for a tent, and tables, and portable coat racks, an instant thrift store, but free of charge, where people could get themselves a change of clothes. They opened up the old chapel and swept it out, and likewise the recreation hall, where there was half a basketball court and some couches under bright lights on the high ceiling. The day before had been a blitz of activity, preparing the cottages, sweeping them and getting donated linens in there.

Across the United States, the same scene played out in hundreds, thousands, of permutations. People had watched the events on television and most responded viscerally the way they had been raised to respond: they wanted to help people in trouble. Before any question set in—of responsibility, fatigue, selfishness—the first thing was recognizing another human, like yourself, in trouble. Not just in the big destinations—Houston's Astrodome, Lafayette's Cajundome—but across the country. Volunteers, urged by their church, or by their service club at their college, or by the Jaycees or the Knights of Columbus or Temple Emanuel, collected canned food and clothes of every description, boxes of juice in plastic wraps on skids, baby food, cereal, socks in bags of a dozen, blankets, toothbrushes, mouthwash, toothpaste, Band-Aids; they brought them to drop points announced on the radio, or at the church or synagogue or college, or the local bank, where volunteers sorted them and tried to get their signals straight with the people who would staff the shelters, with the Red Cross, with Catholic Charities, with the Salvation Army, with the EMS workers and police and hospital liaisons. City and state officials discussed possible longer-term housing for however many evacuees might be coming; they met with landlords and hotel people at the national level. They talked to FEMA and they figured it out, piece by piece, the best they could, on the fly.

For days and weeks, the evacuees came, spilling out of airplanes and buses; they emerged, blinking and dazed, looking around, into a foreign moonscape in Phoenix, or Harrisburg, or Las Vegas, or Atlanta, or Hot Springs, or Chicago, or Albuquerque, or Cape Girardeau. Wherever there was a municipality with shelter capacity, people were taken there, a hundred thousand of them and more, plucked out of

New Orleans and sent out so that New Orleans could set about the process of stabilizing. They would sort it out later. The evacuees were met by confused-looking people who transported them in minivans and buses and cars to hotels or camps or unused church buildings or gymnasiums, where citizens had been busy working against the clock to set up a miniature city in time for their arrival. Down in the church basement, setting up the kitchen, unrolling the futons the ex-hippie with the futon store had just given them, or the box of cell phones the mother of the rock star who grew up in the town gave them. What is this box—it's just sitting here? Nobody opened it? Tell Paula we can't just have all this stuff sitting out here . . . What's in there? Hair curlers? Put these up in the rectory. I don't care—just get them out of here. Does Paula have the sheets and pillows Wal-Mart sent over? Has Bobby got the gas working in that range yet? I don't care what Eugene says we can't fit more than twenty people in here. That's what they told us, right? Twenty? Tell him if more is coming go set up West House; I got my hands full . . .

At Little River Camp, doors opened, people stepped out into the morning and their new lives, leaving the door open behind them, blinking, looking down at the ground, looking around at the wide horizon beyond the fields, looking at one another. The Red Cross volunteers prowled around greeting those who had awakened, telling them to get to breakfast and also announcing a camp-wide meeting, where they would discuss how the camp would work, and how they were going to work on putting them in touch with family and getting them situated in some more permanent arrangement. Ten o'clock, don't forget.

Around lunch some people from the Delphi First Baptist Church came and said hello and brought toilet supplies—toothbrushes, toothpastes, and snack packs. Some folks from the local A.M.E. church came by that evening, with a preacher who sold cassette tapes after his little sermon, which the Red Cross quickly put a stop to.

During the sermon, a small handful of ladies and one or two men sat in the chapel pews, waving their hands halfheartedly in the air; others just sat there, still stunned and disoriented, because it was better being around people than not being around them.

Others tended to family in the cottages, and most walked around hoping to run into someone they knew from back home, and many of them did. At a certain point someone asked if there were any chairs; the New Orleans people were used to sitting on their front steps and porches talking, so chairs were brought in. A small handful of people just sat on the edges of their mattresses, immobilized. The younger men tended to prowl around restlessly, trying their useless cell phones constantly, asking to use the EMS cell phones. Finally, after a day, a wealthy local doctor bought fifteen cheap cell phones with one month's juice in them, which became the property of the camp. Three were attached to thin cables locked to a table outside the trailer, and the evacuees were allowed to make calls under the eye of one of the administrators. That line grew and grew, people calling family in Atlanta, in Houston, in Dallas, in St. Louis.

The Red Cross gradually registered everyone there and put their names on a database available to all the other camps that had sprung up around the country, so that people looking for loved ones would have a better shot at finding one another. The goal was to get people out of the camps as quickly as possible, either into FEMA-subsidized hotels, or apartments, or to relatives or friends' houses somewhere else.

Lucy noticed the two men unloading boxes of clothes from a van. A tarpaulin sheltered the racks and tables on which all the clothes were going to be set out. Some evacuees had brought suitcases with them; these were usually the ones who had left their houses for shelter at the Superdome on Sunday, when there was still time to pack a bag.

Others had stayed in their houses and been plucked off of porches, or roofs, and had nothing but what was on their back.

She tried to size up the situation as she walked over. Looked like the two men pulling boxes and an overwhelmed-looking white lady trying to figure out what to do. Lucy could tell from her distracted manner that she had little or no experience doing what she was doing. This was a good thing.

"You need help setting up the clothes?" Lucy asked, approaching her, smiling, and stealing covert glances at the boxes.

Startled, the lady looked at Lucy as if she were a dog that had just spoken a sentence in English. "I suppose . . ." she said, looking back, vaguely alarmed at the boxes as they came off the vans and were set down unceremoniously on the ground. "None of these is sorted; I don't know how they expect us to put them in order here."

"That's easy," Lucy said, reassuringly. "Just start on 'em one at a time. I can sort them as they come out." The woman looked at her uncertainly. "I got nothing else to do," Lucy said, with a disarming smile.

The woman could locate no immediate reason to refuse, and so they set to work pulling the boxes toward one of the tables for sorting.

"Put all the children's to one side, let people sort through them themselves," Lucy said, scooping armfuls of clothes out and dumping them on the table. The woman hovered by her side for some moments, until one of the men from the vans called to her and she disappeared.

Lucy worked quickly. Emptying one box, she used it for the children's clothes, throwing them in as quickly as she could separate them. The others she separated roughly at first into men's and women's. She kept one empty box under the table right in front of her for especially nice items, which she would toss in for further inspection later. Eventually she was joined by a thin, anemic woman who was a community volunteer, and who had been told by the harried woman to help Lucy. Several evacuees began drifting over, and since Lucy was the one apparently in charge, asked her when the clothes were going to be out.

"Come back in about an hour," Lucy would say. If it was someone who looked slightly prosperous, she would add, "What your size?" The woman would tell her and Lucy would say, "I'm making a special box. I'm-a keep a eye out for you." The word got around quickly that if you wanted to have your pick of the better clothes, Lucy was the one to talk to. If you had a dollar or two to slip her, it helped greatly. Cigarettes were good, too, as a donation; Lucy stockpiled them and resold them for a quarter apiece.

After lunch Steve got Lucy registered with two of the national bulletin boards for evacuees. They plugged in her address, her social security number, birthday, and the same for SJ and Wesley, minus the social security numbers. He asked if there were any relatives or friends whom she needed to contact, and she did mention Aaron and Dot in Houston. Steve said that they could try and contact them later that day. Outside the trailer a table had been set up under a canopy and other evacuees were lined up to use the cell phones. Others were lined up at a table to talk to a man she hadn't seen before, who was taking down information.

When they had finished, Lucy thanked the young man; he had clearly gone out of his way for her, and she couldn't quite grasp why, but she appreciated it.

"Well," he said, "I can't even imagine what y'all have had to deal with, and I'm just glad we're here to help."

She looked at him, guardedly, squinting slightly, trying to read him, as if he were a menu on a wall in a dimly lit bar. He was a specimen she had not seen before, and she wasn't sure what to make of him. "Me too," she said.

16

The Albany airport is small, and Wesley was hard to miss when he came down the concourse. Art and Ell Myers had a picture of him, taken at the facility in Phoenix, which Ell had printed from the Internet. Through their church they had answered a call for members to temporarily house displaced people from New Orleans. Their own two boys, grown up now, had long since moved out of their modest three-bedroom home, to different cities, and Ell thought it would be nice to have someone back in the empty nest for a little while.

Wesley emerged carrying a brand-new duffel bag with the price tag still on it, and wearing a cheap dark blue parka with fur trim around the hood, over a long T-shirt. He had no checked baggage. He turned a couple of heads because of the odd combination of clothes, and also because of his hyperalert quality, looking around like a cat in a cat carrier.

He didn't know how to act, really, out in the world. SJ and, to some extent, Lucy had taught him manners—basics, like saying "please" and "thank you" and to take your hat off inside the house and things like that, but he had no real idea of how the parts fit together in the world beyond the Nine except what he had seen on television. In the Lower Nine if you made a misstep it could cost you your life, or part of your life in jail at least, and he assumed that the same was true everywhere.

Walking down the concourse now, as he had been directed, Wesley felt exposed and anxious, as if he were being processed for prison. He didn't know where the people he was supposed to meet were going to be, or how long he was going to have to walk. It was hard to tell what information was important and what wasn't important. He noticed one or two people looking at him but he was afraid to meet their gaze. Most ignored him completely; there were very few other black faces, and the few he saw didn't really look to him like New Orleans folks.

He came out into a wider area and as he was trying to see which way he should go, an older white couple approached him, smiling, the woman holding a photo of him and saying, "Wesley . . . ?"

"Yeah, that's me," Wesley said.

"Oh, you must be exhausted," the woman said, opening her arms and hugging Wesley, who stood there rigidly, dutifully putting his free arm around the lady. He didn't especially like being embraced by strangers, never had. This woman had thin gold-gray hair done in a permanent, and she was wearing a pink sweatshirt with a bunny appliquéd on the front. Her eyes bulged slightly.

"Welcome," the man said, when the lady had let go of Wesley. The man put out his hand to shake and Wesley shook it. "Art Myers, and that's Ell."

"Which way we got to go to get out?" Wesley said, because that was what he was wondering.

Art Myers wasn't quite sure what to say; a frown came into his manner, if not his face, at the rudeness of the question, the lack of manners. Ell stepped in and said, "We're just parked right out here in the short-term lot. This isn't a very big airport," she said, smiling at the young man, who was looking around as if he expected to be shot at. "Do you need a hand with that bag?" she said, to Wesley but looking at Art. She knew her husband had been annoyed by the young man's response. Art was a good and generous man, but he had rigid ideas about order and manners within the perimeter of his attention.

"No, I got it," Wesley said.

They headed out into the parking lot. It was after rush hour; the sky was still light, although the sun was behind the houses and the hills. They walked without speaking. Wesley had no idea what he should or shouldn't say, so he stayed quiet, and the Myers were in the same boat. Wesley recognized the surroundings as someone's version of normal, but not his.

They left the airport and headed up the Northway. Wesley sat in the backseat, looking out silently at the ridge of silhouetted hills to the west. At one point he said, "Is that the Rocky Mountains?"

Art and Ell exchanged glances in the front seat, unsure if the young man were joking with them.

"Those are the Adirondacks," the man said.

"Adirondacks," Wesley repeated, watching the darkening shapes pass by the window.

That first night at dinner Art and Ell sat thinking variations on the same general thought as they watched the young man eat: What have we gotten ourselves into? The young man didn't seem to know how to make normal conversation, although Ell was more ready to chalk it up to the undoubted trauma of the past week than was Art. They had fixed up their son Richard's old room for him, cleared off the desk, just generally straightened up. Richard was in Savannah at an architectural firm and would certainly not be back before the holidays. Daniel, their younger boy, lived and worked in New Jersey, so they left his room open. There had been a predictable emptiness in their lives after the boys left, which Art filled with his woodworking and Ell filled with volunteer work at a soup kitchen in Troy, volunteer work at the Elba library, and keeping the house straight. She stayed in touch with relatives via the Internet.

Ell had prepared a pot roast with potatoes and carrots stewing in the juice. Although she expected the young man to be hungry, he ate sparingly, and he seemed to be examining each bite of food intently before eating it. Out of nervous politeness, they asked Wesley questions that received monosyllabic answers—about his house, whether he knew where his family was. The longest string of words he put together was, "Do you have any like Crystal sauce or anything to put on this?"

"Crystal sauce?" Ell said, leaning in slightly.

"Like hot sauce?"

"No . . ." she said. "Would you like some ketchup or some A-1?"

"No, that's allright," he said. He made note of her eyes again; it was the kind of face he might have made covert fun of under other circumstances.

"Crystal sauce," she repeated. "Would I be able to find it in a store around here?"

"I don't know," he said.

After dinner, Art went into the living room to read the newspaper. Ell said, "You must be tired; you can go to your room if you'd like, or we usually watch the TV in the living room. Just . . . make yourself at home. For whatever time you are here just act like this is your home."

"Thank you," he said. "When they said I could try and find my people?"

"Well, we can try first thing tomorrow I suppose. It's probably a little late right now."

"Can I try my mama phone again?"

"Of course," Ell said. "Of course. There's the telephone. You go ahead and make as many calls as you like."

"Thank you," he said. He knew to say thank you; Lucy had drilled that into him. If they went to get a snowball and he didn't say thank you to the man, she would give him a swat on his bottom. Even if she was going off about something else, or drunk, if Wesley neglected to say thank you for something she would notice that. "Everybody like to hear thank you," she said. "Everybody like to hear thank you and everybody like to hear their own name." One time for one of his birthdays she had got him a red plastic fire engine, a small thing, but Wesley always liked fire engines, and he had gone and made a big sign for her, just said THANK YOU in red crayon and she had put it up on the refrigerator at the apartment off Jackson Avenue, and it stayed there for years. That was before they moved to Tennessee Street.

Wesley called Lucy's cell number and SJ's cell number and got "circuits are busy" messages on both of them, the same message he got when calling out on his own phone. He tried to think if there were any other number to call, but he assumed everyone else he knew in New Orleans was now in the same situation. He tried Chantrell's phone and it was the same story.

He set the phone back down and stood in the dining room chewing on his lip, staring into the distance.

"No luck?" Ell said.

Wesley shook his head.

"We'll find her tomorrow. Don't worry; we'll go down and get you registered. We'll find your Mom." She looked at the young man standing there in his sweatshirt, and he looked so lost to her that she went over and put her arms around him and gave him a hug. His body was rigid, stiff, as it had been at the airport.

"I guess maybe I'll go to bed."

"You do that," she said. "Sleep as long as you want. If there's anything you want in the night I'll leave a light on and you can just come downstairs and help yourself."

"Thank you," he said. "Thanks," he said, to Art.

"Okay," Art said, letting the newspaper drop to half-mast. "You all set? Ell got you covered?"

"Yeah," Wesley said. "I'm all set."

Upstairs in the room Wesley prowled for a minute or two, looking at the pictures, the posters of unfamiliar faces. He sat on the bed. Then he was up and looking around again. There was a small framed photo of their son, he assumed it was their son, in a tuxedo with a girl in a gown, a prom picture. A small wooden bear, foreign coins in an ashtray, Boy Scout books. Wesley looked out the window into the backyard, which was dimly illuminated by the light from the house's windows. His heart was racing; anxiety was like a constant noise in the room with him. It was harder being here, in this place, with all the evidence of life continuity, in all its foreignness, than it was being in the shelter. In a time of total disruption, disruption was what felt natural. This sense of continuity was what was hard to assimilate. He fought down in himself an overwhelming impulse to bolt, but he knew, he knew, that that was crazy. There was nowhere to go.

He lay down on the single bed with its nubby white bedspread. He did not take off his clothes, not even his shoes, and he left the lights on. All he wanted was to find his family and be out of there in a day or two. He lay there, looking at the ceiling. Within a minute he was asleep.

He woke up all at once, looking around, inside a dream, everything inverted, you wake up out of a dream, not into one, but now he knew where he was. He was in someone else's life. He sat up on the side of the bed, listened hard. The clock on the nightstand said 7:20; the window curtains were light.

Wesley stood up, walked as quietly as he could to the closed door of the room and listened to hear whether anyone else was up. He couldn't hear anyone moving around, no noise from the street, no cars. After some deliberation he opened the bedroom door as quietly as he could and stepped out.

He found Ell in the kitchen, slicing something at the drain board. She turned when he came into the room, wiped her hands on her apron and said, "Well, how did you sleep? Were you able to sleep?"

"I slept all right," he said.

"Was the bed comfortable?"

"Yes," he said.

"Bless your heart," Ell said. "You sit right down here and let me pour you some orange juice."

Outside the window above the sink, the early sun blazed off the rear of a house across the backyard. The kitchen itself had well-used fixtures, a slightly antique stove and refrigerator, but everything was scrupulously clean. There were pictures on the refrigerator, just like at SJ's house.

"That's our son Richard there, with our daughter-in-law, Donna." Ell set a glass of juice down in front of Wesley. "That one over there is our grandson Michael and his sister Caitlin."

Wesley drank the juice. The question of whether his mother and uncle were alive rose around him, like hot quicksand. He felt stifled, hot, and his pulse was racing. Ell kept up a running monologue as she fried eggs for him, about her grandson and her nieces and nephews, about their son Richard whose room he had slept in. Periodically she would ask him questions about his own life, to which he would respond with functional, unadorned answers.

"Daniel is more artistic," she was saying. "I think he was so glad to get out of the house and stretch his wings. Art can be a pretty tough customer sometimes. He's got a heart of gold, but sometimes he makes me so mad that I could almost brain him. Do you like jam on your toast, Wesley?"

"Yes please."

"Art always had a more relaxed relationship with Richard, I guess. He just dotes on Michael and Caitlin. And they love their Paw-Paw. Do you have brothers and sisters, Wesley?"

"No," he said. He attacked the food as if he were starving.

Ell knew that the young man couldn't be interested in what she was saying, but she feared the dread-filled silence that would descend if she stopped talking. She switched tracks for a while, mused about how long New Orleans would take to rebuild. "I just can't understand why it took the government so long to get in there and help those poor people. There is something wrong in this country when people have to live like that," and she went on for a while in that vein, aware that the unanswering young man in front of her was one of the people she was talking about, until finally, defeated, she said, "Art always says I talk too much, and I'm probably doing that now."

"No," Wesley said. He had finished eating and, cornered now, he looked across the table at the woman who had taken him in. Above the shoulders of this morning's embroidered sweatshirt, with its red script letters that read GRANDMA, the golden highlights in her thinning and gamely permed gray hair caught the light from the window over the sink. Her cheeks were slightly puffy under her eyes, and the makeup she had applied too heavily to the wrinkles along the corners of her mouth and edges of her chin had begun to flake off, exposing minuscule pink ravines. The eyes, which he had noticed the night before, still bulged slightly, as if she were being squeezed around her midsection by a giant, invisible hand. On first glance it had given her a cartoonish aspect in Wesley's mind, but sitting there now he recognized something else in them, hard to pin down, which he had previously seen only in his own mother's eyes, a look that he had no name for, a sympathy that bypassed any shell he had managed to construct. He feared that connection, even as he desired it. In any case it lasted only a moment, and then plates and glasses were cleared, and they made ready to head out into the day. Their first, brief, stop would be the Lutheran Church where Art and Ell had registered for the program that sent them Wesley.

The church office, ten minutes' drive away, was lit by gray fluorescent ceiling lamps and furnished with beat-up wooden salvage furniture that sat on bare, ancient green linoleum tile. One of the women there took down all of Wesley's information—home address, names of his relatives, his social security number—and loaded it into one of the national information-sharing databases that they, like thousands of others around the country, had been trained to set up to process the tens of thousands of evacuees who had been separated from their families.

Wesley sat on a gray metal chair with a green vinyl seat, next to the desk, watching every move the lady made, his knee jiggling up and down. He asked when he might hear something, and the lady who had taken his information said, "The information is in the system right now. Once it's in the computer, it will match up with any of the names you're looking for as soon as your people are registered. We have Mrs. Myers's contact information and we will be in touch as soon as we have anything to go on."

"When that could be?"

"Well," the lady said, raising her eyebrows and pursing her lips, "let's have a look right now."

The woman peered into her computer monitor, scrolling down. Ell took Wesley's arm and rubbed it vigorously once or twice, encouragingly. After a minute the woman said, "Well . . . it doesn't look like we have any matches yet, but that doesn't mean anything. They told us that they've been adding sometimes four or five hundred names to the rolls in an hour. So we will contact you as soon as we have any information at all. Promise," she said, smiling at the young man.

As they walked out the door into the snappy fall air Wesley seemed slightly relieved. As they approached the car, he even said, "That's your name? Myers?"

"Yes, it is," Ell said. "That's my married name. My maiden name was Swierdza."

"What?" Wesley looked at her, trying not to laugh.

"I didn't say 'weirdo' if that's what you thought," Ell said. "Swee-eerd-zuh."

Wesley laughed politely at her attempt at a joke. "What kind of name is that?"

"It's Polish," she said.

Their next stop was Hudson Lake Mall, where all the big department stores were, to get Wesley some clothes. Wesley picked out some underwear and socks and two baggy sweatshirts and an extra pair of jeans.

"You need more than that," Ell said.

"No," Wesley said. "I'm good."

"Are you sure?" Ell said. "The church put in some money to help out. Don't be afraid you'll break the bank." She smiled at the young man; she remembered shopping for fall clothes with her own two sons, and this excursion made her happy.

In the car on the way back to the Myerses' house, Wesley's thoughts jumped all over the place as they drove through the unfamiliar landscape, the suburbs, the unfamiliar trees and roads. His mind was a battlefield of incompatible emotions. Agonies of worry and panic over his mother, and SJ, attacked him like an ambush in a strange neighborhood. Then the imagery would recede for a while, diluted and temporarily supplanted by the process of the day, the undeniable reality of this woman's kindness, which bore in on him despite his distraction, and touched him. Then the thoughts of home would reassert themselves with a brutal force upon his thoughts. He was sure his Uncle J would have found a way to get them out, but he would be beside himself until he knew something about his mother and uncle. They must have been worried about him, too. Maybe at that moment they were trying to call . . .

At one point, because it occurred to him at that moment, Wesley asked Ell why she and Art had decided to volunteer to take him in.

"Well," Ell said, "it's just what you're supposed to do. When people are in trouble you are supposed to help out. That's really all there is to it." She looked across at him, then back at the road. "We all can do something to help somebody else. Somewhere somebody has done something to help each one of us, and you are supposed to give that back, or pass it along I guess you'd say. And, you know, in our church, we believe that Jesus gave his life for us, so if you believe that way, you are just acting by his example, but you know, every religion has some version of that in their own way. We're all very lucky to be alive and we should treat each other better than we do."

Wesley sat back in his seat and watched the road.

They arrived back at the house around five o'clock, scooting in just under the wire before the evening traffic began in earnest, the Albany commuters and the Schenectady people. They came in with the packages and, first thing, asked Art if there had been any calls, which there hadn't been. Then Ell said she was going to "busy herself" making supper.

Art asked the young man a few questions about the day and then they watched the five o'clock news for a while, still full of images of New Orleans, which Wesley watched attentively. Afterward there was still time before dinner and Art said, "Want to see how I spend my golden years?"

He led Wesley through a door and down some stairs into the basement, a large, damp-smelling cement-floored room of a type Wesley had never entered, since nobody built cellars in New Orleans; the ground was too wet. Art had turned on the light going downstairs, and now Wesley saw a room something like a bunker in one of the war movies he had watched with his Unca J, but this one full of hardware under the overhead lights, woodworking materials that Wesley recognized from SJ's workshop.

Art walked around the room, tapping his hand on different tools, as if ticking off inventory. "Band saw . . . Jigsaw . . . Table saw . . . Lathe . . . Over here I do my sanding; I got her rigged up with oversized exhaust fans for the varnish; it's nasty stuff first of all, and Ell's sensitive to the fumes. Over here is for painting; double vises over there . . ."

Wesley listened to be polite, although he knew what the tools were. Art took him to a low table against the far wall and pulled the cord on a double fluorescent light under a hood and it shone down on three wooden model planes, done in meticulous detail, and one apparently in process.

"Do you like planes?" Art asked Wesley.

Wesley shrugged, smiled a little.

"This is a Spad, here. That's a Fokker triplane, like what the Red Baron flew."

"Like in Peanuts." He remembered that from the Christmas TV show.

"Right," the man said absently. "This is the Flying Tiger, and I'm working on a Sopwith Camel."

"What do you use them for?" Wesley asked. "They fly?"

"No," Art said. "I just like them. They're beautiful. Or I find them to be so."

Wesley sensed that the man was slightly disappointed in his reaction. So he pointed to the jigsaw and said, "What does that one do?"

"That's the jigsaw," the man said, turning off the fluorescent light and walking over to the high bench with the tool on it.

"Like what they make the puzzles with."

"Well, yeah, you've got the idea anyway. Nowadays they make the puzzles with big stampers. You couldn't work each one individually with a jigsaw; it would be prohibitively expensive, and it would just take too long."

"Why they call them jigsaw puzzles then?"

"I think they just got started when some carpenter had a little too much time on his hands and decided to cut up a picture somewhere and they found out it was fun trying to put it back together."

"My uncle have a shop."

"A wood shop?"

Sudden drop in Wesley's stomach, sinking, Unca J . . .

"Yeah," Wesley said. "He has a shop in his backyard." He was looking at the jigsaw. Thinking about SJ, or talking about him, made him feel bad suddenly.

"Does he have his own business?"

"Yeah," Wesley said. "He make things, fix houses. I help him." Then, looking at Art with a look that Art would later remember as sudden and frantic, like an animal that spooked, or a cat struggling to get out of your arms, he said, "You think I can make my calls yet?"

Slightly startled, Art looked at the young man, with his scared eyes, skinny, standing there in his long T-shirt, and he felt a sudden rush of tenderness come over him. Yesterday, the abrupt response would have bothered him, but now he saw a kid a couple thousand miles from home, with nobody in the world. The poor fellow, he thought. "Well . . . let's go see." Then, out of nowhere, he looked the young man in the eyes and said, "It's going to be all right, son. We'll get you hooked up with your family." Wesley looked at him, then looked at the floor, said, "Thank you."

"Come on," Art said, putting his hand on Wesley's shoulder. "Let's go find Ell. She's the boss." And they went upstairs into the kitchen to find a pot of water boiling, unattended, on the stove, and Art's wife of forty-two years lying unconscious on the floor.

Three hours later, at Albany General, the doctor came out to the waiting lounge and told Art and Wesley that Ell was doing fine. She had

had what they called a transient ischemic episode, which they said was nothing serious, although they wanted her to stay in the hospital for another day or two for some more tests. She had a nasty abrasion on her forehead, but the X-rays showed no concussion. "Sometimes," the doctor said, smiling reassuringly, "wires get slightly crossed and the power goes out momentarily. We don't know why, but it does not make a large problem mostly." Art put his left hand over his eyes and made a kind of stifled sobbing sound, and Wesley looked away. The doctor said they were welcome to come in and see her.

In the room, which she shared with an old woman who seemed to be dead already, Ell looked up at Wesley from her bed. "You poor thing," she said. "After all you've been through and here you come into all this."

"I'm glad you all right," Wesley said.

"You two ought to go out and get some dinner. I had those perfectly good pork chops at home, and cabbage and all; it's a shame to see them go to waste." She smiled at Wesley when she said this. "All Art can cook is meat loaf." She smiled up at Art when she said this. Wesley noticed that they were holding hands.

"I mean, I can cook pork chops," Wesley said. "That's easy."

"You have been through too much; you need some taking care of right now."

"It ain't nothing. It give me something to do at least."

"Well, whatever you both decide to do, have fun and don't worry about me. I'll be fine. Don't forget to check the answering machine and see if any calls came in from the church people."

"We'll do that, sweetheart," Art said. Wesley saw that his eyes were red.

"Here, I guess these are thawed out," Art said. Wesley was looking under the drain board cupboards for a frying pan. "I think she keeps the pans over here," Art said, pointing to a cabinet next to the stove.

Wesley got the chops into one skillet and the cabbage into another; on the chops he sprinkled salt and some garlic powder he found in a cupboard. On the cabbage he put the same, along with some lemon juice, which was a trick of his Uncle J's.

"I'll tell you, I wouldn't know what to do without Ell. You come to depend on these women for everything. Have your mom and dad been married for a long time?"

Wesley was slicing an onion with an intense concentration. "My mama wasn't married to my father. I don't know where my father is."

"Oh," Art said, embarrassed. "I'm sorry. That was a personal question, I shouldn't have . . ."

"It's allright," Wesley said, scraping the onions into the skillet with the cabbage.

Art watched the young man preparing dinner for him, and he felt a weird sense of vertigo, this person he hadn't known three days before, and about whom he had had more than a few unexamined preconceptions. "We almost lost Ell about six years back," he said. "She had to have a hysterectomy and she almost didn't make it out of that. There was a bleeding that they didn't know the cause of, and we had a heck of a time getting her stabilized. I'll tell you the truth . . . I didn't know if I wanted to live if she didn't make it. I really thought to myself that if she wasn't going to be here anymore I would go where she was. Does that sound crazy?"

"No," Wesley said. What the man said didn't sound crazy to Wesley. Wesley knew what it was to feel that there was no point to living. He had felt that. And he had seen Uncle J after Aunt Rosetta died, although Wesley was a little young to really grasp what was going on. But he knew that something had seemed to go out of his uncle then.

Over dinner Art asked Wesley if he played sports, and that opened a conversation about football. Art, it turned out, had played halfback in high school, and they began a lively discussion of various teams' chances for the fall, which was interrupted by the phone ringing.

Art stood and went to pick up the phone, which was on the drain board under the cabinets. Wesley heard him say, "Uh . . . hold on . . . hold on one moment. Just a moment," and held out the phone to Wesley with a look on his face that Wesley couldn't read.

"Hello?" Wesley said, into the phone.

"Wesley?" he heard the voice say. *"Wesley . . . Oh, Lord . . ."* he heard her voice say, away from the phone, *"oh, Lord . . . it him . . . Wesley . . ."*

"Mama," Wesley shouted. He heard weeping and hollering and confusion on the other end of the line. "Mama," he said, alarmed, elated, scared; his nerves glowed red under his skin like burning wires; he would have jumped through the phone if he could have, but not knowing what was going on . . .

Then another voice came on the line, a slight Southern accent, saying, *"Hello; is this Wesley Williams?"*

"Is my Mama all right?" Wesley said, panicky.

"Yes," Steve said. *"She's fine; she's just kinda emotional hearing your voice. She'll be okay in a minute."* In the background, Wesley heard Lucy's voice saying, *"That my boy . . . My boy allright . . . Oh Lord . . ."*

Art watched the young man begin to weep, and he started to go to him, then thought better of it. He could not figure out what he should do. Ell was the one who knew what to do in a situation like this. Finally he decided to give the young man some privacy and stepped out of the kitchen.

When Lucy had pulled herself together she got back on the phone and they told one another where they were, some of what had happened. "SJ all right," Lucy said. "I talked with him just before.

He in Texas by Aaron. They going to fly me there tomorrow." They had both been in the Superdome, unaware of the other's presence. "I ain't lying Wesley, I thought we was going to die. The water come like a tidal wave. SJ swam to get a boat and he put me on the bridge. Then he stayed and I didn't know what even happened to him. He with Aaron." Lucy said Wesley should come to Houston and that FEMA would likely get them into a hotel or an apartment.

When they finally got off the phone, Wesley stood in Art and Ell's kitchen, stunned, trying to get his bearings. As the initial wave of emotion receded, he saw the strange room in which he had found himself surrounded by these other lives not his; it would take a few moments to regain his balance.

Art came back into the kitchen and said, "She's all right, your Mom?"

Wesley nodded, looking at the man. They looked at one another for several moments. "When you think I can go?" Wesley said.

Art was getting used to the young man's abruptness, and he answered that they would need to ask Ell what the procedure was, but maybe he could even get out of there tomorrow.

Wesley left the room to go to the bathroom. Art cleared the plates off the table and put them into the sink, scraped the few remaining strands of cabbage into the disposal. He gave thanks inside himself that Ell had set this up. They had done something good. He couldn't wait to tell her. Once or twice he had to struggle to keep his composure as he reexperienced the shock of seeing her on the floor earlier. He had had periods of mild depression lately, an occasionally overwhelming sense of melancholy at how quickly everything seemed to go. It all went too damn quickly. This young man's presence had somehow, for short bursts here and there, almost made it feel as if time had slowed down, or gone backward just a little, as if new things were still possible. And, of course, it reminded them both of when the boys were still young.

Upstairs, Wesley stared absently at some plastic flowers in a small vase on the toilet tank. His mama was all right, and Uncle J was all right. When he was finished he zipped up and went to wash his hands. To the side of the bathroom mirror were two little shelves bolted to the wall. As he washed, his eyes grazed over a haphazard arrangement of small, neglected treasures placed there. A pinkish jar with a lid that looked like a bouquet, a tiny, dusty glass dish with a chipped edge, shaped like a heart, a small ceramic urn with partly effaced lettering that read QUEEN'S SILVER JUBILEE.

He found himself staring at them after he turned off the water in the sink. Why were they making him think of a small plastic fire truck his mama had given him a long time ago? He remembered that truck suddenly and fully, as if he could see it in front of his eyes. It was so vivid it almost scared him. He had carried that truck with him everywhere. He would get right up close to it on the floor or along the edge of a table, and try and imagine himself inside it, like he could live inside that little truck until she came back from wherever she had gone off to.

He dried his hands and left the bathroom.

In the kitchen he found Art, putting the pots away in the cabinets under the sink. He had the skillet in his hand and was looking around like he had forgotten where he parked his car.

"That one went next to the stove," Wesley said. "Down there."

Art shook his head, bent down to the narrow cabinet next to the stove. "I think I'd forget my own head sometimes if it wasn't stuck on my neck." After he'd put the skillet away, with some difficulty, he stood up and said, "How are you making it? This is some pretty big news for you." He pulled out one of the kitchen chairs and sat down.

"Yeah. She going to stay in Texas with my Uncle Aaron. My Uncle J there already. I was worried they might be dead."

Art nodded slightly, looking at Wesley.

"Your Uncle J is the carpenter?"

"Yes," Wesley said. "His name SJ but I call him Unca J. He partly raised me sometime, like when my mama sick or someplace, he and my Aunt Rosetta would raise me."

"Is your Aunt Rosetta still alive?"

"No."

"How does your uncle do alone?"

"He all right. My mama always say he need to find somebody to be with, but . . . He takes care of shit. I'm sorry . . ." Wesley said, trying not to laugh and looking to see whether Art was offended by the word.

If Art noticed, it wasn't apparent. "It's hard for men alone," Art said. "In a way, I think the women have an easier time of it after their husbands are gone than the other way around. I think you just fall back on discipline."

"That's what Unca J say."

"Was your uncle in the service?"

"Yeah," Wesley said. "Can I sit down?"

"Of course. Help yourself."

Wesley sat down.

"What branch of the service was he in?"

"I don't really know," Wesley said. "I guess the army. He went to Vietnam."

"I spent two years in the army in Germany in 1959, 1960. Here." He rolled up his sleeve and Wesley looked at the tattoo, a blue eagle with red tips on the wing feathers. Wesley had a tattoo of his own, above his left bicep, which read, simply, "Chantrell," in blue script with little starbursts of the ends of the *C* and the final *L*, but he didn't show Art. He planned to get it erased when he could.

"I'm sure glad we were able to give you a place to stay, even if it was just for a short time. Ell and I both said it was almost like having one of our boys back for a while. I don't know where the time goes. As you get older, it just makes your head spin. I'll tell you, it was such a shock seeing Ell like that." He fixed Wesley with a look that seemed to Wesley both guarded and pained. "I'm real glad you were here. Thank you for being steady. Your uncle would be proud of you."

Nobody had ever thanked Wesley for being steady before, or a source of strength. It was a strange thing to hear, but it made him feel like he had done something good, himself. He liked the idea that Uncle J would have been proud of him. But he wasn't really sure what he had done. "All I did was cook some pork chops," he said.

"Well . . ." Art said. "Sometimes that's enough."

They went and watched the news, and then Art asked Wesley if he liked Western movies and Wesley asked him what he had, and they looked through Art's stash of war movies and Westerns and finally settled on *The Searchers*. They both fell asleep about halfway through.

Okay, you're on the air, Bill from Grafton, Wisconsin, Get Wise.

Bobby?

You're on, sir.

Hi. What I'd like to know, is [garbled].

Bill, you broke up a little there.

Sorry, what I said is some of these people if they sat in the middle of a railroad track and a train hit 'em they'd sue the railroad. How much money are the trial lawyers milking out of the rest of us for these lawsuits, and—by the way—now they'd call it a 'hate crime.' What I'd like to know is when are these people going to realize that they need to [garbled] . . .

Bill? Okay . . . looks like we lost you there, Bill; thanks for your call. Ray, from New Braunfels, Texas, Get Wise.

Yeah, Hello Mr. Wise.

Hi Ray. What's on your mind?

I'd like to know this. Two things.

Okay.

One is, these people are trying to turn the federal government into the place of God almighty. What I mean, instead of praying to the Lord to provide, and then helping themselves some, what you call lifting yourself up, and placing faith in God, they want the government to do everything for them. That's number one.

Well, that's because they have no other God to believe in. I guess they have to believe in something.

That's number one. Number two—I don't hear anyone talking about what's been going on in these places to where the Lord would get angry enough to send the storms on them. There's fornication, gambling—some of these casinos, which I have seen in pictures, you can't even see past 'em they're so big—crimes, robberies, holdups, what have you. I mean, people don't see a pattern in this? When the Lord got angry with the city of Babylon, what happened?

He razed it.

He razed it. And the Lord is bringing the waters now upon them, but instead of praying to Him they praying to the government and the television with all its filth. And they wonder why their roof falls in. You see them on TV crying about this or that. If I warn you about something five times and you don't do anything about it, don't cry to me. Like that last caller said about sitting in a railroad track. Don't ask me to pay your hospital bill if you're too stupid to get off the tracks . . .

Well, Ray, first of all we want to say that nobody wants to see people get hurt, and of course for the elderly, or little children . . .

I'm not sayin' that, Bobby . . .

Hold . . . hold on, there, Ray . . . I know you're not. But I think you touched on something important there. You know for liberals, if there are any liberals listening right now, I'll tell you exactly what they are thinking. They are laughing at you because they can't even conceive of what faith is. To them if you can't see it, it doesn't exist. They call that materialism, and it goes straight back to Karl Marx, even though some of them have gotten smart enough to say they don't believe in Communism anymore.

Well, it fell apart on 'em . . .

A lot of them haven't noticed (*laughter of guest over phone*). But they still have that faith in the government being the Great Father who's supposed to do everything for them. And now you see what has happened. And they see all these faces of people crying on the TV, which of course the media is milking this for all it's worth, crying people, going "Why don't you help us?" Well, I'm sorry, but unless you are a little baby, the question really should be, "Why didn't you help yourself?" Ray, we're going to have to move to the next caller; this is Sheila from Kennett, Missouri. Sheila, Get Wise.

Mr. Wise?

You're on the air.

Yes. I have been listening to these last few callers, and what I wanted to say is this. You all believe in Our Lord Jesus Christ. You have a personal relationship with the Lord.

Yes.

What I don't hear in what the people has said is any compassion for people in trouble. You seem so mean . . . I haven't listened to your show before this, but we had to evacuate here and I heard your show . . .

Where did you evacuate from, ma'am?

We are from New Orleans.

Well I am glad that you listened to the warnings and got out and made it to safety.

Thank you, praise God, but there was a lot of people in New Orleans and other places who weren't . . . who didn't have the means to get out. And also the people whose houses got flooded out, that was the fault of the levees. They had levees that cracked and that's what sent the water. Now people can't fix a levee by themselves. But what I mean is, how can you look at people when they suffering, some of these people lost their parents or children . . . My brother had his two children had to be sent two different places. Families got tore apart, and some of these people had nothing to begin with. And it seem to me that if we are talking about what Jesus would do or say, how can you look at people suffering . . .

Ma'am . . .

. . . and say "I wash my hands of him." You almost sound like you're making fun of people who lost their house . . .

Ma'am . . . If that is how I sounded I didn't mean it to sound that way. But now let me ask you a question. You say you are from New Orleans.

Yes, I am. I live in the Seventh Ward, and I lived there my whole life.

Did anybody ever tell you that it wasn't smart to build a house below sea level?

What you want people to do? Your mama and daddy are there, and your grandparents, and the church you go to . . . You didn't just get dropped someplace and pick up and leave . . .

Answer my question: Did anyone ever tell you it wasn't smart to build a house below sea level?

Look, motherf—

Okay, next caller; Frank from Arlington, Virginia. Frank, Get Wise . . .

One afternoon early in their third week in Elkton, Craig found Gus in the kitchen listening to the radio and shaking his head. Craig recognized the voice; everyone knew that voice:

Nobody wants to see anybody lose their homes, and our thoughts and sympathy go out to everybody who listened to the weather service and got out of town, took the kids and the most valuable stuff and acted like responsible adults. But I think most of us wonder why we should be stuck cleaning up after people who didn't bother listening to the warnings, who just sat around and said, "Why should I bother? Somebody'll give me a handout like they always do . . ." It's another case of wanting Big Brother to do everything. Like—do you remember this one?—the lady who sued McDonald's when she spilled coffee all over herself, saying the coffee was too hot? And won? Do you remember this? Okay we're going to go to Billy in St. Augustine . . .

"Tell 'em, Bobby," Gus said.

Craig took a deep breath and looked in the refrigerator for the soy milk he had bought the day before. Bobby Wise's voice was a sound guaranteed to drive him up a wall. The show was hard to escape, especially through the South and Midwest.

"I can't see," Gus said, "why people would just sit around scratching themselves when they know something like this is on the way. Can you explain this to me?"

Calmly, Craig thought to himself. It would be so much easier if Gus were a bad drunk and you could blame it on the booze talking, or if he were just a coldhearted son-of-a-bitch. But he was a loving, generous-hearted man who had worked hard his entire life. How could he be so susceptible to this vile crap? Craig usually tried to avoid the kitchen during the times when Gus was listening to Bobby Wise.

"Well," Craig began, "a lot of the people I think you're talking about don't have cars and couldn't get out. The city was supposed to provide buses, which they never did. And a lot of them aren't particularly sophisticated . . ."

"How sophisticated do you have to be to get out of the way of a Category Five hurricane?"

Craig kept on. ". . . people; they hear year in and year out about storms coming and it's always a false alarm. Evacuating is expensive and a lot of them have big families . . ."

"That's part of the problem right there," Gus said. "They have five or six kids on the welfare that they can't take care of, and it's everybody else's problem."

Craig was about to say that "families" could mean aging, sick parents, it could mean a lot of things . . . But he stopped himself. The gray-haired, crew-cut man with the craggy face looked up at him from the kitchen table as if he really expected an answer from Craig, and at that moment Alice walked into the room and a quick glance between them told her everything she needed to know.

"Uncle Gus," she said, kissing him on the cheek, "I'm going to have to steal Craig away from you. We have to go to the store and then he has to go do an article."

"Okay, Allie," he said, kissing her back. "I was just giving him a hard time anyway. Sorry, there, Craig; there's a lot of things the old flight mechanic doesn't understand too well."

"There's a lot of things I don't understand, too, Gus," Craig said, jollying it along. "I guess we'd better be going. See you for dinner?"

"You bet," Gus said.

Outside, Craig thanked Alice for saving him. "I really thought I was going to lose it."

"Well, don't lose it; they are putting us up and being incredibly generous to us."

For his second column, Craig had decided to track down some New Orleans evacuees. By talking to Catholic Charities, the Red Cross, and the Salvation Army, Craig came up with a provisional list of sites, mostly churches, where groups of New Orleans evacuees were being temporarily housed. Small groups of evacuees had landed all over Chicago, awaiting the next step, whatever it might be.

That afternoon, Craig visited a church, Our Lady of Lima, which was embedded on a short street that connected two longer streets in Old Town, on the North Side. Eight New Orleans families were reportedly quartered there. As he approached the church, Craig found three people sitting on the front steps of the brick building next door, two women in their thirties and a boy who looked to be about nine or ten years old, who was bouncing up and down in place, shaking one of his hands. The women returned Craig's tentative nod, warily, watching him. On a hunch he asked them if this was where the "folks from New Orleans" were.

The women looked at him guardedly. The one wearing a kelly-green T-shirt, culottes and sandals, said, "We from New Orleans."

Craig's heart quickened. He introduced himself and told them what he was doing there.

"You from New Orleans?" the one in green said. "You evacuated up here?"

Craig told her the short version of their story, and how he came to be doing these articles, told them he was the editor of *Gumbo*, which she had not heard of.

"I heard of it," the other said. "It like a magazine."

"Where you stayed at in New Orleans," the other asked.

Craig told her.

"When they going to let us back in?"

Craig, slipping his tape recorder out of his bag, tried to establish control of the conversation by asking her, in return, where they lived.

"Lafitte Projects, baby," the second one said. "Orleans Avenue." They both eyed the tape recorder hesitantly. The boy was shaking one of his hands in the air, bobbing his head down, shaking his hand. "Stop that joogin'," she said to him, sharply, and the boy stopped.

"Would you mind if I interviewed you on tape?" Craig said.

"What this for," the woman in green asked.

"It's for a weekly paper here called the *CHI EYE*," he said. He added, "It's sort of like Chicago's version of *Gumbo*."

"You doing a article?"

"Right," Craig said. "I'm doing a series of articles, actually, on people who had to evacuate from New Orleans who landed in Chicago, and what's happening with them . . ."

"You going to pay us?"

Craig immediately knew he should have anticipated this question. He, after all, was getting paid for doing this, and they were undoubtedly in worse shape than he was.

"I hate to say this," he said, "but I don't have money to pay you. The paper doesn't give me money to pay the people I interview. I understand if you don't want to take up time to talk for free. I completely understand that. I'm hoping to be able to talk to as many people as possible, because people's stories have to be told. That is the only way New Orleans is going to get the help it needs. What happened in our city should never have happened . . ." Craig stopped talking for a moment, surprised as always by the onrush of overwhelming emotion.

"That's allright," the other woman said. "Go on ask your questions. People got to know what happened."

"I'm sorry I can't pay you . . ."

"That allright. Ask your questions."

Craig talked to them for half an hour. They had awakened Tuesday morning to find themselves in a lake; some men they had never seen came in a boat and got them off the steps. "Look like it had to be 'bout six feet of water. Dooky Chase was underwater. You know Dooky Chase's?" They were deposited not far from the Superdome, walked there with the boy in a shopping cart they found ("He can't walk good for too long"), only to be turned away because the Dome was full. They ended up at the Convention Center for three days.

"A woman died right next to us on the sidewalk. We was trying to fan her. It was a white lady in hospital clothes; they had her in a wheelchair. I don't even know where she come from. Wasn't nothing we could do but fan her; wasn't even any water. She died and they put a blanket over her head."

Then on a bus to Baton Rouge, then on a plane and another

bus, and here they were. "People just told us where we needed to go and we went."

"What's going to happen now?" Craig asked. "Are they putting you in touch with relatives?"

"We don't even know where they at," the one in green said. "The FEMA supposed to get us in a hotel. We been here a week. But we don't know nobody in Chicago. Raeann got a brother in Cincinnati. Is that close to here?"

Craig asked if they had ever been out of New Orleans before, and the one who hadn't wanted to talk said, "I was in Baton Rouge one time."

That day Craig talked to three other people, all of whom seemed to be in some degree of shock. The last was a woman who looked to be in her early sixties, wearing a bright paisley blouse and a wig of straight, styled black hair, although her eyebrows were gray. How, Craig wondered, had she managed to keep the wig with her through all the evacuating? They spoke at a table in a green-painted cinder-block common room inside, while several people watched a soap opera on the television. She filled him in sketchily on some background facts: she had been a schoolteacher, she was leaving the next day to stay with her brother in Indianapolis, she had raised five children at her house in the Lower Ninth Ward. She spoke in an educated manner, with a formality that Craig had heard before in black people of a certain generation.

"I am going to tell you something," she said, regarding him across the coffee table. "This event is a tragedy for the country. Do you understand? It is not just a tragedy for our people, black or white, people from New Orleans. This is a tragedy for everyone in this country. This is the greatest country on earth, and if this is the best they can do then it is a shame on all of us. It is an embarrassment in front of the world."

Craig took notes in his notebook as she watched him. "How old are you?" she asked him.

Craig stopped writing, smiled a little, looked at the woman. "I'm thirty-six."

"You're not old enough to remember Martin Luther King."

Craig chuckled, self-effacingly, said, "No, but I certainly know his story and his speeches."

The woman did not smile along with him. "I am a teacher," she said. "I have taught young people for almost fifty years. I am seventy-four years old." At Craig's unfeigned look of surprise, she said, "Does that surprise you? I was born in 1931 during a rainstorm in Algiers, Louisiana. You know where that is. Right across the river from downtown. There was no bridge at that time; you took the ferry if you wanted to come to New Orleans. My parents raised me and my three brothers through the Great Depression and the Second World War, what they called Jim Crow times. I have seen many things come and go. We had to sit in our own place in the movie theaters, we could not go to the public pool, or the beaches by the Lake. But I have never seen a time this bad in our country. I am not just talking about this particular event of Hurricane Katrina. There was an aspiration toward something better that does not exist today."

The woman's sound was one Craig had heard on many occasions from older African-Americans—the formal diction, the essential seriousness, the indifference to making an impression—the gravitas—a word that Craig hated although he used it all the time. Listening to these people, usually older, he always felt exposed, as if his measure were being taken and he was being found wanting. What, after all, had he done to help things? He asked this woman, who gave her name as Mrs. Gray, where she had taught.

"Lawless High School, and then at McDonough 35 until I took my retirement. What people need to know is that there are schools in New Orleans with no books, with no light fixtures in some classrooms. Where there should be a toilet in the lavatory, sometimes it is only a hole in the floor. And no toilet paper; some children had to bring their own toilet paper to school. I am telling you the truth. How are young people supposed to learn in such an environment? How are they supposed to feel that something is expected of them? School is a place where you learn values, and among them is the value of yourself as a part of a larger group. What are these conditions saying to our young people?"

"Do you see this as a function of racism?" Craig asked.

The lady regarded him with that look again, which he did not know how to read; it was not appraising, exactly. She seemed to be sifting, weighing, feeling the texture of his reactions and their timing, thinking, Which kind is this one? How far has he gotten; how much distance is there? How real was the concern? The tacit assumption was that white people with any grasp at all of what racism actually was, and how it worked, were as rare as albino elephants.

"It is not really just about racism," she said, "as far as it goes. Our society has always faced racism. You notice I say 'our society,' because I don't believe that racism affects only the people of color, as they call us now. The racism hurts the people who have it, also. I will explain it this way. When integration came many white people left the city of New Orleans because they did not want to have their children attending integrated schools. This, really, is where the collapse of the public schools started. But, now . . . these people who moved may have felt they were doing the right thing by their children, but look at what the long-term effect has been, with the increase in crime, and poverty and public assistance. As long as we are thinking about an 'us' and a 'them' we are thinking the wrong way in our society." She stopped talking, and fixed him with the look again. Uncomfortable, he asked her in what part of town she lived.

"I lived in the Lower Ninth Ward on North Derbigny Street. My husband died six years ago. My entire life was in that house—photos, my teaching awards, scrapbooks. I imagine I have lost everything I own except what I was able to take with me to the Superdome on that Sunday. But it is not really about what we each have lost individually. It is about what we have lost collectively."

The woman's calmness and clarity and intelligence affected Craig strongly, and he hoped he would be able to re-create that sound and that affect on the page. When the conversation seemed to have come to a close, Craig thanked her for her time and she offered her hand, still seated on the couch. "Good luck writing your article," she said. "Do the best you can. Let people know what you are hearing."

Craig worked on the piece for three days; the teacher's words had both unsettled him and given him a compass, of sorts, for how he might proceed—for what, in fact, he might be able to make of this disruption. Through his own questions about whether to stay, his own wrestling about what all of it meant, he could still do something to help, by telling the stories, by making sure that it stayed on people's minds, in their mailboxes.

Those thoughts were backlit by the eerily quotidian nature of apparently normal life going on all around him in Chicago. People in stores, walking on the sidewalks, evening dinners and fall clothes, school buses and post offices and firefighters washing down their trucks in front of the brick station house in the bright September air. And even the necessary steps within his own family—Annie back in school at St. Lawrence Montessori, Alice's attempts to stitch together a regular schedule of meals and homework and shopping—felt unreal to him. Craig couldn't help thinking of *Invasion of the Body Snatchers*, the thin crust of normalcy covering the erosion of humanity underneath. They needed this routining in order to stay sane; the kids, especially, needed it. But at the same time it felt obscene to him to act for even a minute as if all were normal. Their own lives had been knocked over so easily; how could they ever again act as if there were such a thing as normal? And yet normal was what he found himself yearning for.

The question that pressed on him hardest as the days went by was what was going on in New Orleans itself. He had been waiting to make his first trip back until he could be sure that there would be gasoline available along the entire route, and by now necessary services had reportedly been restored along the interstates. New Orleans itself was still an armed camp controlled by the military, but emergency workers were being allowed in, and press as well, so Craig's *Gumbo* credentials were an advantage.

He had talked to Bobby and Jen several times, and he and Bobby had agreed to make their first trip back in together, for moral and logistical support. Craig would rent a van so he could retrieve things from his house, and he would drive down and pick up Bobby in Baton Rouge. Craig was certainly going to write a column about his first return to the city, and in the back of his mind he thought that going in with his friend would lend an added texture to the story.

1 8

Through the mid-morning traffic, Alice drove Craig to O'Hare Airport, where he was to pick up the minivan he had reserved for the drive to New Orleans by way of Baton Rouge. He would not make it all the way that night; he planned to stop as far south of Memphis into Mississippi as he could get, stay at a hotel, then make it the rest of the way to Bobby's the next day. The day after that, Craig and Bobby would head into New Orleans to see the city and find out what had happened to their houses and neighborhoods.

Craig had filled the trunk and backseat with all the supplies he had bought at Home Depot, every possible thing he anticipated needing on the trip: disinfectant wipes, cleaning spray with bleach to kill mold, three types of rubber gloves—thin, heavy duty, extra heavy duty—cheap, disposable rubber boots for wading through toxic muck. Two different kinds of surgical masks, an extra-large pack of heavy-duty garbage bags, a flashlight and batteries, six empty plastic tubs and a skid of twenty-four bottles of spring water, snacks, a big pail and two brushes and sponges. "I feel," he had told Alice, "like I'm going to the hospital for an operation and I don't know if I'm going to come out in one piece." He had with him a short list of things Annie wanted him to bring back from the house, and she had appended a briefer list of requests from Malcolm.

By this time they were reasonably certain that the flood waters hadn't reached their neighborhood, or their block at least. Or if they had, they weren't deep enough to have gotten into their house. It was hard to tell. The sketchily available flood maps had bloomed slowly on the Internet, like photos developing. Bobby and Jen's Mid-City house had almost certainly flooded, although they couldn't be sure how badly. The ground in Mid-City was full of dips and rises, and the damage would vary from block to block. Hard information had been slow getting out because of the lack of coordination of local agencies and the failure of cell phones and telephones. Some people had blogged out piecemeal information, neighborhood by neighborhood, street by street, and they pored over the entries, trying to get a reliable picture (*btraven 9:01 a.m.: I'm on Oak Street and all that area is dry and up Leonidas to around Hickory . . .*) (*carrie1974, 2:43 pm: I was on leonidas and didn't see any water there :*) *biked around Irish Channel and okay up to Carondelet*), but since the forced evacuation of everyone, news had gotten sparser, and the situation had been changing, too. Everyone had been siphoned out of the city and there were, reportedly, checkpoints almost everywhere.

In the days immediately before the trip Craig was sleepless, anxious. He even snapped at Annie for leaving a toy on the stairs. He had diarrhea and headaches. Craig was aware that the attention he was paying to detail was a large channel into which his dammed-up anxiety and worry could flow. You held a torn world together with stitches of manageable detail. The trip was an excursion into a giant howling blur, a place that used to be the most welcoming place he had ever known, now full of potential threats of almost every type.

At the airport car rental station, a large open lot, they found the Windstar in space 23 and Alice helped Craig transfer everything from the car into the minivan. Craig oversaw the deployment of every tub, every box of trash bags, with a gradually mounting intensity;

nothing should shift as he drove, everything should be retrievable in a logical manner, he didn't want to have to climb over storage tubs to reach the things he would need immediately. He focused on the arrangement of the boxes as intensely as if he had been performing open heart surgery.

When Craig was all packed they stood in the rental lot and looked at each other. Steadily, Alice put her hands on Craig's upper arms, held him and looked into his eyes and said, "You're going to do fine. Whatever happens will be fine, and we will get through it."

Through all the anxiety, Craig heard this, and the words soothed. He wanted to hear that some part of the future was knowable, that it could be counted on. He looked Alice in her eyes—the brown, wounded, intelligent, understanding eyes that he loved—and said, "Thank you. I needed to hear that." Then he said, "Are you going to be all right?"

"Yes," she said, still looking him in the eyes. "I love you. Please be careful."

"You know I will," he said. At that moment it occurred to him, suddenly, that this arc of understanding and trust was where home was, and New Orleans was not home, for that moment at least, and he realized that it might never be home again. After embracing Alice he got into the van, adjusted the mirrors and the seat, and, with Alice waving at him, he drove out of the parking lot to find his way to Interstate 57.

Alice had been secretly combing through the real estate ads, the rentals, to see whether there might be something they could afford as a temporary base that would keep them in more or less the same neighborhood around OffWabash, near St. Lawrence Montessori. She knew that they couldn't stay much longer with Uncle Gus and Aunt Jean. Her aunt and uncle were generous, good people, but it was all too obviously not a match made in heaven, and despite the protestations that they should stay as long as they liked, she could imagine the sigh of relief that would follow their departure.

She knew Craig wanted to move back to New Orleans. She also knew, without letting it be wholly conscious, that this was an opportunity to set themselves up in a place where life might be a little more as she had pictured it. This motive rode, like a stowaway, underneath other, more global concerns. The ecological questions around moving back to New Orleans were huge, especially for the kids. Even in a best-case scenario, wouldn't there be toxic dust spread all over the city from the floodwaters as they receded, and wouldn't kids be more susceptible to the long-range effects? How long would it be before the schools were back up and running? How long would it be before there were hospitals? What kind of childhood would Annie and Malcolm have in that damaged, stunted city?

These were questions that she entertained as questions, while keeping open the possibility that they might move back. But if Boucher were closed, if *Gumbo* was history, if their house was a shambles . . . She didn't want to live her life as an urban pioneer. New Orleans had been challenging enough as it was. In principle she understood wanting to help out, pitch in, rebuild. But everybody had different tolerances for the sacrifices involved. It would be one thing if they were both ten years younger and childless. But now she wanted to have a life. The image she had in her mind was of pulling herself up out of a well and sitting on dry land. She could even imagine getting back some of the pleasure and openness that had been there with Craig. As part of a well-balanced diet. But the idea of making love in the middle of New Orleans' decaying, over-ripe landscape was too much; she felt swamped, overwhelmed. She had to draw the line against the encroaching chaos somewhere, and she drew it at the one place over which she had some control. She imagined walking in the park, going to plays in Chicago . . .

Driving back into town, she opened the car windows and en-joyed the fall tang in the air, the implicit urban tempo, the interlock-ing parts of a functioning city just offstage. She turned on NPR and listened to the morning classical music. Vivaldi! The entire land-scape, the fresh air, gave her the closest thing she had felt to an erotic charge in months. She could feel her body in its environment, in-stead of resisting it.

Alice had made a few calls to rental agents, left messages, and had finally set up an appointment with a broker to look at three apartments just after lunchtime that day, leaving Malcolm with Jean and Gus for a couple of hours. The first place she saw was a walk-up over a block of stores right along the main drag in Off-Wabash, a dismal entryway between a bakery and a shoe-repair shop on the less-developed end of the stretch, with three mailboxes at the bottom of a long, straight flight of linoleum stairs leading up to a door without even a landing. Inside the apartment, the kitchen had a thirty-year-old avocado-colored range with burnt-on spills and a window looking out onto a tenement-style fire es-cape; aside from that dismal window there was no light at all in the two-bedroom place, except for the bedroom window onto the street, which would certainly be too loud. Why, Alice wondered, had they put the living room in the rear and the bedroom on the street side?

The second place was worse, a basement apartment with very low ceilings and a damp smell, and no refrigerator. The bathroom turned out to have no toilet either, only a big hole in the vinyl-tile floor, and when Alice expressed surprise the broker said, "You get to choose your own. Some people think that's an advantage." She checked herself from snorting at the absurdity of the lame ploy, noticed something on the molding—a line of little stickers of the type you would find on fruit. They hadn't even bothered to take them off the molding. There was stained beige shag carpeting in the bedrooms and the living room, of which one wall had been painted solid black.

"This is a very desirable area," the man said as they walked out. "This one won't last."

"Well, it just isn't right for our needs," Alice said, offering an unconscious thank-you that Craig wasn't there. She could get rid of all these places without negotiating his resistance to the whole project on top of everything else.

After seeing the third apartment, half of a shingled, two-family double, she began to feel a little depressed herself. The family living in the side to be rented hadn't yet moved out, and the place was a mess—kids' toys and underwear all over the living room floor, someone watching the television who didn't look up when they came in, a little boy who couldn't have been more than a year and a half walking around in a torn shirt. The broker whispered to her "They'll be gone in a week, and they have to clean up the property, or they forfeit their security deposit and, believe me, I don't think they're in a position to do that." Alice looked at him and saw the little invitation to smirk along with him. She was losing her patience with trying to seem nice to him. The kitchen was a nightmare—dishes overflowing from the sink, pots and pans on the floor—how did they get on the floor?—and the overhead fixture missing one of the two bulbs intended to be there. "The landlord will fix all that," the broker said.

Alice headed back to Uncle Gus's with a draggy feeling; there is nothing like looking at beat-up, vacant apartments with no refrigerator and scuff marks on the walls and stained carpeting to make you long for your previous home. As she pulled up to Gus's house her cell phone rang; it was from another of the listings where she had left a message. Alice was tired and hungry, but the woman on the line sounded nice, refreshing after the snark she had spent the previous two hours with, and she drove to the address the woman gave her, which was only two minutes away.

Alice pulled up to a large Arts & Crafts–style house that she immediately loved. A deep-set porch overhung with wide eaves, and the house itself finished in cream-colored stucco. It felt cozy and welcoming. An intelligent-looking woman in her early sixties met her at the door, with sharp eyes and reading glasses up in her short, salt-and-pepper hair. She introduced herself as Grace Olsen and was, it turned out, a political science professor at Northwestern. ("I realize that many people think of 'political science' as an oxymoron," she said, disarmingly.) She wore a cardigan Fair Isle sweater, and the interior of her house was full of art and nice furniture; on one wall floor-to-ceiling bookcases framed a large window, and a floor lamp stood next to the couch where an open book lay, waiting to be taken up again. A long-haired black cat rubbed up against Alice's leg immediately. None of it felt overstuffed, neurotic, it was just . . . like what Alice wished her own life looked like.

"Would you like a cup of tea before we look at the apartment?"

They sat and talked for half an hour before remembering to look at the apartment downstairs. The woman's husband had died several years before. The woman asked questions and expressed concern about New Orleans, mentioned that a number of students from Northwestern were planning a program to help clean up or do whatever seemed necessary.

"Then you are only looking for a short-term rental? Six months or a year, I would imagine? Surely you want to return to New Orleans. Or do you?"

"Well," Alice began, "we don't know. Craig is heading down today. We don't know what is left of the house, or what is going to happen in the city . . ." She looked in the woman's searching eyes. "Honestly, I don't personally feel that it is the best idea to move back. Craig wants to, I know that, but even if our house can be fixed and the city is working, I don't know if that is where I want to raise my children."

The woman drew herself up slightly, nodded a little bit. "Well, let me show you the apartment. It is very nice, and we'll see if it suits you, and then we can talk some more." She stood up, retrieved a set of keys from a dish on a beautiful antique sideboard, and they walked out the front door and around the house's left side, across a private parking area for the apartment. "This would be yours," the woman said. "We—I'm sorry; force of habit—*I* park in front."

Approaching the door Alice noticed a large window to the left, with small panes, and through it she could see another matching window on the house's rear wall; the room must have high ceilings, and they walked in and the woman flicked a light switch on the wall next to the door and Alice exclaimed, "It's furnished?"

The woman laughed and looked up at the ceiling. "That's what getting older will do for you. I didn't tell you it was furnished?"

"No," Alice said, looking around.

"The ad didn't say it?" the woman said, puzzled.

"You know," Alice said, "maybe it did. I've looked at so many ads . . ." In the corner between the two windowed walls was a fire-place, and facing, two couches at right angles, cozy, a perfect area for reading.

They walked through the apartment and Alice knew that this was where she wanted to live. At the end of the visit Alice said this to Grace and asked if she would be able to give her a couple of days to talk to Craig about it. The woman agreed, saying that the first of the month was a ways off, and Alice drove back to Gus and Jean's with an unreasoning feeling of joy and possibility inside.

Illinois was a long, flat fact, Interstate 57 a thin scar down its midsection, eventually joining I-55 just across the river from Cairo, Illinois, around Cape Girardeau, Missouri. Craig, in the van, was a moving dot, making his way south, a dot within the moving dot of the car, with tense shoulders and a grim expression on its face as he listened to the radio in the endless afternoon:

Now, see, Bobby, what I'm saying is what's interesting is the people complaining about the government are the same ones that's been living off the government. "You didn't come fast enough, you didn't take care of us." The government's been taking care of them and giving them no-work jobs and doing everything but wiping their nose and someplace else, too, and now after the government tells 'em get out, we got shelters, they just sit there and cry when what the government says is gonna happen happens.

And help themselves to some free loot.

That's right. But you don't see that on the CNN. All you see is these women with fifteen kids that they feed off a government check in the first place, crying about how the government won't support their [BEEP]. *None of 'em look like they been going hungry too much either.*

There was a good line that Nelson Rockefeller, if you remember Nelson Rockefeller was governor of New York State some years back . . .

And . . . and . . . Bobby . . . he wasn't any kind of a Republican either . . .

He was campaigning and one of these big Welfare Gourmets stood up, she was pretty big, you know, and she said, "Mistuh Rockafellow, you don't know what it is to be hungry." And Rockefeller said, "Madam, from the looks of things neither do you."

He said that?

He sure did, and it effectively ended his career. The liberals didn't want to hear that. Mr. Steve, we're going to go on to the next caller here.

Allright, Bobby, but one more thing that Rockefeller quote shows. Nobody's all bad.

Except Hillary Clinton. [Laughter.] Next caller, Michelle from Greensboro, Get Wise.

Bobby?

Yep; you're on the air, Michelle.

I just wanted to say about what that last caller said about people having babies and feeding them off the government checks?

Yeah.

Why isn't the president doing more to stop that kind of thing?

Michelle, I think he wants to, but this country isn't a dictatorship, thank God. If it were a dictatorship Bill and Hillary would still be sitting up there on a throne in the White House and you and I would be paying to have Willie Jackson's Cadillac souped up, or gold teeth put on his grandchildren. The president has to go through the Congress, and they are worried about getting reelected. Right now we have a media that is completely controlled by the liberals . . .

Craig reached for the knob and punched it angrily, catapulting himself into solitude and road hum, his heart pumping pure anger. He shook his head, opened the window. No more, he thought. He had turned the radio on to get away from the constant scenarios and questions his mind was generating about what he would find in New Orleans. What would he do if the house was wrecked? The entire city had been emptied; what would that look like? Should he have brought a gun? What was he going to do with a gun? The *Gumbo* offices were in Mid-City, and they knew Mid-City had flooded. Was New Orleans still New Orleans if the houses had been flattened and the oak trees blown down and there were corpses floating in the canals?

It took Craig six hours to get to Cairo, where a tangle of construction detours added half an hour onto the process of getting across the Mississippi River to Missouri. This was hilly country now, a nice change of pace from Illinois' nearly unrelieved flatness. He picked up I-55 and took it down through the Missouri Bootheel and into Arkansas as the sky slowly lost its light. What, he wondered, did New Orleans look like right at this moment? Was anyone walking down Cypress Street, looking stunned and crazy? Were there soldiers? Was there anything?

Moving back home had been a topic he and Alice had tacitly avoided in the past two weeks. He couldn't know the true dimensions of the question until he had seen the city himself, gotten a feel for what they were up against, what it would take. Some of that would only be answered with time, too—the fate of *Gumbo*, of Boucher, of their friends . . . He knew that he wanted his house, his food cooked in his kitchen, their kitchen, with their friends. One of the hardest things was talking every day to people who had no idea what it was like, who thought normal was . . . normal. It had felt so refreshing to speak to the evacuees. But who knew who he would speak to in New Orleans? At least Bobby would be with him.

He crossed the bridge into Memphis around eight-thirty and fought an impulse to stop and get barbecue, which would have used up at least half an hour. Instead, he stopped at a McDonald's drive-through south of the city. Around Batesville he found himself getting too tired to go on—it had been a long day of driving but also long emotionally, and he pulled into a motel and settled in for the night. After he got undressed he called back to Elkton to talk to Alice and to say goodnight to Annie and Malcolm.

Alice had planned not to say anything that night to Craig about the apartment she had looked at that afternoon, but she was so excited she couldn't help it. After Craig told her about the drive and spoke to the kids, Alice got on and told him about the house, about how nice the landlady was, how warm and comfortable the apartment was, and furnished, too, and there were books everywhere, and a fireplace and close to the Montessori school. "I know you're thinking about a lot of other things," she said, "but I can't wait for you to see it."

Craig, sitting on the bed in the motel room, found himself almost breathless with anger. Here he was on his way back to New Orleans to see what, if anything, was left of the life they had been living—their life, he thought, not a fantasy; the one they had been living—with friends, and a school already there, and a culture they had been part of—and to hear Alice so excited about beginning a new life in Elkton was so jarring he didn't even know how to express it. He imagined all her class anxieties being played on by the iconography of this place; this, she thinks, is the ticket to the white middle-class dream she has been looking to live out. Even if she couldn't wait to get out of New Orleans, what about his feelings?

He stammered out some version of all this, trying to keep his voice even but almost blind with rage. "We already have a life, Alice," he said, feeling vaguely nauseated. "I can't think about starting another life someplace. I'm in the middle of the life I'm living; I don't know what life you think you're living. This is a fantasy. Books and a fireplace . . . I need everything I have just to get through the next few days and I just can't believe you are saying this . . ."

"This is a fantasy?" Alice said, in disbelief. "You want to know a fantasy? Right now going back to New Orleans is a fantasy. Nobody even knows if anybody's going to be able to live there. We're going to be in Chicago for at least the rest of the fall and probably the rest of the school year. What do you want to do—stay up in Gus and Jean's attic for six months?"

This logic was unassailable, but the logic wasn't what was really bothering him. It was what he picked up underneath the logic—the unshared thing, the agenda, or put better, the bald fact that they were not going through this with one purpose. He felt betrayed and sick; the closeness he had felt that morning had now disappeared, and here he was sitting in the middle of Mississippi in this motel room, on his way into God knew what . . .

They got off the phone with no good resolution to the conversation, both hurt, both anxious and far away from home. When the cell phone was folded up and silent, Craig stood and paced back and forth a few times, looked outside the room door and thought about pacing outside, decided not to, closed the door and stood with his hand against the wall, leaning, looking at the rug. For the first time, standing there, he had a feeling that they might not make it through this. It wasn't just that they wanted different things; it was that the things they wanted had accrued such symbolic force for each of them that it was hard to see any way of reconciling them. Where was the loyalty to New Orleans, and to the life they had bought into together, he thought? He was not going to be a suburban squire in Chicago while the city he loved sank. The last thing in the world he wanted was to give Annie a broken home. But would a broken parent be better for her?

After a long while, Craig got into bed and turned out the lights and lay staring into the space above his head. It was a long night in Batesville, and it was a long night in Elkton, while in the countryside and the streets around them people spun out their own lives, with who knew what kinds of interruptions, losses and sadnesses.

1 9

Silence.

Parking lots baking in the sun. Long avenues and short side streets.

Shaded, broken sidewalks. Buckled porches. Winding bayou placid and empty except for twisted dead helicopter.

Traffic light boxes silent at empty corners. Telephone wires, birdless; air humid and undisturbed.

Three weeks after the storm, the city empty. Where water had been, now unmatched sneakers, rags, branches, tires, flotsam come to random rest. Cars empty, trunks popped open, windows broken out, striated with muck left to dry as flood water slowly drained. Motorboat at rest on broken glass storefront sidewalk.

No bird; no insect. No sound, no radio, no passing car, no car waiting at intersection. Sun, empty, silence.

They had started toward New Orleans from Baton Rouge that morning before sunup. It had been an emotional reunion the night before, when Craig arrived at Pam and Mike's, where Bobby and Jen were staying. The usual joking and deflective parrying was replaced with serious eye-to-eye looks and gratitude at seeing one another, alive.

Bobby had developed a small rash on his cheek by the corner of his mouth, and his eyes were red around the rims. Jen was subdued, a little stunned seeming. Pam and Mike prepared a Mexican dinner that night, and they talked about the past three weeks. Bobby and Jen had seen Doug and Connie, who were both now in Hammond, an hour away. Doug had reported that aside from wind damage, things seemed more or less stable in Craig's neighborhood.

Mid-City, where Bobby and Jen lived, had flooded. "It's hard to tell where the water is, and how deep it is," Bobby said. "I think where my mom's house was they had about ten feet. It used to flood if there was an afternoon rain."

"What about yours?" Craig said.

"Don't know. Can't tell. Could be two feet, could be ten."

"We got the second floor, though," Jen said. Then, an afterthought: "We don't know if we have a roof or not, but we have a second floor."

It was a Jen-ish remark, but delivered in a more muted tone than usual. Craig found himself, as he listened, taking mental notes—like that "could be two feet, could be ten"—for use in the article he would write. The columns were a godsend, he thought; they gave him a way to process and manage all this potentially overwhelming material.

The next morning they headed out from Baton Rouge on the nearly empty interstate. The press credentials got them easily past a checkpoint at Laplace. As they got closer in toward the city, they gaped at the wrecked suburbs of Kenner and Metairie, silent, roofs covered with blue tarpaulins, streets impassable, branches, tree trunks, splintered wood and pieces of roof everywhere . . .

They took the familiar exit for Causeway and headed south toward the river, alone on the four-lane road. A traffic light had blown off its wire and sat upside down in the middle of its intersection. From a smashed storefront across the way a motorboat protruded like a fish in a bird's mouth. A billboard bent over backward, and next to it a storage facility with its side ripped off, furniture inside spilling out as if from a ruined dollhouse.

They had decided to go to Craig's house first, since the neighborhood hadn't flooded. Apricot Street was an obstacle course of downed tree limbs and electric lines hanging down like thin, deadly snakes. All the houses had fluorescent orange and green spray-painted markings left by search teams to indicate the day they had passed, and whether bodies had been found, of humans or of animals. They made the corner onto Cypress Street, Craig's block, and parked.

Withering heat in the oak tree shade. One tree had blown down and blocked the street three houses down; as it fell the roots had torn up the sidewalk. Craig approached the front door of his house, with Bobby, looking up and down the deserted block.

The air inside was as still as a tomb, suffocatingly hot and foul smelling. Everything was exactly as they had left it two weeks earlier. One of Annie's toys on the picnic table where they ate, the television, the stacks of kids' videos next to it, a copy of *Charlotte's Web* sitting in the middle of the sofa, sheet music open on the piano. Craig had the sensation of having entered the house of a person who had died suddenly.

In the laundry area in back of the kitchen, a fresh stack of towels and underwear on top of the washing machine. Craig opened the refrigerator before he thought about it, and he slammed it shut immediately and retched, briefly, in the sink.

"Sorry," Bobby said. "I should have reminded you not to do that."

"We have to get that outside," Craig said, wiping his mouth with his sleeve.

"You can't just set that out," Bobby said.

"We can duct tape it or something," Craig said. "I've got some somewhere. I want to look upstairs."

The second floor was untouched, like the first floor, and even hotter. Only the rear room, which Craig had used as an office before it got turned into a storage room for boxes of books, had suffered any damage at all—a broken window had let in some rain, and there were some streaks and a couple of spots of black mold that had taken advantage of the heat and moisture to grow, and likewise some green mold on the ceiling around a brown ring that showed where water must have entered through some missing roof shingles. But there wasn't much, and before they left Craig would get some spray cleaner with bleach out of his car and wet it down.

Craig spent most of half an hour retrieving the items on Annie's list, some things Alice had asked for, and some important books, financial records, photographs and papers. Everything else he left, reasoning that their possessions were likely as safe there as they would have been anyplace. He found the duct tape and with Bobby's help wrapped tape around the refrigerator several times to make sure that both compartments stayed closed, then they dragged it out Craig's back door, thumping down his rear three steps and out to the curb on Apricot Street. A quick walk-around revealed one broken windowpane high up on the Apricot Street side, the one that had let the water into his office, and some of the missing roof shingles, too. Aside from scattered debris here and there, that was it for visible damage on his property. After that they sat on the front steps and drank some water from the skid of bottles Craig brought along.

In his mind, after the initial shock of the deadness of the neighborhood and the stillness and eeriness of the house's interior had subsided slightly, Craig let himself be grateful; he knew they had been very lucky. The neighborhood, despite the wind damage, seemed intact. But even though he knew this, Craig's emotions skittered like ants through his veins; his mind and heart were trying in a panic to regain a sense of reality. They were in New Orleans, but it wasn't New Orleans. It was like seeing someone for the first time after they had had a lobotomy. It was not something that happened, to see a whole city deserted like this, as if after some apocalyptic battle. You couldn't get the weirdness just from watching the television. The shock of streets that had been vibrant with life, houses, all empty. What had happened here?

He wanted to call Alice and he didn't want to call her. They had spoken only briefly the day before, en route to Craig's brief conversations with Annie and Malcolm. Annie asked if he were in New Orleans yet, so he explained again about the timing of the trip.

"When can I come down with you?" she asked.

"Let's talk about that," he had said. "I want to make sure it's safe before I bring you down."

"I made an angel in art class today; they had cell-o-phane and we made wings out of wires and cellophane."

"That's great, sweetie."

"I miss you."

He missed her, too, and the feeling clutched at him in the cold space around his businesslike exchanges with Alice. Neither of them, apparently, was in the mood for a peacemaking gesture after the previous night's conversation, a stance which they both knew could lead to deeper problems, yet neither of them made the first step. This, he thought, is how the battle lines get drawn. He needed an extra degree of understanding from her during this visit, especially, and he would not easily forgive her leaving him to experience this grief and weirdness by himself.

Could he imagine a life there without her, which also meant without the children? The pain was more than he wanted to try to process on top of everything else at that moment. But neither did he want to imagine moving to Chicago and leaving behind the city that had expressed everything he'd always wanted to express himself, in its time of need, and picking up a comfortable upper-middle-class life among people who'd had no idea what they had been through. The ants skittered in his mind and his veins . . .

Along Carrollton Avenue on the way to Mid-City, Craig and Bobby watched the greasy brown horizontal high-water lines creep higher on the sides of buildings, block by block, as the ground got gradually lower. The lines marked where the water had finally become level with the surface of Lake Pontchartrain before beginning to be drained out. It was one thing to hear about it on television, but it was another to see it in 360 degrees, with nothing but silence and stillness to fill the space.

The streets of Mid-City were full of debris, garbage coated with the toxic greasy mud from the floodwaters. Some of the streets had been cleared, some were still blocked with downed trees and parts of houses, waterlogged cars with smashed windows and trunks popped open. The smell was different in the air, sour, and with invisible clouds of instantly nauseating decay hanging in ambush. Craig and Bobby had once shared a house in the area, for a year after Craig moved to town. As Craig drove, he glanced at Bobby in the passenger seat. It was hard to tell what Bobby was thinking, even after years of knowing him. Same expression of faint surprise and almost amusement, but the eyes registered nothing.

They pulled up in front of Bobby and Jen's two-story wood-frame house off Orleans Avenue, not far from City Park. The house sat on brick piers, three feet off the ground, and a horizontal brown line ran across the thin weatherboards about three feet above where the floor was, with a greasy residue coating the boards below it, and two thinner, fainter secondary lines where the receding water had come to a temporary rest. Six feet of water had sat in the street for over a week.

They made none of their customary jokes or asides as Craig followed Bobby up the steps. They had put on the disposable rubber boots Craig had picked up at Home Depot, and they carried medium-grade surgical masks and rubber gloves. As Bobby turned the key in the lock, Craig looked up and down the empty street at the garbage, ruined cars, dead trees, brown grass coated with muck . . .

Door opened, and they stepped inside to the large living room, which was shadowy from plywood over three of the four windows. "Watch it," Bobby said immediately; his foot had slid on the wooden floor, which was coated with a layer of slick scum. The smell of damp and mold was sickening. They both slid their surgical masks over their mouth and nose and got the rubber bands set in back of their heads.

Once their eyes adjusted, the impression they both had was that someone had come in and ransacked the house. The couch was set at a crazy angle, and the television was facedown in the middle of the floor. They closed the door behind them. Two cheap bookcases had apparently come apart and leaned against mounds of sodden, soaked books. A shattered ceramic pot with a withered, drowned brown plant next to it.

They walked in across the slick floor, tentatively. Three rugs that had once been brightly colored were now black; water squeezed up out of them with each step across. Bobby's acoustic guitar lay on the floor; the back had come unglued and had warped away from the rest of the body like a potato chip. He bent to look; it was draped with grease or muck that hung off of it in translucent folds to the floor, which it also covered. One wooden chair on its side, the same. The sound system had not moved from its low shelf near the passage into the kitchen, but on examination it was covered with a film of the same stuff. Everything, in fact, had been draped with the greasy muck, which had been floating on top of the water as it set. From the evidence on the walls, the water had indeed reached about the three-foot level, and then gradually went down like the water in a slow-draining bathtub.

"Look at this," Craig said. Bobby came to look; an antique table that had belonged to Bobby's grandfather had been stripped of varnish below the waterline, although the varnish had been left intact above it. "What was in this shit?" he said, looking around.

The news reports had been full of dire speculation about the contents of the water, since chemical spills, battery acid, human remains, raw sewage, dead animals, and countless other ingredients had spilled into it without a doubt. Craig and Bobby both put on the rubber gloves. Bobby had squatted down and lifted up a corner of a small oriental rug; Craig remembered Jen talking about her mother giving her that rug specifically before she died of cancer; it had been one of the few times Craig remembered her letting her emotions show without some kind of deflective humor. The goo came up with it like cheese on a pizza slice, and liquid dripped from it.

"This is toast," Bobby said.

"What do you want to do with it?" Craig said, through the mask.

"I don't know," Bobby said. He looked around, still squatting.

Mold, green and black spots of different sizes, had bloomed tentatively on the walls below the waterline and, in a couple of cases, above it as well. A few posters that hung high on the walls were apparently all right. They went into the kitchen, where the floor was littered with sodden boxes and cans. Bobby opened a cabinet containing cereal boxes covered with fuzzy mold, rusted pots and skillets . . . He opened the oven door and water spilled out on his boots, along with an unendurable stench. Making the same mistake he had failed to warn Craig about earlier, he opened the freezer before he thought; a package of once-frozen bacon was now a pullulating mass of maggots. He shut it again, quickly.

In the dining room, Bobby's Les Paul guitar seemed all right at first glance on its stand, for some reason it had stayed put, but on closer examination the strings and pickups were full of corrosion and the leather strap was coated with fuzzy green mold.

The heat was amazing, and the masks got irritating with sweat and Craig slipped his off for a moment until he took a breath of the air without the mask, then he slipped it back on again. They walked upstairs, and, miraculously, the upstairs rooms were unharmed, except for the rear one, where a tree had fallen and broken a window and some glass had smashed on the floor and some books in a case under the window had gotten wet.

It was more than the mind could take in. Every house on that block and the next and every other block for miles in each direction contained some version of this scene, marinating in the murderous heat. Craig felt a gaping pain for his friend, who walked next to him surveying the wreckage of the life he had led. What could he say to help? He was there with Bobby; they would do some work, but what was there to say? He also noticed in himself an unmistakable feeling of guilt. He and Alice had been spared this scene.

Back downstairs, as Bobby examined something in a corner, Craig leaned against a wall, allowing his mind to coast for a minute or two, staring at Bobby's poster of Professor Longhair, playing piano in the yard of the parish prison, a famous image, hanging on the wall above the waterline in the dining room. Suddenly it occurred to him consciously that the poster was intact. Professor Longhair was all right; this was a good omen . . .

"Hey," Craig said. He looked around for Bobby, who was still crouched in the corner, looking at something he had picked up. "Hey, your poster is good to go, man. Check it out." A moment or two. "You okay?"

He walked across the room to where his friend was.

"You okay?"

Bobby was holding something in his hands, crouching and staring at what looked to Craig like a limp, browned slice of sautéed eggplant. Craig leaned slightly to put his hand on his friend's shoulder.

Without looking up, Bobby said, "My mom's gloves, from her wedding."

Bobby stayed in a crouch, looking at his mother's gloves, and Craig stood with his hand on Bobby's shoulder. Bobby's mom had cooked the first Thanksgiving meal Craig had eaten in New Orleans. A large, sunny woman whose working-class family went back generations in the city; she liked to laugh and to cook, and she adored Bobby and she had died a long, horrible death from emphysema and diabetes, four years before. Craig noticed a filigreed picture frame on the floor, facedown. He stayed there with his hand on his friend's shoulder, feeling the slow rise and fall of his friend's breathing. It was the best he could do.

They spoke very little on the ride out of town. As they left Bobby's house they had been stopped by four members of the 82nd Airborne patrolling the streets in a Jeep. The soldiers asked them for identification and to state their business. Bobby and Craig ended up having a cordial three-minute conversation with the young men, none of whom had ever been to New Orleans before. But after thanking the soldiers and heading out, they got quiet. Some strange discomfort had entered the car, as if they had seen something shameful and were embarrassed to look at each other. What was that, Craig wondered? Where could shame have possibly entered the picture?

As he drove, Craig realized that, for the first time in his life, he was happy to be leaving New Orleans. He was aware, to his surprise, of a voice inside himself saying, "Get me out of here." Some unlicensed neural channel was broadcasting subversive propaganda, insisting that New Orleans, as he knew it, was over with. "Much as you love it, New Orleans is not your whole life. You can get away; you have the resources. Save yourself and your family."

Craig was astonished and repelled by this reflexive, seemingly autonomous, and nearly overwhelming voice. Leaving New Orleans was, in fact, an option for Craig. He had lived for many years before moving there. But New Orleans was Bobby's entire life. The streets they drove, the corner stores they passed, the churches and schools, all of it carried echoes for Bobby of childhood adventures, playground fights, first Communion, early girlfriends, funerals of grandparents, holiday dinners . . . If New Orleans had been an exoskeleton for Craig, which conferred meaning from outside, for Bobby it was his very bone structure. It wasn't a refuge; it was life itself, from the inside out. And that difference, which, under normal circumstances, created a nice tension, a fruitful source of mutual stimulation and interest, had settled into the car and was the source of the embarrassment he was feeling. The fact was that Craig could, in principle, walk away, but Bobby couldn't leave. It was like driving with a condemned man.

Bobby gave no evidence of those feelings, nor of much else. Craig wondered how he felt, but to ask him questions about it would only underline the fact that they were having very different experiences. In New Orleans, the one place where Craig had come to feel like an insider, he was suddenly an outsider.

Or was he? If he shifted positions in his mind just a bit, reminded himself that he owned a house, that they were raising children there, and that they had a stake in the city even if they didn't go back generations, Craig could bring himself back up in the mix enough to take a deep breath and feel his own sorrow, his own shock and anger, and his own set of questions about the future. Yet even as he rehearsed these steps, the other voice slithered in again, saying, "You need to establish an alternate plan."

He would not be able to speak about this with Alice. Such thoughts were her end of the tug-of-war, and if he began to slacken his hold on the other end, the game would be over with. He wasn't ready for that, and he would need to sort it out. But the thoughts would not leave him alone all the way back to Baton Rouge.

20

They were some long days, in Texas.

Breakfast at the table in the kitchen; one end of the table up against the paneled wall, under a travel poster for Jamaica, picturing a sand beach stretching off into the distance. "I like looking at that," Aaron said. "We ought to all go down there for a break, maybe January."

If SJ agreed or disagreed, there was no way to tell. Dot set a plate of eggs and country ham down in front of him. The only thing that could get SJ to smile or focus much was when Ali, their Pomeranian, would come into the room, with its bulging eyes and bodacious attitude. The dog would get on her hind legs and put two paws on SJ's thigh and stare at him, and if SJ didn't acknowledge her she would let out a sharp yap at regular intervals until he did. When Aaron and Dot were off to work at the post office SJ would often hang out with Ali on the couch. SJ couldn't seem to focus on a book; he tried a few times, but he couldn't concentrate. But he could talk to Ali for a long time.

"Where's your mama?" SJ would say. Ali's head would cock to one side, staring at SJ on high alert, as if he were transmitting important messages. "Where she, Ali?" Ali would snort and shake her head a little, maintaining that eye contact. "You talking, Ali? You trying to talk with me?" No response, just holding SJ's gaze, until SJ's attention would get distracted by something, maybe the TV, and he would look away for a moment and Ali would issue a quick bark to draw SJ's attention back to the important business at hand. At those times SJ would smile and might even chuckle slightly. Eventually SJ would get caught up watching the TV and Ali would curl up next to him and go to sleep and SJ would go to sleep, too.

Hammer, drill, sander, saw . . . his tools were phantom limbs. SJ would sometimes wake up almost physically hungry for his tools, for his truck. But even if he had them, what would he do with them? What would he work on? And why? As the long days and weeks went by, there seemed no answer to that question. Aaron's house was all of twelve years old and needed no work. The whole subdivision could have been dropped down by a spaceship for all it had the character that SJ was used to, and used to caring for.

There was work if SJ wanted it, or needed it. Aaron had a friend with a carpentry and construction business something like SJ's own, and he could have used SJ's expertise "in a New York minute," as Aaron said. But SJ wasn't ready to go to work on a small team of people he didn't know, in a place he didn't care about. And even the possibility that he could begin to care about any of it was something to be avoided. He was in no way ready to have a stake in some other place not his own, meeting the new people, explaining why he didn't go out to the bars . . . He wasn't ready at age fifty-seven to start thinking of himself as a Texan. It would have been like turning away from his father and his grandfather and the houses they had built, Claiborne Avenue, memories of Camille as a girl, cookouts on the neutral ground, the Mardi Gras Indians, Mr. Doucette and Mr. Broussard and Ronald Riley and Bobby Encalarde and Sister Neeta and Charmaine Thomas and St. Claude Avenue, the Second Lines up on Galvez, sitting with Bootsy out on the porch, Rosetta. But it was all gone anyway, the houses they had built gone, Bootsy gone,

Sister Neeta gone, breathed in all that water with her head knocking on the wood beams in her attic, her feet all wet . . . Thrown away like garbage, floating like garbage for the animals to eat, what did it matter where he was if that was all gone? And if it didn't matter where he was, then what did it matter if he was anywhere? What was the point in living if it didn't matter where he was? If there were something left to build on . . . but how could there be? It was all gone. And he would never be a Texan . . . There was no point.

"SJ," Dot said, taking his plate, "looking toward the future isn't giving up. You can't live in the past. Not looking into the future is giving up."

"Where's the future?" SJ said.

"I don't know the answer to that, SJ. But I do know that flood was God's will. Nothing happen without it have a reason. You have to live so God can use you."

"That flood was not God's will," SJ said, anger flaring up in him with startling and frightening speed, as if he were talking to a stranger who had threatened him. "How can you tell me that was God's will? That flood was somebody's mistake. The hurricane was God's will, if you want to see it like that, but that flood was man's mistake." His veins, tensed, muscles, in his mind, it ran out of control: God has a goddamn plan? What kind of plan involved a three-hundred-pound paraplegic drowning in her own attic in motor oil and human shit? Where's the motherfucking plan in that? People seventy years old been together their whole life, owned the house, holding hands while they die? Where's the fucking plan? "They going to find out. Some motherfucker didn't do his goddamn job."

"Samuel." Dot said, sternly. "Please."

"I'm sorry," he said. "But they will find out. And what man has broken, man can fix."

"It don't look like nothing left there to fix, SJ."

SJ stood up from the table, shaking his head. But what if it was so? All the streets he ran on as a boy, as a young man, he lived on as an adult, had bodies of his friends and neighbors floating in them. They were finding bodies all over. Sometimes it was too much for him and he would not talk for an entire day at a time. The stress sometimes triggered other memories and feelings and responses that felt almost physical to him, things he had known for a long time, from after his time in the army, and he would sometimes lie on his back at night in bed practicing breathing, thinking about Rosetta, thinking about good times he could remember, but every thought of a good time stabbed like a knife that said, gone, gone, gone . . .

On the phone one day with Camille. Camille had made a good life, with two sons, in Raleigh-Durham; her husband was a good man with whom SJ had not much in common, but he was good to Camille; SJ and Rosetta had raised their only child to know the difference between fool's gold and real gold, to look for a man who respected her. They had a beautiful new house there; their boys were in Catholic school, well behaved and bright.

"Daddy, you know what Mama would have said. 'You got to get in that church.'"

SJ standing in Aaron's living room, looking out over his driveway at the house across the street, somebody's child riding a tricycle past, a beautiful, sunny day and him inside with no lights on. They had all gone to church until Camille had made her confirmation and SJ even kept on after Rosetta had died and he lost his own faith, until Camille had graduated high school and went off to college. All those streets, those neighborhoods, the stores, the people . . . how did the entire population of your life disappear? Anyone he thought of from those days he thought of in wet clothes wondering where help was, wheelchair-bound, taking water in their mouth. He knew he had to control it and sometimes he could and sometimes he couldn't. Why the mouth, he thought? Why was it always the water at the corners of their mouth, and what was the last thing they saw.

"Daddy, may I speak with Aaron for a minute?" SJ handed the cordless phone to his cousin, who stepped outside with it onto the back patio.

Days and weeks of waiting, of drifting.

One late September day he woke up feeling allright, for no reason he could think of. He looked at himself in the mirror, put on a light-green ribbed shirt he had gotten at Target with Aaron and Dot who took him shopping one day, and some slacks, clothes he had never even taken out of the bag. He went downstairs for breakfast, and Aaron and Dot brightened to see him looking fresh.

They had a fine time over breakfast, talking about nothing in particular, a break in the clouds, relief for everyone. At one point SJ was drinking some orange juice and something unfamiliar came over him; he spit the juice back in the glass, looking down into the glass, and then he was sitting with his head bowed down and his lips pressed together and shaking, trying to contain it. His neck muscles rigid. Some of the juice dripped down the front of his new shirt and Dot stood up and went over to him and put her arms around his shoulders; his body rigid and shaking.

He would go two or three days without shaving, sometimes more. He noticed one day that part of his beard had started coming in gray. He had never had any gray at all, anywhere. It didn't seem to matter much.

Aaron would get him to go out for walks. Aaron, who had also been in Vietnam, knew a fair amount about the traumatic syndrome that SJ was struggling with, and exercise and talking through things could be important. Some days they would walk and SJ was silent, some days he would talk for a while, and then get silent. Often he had violent fantasies that would crumble apart into debilitating grief. "I don't want to be angry like this A," SJ said. "I spent long enough dealing with it. I never thought I'd have to be back in this."

"You know more now," Aaron said. "You equipped more to deal with it."

"I get imagery, just like after discharge. Just like it. But it's different. I can't get some of it out of my mind."

"You could go see counseling section down at the V.A."

"I don't want to talk to nobody about it who wasn't there, Aaron. Except you. I'm not going to act out nothing, A. Even if I was going to take me a mad moment, A—who I'm gonna shoot? Who's responsible?"

One thing that did help was that Lucy and Wesley were around. It had felt to him like a miracle, really, when he saw them each again for the first time. Lucy had come in first, on the plane; he went to the airport with Aaron to meet her. They saw her before she saw them, as she walked down the concourse looking around for them, and then when she saw them her face first expanded in recognition, her eyes widening, and then she walked toward them quickly, carrying some heavy bag, and she fell apart in SJ's arms, sobbing as SJ embraced her and said, "It's all right. It's all right. We together now." Wesley arrived two days later, and they all stayed at Aaron and Dot's for a week and a half, Wesley on the day bed in the den. After the initial excitement of reunion, though, SJ sank back into his numbed, paralyzed state.

Through FEMA, which Lucy had a knack for dealing with, Lucy and Wesley got "relocated" to an apartment just outside of Houston in the third week of September, half an hour from Aaron's on the bus, a second-floor two-bedroom place in a glum four-story apartment house of ochre-colored bricks on a long tree-lined, arterial boulevard of apartment buildings in a residential neighborhood a mile or more from any stores. Grateful for the space, the perch, still Lucy didn't know what to do with herself.

"It nice, Samuel," Lucy said. "It ain't that. It just like being on the moon. Shopping malls all over but no place I can walk to."

"They have the bus," SJ said, sitting next to her on the couch at Aaron's, watching TV.

"Where I'm a take the bus to? I can't walk two blocks to the Tip-Top and buy me a pack of Kools and walk back. It like going to the North Pole if I want to get a beer."

Lucy was being dramatic for effect. In fact, two friends of hers from back home had also been relocated in that group of buildings, and they had cooked up some gumbo the best they could with what they could find in Houston. One of them, Wandrell, had gotten a car and they would drive to the mall and walk around like visitors from another planet among the cool, smooth, bright stores, the fountains, the lush plants watered by hidden watering systems. They would get looks sometimes from the slightly more cosmopolitan Houston women. Many of the New Orleans transplants still had some country clinging to them, even if their families had lived in the city for generations, and Houstonians, welcoming as they had been by and large, had taken to identifying the New Orleanians by their dress, their speech, their tempo. Of course the New Orleanians noticed the Houstonians noticing them, too.

Aaron had delivered mail to Buddy Ermolino, a white guy who worked for Westco Cable, and through him Wesley was able to get a job training with the cable company to do installation in people's homes. Wesley was a very quick study. "Basics" class took two weeks, after which Wesley had a full command of the basics of cable installation. The carpentry aspect was easy for him—drilling the holes in floors and walls with a kind of auger, threading the cables through, splicing . . . Wesley was coordinated and he was dexterous, and through his uncle he had already had plenty of carpentry experience. The day after the class ended he was out making calls on his own, and he was quickly up to four or five a day.

In the truck, one of three floaters the company had on hand (after four months you were expected to get your own), Wesley got to know the city, studying his Hagstrom city map book for Houston and suburbs. Driving around, he kept his cell phone on and talked to Lucy three or four times a day. A week into the training he got his hair trimmed neatly and his beard shaved to a thin, sharply defined ridge along his jaw. For the first time in his life he was making decent money, acquiring a skill and dealing with the discipline of a real job. In the evening he would sit in the living room in the apartment he shared with Lucy and watch sports on the television, which he had hooked up himself.

One day a large package arrived at Aaron's house addressed to Wesley, with the words "Please forward" written on it, and that evening Wesley came over and opened it and it was from Art and Ell Myers, wrapped in newspaper and masking tape. Inside was what looked initially like a flat, jagged, random piece of wood. Flipping it over, Wesley saw painted lettering and, righting it, the random piece became a silhouette of Louisiana, carved, Wesley knew, by Art in his shop downstairs. Along the wide bottom of the boot was the word LOUISIANA, with a couple of musical notes and hot peppers, and coming down the top, stacked one-two-three, were the names WESLEY, LUCY, SAMUEL.

There was a folded-up note with it, too, but Wesley left the room quickly, without reading it, while they all stood looking at this message from people they didn't know. "Isn't that something," Dot said, picking up the wooden artifact. "Those people went to all that trouble."

SJ looked at the wood with a professional eye, turned it over to look at the back, where they had written with a black marker, "To Wesley, with love From Art and Ell; September 25, 2005."

Dot asked Lucy if Wesley was all right, and Lucy said, "He allright. He just don't like to show his emotion sometimes."

The next day, a Saturday, Lucy and Dot's half-sister Leeshawn took Wesley to buy a thank-you card. Lucy and Leeshawn had formed a friendship, and Lucy would ask SJ if he was going to "hook up" with her. "She like you a lot, Samuel. You need someone around take care of you. Look like she good for you."

Leeshawn. SJ had known her for a long time, she was younger than the rest of them, ten years younger than SJ. Leeshawn had had ups and downs, had a bachelor's degree in communications from Texas State, but had logged some time on the dark side of the street, years ago. She had gotten married, moved to Los Angeles, where she had been for years, and had moved back a year and a half before. She worked now as a secretary for a law firm and did well, had her own place, had raised a son who lived in Albuquerque by his father.

One day, after a dinner or two in the group at Aaron's, at the beginning of October, Leeshawn called SJ at Aaron's in the mid-morning, saying, "I'm off for a day. Would you like to go for a walk?"

SJ, who was watching the television in his pajama bottoms and a flannel shirt, didn't ask where or anything else, only said, "Can you come by in about an hour?" He showered, shaved for the first time in three days, put on a fresh shirt that he had bought on a trip to the mall with Dot.

At the park, walking, Leeshawn pulled out a pack of cigarettes and offered one to SJ. He declined, saying, "I quit when the doctor told me I needed to."

"He hasn't given me the red light yet," she said, lighting one.

They talked, they walked around. Leeshawn asked sensible questions about what SJ thought about the possible future in New Orleans, asked whether he was in touch with friends. She asked if he thought they had dynamited the levees, as some black residents of the Lower Nine were claiming.

"I would be very dubious on that," SJ said. "I'm not saying they couldn't, but I don't think they needed to even do that. The levees broke all over. I don't really see that they did that."

"It does seem like folks are having a hard time getting in to look."

SJ appreciated the concern, but it was one step too much for him to go into the conspiracy thing. Who was going to make the decision to do it? The City Council? Not with Oliver Thomas on there, a son of the Nine. The Mayor? Highly doubtful. Who else? Too much chance them getting caught. They didn't need to anyway. All they had to do was make weak levees and that was it. He was sick of thinking about it, and he found anger hissing inside him like a python. Except pythons, he thought, didn't hiss. Boony had carried a book on snakes all the time they were doing reconnaissance until a mortar broke his sternum and that was something that was not to be thought of, dismissed. They used to catch snakes when they were kids over by the canal or they would go and play by the St. Maurice wharf, G-men or whatever it would be at the time and I like grape and you like strawberry and Bobby's sister like mixing lemon-lime and peach and your mama got a pussy like an old man's dick if I catch you say that again I will whip you until you can't walk do you hear me Samuel and they would stand on line to see Butch and sometime Mama asked them to bring her a root beer and they would sit out on the front steps over on Dorgenois and if it was a Sunday sometimes they would hear a band coming, no big fancy police escort necessary in those days, not in that part of town, and they liked the Lady Buck Jumpers and the Jolly Bunch, and some did plaster and some did lath and sometimes you find old bottles in the dirt and he remembered when Hurricane Betsy came and everything flooded but not like this, not like this, not like this, not people thrown away like garbage, and where Butch where Mama where Bobby where Boony where Mary where Rondell where Roland and Charles and Erving, where Antoine, where Bat, where Sweets and Junior and Pops and Roderick and Sharonda Serena Bailey Annie and Mr. Joe and Mr. Jimmy and Miss Emily and Bootsy Dee Minnie Buster Too-Tall Jawonda Latrell and Shondra and Toots and Toot and Turnell . . .

"SJ."

He felt hot tears coming to his eyes that he couldn't stop and he turned away to weep and so couldn't see Leeshawn watching him, fighting back her own tears, unsuccessfully. For a few moments she let him get a hold of things, but when he didn't, she approached and put one hand on his right shoulder and stood close to him. "I'm right here," she said.

Later, when she dropped him off and they were saying goodbye, Leeshawn let her eyebrows go up just a little bit with the question, but not much, aware that it might be premature. SJ saw it, knew it, part of him wanted it but he wasn't ready. That was so clear that he didn't even think to himself, *You getting old, man*, as he might once have. And he saw, too, in her expression a hunger that was not just physical but emotional, which he did not want to disregard or disappoint. SJ hesitated as he was about to get out, and he saw her ready to take him up on any invitation to take another step.

"Give me a couple of days."

"Allright, SJ," she said, with just a scrim of self-protection in the tone, not distancing exactly, but a slight glaze, and SJ got out without looking back and Leeshawn started up the car and pulled away and SJ walked by himself up to the front door and inside.

Two days later he called her and she picked him up and brought him directly back to her house, where she made a vodka and orange juice for herself and plain orange juice for SJ. They sat on the couch and talked, not the easiest conversation, not the least stilted that either of them had ever had, and Leeshawn brought out a photo she had kept for more than three decades, a picture of a twelve-year-old Leeshawn with a twenty-two-year-old SJ, maybe a month back from Southeast Asia, for some reason wearing his fatigues although he remembered getting them off as quickly as he could and never looking at them again. His hair was pushing outward into a good-size Afro and he wore thick-framed black glasses and a big, thick dark black mustache that curved down alongside the corners of his mouth almost to his chin. He looked at it wordlessly.

"What happened to those glasses, J?" she said teasingly.

"I don't need glasses anymore except for reading. You kept this picture all this time. Out to California and back."

"I had a big crush on SJ from New Orleans."

He wanted to and he didn't want to. Years, decades, really, putting such funds of energy, such resourcefulness, into functioning well, not blowing; the levers and gears and pulleys involved in keeping down the anger, and then the grief, stowing it; like a pain in his side it would sometimes obtrude and then his discipline, his strength, and yes his fear, fear above all that he wouldn't be able to control the anger and the grief, pushing it back and keeping it in line. Now they stepped onto the first stepping-stone of what there was no keeping a lid on. Yes, you could turn it into a control situation, but SJ couldn't stand that; he had been in a different place with Rosetta and it had changed him and he had never wanted to smudge or deface that memory by turning it into something simpler and coarser, and so he had acted in his mind as if he was in love with some women he never should have taken seriously, and finally ended by staying alone, paying out his time the best he could. And now after the grief, the holding even tighter, the aloneness magnified and the things he saw, this sound of caring, of undeniable humanity, this skin, this goodness that was different than Rosetta's but good, too, in her way, the birthmark on her left cheek and her wide-set eyes, her smooth chocolate skin, and the subtle waft of scent coming off of her, part shampoo, part cologne she had put on, part her, and they threaded their right-hand fingers through each others' fingers and SJ pulled her close to him, wanting this and not wanting this, but finally the softness in her skin and the rustle of her clothes as she moved toward him on the couch and he kissed her lips, which gave and gave back, he abandoned any attempt to hold out, he needed this contact, even if it was just to know that he was still alive and capable of this, this thing he didn't want because he had for years carried around the certainty in his muscles and veins that it cost too much. But there was something here, he sensed, that to deny or push away would mean closing the door on his own best possibilities; if he didn't meet this moment, he would never again have any moments worth meeting.

Her hand found his belt buckle and slid down slightly over the bulge in his slacks, and SJ pulled himself back from driving down that road too quickly, and he took her hand and they went into her bedroom. There on the bed, suddenly nervous, or hesitant, she said, with a look half afraid, half almost hopeful, "I can still make a baby, Samuel," and it was impossible to tell if she were warning him about using protection, or if she were sending out one vote of hope for the future, the two possibilities tangled together, and the intimacy of that moment hit him like a blast of wind, spoke to his own mixed impulses, a buried hope, a desire, a vision of a future that he had closed up like rooms in a house never to be used. He needed more than just to relieve himself, with the wind sucking the emotional door shut afterward with a slam. She needed more, too, but she found herself suddenly nervous about meeting him as an equal, a part of her stepping back and thinking, This, finally, is SJ. The surest and most familiar path was to give pleasure. SJ saw it without naming it in his mind—the weakness or insecurity— whatever it was he needed her right there with him, one to one, and he ran his hand through her processed hair, again, and they kissed, and kissed, and he unbuttoned her blouse and unhooked her black brassiere. Her breasts were large and all but firm, with large dark-brown aureoles around the nipples, and as he bent to lick one he saw several thin black hairs sprouting from around the nipple, and one long one. He took her breast in his hand and kissed her nipple, licked it and kissed it again and heard her lightly moan. Instead of licking it some more, using her pleasure as his power, he began kissing the breast around it, licked her salty skin, starving for this, kissing the side where it bellied down near her rib cage, licked her skin, then kissed, then went back to her nipple again, which he licked and sucked and, finally, bit softly, eliciting a small yelp of surprise from her, sending her up on one elbow, pushing him down on his back by his shoulder and throwing one leg over to straddle him, both of them still dressed. Looking down at him, her skirt up and her sex pressing against his through her underwear and stockings, she removed her blouse, and her bra, and the sight of her breasts, and her graceful neck as she looked down at him inflamed him and he thrust subtly against her, rotating his hips and his own hard cock against her, holding her gaze, and she looked down at him now like a slightly mocking princess deciding whether to bestow a royal favor, and on whom, moving her own hips just slightly in answer to his motion, as if to assure him, finally now, that this was indeed a matching of equals for as long as it would last, whatever it would be, and she raised one eyebrow slightly and said, "Yes?"

Something in her manner, her salty, resilient manner, hit him as funny, and he chuckled, slightly at first and then more; he had not been so happy for as long as he could remember. "What are you laughing at, Mister Man," she said, in a fake menacing whisper, falling forward slightly and placing her hands on his shoulders, pinning him down. This made him laugh a little harder, a rumbling chuckle that came from his stomach. What, indeed, was so funny? He didn't know, but he recovered himself; too much of a laugh discharged the tension that gave intensity to sex, after all, and he put his hands on her hips and pressed against her harder and said, "I'm laughing at you thinking you can wrestle me."

"Is that so?" she said, unsmiling, don't-carefied, looking into his eyes not a foot from his face, a coolly appraising look, a cat regarding a trapped mouse, eyebrow arched now in mock hauteur and disregard. "I believe I can take anything you can dish out, Mister Stuff. I don't know if you can take it."

SJ gave one grunting, grudged, half-laugh at this and brought one of his hands up behind her head and brought her face down to his, saying, "Let's see about that."

Afterward, after they had both taken showers and lounged around some, SJ wanted to speak to Leeshawn, to tell her that he was in no way sure what could be possible, that he couldn't know where this storm would finally leave him, but she stopped him even before he could speak.

"You don't need to say a thing, SJ. I'm not expecting anything from you. And I got my own questions I deal with, so don't worry about I can't handle it or anything like that. Let me tell you something," she said, sitting next to him and putting her hand on his chest. "You gave me a gift today. We both got a gift. I'm grateful for that gift, do you understand what I'm saying? It is a blessing just to be in the world, and sometimes we forget we're in the world. You understand what I'm saying, Samuel?"

She hadn't called him Samuel before. "I wanted to make sure," he said.

She nodded, not smiling, looking into his eyes. "You also need to make sure for yourself," she said. "Don't worry too much about me. You've been through a lot and I'm not talking about just this hurricane. All I'm trying to say is you need to figure out what you need for your own sake, not for mine. I'm not a schoolgirl anymore, SJ."

SJ wanted to say that he understood, but saying it would somehow have undercut the very thing he wanted to say. And anyway what he wanted to say was more than just that he understood. He wanted to say that he was grateful for this understanding, and for her strength and clear-sightedness.

"I can see that," he said.

"Mmm-hmm," she said, tartly, regarding him as she stood up and finished getting dressed. "We'll see."

21

SJ looked at his shirt, felt it between his fingers, like a phrase in a foreign language out of which he could understand only a few words. The grammar manifest, yet inscrutable. The bedspread at Aaron and Dot's a presence, again; he ran his hand over it, mystified, like an amnesiac. Water, in the sink, his own torso, the feel of the razor as he shaved. You remember this. Don't you, SJ? Yes you do. This was called life, this call-and-response of senses to mind and back again . . . The tactile, the way things fit together and spoke to one another physically. Or at least, for starters, the sense that they did, that the relations comprised a language. Food in the mouth, sun on the skin, air in the open car window (driving to Sun Village Mall, for example, to buy linens with Leeshawn). Or simply the grain of wood, the density, the language of pine, of oak, of cypress. The door, the molding, the varnish, the paint. There it was; there he was.

One day he saw something he had seen every day for a month and a half, a loose hinge on the closet door. He went downstairs to Aaron's utility room, rummaged around and found a Phillips head screwdriver and an assortment of screws and simply replaced the screw that was in the hinge with a larger one. That would hold it until he could really fix the hinge.

This was how you came back, if you came back. One thread at a time, one nail at a time. Make each one good and the pattern would reveal itself.

By early October there were over 150,000 displaced New Orleanians in the greater Houston area. Two hundred thousand more landed all over the country, like unsorted nails in a toolbox, like clothes thrown into a bag quickly, to be sorted later. Many migrated an hour upriver to Baton Rouge, where the housing prices doubled within three months. They landed in Atlanta and Dallas and Memphis, in Chicago and Little Rock and Hot Springs and Phoenix. But the largest concentration was in Houston.

It took a while for people from a given neighborhood to find one another, but little by little they did. Lucy found Jaynell, who had already started doing hair "New Orleans style" for some of the evacuees in the living room of her cousin's house on the East Side, and Lucy was able to pick up a little extra money helping her out. New Orleanians ran into one another at the store, at the Home Depot, at malls. They gave each other news of neighbors, of family, shared information about troubles getting aid from FEMA, or from insurance. There was plenty of news about members of the community who did not make it through, and it wore on the mind and the heart. And at the times when they saw someone for the first time and knew that they had, in fact, made it through, there was a deep sense of gratitude, thanks offered to a God most of them still believed in and thanked for what they had, even as they wondered how to construct a future out of the fragments that were left.

Across the country, the displaced citizens of New Orleans wondered why they couldn't come back home. Those with resources were able to rent apartments in upscale areas of New Orleans at the inflated rates that landlords suddenly realized they could charge, or they bought one of the houses that suddenly hit the market in the twenty percent of the city that did not flood, sold by owners who suddenly realized that they could sell at fifty percent above the price they might have gotten six months earlier and move out of New Orleans.

The people without those resources, who had just been hanging on in life as it was before the storm, who had to take three buses to work across the city and back from work every day and support aging parents and nieces and nephews of siblings or cousins in jail, or sick, ended up in far-flung places: Salt Lake City, Hot Springs, Memphis, Atlanta, and hundreds of temporary shelters in the countryside of America. They wanted to come home, and they waited and watched as the weeks, and then the months, stretched on.

Huge tracts of the city sat without electricity. There was no water, and there was no gas. Even after gas service had been restored, water got into the gas lines and rendered them inoperable. A year later, there would still be no telephone service in large areas of the city. There were no traffic lights for months, even at major intersections. And in many cases there were no houses to come back to. Hundreds of displaced people ended up living under the Interstate 10 overpass along Claiborne Avenue in abandoned cars that had been flooded and which reeked of mildew. If you found a dry piece of cardboard and laid it down across the backseat you had a place to lie down at least. It smelled bad and you developed a cough, but you could say more or less the same thing about anyplace.

To address this, the government ordered thousands of mobile-home trailers, universally called FEMA trailers after the agency in charge of providing them, which cost the government over fifty thousand dollars apiece. The move was announced with great fanfare and many of the displaced applied for the trailers, making their way through a jungle of recorded messages, inexperienced voices on the phone, contradictory information, inexplicable delays, duplication of effort. There was no coordination among the various agencies set up to provide aid. Insurance companies dragged out their response as long as possible, haggling over whether damage to peoples' houses had come from the wind, which took their roof off, or the flood water, which sat in their house for a week and had been, ultimately, caused by the wind, so was ineligible for flood claims.

The few trailers that did trickle into New Orleans (thousands more sat, inexplicably, like rounded-up cattle in pens in rolling fields in Alabama and Arkansas and Mississippi, where they still sat a year later), were dutifully installed in front yards and then left there, locked, since there was often no key. A year later, people who had long since resettled themselves elsewhere were getting calls telling them their FEMA trailer was ready.

The repairs on the actual houses were another story. If you got your insurance money and had a house to repair, which meant you were one of the very lucky ones, the repairs were slow, tedious and unreliable at best. The contractors, not to mention the scattered members of their crews, had also been displaced and were struggling to get back to town to live in damaged houses, or commuting in from Baton Rouge or Laplace or even farther every day in brutally swollen traffic. They were overwhelmed with requests to do work that would have been too much even with full, experienced crews. Now they competed with one another for the few workers who were able to make it back.

Some contractors rounded up illegal alien workers, many of them young men from Mexico or Honduras, found shaky and often substandard and dangerous housing for them, where they lived ten and twelve to a room, made the appropriate payoffs to city officials who might otherwise have been expected to make sure that didn't happen, and set to work making shoddy repairs, often being none too careful about electrical codes, plumbing codes and other safety regulations. But they filled a need. Then there were a certain percentage who had signs printed up, took the calls, took the down payments, and then simply disappeared.

People somehow made it back to pull the refrigerators full of rotten and spoiled food out to their curbs. They put on rubber gloves and boots and heavy-duty masks and set to work dragging the soaked and moldy couches out of the shells of their houses, the soaked and heavy carpets, the wrecked appliances, the sodden, unrecognizable clothing, the old rocking chairs with their wood split by the water, the desks and computer equipment and scum-coated flat-screen televisions, the lamps with torn and discolored shades, the vases and broken dishes and corroded flatware, the collapsed bookcases and the bags of soaked and ruined books, the beds and bedspreads and quilts that were unsalvageable, the framed diplomas, browned and ruined in smashed glass. At the end of the day's work they drove back to their sister's house in Baton Rouge, or their cousin's in Hammond, or the hotel that FEMA was temporarily paying for in Lafayette, and they stood under the shower for half an hour. It was after the work they were able to do themselves had been done that the depression and anxiety and frustration began to set in deeply, the waiting and the contradictory and incoherent answers from the various agencies that never seemed to know what was happening, and everyone started knowing people who had committed suicide, or who had gone crazy publicly or privately, or who just sat on a bed or couch all day, watching television in a room somewhere far from home.

Those were the people with some money, who were able to come back to oversee rebuilding, in parts of the city where there were houses to rebuild and insurance money paid out. But those who lived in areas where the houses had been leveled or smashed to kindling, or pushed off their foundations and left in the middle of a street, or upended from behind like horses with their front knees broken, in areas where any vestige of property lines had been erased and surveying was a problem for the distant future, like parts of the Lower Ninth Ward, or Lakeview or Chalmette, it was almost impossible to know where to begin.

Around the country, people who had done all they could do

finally had to sit and wait. They had filled out the applications, tried to get information, made the phone calls, and eventually they put their children in local schools in Houston or Atlanta or Chicago, got jobs and began rigging up a provisional sense of community, because it was plainly an open question when they would be able to return home. Or they sat, in shock and grief, with no counseling to help them manage the intrusive imagery they had of their mother, who refused to leave, drowned in the living room where they had grown up and had graduation parties, everything they knew transfigured as if in a nightmare, or their wife's hand slipping out of theirs and watching her sucked underwater, or their neighbor's calls from inside their attic as they sat helpless to aid them, and then finally no more calls, and there were no mental health clinics to help them, and others couldn't understand why they didn't just pull up their socks and do something to help themselves.

SJ had found an apartment, with Leeshawn's help; she had had fun setting him up there, taking him to Target. Bed, mirror, couch, lamps, bathmat. He acquired a car through a friend of Aaron's and set up an informal shuttle service for a handful of New Orleans people who lived nearby who were without transportation, driving them to unemployment offices, or to the store, or to see relatives, and little by little, like a woven bridge across a ravine, or a spider web, a network of vital connection slowly began to construct itself, like a brain and body recovering from a stroke, learning how to work around the damage.

Those first weeks with Leeshawn were for SJ an oasis in a strange dream. Something unreal about it, yet connected to something essential from long before, some long-ago self. They went to movies, held hands. And yet there was a moat between his experience and hers, and it would become apparent at unexpected times.

One evening SJ and Leeshawn were sitting down to dinner at Ruby Tuesday's when a waitress came over to the table, tentatively, saying, "Is that . . . ? Oh Lord . . . Mister J . . . I'm Anita; do you remember me? I stay by Law Street."

SJ remembered her. She worked for the Sewerage and Water Board. He stood up and embraced the woman, introduced her to Leeshawn.

Anita told the other waitress who would normally have waited on their table that she would take the table herself. She brought SJ up to date on the people from the neighborhood whose where-abouts she knew. She heard that Mrs. Gray had evacuated but she didn't know where. Bootsy and his wife she did not know about. Earl and Madeline had been rescued off their roof and she didn't know where they were. Jawanda—nobody heard from her; I don't know if she made it, Mister J. Bobby was staying a block from them in Fernwood, the little apartment complex where a number of New Orleanians were staying.

"The Coast Guard come and got us, Mr. J. I took the helicopter ride; I held on to Kiann tight, tight, like we was going to the moon but they got us in there and dropped us at the airport and next thing they was telling us where to go and here we are. We are blessed we made it through alive. Where Lucy at?" SJ told Anita about Lucy and Wesley, to the woman's under-the-breath responses of "Praise God." The same alternation between gratitude and anger, the grappling for equilibrium. "I have a job, my baby okay, she in school. But Mister J how they let this happen? How a whole city go underwater and we still out here and nobody know when we can get back?"

At the end of the meal, when SJ asked for the bill, Anita said she was taking care of it. SJ protested, but Anita straightened up and shook her head twice, decisively.

"Mister J, I don't give a fuck about no money—pardon me,

ma'am—but anybody from New Orleans gonna eat free as long as I am working the goddamn shift."

SJ left a twenty-dollar bill under the plate for her anyway. In the parking lot, on the way to the car, Leeshawn said, "She won't have that job long."

SJ looked around at the people coming in for dinner, at the traffic going by on Route 28, and said, "People can't understand what it was to be there. Even people who want to can't get it. There is a wound."

Perhaps Leeshawn felt hurt or excluded by this way of putting it, as if SJ was drawing a line between himself and her, but she said, "But people are going to have to learn how to deal with it. Isn't that true, SJ? It is going to take a while for people to get back, if ever."

They walked along and SJ felt her warm hand in his. The past three weeks had been a time he had never expected to see or feel again. And although what she said was true it also spoke another painful truth behind itself—echoed, in fact, what SJ had himself said immediately before. There was a gulf between those who had had their community smashed and their future thrown completely into question, and those for whom life still moved in an intelligible stream. It was not unlike the line that separated those who had come back from the war and those whose lives had been going on continuously while they had been away. There was an understanding among those who had been there, and a gap between them and those who had not. And, too, SJ could feel under the surface of her remark, like something hidden under a sheet, the worry that SJ might leave her, and he knew this was something they were going to have to discuss. Leeshawn was strong, smart, independent, and yet, despite all their caveats, SJ knew she had let herself fall in love with him.

Was he in love with her? He didn't suppose he knew. Everything around them was too much up in the air to know. There were too many unsettled questions. She had brought him back to planet earth again, and he knew that. He felt alive, and in his body, in a way he hadn't in years. But there was a disjunction between this self, walking along in the Houston October twilight in nice new clothes, and the continuity of all that interrupted life in New Orleans. Somehow they would have to be brought into line. Or not, as the case may be. But it was going to take time, and he needed to make sure that she understood that.

One night, SJ had a dream about his father. He didn't often remember his dreams or pay them much mind, but this one was almost real. There was a crowd, on the street, a second-line certainly, and the band was playing, and the whole river of everyone they knew and their family was there, and he was dancing with his father, showing each other steps, surrounded by an aura of weird ecstasy. They had never actually second-lined together in life, that SJ could remember, but here they were in this dream, both of them part of the music and the river, ecstatic, relaxation and precision, wit and seriousness, transcendent . . .

He awoke, with his heart pounding, with the dream going, and wanting to hold on and stay in it. Leeshawn was asleep in the bed, next to him. He lay there silently in the dark, staring at the ceiling, until the first dim blue light could be seen through the blinds, and then he fell asleep again.

SJ closed the door after her when she left, and he stood alone in the silent apartment. He walked to the middle of the room. Couch, poster, end table, lamp. Telephone. Ingredients in a soup that hadn't had time to blend flavors. There was the coffee table. There was a bed in his bedroom and, because Leeshawn had insisted on it, there was a rug on the floor next to the bed. There was a toilet seat cover and a matching mat on the floor of the bathroom. All of it bought at Target that week. He had everything he needed to live except a life.

There were days, now, when he could look in a mirror and almost recognize himself. Not just his face, but his energies, and not just from before it had all happened, but from longer ago than that. Parts of himself that had been wrapped and put away in a drawer, exposed now by all that upset. It was not necessarily a bad thing. But as it healed and he began to piece the parts of himself back together and he felt familiar energy, he got restless to use those energies, to begin building something connected and coherent, a life.

Outside the window he looked across a pathway between his building and another building exactly like it next door. A place with no roots, no reason, no echo, no flavor. Not for him, anyway. This will not last forever, he told himself. As long as you can begin again, he always thought, have a place to start, you could build, you could continue. But he didn't want to get started here. There was unfinished business in New Orleans. They were still not letting people back into or even near the Lower Nine yet, and SJ knew he wouldn't know exactly what he was doing until he had had a chance to see for himself. He began to think about how to get back in, official go-ahead or not.

They had gotten him a new cell phone at Wal-Mart, one where you bought minutes and added as you went, and SJ spent time calling the numbers he remembered or could find for his crew, trying to track them down. Lester, when he finally found him through his sister, was in Little Rock, which was good. Ronald's trail was cold for the moment. He knew that Curt had cousins in Baton Rouge; through them he tracked down Curt in Atlanta. SJ registered with a couple of the national data bases for displaced New Orleanians.

His crew had different ideas about returning.

"Where I'm gonna stay, J?" Curt said. "I'm not coming back to that motherfucker. My daughter in a school where they got books and the lights stay on. FEMA got us into an apartment where it ain't like the Wild West every night. You know God-damn well they blew up the levee on us. What I want to come back for?"

"We managing, J," Lester said. "If I could get a trailer I'm happy to come back. I want to come back. Little Rock got nothing for me. How you doing? Lucy and Wesley make it through all right? People here try, but you know . . . This lady made some red beans at the church the other night I almost started walking back home after the first bite. Didn't taste like nothing. Look here, the whole city like that. Not to put nobody down, 'cause they being real nice to us, but I want to come home."

Sometimes SJ wondered if it would be possible to conceive of another life entirely, outside New Orleans. Aside from himself, where would Lucy live? And Wesley? Wesley was working, he was doing very well, actually, and Houston worked as a city, unlike New Orleans at the moment. Lucy missed New Orleans very badly. But what if there was nothing to go back to?

It had been decades since he had even remotely entertained the idea that he might live somewhere other than the Ninth Ward. But now, in between the errands, and the calls to his crew members, the visits with Lucy and the trips to shop for Aaron and Dot, life began to assume a pattern again, inevitably; you fell into it like hypnosis, it seemed real, until you woke up again and realized that your real life had been interrupted, that it was on hold, trying to reassemble itself in your sleep, like the dreams you might have when you were in a coma. But what if you never woke up? What if someday this life began to be your life?

When he spent time with Lucy and Wesley, they kept each other warm, restated the fact of continuity with the past and the future. But they were subject to the undertow, also. Lucy seemed to be doing well in some ways, not in others. She seemed a little depressed, to him. He worried that she might get started with her bad habits again, out of boredom if nothing else.

"You taking your medicine, Loot?"

"That the first time you called me Loot since we been here, SJ.

You remember one time Wesley call me Lootie when he was seven year old and you told him you'd go upside his head if he didn't call me Mama?"

"You taking it?"

"It back on Tennessee Street, Samuel. Don't get mad. I didn't like it. The Humixtra give me diarrhea like I couldn't even get my drawers down in time, and the other give me a female problem, and I'm a go see Wandrell doctor over in Holly Ridge see he can get me something don't make me have to run every half hour. But look here, SJ—if I die and we still here don't bury me in Texas, allright? Promise me that. I don't care about buried or cremated; just take my dead ass back to New Orleans."

22

A bright Wednesday in mid-October, and Alice stood at the corner of East Forest Avenue and North Mankato, sipping the mocha latte she had bought at Brew Horizon and waiting for the crossing light. She had an entire afternoon to herself; Craig was in New Orleans doing another column, Gus and Jean were watching Malcolm, Annie was in school, and Alice was walking the three-block strip of Forest Avenue that formed the main drag of OffWabash. She hadn't felt so happy in months.

Alice loved the change of seasons; it was one of the things she had missed most, being in New Orleans. This autumn snap in the air brought back Ann Arbor, the early days with Craig; it brought back acting, and painting, college lawns, possibility, new classes and new clothes. All around her, early-afternoon light glinted off of car bumpers and shop windows, and the latte warmed her as she drank.

The light changed and she crossed Mankato and passed Salon Elegance, the tired-looking hair place on the corner with its perpetual "Help Wanted" sign in the window (Our Lady of Perpetual Help Wanted, she thought—one of her and Craig's old games). She was headed to La Bahía, figuring that she would work her way back down to the other end from there. La Bahía had great scarves and block-print skirts and blouses. It reminded her of Gae-Tana's, on Maple Street in New Orleans, where she used to go with Connie and Kelly, and then they'd have lunch at the Maple Street Grill. In front of the store Alice first stopped and looked at the display windows, which were featuring cotton sweater jackets in a sort of brick orange and olive green. Big cloth buttons, which she never understood; they were hard to fasten and they lasted about three wearings. The scarves, on the other hand . . .

Inside, Alice tried on a scrunchy velvet hat, black with dark red flowers embroidered on it, looked in the mirror, put it back. She gave some attention to an oatmeal-colored cotton sweater, loose-knit, with off-the-shoulder seams and an oversized crew neck. She held it up to herself in a mirror, imagined it over her black slacks, maybe with the small pearl pendant on the fine gold chain . . . She decided to wait; she wasn't in love with it.

After browsing for a while more she left La Bahía and turned left on the sidewalk, walking east. The air was crisp and invigorating, and her beige parka kept her nice and warm. One day before too long she wanted to buy something a little nicer for herself for the winter. She nibbled at the lemon tart she had also picked up at Brew Horizon— a guilty pleasure, which reminded her to call Stephanie and see about finding a health club that held yoga classes. She crossed back over Mankato, past Brew Horizon. The only real goal she had for the afternoon was to hit Planka's, where she wanted to buy some pastels, a set for her and a set for Annie. Alice missed painting, and the pastels were so much easier to use than oils, certainly as far as cleaning up was concerned, and with the limited space back at the apartment it would be a good solution. And it would be something she and Annie could do together.

She had been short with Annie lately, and at the same time she had been yearning to make more of a connection with her, for them to be there, together, where they were. A few days earlier, Alice had found her sitting on the floor, with her big sketchbook open to swirls of pink and bright yellow, fluorescent orange. "What's that, Annie?" she asked.

"It's Wild Magnolias," Annie answered. This was a gang of Mardi Gras Indians.

"Wow," Alice said. "Pretty. What's the house?"

"That's the H&R Bar." This was a place Craig insisted on bringing them every Mardi Gras as if it were the Taj Mahal. Alice could understand Annie drawing pictures of the brightly colored Mardi Gras Indian outfits, but that her daughter would choose to draw a low-life bar as a place to which her imagination returned felt wrong. And one that had burned down, in the bargain. Even before it burned down, that was one place Craig had brought her that made her feel nervous.

"That is real pretty, sweetie," she had said. "Listen—how'd you like to go out to Herman's?" Herman's was an ice-cream parlor in OffWabash that was always a big hit with the kids.

Without really intending it, Alice found herself trying to sell Chicago to Annie and Malcolm. But Alice used to like the Mardi Gras Indians. She had enjoyed the neighborhood bars, the second lines. It had been fun, and mysterious. But the fun had disappeared somewhere along the line, like the smell of flowers, replaced by this fist she carried in her stomach. And she felt a sadness wafting off of Annie that worried her. Annie had an iPod mini that Craig had given her, stocked with New Orleans music, to which she listened constantly. Alice felt that it was unhealthy for Annie to be so emotionally focused on what could well turn out to be an irretrievable past. Alice was trying with everything she had to project a vision of a life that would be healthier and full of more possibilities for her children than what she honestly believed New Orleans had in store for them.

Alice looked up and down the sidewalk and thought, This is a beautiful, sunny afternoon. Across the street was Szarky's Market, and Alice reminded herself to swing back later with the car and pick up some of their good Polish sausage for dinner. Right after Brew Horizon on her side of the street was Alizé, and she stopped in there for a minute to look at the lingerie.

She moved among the tables with the frilly satin pillows and ribbons. Who bought this stuff, she wondered? Some of the lingerie was all right, although her style tended toward the more straightforward. She thought about an item or two, maybe a new pair of the colorful string bikini underpants they had arrayed on tables, fanned out like cold cuts on a tray. She couldn't do the whole deal with the negligees, the garters and stockings . . . it just wasn't her. She didn't like the thongs either . . . One table had very sheer underpants of a type she could wear, with lace cutaways in front and a full-cut back. She could surprise Craig with something like that; the idea made her feel a little racy, until she checked the price—forty-eight dollars, and she put them back on the table. Fifty dollars was too much for a pair of underpants, no matter how cute.

It was hard for her to work out a balance in how she felt about Craig being gone so much. This was his second trip, and he had another scheduled for later in the month. Obviously they needed the money from the columns, and she knew, too, that it was important to Craig to not feel totally cut off from New Orleans. At the same time, the nonstop tasks of parenting and housekeeping were a lot heavier to carry solo: getting Annie and Malcolm dressed in the morning, then taking Annie to St. Lawrence with Malcolm in the car, and juggling the shopping and picking up Annie and making sure Annie did her homework, and dealing with Malcolm's stubbornness around certain toilet-training issues, and doing the cooking and getting the kids to bed . . . it was a grind. On the other hand, she had the occasional day like this, which felt like a blood transfusion to her. But even in the middle of such a perfect day she missed Craig, even though they were having a difficult time right now. She missed her partner, and her friend. And on days like this, when she felt so alive, she missed her lover. Sometimes that felt like such a long time ago. She picked up the underpants with the cutaways one more time, held them out by the strings. She'd wait; maybe she'd come back and buy them. Anyway, Craig wouldn't be back for another three days.

Planka's was almost at the end of the block. Alice liked the place, an older store run by a family, with all kinds of mismatched stuff— mostly art supplies but also straw hats, tarot cards, greeting cards, coffee mugs, little statuettes and Halloween costumes and posters. The floors were charmingly unreconstructed—linoleum green in some places and black in others, and the art supply section was in back, up a couple of stairs, on bare, worn wood flooring. There she picked out two sets of pastels, a nice starter set for Annie and a slightly larger one for herself—Caran d'Ache—pricey, but this was worth the investment. Annie loved to draw—she was crazy about Ms. Ritter, the art teacher at St. Lawrence—and Alice looked forward to teaching her daughter a little bit about the more sophisticated techniques involved in pastels. And also just drawing herself—she imagined the feel of the pastels in her fingers, the simplicity of the experience, the direct pleasure of making a mark on a piece of paper, the immediate return.

She also picked out two sketchbooks with heavy-duty paper and went to check out. Waiting there behind two other customers, she mused idly over the little impulse-buy items, the mints and gum, the talking key chains, the eyeglass-repair kits. She looked at her pastel sets, which made her happy. As she looked at them, she noticed her hands, the slight redness and dryness in the knuckles in the fluorescent overhead lights. She stared at the backs of her hands. Not an old person's hands, not by a long way, but it seemed that she could read a map of the past eight years in them. Her nails, trimmed short and unpolished, like a nun's haircut . . .

"Will that be all for you?" came the polite, older man's voice, Mr. Planka.

"Yes, thanks," Alice said.

"These are wonderful," he said, tapping the pastel sets lightly, ringing them up.

Outside, she stood in front of the store for a few moments, looking around at the crisp shadows on the street, the bright blue sky over the two-story buildings, the people coming and going, and she willed herself to be happy. This is life, she thought. Come on.

She decided to make one more stop, turned left and crossed North Oliphant onto the third block of OffWabash. Plume was an upscale stationery shop, one of the strip's new jewel boxes, which sold handmade papers and expensive pens, fine notebooks, custom letterhead, engraved wedding invites. She had been thinking about getting a journal for herself, someplace to keep the thoughts and feelings and experiences she was having in Elkton. If she could start stockpiling these images and good feelings maybe they would begin to accrue interest, maybe before long they would start adding up to a life.

Inside, she looked at one leather-bound journal, pretty, a rich, soft brown leather with an elastic band to keep it closed, and cream-colored paper inside. It would have been an extravagance, at forty-two dollars, and she looked around at some others to find one at a slightly more reasonable price. Here was one—red leather, or imitation leather, with a softer cover. Maybe? She opened it, white pages, and for some reason they had put a thick, annoying border around the lined part, and she put it back. Here was a black one, with a rose on it. A rose on the upper-right-hand corner of the front. Craig had bought her a journal very similar to it, not long after they had moved to New Orleans. He bought it at Scriptura, one of her favorite stores, on Magazine Street. He knew she would like it. She set the journal back down and walked out the door.

Alice cut around the corner onto Oliphant, weeping, sat down

at an empty bus stop bench, furious with herself. Why was she crying? Something inside her had betrayed her, some part of herself that
she didn't even know. Almost like wetting the bed—that sense of
affront, of part of her acting on its own, without her permission . . .
It was a strange thing to remember at that moment. Her father had
made her feel like a leper about it, but her mother showed an odd
sympathy; they had never had that great a relationship, but Alice
remembered some feeling of tenderness around that one question. A
bus rolled past, down Oliphant.

She hated this; there was no room for her to have her own grief
about their life, or to miss New Orleans; Craig's missing it took up
all the air there was; it sucked the air out of her lungs. She wanted
to be here, where she was. It was a chance at a fresh start, which she
had wanted, and it was evaporating before she even had a chance to
experience it. Annie had had a bedwetting problem, too. It was a
couple years back, and Alice had a hard time with it; she got angry
with Annie, kept telling her to pull it together. Why was she thinking about this now? What an idiot, she thought. Craig had been so
gentle and understanding with Annie, too, during that time. Their
daughter. Where are you, she thought, sitting there weeping . . . like
an idiot, she thought . . . Craig, goddammit, where are you?

All along the grassy neutral ground on Carrollton Avenue, on either
side of the dormant streetcar tracks, the little signs bloomed like
wildflowers. Little thin wire stems, blowing slightly in the breeze—
*Oak Street Grill Now Open. Jefferson Chiropractic Open. Crescent
Ford Now Hiring. Drywall and Painting Specialists. Ochsner Welcome
Home—We're Open, Walk-Ins Accepted . . .*

Craig was driving up Carrollton toward Mid-City to visit Bobby
and Jen, who were staying in Baton Rouge and driving into New
Orleans every day to gut the first floor of their house. He wished

Alice could see these little signs. He took a couple of snapshots with his digital camera. He would tell her about them that evening on their nightly call.

What he would not tell her about was how hard he found it to be in New Orleans, even in their neighborhood, which had been spared the devastation of most of the rest of the city. The community had been so wounded; everyone had the worst stories, so many people were absent—temporarily or permanently. It was heavy on the heart, being there, and everyone showed it in unexpected ways. Craig, for example, could apparently not eat enough doughnuts. He would buy a box of Krispy Kremes and eat three right off the bat walking through the rooms of his house.

Yet there were also all these little signs of hope—a restaurant opening, a friend seen for the first time . . . Slowly, some parts of the city were making witty and defiant gestures toward normalcy. Bacco, a high-end French Quarter restaurant, had opened at the end of September, when there was still no safe running water in the city, serving meals on paper plates with plastic utensils and a Xeroxed daily menu consisting only of cheeseburgers. People huddled together in the one steamy coffee shop that might be open within a mile's radius.

But to get to these outposts, one walked or drove through streets where the dust blew down the sidewalk and the houses sat in comas, waiting for life to return. After nightfall, the areas of the city that had flooded were submerged in darkness. Nighttime drivers passing through on Interstate 10 looked down upon two cities, on either side of the elevated roadway; toward the river, the French Quarter was brightly lit, although the streets were empty. To the other side, looking toward Lake Pontchartrain, Mid-City was utterly dark, dark as the inside of a fish tank filled with black ink—no streetlights, no lights in any house. It was like driving along the very edge of the world at night and looking off into deepest space. The occasional adventurer or curious resident driving through those streets followed his headlights, like a diver searching a sunken wreck, down tunnels and corridors of lurid desolation, the furniture of wrecked lives caught in the glare of momentary revelation, like one of Weegee's famous crime scene photos—ruined houses, piles of debris, duct-taped refrigerators, waterlogged cars streaked with muck, their windows broken out and trunks popped open, random garbage everywhere, dead houses with doors open to the empty street—which sank back into a starless blackness again as the headlights moved on.

Alice had asked Craig to at least speak to a realtor about the real estate market and the possibility of selling their house. There was, apparently, a strong demand for houses in areas of the city that hadn't flooded. Predictably, they had a huge argument about it. One added element was a call from Borofsky, announcing that *Gumbo* was indeed going to relaunch, probably in January, from temporary offices in Metairie, and he wanted Craig to come back as the editor. Boucher School, too, claimed that they would reopen in January. What the actual texture of life would be in the city, with its strained or nonexistent resources, bankrupt energy company, one partially working hospital, half the people they knew gone, along with three quarters of the people they didn't know, the wreckage of so much infrastructure, nobody could tell.

"Craig, how hard could it be to ask? Just go to Latter & Blum on Maple Street and get a feel for it. Please? Just ask them for some sense of what the market is like?"

It had been a step he could not bring himself to make. Yet part of him was besieged by a debilitating anxiety that the city could never come back, that getting out was the only smart thing. The emotions involved were hard for Craig to explain, even to himself. Getting them, in all their contradictions, into the fifteen-hundred-word columns he was writing was proving to be more than he could manage. So Craig ended up writing what he told himself was necessary—

columns about all the signs of hope, and bravery, and occasional pathos. He kept his own dark doubts to himself.

Like the column he had just sent off. He had been in the Quarter two nights earlier, looking for signs of life, and three blocks from Rosie's along Decatur Street he had found a ragtag pickup band playing in a little corner joint. The night was wet and chilly, but they had the front door open and the sound of that little band—trumpet, guitar, and a guy playing with brushes on a single snare drum, in the middle of the empty blocks, like an outpost at the South Pole— drew him in and he sat down and got some chips and a can of Coke, and sat along with the dozen or so others who had found their way there.

He tried to let his mind relax to the sound of the group, and he pulled out his notebook and began making a few notes on the others who were there, the guitarist playing with the hood of his sweatshirt over his head for warmth, shaping it for his column. But even as he did this he felt the undertow of all the places that were no longer and that might not be again—Palm Court, Preservation Hall, Mandina's, Crescent City Steaks, Liuzza's, Domilise's, Bruning's, Sid-Mar's. The sheer fullness of life as they had known it. It was one thing to be grateful for the human spirit poking up like a little shoot of foliage in a bombed-out landscape. But New Orleans had been the most lush garden in the world, to him, and now here they were huddled around these few remaining stalks, trying to warm themselves . . . It was like living in an optical illusion; from one angle the city was a ruined shell of itself, where people hung onto the wreckage for dear life; from another angle it was already coming back, insisting on not dying, full of examples of the human spirit defiantly asserting itself in the face of the worst that life could dish out. If Craig's own conflicts hadn't been so overwhelming for him, he might have been able to write his column about how the city was both, at the same time. But as it was he chose door number two. He called that column "The Outpost."

Now as he drove across Claiborne, headed toward Bobby and Jen's, the little signs along the neutral ground stopped abruptly and the evidence of flooding began. The by now familiar high-water lines crept higher as he made his way up Carrollton, past the huge piles of broken furniture and soaked couches and garbage and refrigerators and moldy Sheetrock at curbside up and down every block. All this was, in fact, evidence of the cleaning-out that needed to take place before rebuilding. It was simultaneously inspiring and depressing.

As he approached Canal and Carrollton, Craig decided to swing by the first place he had lived in New Orleans, the house he had shared with Bobby on South Cortez Street. It was right around the corner. Driving carefully to avoid the ubiquitous lengths of wood and roofing and weatherboard with nails sticking out of them, and all the other nails everywhere—flat tires were epidemic—he turned slowly from Canal onto South Cortez and crawled along the block.

The old house showed a waterline about seven feet off the ground and one refrigerator out front but not much else. Beyond the house, he saw what, for a moment, he thought was a hallucination— his neighbors from ten years before, two lesbian partners, Chris and Babe, wearing rubber gloves and surgical masks, hauling out trash in front of the next house down, and a battery-operated boom box on the porch blaring the Meters' "Hey Pocky Way" into the deserted street. Next to the boom box sat a bright red cooler. Craig slowed to a stop in the middle of the street. He waved, and Chris walked over to the car and hollered, "Hey Babe—look who's here." She leaned down, sweaty, to look in his window. "You allright dawlin'? How's your little girl?"

Babe came up to the car, sunburned skin, short-cropped blond hair, tough. Craig shut the car off, stepped out.

"You don't want to hug us, dawlin'. We too dirty."

It had been a wild place when Craig had lived next door, especially on Mardi Gras, when it seemed as if every lesbian in the city converged on their house. They had a rugby team, and Craig and Bobby used to watch from their balcony as the whole gang of rowdy dykes, some of whom they found drop-dead beautiful, would do a group striptease at midnight on Lundi Gras, hollering encouragement to one another. Craig and Bobby would watch, laughing, asking themselves how they could ever live elsewhere.

Babe brought Craig a beer from the cooler and they stood in the street and talked. The two of them had been staying out in Laplace and coming in every day to gut the house. They talked about the neighborhood, and who was back, and do you remember Mr. Arceneaux, he died at the airport, we heard from his wife. She moved to Phoenix by their son. And Lorraine is talking about moving back. FEMA trailers? What fucking FEMA trailers? They gonna finally deliver the trailer next year after we back in the house. Are we moving back? Where the hell else are we gonna go? They gonna have to drag us out by our ankles. We gonna have Mardi Gras this year. Bet on dat.

"With the rugby team?"

"Yeah—bring your camera, Craig. We used to see you sick bastards up there on your balcony." The two of them laughed and laughed, and Craig said the hell with the dirt and hugged them both. Eventually he drove off and they waved at him as he disappeared around the corner onto Cleveland Street, waving at them out the window.

Bobby and Jen's was not far away, across Carrollton and a block off of Canal. He made the eerie drive down the block with its canopy of oak trees and its giant piles of rubbish on each side. Craig pulled up as Jen was dragging out a gray plastic garbage can, wearing a surgical mask, pulling it, bumping, bumping, down the three steps from their porch to the ground and out to the sidewalk. It was filled to the top with strips of wood and chunks of plaster and drywall.

"Bobby's letting you do all the heavy work?" Craig said, getting out of the car.

Jen pulled down the surgical mask. "Just like when we fuck," she said. "The difference is I don't have to do this if I don't want to."

Before he had a chance to approach, Jen put up her hands and said not to touch her; she was filthy. Bobby emerged onto the porch, pulling down his mask, wearing shorts and rubber boots. "Hiyo Silver," he said, in greeting. "Get your hands off my wife."

"Place is looking good," Craig said, breezily, stepping up and giving Bobby a soul handshake.

"Sorry for the rubber glove," Bobby said. "Reserve judgment on the visuals until you see inside."

They walked through the familiar doorway together, with Jen following a moment later. The living room and, beyond it, the dining room, were empty of furniture, the bare, dirty floors littered with plaster pieces and papers and one folding chair. The floor was covered with a fine, damp, gray dust in which shoes and dragged furniture had etched lines and smears. The walls had been knocked out from the floor up to about waist height, exposing the studs and the back of the exterior weatherboards. Lengths of molding leaned in a corner of the room. Their house had taken on only about three feet of water, but that, as Bobby said, had been enough to ruin the plaster, most of the furniture, and the electrical wiring. Only small signs, here and there, of the green and black mold that had grown riotously in so many homes; on one wall a large chunk of plaster torn out, floor to ceiling.

"What happened there?" Craig said.

"That happens to be an interesting thing," Bobby said. "The one place where the previous owners had patched the plaster and replaced it with Sheetrock, it was like a mold farm. We thought about putting a frame around it, but we decided to toss it instead."

"What, the mold doesn't like plaster?"

"Apparently not. I mean, you can see—it likes it a little bit . . ." He pointed to a few spots.

"So you're going to replace the plastering?"

"Probably not; it's too expensive and there's like two guys left in the city who know how to do it and they're busy until 2015."

"We're getting this expensive treated Sheetrock," Jen said. "I told him if the place floods again we're out of here anyway, so who cares if the Sheetrock is mold resistant? But he's like, *'I'm a big-time reporter . . . I write for the 'LifeStyle' section and I make sixty-five thousand dollars a year . . . I'm rich . . .'* I'll probably end up having to give blow jobs outside Café Brasil just to pay for the fucking Sheetrock."

Bobby gave Craig his "Not bad, huh?" smile, and Craig smiled back at him. There they were, Craig thought. Still alive, still there. They had made it through.

They walked through the dining room into the kitchen, which was bare, too; they had had to throw out all the appliances—stove, refrigerator, sink, dishwasher. So many parties there, Tuesday night movies, nacho chips and salsa, the kids of their large extended family as years went on, running between adults' legs, Doug singing a cappella Coasters songs . . .

"I'm going to take this bag out," Jen said. "You want to put anything else in it?"

"No, I'm happy," Bobby said. Jen tied off the bag and dragged it out through the dining room, toward the front door. A piece of wood that had poked through the bottom of the bag scored a wavering scar behind her on the grimy wood floor. As he watched her, Bobby said, "We're gonna have to refinish the floors anyway. You want to see upstairs? It's the same as it was, except we got a hibachi on the balcony."

Craig stood quietly, looking around.

After a moment, Bobby said, "Yo . . . Craig . . . Are you visiting the Giraffe People again? What's up?"

"I just don't fucking know why we're in fucking Chicago; we should be back here."

Bobby frowned, laughed. "Hey, one step at a time. You'll be back."

"Alice wants to stay in Chicago. She wants to sell the house."

"That's an old story, right?"

"I don't know," Craig said. "It's crazy. I should be here helping you out, doing rebuilding . . ."

"You're writing the articles, honcho. You're spreading the word."

"Yeah, but it's not the same as being here."

"Hey man," Bobby said, "you know what? If you feel like you should be here, then be here. If you have to leave, you have to leave. It just doesn't seem like it should really be all that complicated." Jen walked back into the room. "It's like you're asking me to tell you it's okay that you're not here helping me out."

Craig was a little taken aback by his friend's tone, through which he easily read, and amplified, the mild annoyance that was there.

"He's not thinking about moving out of town is he?" Jen said.

"Alice wants to stay in Chicago," Craig began.

"So let her stay in Chicago," Jen said. "Let her go chew on a cheese steak."

"That's Philadelphia," Bobby offered.

"Who gives a fuck?" Jen said.

"Well," Craig began, feeling defensive and annoyed now, himself, "she has some legitimate concerns about the schools . . ."

"You said Boucher is opening again."

". . . and about health care and about the state of the whole city in general. She wants to raise Annie and Malcolm someplace a little more secure, and I can see where she's coming from, even if I don't agree." Craig felt sick with himself, defending a point of view that he had spent the past couple of years arguing against, but it couldn't be dismissed out of hand, after all. If it could, then they would have to stay in New Orleans. Or he would. And his marriage would be over.

"So I guess you haven't told him?" Jen said. She was speaking to Bobby. Craig looked from one to the other.

"We're going to be contributing to the repopulation of the city by at least one new citizen sometime next June it looks like," Bobby said.

"He forced me into it," Jen said. "I told him it might be yours. But now it turns out you have no balls, so . . ."

"Hey . . ." Craig said, frowning and laughing, a little hurt.

"Oh come on, you big fucking baby," Jen said. "You aren't moving."

"I am so happy for you guys," Craig said. "That is incredible news."

"So anyway," Jen said, "little Gertrude is going to need a babysitter, and Annie will be the right age."

"Gertrude?" Craig said.

"If it's a boy we're calling it Hercules."

Bobby gave Craig his "What am I supposed to do about it?" shrug, and they shared their standard chuckle.

Eventually, Craig headed out with his mind in a tangle of confusion.

The next morning, he drove through the uptown streets, to the coffee shop on the corner of Nashville and Magazine, his temporary outpost until PJ's on Maple Street, much closer to his house, reopened. This new place was always filled with the most disparate types of people who made their way there through the empty streets, mismatched, thrown together sitting at the small tables or waiting on line for the rare and precious coffee: emergency workers, contractors, FEMA officials, real estate speculators from out of town, police officers.

On this afternoon, Craig found himself on line behind a short, youngish man wearing khaki shorts, a white Izod shirt, sunglasses hung from around his neck with Croakies, Top-Siders . . . Not New Orleans; probably a claims adjuster, he thought absently, or maybe a FEMA man.

Craig stared into the display case, trying to decide between sesame and poppy seed bagels, sensing that this fellow was watching him. He was not in the mood to talk to anyone, and he tried to convey this through his body language. Then he heard, "Hey there—Chuck Bridges."

Craig looked up from the display case and saw the face, the vacant alertness, vaguely familiar.

"You live in the house on Cypress Street?" the man said. "A block from Boucher. I came to your party right before the storm." The short, athletic-looking man was putting out his hand for Craig to shake. This was the guy he and Bobby had made fun of. To his surprise, Craig found himself mildly but reflexively happy to see the man. Craig had noticed this before; there was a happiness at seeing just about anybody you had known before the hurricane. If they had made it through, you were comrades, of a sort. For a little while anyway.

"Are you still in your house?" the man said. "That block didn't flood."

"Uh, yeah," Craig said. "We're still there." No need to tell him that they were in Chicago, or thinking about selling. Now it came back to Craig—the unpleasant feeling he had had from the guy asking him so quickly if he was thinking of selling. "How did you do?" Craig asked, to be polite.

"Did fine. We're out in Metairie. A little roof damage but we got that cleaned up pretty quick. Want to sit down?"

Craig could not easily find a credible excuse, and so, reluctantly, he followed the man to one of the small tables in the back.

"Thinking about selling?" the man said.

Craig was struck again by the man's directness and apparent guilelessness. Small talk didn't seem to occur to him. "A lot of people in your neighborhood are selling and making beaucoup profit."

Craig shook his head, looking down at his bagel, spreading the cream cheese as if he were putting the final touches on a painting. "No," he said. "No. We like our home."

"If you're thinking of buying more property," the man went on, helpfully, "now's the time to buy houses in flood areas. Mid-City especially. Broadmoor maybe not so much."

"I don't think we're in the market for more property, either. We kind of have our hands full as it is." Craig said. He didn't want to telegraph any sense that he was unhappy. He didn't want to give the guy an opening. Trying to sound upbeat, he said, "You said a lot of people are selling up around Boucher?"

"We've moved six houses within a twelve-block radius in the past week."

"Really," Craig said, noncommittally, still looking down at his bagel.

"Yep. It's a land grab. Houses that didn't flood are in big demand. It's going to get bigger. As soon as all the Lakeview insurance money starts rolling in they'll all be looking for houses that didn't flood."

Craig silently, tortuously, debated whether to mention that they were . . . considering selling. Just out of curiosity. It was information, nothing more than that. He had yet to have a conversation with one realtor. This could be a bone to throw Alice; he could use it to stall for a little more time, make it seem as if they were moving forward . . .

With half a smile, Chuck Bridges said, "You sure you're not thinking about it? I could have a buyer for you within a week. Guaranteed."

"Well," Craig said, playing for time, "everybody I know has 'thought' about it. Given everything that has happened you'd be crazy not to at least think about it. But this is our home, you know?"

"Let me tell you something," Bridges said. "Your house is one of the most desirable houses I have looked at. A block from Boucher, all that space, the nice yard, convertible garage . . . You could do well."

"What is 'well'?" Craig heard himself saying.

"Shoot for 450K," Chuck Bridges said, "and maybe she'll weigh in around four twenty-five."

Craig was genuinely shocked by the figure. "You're kidding," he said.

"When did you buy the house?"

"Eight years ago."

"So you paid maybe one seventy?"

"One fifty-five," Craig said, disgusted with himself for playing along.

"Sweet. After you pay out the closing costs and all, you walk with close to a quarter mil in profit. Not bad. Put the money right into the kids' college fund."

Craig had not thought about the profit as money in the bank for Annie and Malcolm. Even if the house sold for $400,000 it was an inconceivable profit, to Craig. Even $300,000. He had known in the back of his mind that they could make a profit if they sold, but he had never wanted to think about it too directly. The provisional number he had in mind was somewhere around $80,000 in profit, which he had thought made him something of a real estate genius. But these figures were like science fiction. These weren't just numbers to make life easier or more comfortable. These kinds of numbers represented a paradigm shift.

"A lot of people are doing it," Bridges went on. "It's just timing. There's an inflated demand right now. In another year, fourteen months, it'll all start cooling off once the market stabilizes."

Never had Craig thought of being able to make a one-shot coup of this sort. Years ago, when he had assumed the harness of the editing job at *Gumbo*, it was with the recognition that the kids had changed everything in the equation. But the kind of money Bridges was talking about meant being able to knock their potential mortgage way down if they bought a house in Chicago. Alice wouldn't necessarily have to find a job right away; she could stay home and take care of Annie and Malcolm. The money from the *EYE* would be enough to take care of them. Assuming that Bridges was telling the truth and knew what he was talking about.

"I'll tell you something," Bridges said. "The market around by you was hot before the storm. But right now it is on fire. The time isn't going to be right for everybody to sell; I understand that. If you have your kids in school, and a solid job, or you need to be here for family, whatever . . . Hey, that's the way it is. But anybody who's even thinking of moving . . . Hey, do it now. There'll never be a better time. And, you know, once the next storm hits, if the city floods again, property values will tank all over the city. Here," Bridges said, holding a card out between his thumb and index finger. "You don't want to be rushed into anything, and I respect that. Take my card and call me when you decide. I'll deliver for you better than anybody else can. I live this stuff and I know it like the back of my hand."

"I don't doubt that," Craig said, looking at the type on the card for lack of anything more sensible to do while he grappled for a little equilibrium.

"Actually, that's the old card; let me write my cell number on that for you."

The man took it back, wrote something quickly with what Craig recognized as a Mont Blanc pen—an odd dash of flair that he wouldn't necessarily have expected from Chuck Bridges. "There you go," Bridges said, handing the card back to Craig. "Day or night."

"Thanks," Craig said, placing the card in the breast pocket of his shirt. "I'll call you if we decide to . . . sell. Some day."

"That'll work," Chuck Bridges said, standing up. "Don't wait too long."

23

When Craig was back in Chicago, the old routine reasserted itself—Alice reading a book on the couch after the kids were in bed, and Craig watching movies or TV, or working on one of his columns. The apartment Alice had found was undeniably a good place for them to have landed, and both Craig and Alice knew how fortunate they were. Yet for Craig the very comfort of the place—the tasteful furnishings, the maple veneer table where they ate, the kitchen utensils, the linens, the couch—was jarring, incongruous. And yet, secretly, he was glad for it. It was a secret even to himself.

In the evenings, husband and wife watched each other covertly. Craig hadn't told Alice about the conversation with Chuck Bridges, nor about the part of himself that wanted to run from New Orleans. And Alice didn't ask Craig about Maple Street or the places she missed in New Orleans, or the depression she was experiencing, and she didn't tell him about the cute underwear at Alizé, nor about seeing the journal. They didn't tiptoe around each other, exactly. But each carried secrets that they were afraid the other might sniff out. So they talked to Annie a lot—about school, about her teachers, about her homework. Craig found ways of inserting New Orleans into the conversation. Despite himself, he didn't want Annie to get too attached to St. Lawrence

Montessori and lose her hold on the life they had been building those past years. At her age, roots were shallow. While cleaning up the kitchen, making coffee, Craig would slip a Professor Longhair CD into the boom box on the drain board, or the Wild Tchoupitoulas.

Annie seemed the most self-contained, the least fazed, of them all, from outside at least. Malcolm had decided that, of all things, the Teenage Mutant Ninja Turtles were the most interesting thing on the planet—where he had found out about them, neither Craig nor Alice knew—and he watched the old videos they found for him over and over. Alice and Craig both worried about him watching so much television, but it was a provisional solution to the question of where to direct his attention. Annie, on the other hand, read every book they could take out from the children's room at the Elkton Public Library. She filled sketchbooks and books of newsprint paper with drawings. She dutifully let her mother show her how to use pastels, then she used them to copy a picture of an ostrich from a book which shocked both her parents with its assurance and quality.

If Annie was worried or upset, she didn't show it. Without realizing it, she was practicing a skill that both her parents had acquired as children, a way of maintaining a substitute life while hanging over the abyss of her parents' unhappiness, as if hanging between two railroad cars running along not-quite-parallel tracks. Obviously an impossible situation, so she summoned up a world that she could have some control over, at the tip of a pencil, or Magic Marker or crayon or pastel. When she got tired of that, she escaped into a book.

Secretly, she had a fantasy about having a cat. She wanted a cat to hug because she got cold sometimes. She could play with a kitty and it would be her friend. More than anything, really, Annie wanted a cat. But she never mentioned it to either of her parents.

• • •

On a brilliant, cloudless fall day in the third week of October, Craig headed down to the Loop for lunch with Peter Morehead. The *CHI EYE* offices were in a building a block and a half from the Art Institute, amid all the good urban bustle of downtown Chicago. The fall tang in the air, the sense of people heading someplace, the old steel and stone Chicago of Theodore Dreiser and Bix Beiderbecke. Not manic and hell-bent like New York, but solid in some hard-to-define Midwestern way. The marble-and-terrazzo lobby spoke of the mid-1920s, with brass fittings on the elevator call plates and the edges of the building directory kept shining, on this afternoon at least, by a white man in his forties wearing a blue workman's shirt and wielding a rag with detached, professional concentration. Craig wasn't impervious to the urban caffeine, the fizz, and despite himself, and periodic intrusions of vertigo when he thought of his life in suspended animation in New Orleans, he enjoyed being dressed in jacket and tie, on an errand in a downtown filled with activity.

The *CHI EYE* offices, on the eighth floor, turned out to be a Bizarro-world version of the *Gumbo* offices, which had been very funky and unbuttoned. Alternative newspaper offices almost always are, but here, young interns passed down a warmly lit hallway lined with framed *CHI EYE* covers. A woman whom Craig checked himself from staring at too intensely, shockingly beautiful with red hair and stylish glasses, wearing black slacks and a red silk blouse, gave him a smart, brief smile as she passed him. A young man sat at the reception desk, wearing a black open-necked shirt and moussed hair, reading *The Wind-Up Bird Chronicle*. Craig gave his name and said he was there to see Peter Morehead.

The receptionist's eyes focused and he said, "I've enjoyed your New Orleans articles, Mr. Donaldson."

Slightly startled, Craig fumbled out a few words of gratitude, then he stood looking around as the young man hit Peter More-head's number on the intercom. At *Gumbo*, he was lucky if Alison at the front desk could take down a phone number accurately on a message slip. Everyone he saw, walking past, or down the hall next to the desk, talking in office doors, seemed bright, plugged in. Craig sat down on a leather couch in the reception area; on the end table were copies of the *EYE* with his name on one of the cover lines.

He had trouble admitting to himself just how much he dreaded the idea of going back to work for Borofsky at *Gumbo*. That had been another conversation he'd declined to share with Alice. On his last visit he had met with Borofsky to discuss Craig moving back to steer the "book," as Borofsky called it, back to weekly status. Borofsky held forth about revised demographics and New Orleans' "new profile," and his vision for the paper's future, which was characteristically both grandiose and venal. Craig mentioned a letter he'd received, part of a theme that was coming out of the closet more and more, asking whether the city wasn't better off without its poorer black citizens, and Borofsky had tacitly defended the letter-writer's point of view.

"Craig," Borofsky had said, with his condescending smile, "No-body loves the Mardi Gras Indians more than I do. But you and I are the Outsiders' Club, here. Because of that we can see things with a healthy degree of perspective. I, like you, see the city as a dynamic set of tensions among its different neighborhoods, and I, too, read its culture as a dynamic mixture of African and European streams. I realize full well that the culture that we love and share in our city comes out of, and serves, a community. What I am saying is that communities are living organisms, and living organisms do not re-main static. I completely agree with you about the apparent agenda behind this note and others like it and, like you, I find it reprehen-sible. And at the same time the fact does remain that some of these neighborhoods do not express, have never expressed, something es-sential about the city."

"Like which neighborhoods?"

"Well, my young friend, just to show you that this is not a racially based argument, let's take Lakeview. Lakeview could be anywhere. From a preservationist viewpoint there is absolutely no reason why Lakeview should be rebuilt or preserved. The houses are 1950s at the earliest, characterless—and populated, I might add, by white-flight types who were attempting to escape the inner city, or at least alter the fuel-to-air mix of the cultural realities we prize so dearly."

"But they are still New Orleanians. They are still part of the mix. And they stayed in the city at least. They didn't move to the suburbs. That's got to count for something."

"I'll let that pass for a moment. Let's take New Orleans East. Same thing, different color. Middle-class, black, flavorless, could be in Atlanta or Los Angeles . . . Why rebuild it?"

"Because people made lives there. They raised families there. They worked hard to build those houses and to afford them . . ."

"Craig, please. Sentiment aside, the reality is that the city has a reduced footprint, and greatly reduced resources. We need to think about how to deploy what we have most effectively. I and you and everybody else would love to just wave a wand and have everything back the way it was, but that is simply not going to happen. So we have to make hard decisions about what we spend money and effort on, and what we don't."

"I disagree that everybody would like it back the way it was. What about the guy who wrote that letter, and the others like him?"

"Okay, I relent on that point. I overspoke. Let's say everyone of good will."

"And anyway," Craig went on, "it's not about having it back exactly as it was. Maybe there's a chance to have people come back and this time make sure they have decent schools. With books, and working bathrooms. You know, you don't have to be blind to the poverty and crime to recognize that the Ninth Ward was a living community.

You don't have to bulldoze it to make it function. That was like the whole Vietnam thing, right? Torch the village to save it?"

"Slow down, Craig," Borofsky said, his smile fading just a bit. "The Ninth Ward is not the alpha and omega of black New Orleans. The most motivated, most talented citizens, black and white, whatever neighborhood they lived in before the storm, will come back. And they will be the ones most likely to make a contribution to the city's growth and rebuilding and eventual well-being. And the ones who want to sit on their ample posteriors and cash a monthly check to buy potato chips and watch their High-Definition TVs that they bought with their FEMA money will be just as happy in Atlanta or Houston, I daresay."

Craig was stunned; he felt his face redden. Borofsky's knowing smile, the cultured façade that hid the old nasty reflexes, the easy cleaving—keep the good ones, get rid of the bad ones; the strong and good would come back, the others would disappear and they weren't our problem . . . As if it could ever be that simple. What about the hardworking people who were just hanging on, who had worked their entire lives, doing the best they could, stuck two thousand miles from home? If they couldn't muster the resources to move back, in this climate of no insurance, no electricity, no jobs, no schools, no services, then the hell with them? Easier just to airbrush them and all their troublesome complexity out of the picture, one less set of problems to deal with. How were they supposed to make a life? Or were they? If you lacked the energy to overcome problems that would have crippled the strongest and most privileged among us, then it was just tough luck . . .

Craig sat in the chair, overwhelmed and depressed at the prospect of continuing to work for this windbag. The sheer weight of that point of view, of knowing how ingrained it was, how widespread, felt like overpowering fatigue.

"Craig, are you much of a poetry devotee?"

"Why?" *Devotee?* Craig thought.

"There's a marvelous poem by the Irish poet William Butler Yeats"—*as opposed to the French poet William Butler Yeats, you jackass*—"called 'Lapis Lazuli.' It's about how people—Yeats calls them 'hysterical women'—think their society has to last forever or the world will end. And he delineates all these different civilizations that 'go under the sword' and how the world lasted through art; the people themselves didn't matter all that much in the final analysis. Telemachus made sculptures and they were all destroyed . . . 'Things fall apart and men build them again; in the building is happiness.' I remember my Yeats fairly well," Borofsky said, with a self-satisfied smile. Craig was almost sure Borofsky had misquoted the poem, which Craig remembered dimly from a twentieth-century-poetry class in Michigan . . . *And Telemachus wasn't a sculptor . . .*

"The art that you and I both love is the only thing that matters in the long run. The world will not long remember or care whether Fred Johnson or the waiter at the Camellia Grill ever lived—much as we might love them now. They don't matter. What did Faulkner say? The 'Ode on a Grecian Urn' is worth a thousand old ladies?"

You probably have that quote wrong, too, Craig thought. Borofsky was looking across the desk at Craig, with his ironic smile, inviting Craig into complicity. What was he supposed to say to this? Should he call Borofsky a pretentious fool? A moral degenerate in the guise of an aesthete? He stood up as Borofsky said, "Craig . . ." in the voice that Craig thought of as his Great Conciliator voice, another intolerable mask.

"I need to step out of this conversation for right now," Craig said, and he started for the door.

"Peter will be right out, Mr. Donaldson," the receptionist said. "Are you living in Chicago now full-time?"

"Yes," Craig said. "I mean, no, we are based here for now, but we don't really know what the future has in store. We still have a house in New Orleans, and, I don't know . . . It's like . . ."

"Craig," came the familiar voice, his old friend Peter, walking down the hall toward him.

Craig turned toward him; he put out his hand and his friend said, "Stop . . . A handshake instead of a kiss?" and gave him a big hug. "You look great."

"So do you." His old pal wore a pair of fine brown wool slacks, a white linen shirt with the sleeves rolled up and, like everyone he had seen so far at the *EYE*, very expensive-looking glasses.

"Come on down to the office." He clapped Craig on the shoulder and they headed off down the hallway past more framed covers, and around occasional stacked-up boxes of copies of the paper, books, office equipment.

"I don't know how you're holding yourself together, bud," Peter said to Craig as they walked. "How's Alice doing?"

Craig thought about how to answer this one. He didn't even know how to answer it for himself. "It has been tough on all of us in different ways" is what he said. "I think she's trying as hard as she can to make a normal environment for Malcolm and Annie. But, you know . . . how can it be a normal environment?"

"Michelle and I want to have you guys over for dinner; we'll get out the calendars and see what works. Here we are."

Peter ushered Craig into a wide, comfortable office that looked out over Michigan Avenue. "Have a seat."

"I want to look around a little," Craig said, smiling. Theater posters, a Walker Evans photo of a railroad yard, and, unmistakable, a poster from one of the old UMich theater productions they'd been in together.

"Ring a bell?" Peter said, joining his old friend.

"Goddamn I can't believe you have this thing hanging up."

"Wait until you see this."

On top of a long, low black lacquer bookcase Peter plucked from among fifteen or so small framed standing photos of his wife, children, vacations, one small one, slightly bluish and faded with age and handed it to Craig, an image of two young men and one young woman, the shorter of the two men with a huge nimbus of curly hair, holding a guitar, the three of them singing into a microphone. The tall guy with the shoulder-length hair in the middle was Craig, the guitarist was Peter.

"Unbelievable," Craig said, looking pointedly at Peter's well-groomed, thinning hair.

"Time marches on," Peter said.

"Whatever happened to Barbara Cohen," Craig said, shaking his head and peering at the woman in the photo. "Where is she now," as if no answer could be forthcoming.

"She lives in Winnetka."

"You're kidding," Craig said, looking at his pal to see if he were joking.

"One husband, three daughters, two dogs. At last count."

They sat down and chatted for a while, then they headed out to lunch at a steakhouse with heavy, dark wooden walls and floors, a 1920s-era temple of beef abundance, stockyard muscle, that had supposedly been one of Nelson Algren's favorite spots. Craig enjoyed the vitality in the place, the energy. After they had ordered, Peter came right to the point and offered Craig a full-time writing job at the *EYE*, if Craig thought they might want to stay in Chicago.

"I know I've told you, Craig, but the column has been just what we wanted. Alan has been looking for a feature writer with a strong personal voice, and he seems to be convinced that you can fill the job." Peter went on to praise Craig's work, adding specific things Lee Binner, the editor, had said. "We know that your living situation is still an up-in-the-air question for you. But the offer is on the table, when and if you want it. The benefits package, may I say, is exemplary. We can talk salary if you decide you want to talk more about it. No pressure at all."

This offer found Craig's most vulnerable place, professionally. After years of editing, rather than writing, of Arthur Borofsky trying to steer *Gumbo* away from the kinds of substantial reporting Craig favored, toward the restaurant guides and home furnishing supplements and lifestyle gewgaws, hearing praise for his writing was the thing that got Craig at his most susceptible. Not to mention the fact that sooner or later the question of a steady income and insurance for his family would begin to loom larger than any other concern.

He said the only thing he could say, which was how flattered and happy the offer made him, and how he would have to sit with it, discuss it with Alice, all of that. After lunch they parted in front of the restaurant, and Craig walked for blocks through the Chicago streets and the afternoon crowds, exhilarated, shaking with anxiety.

"Peter says hello, by the way," Craig said as he set his laptop case down on the couch and loosened his tie.

"Oh," Alice said, absently, doing something in the kitchen. "Great. How's he doing?"

"He's great," Craig said. He was not going to tell Alice about the job offer yet. Add it to the list of secrets.

"Did you meet the editor?" Alice said.

Annie came skipping, excitedly, into the room.

"Uh, no," Craig said, picking his daughter up and hugging her. When he set her down she jumped up and down a couple of times and Craig gave her a questioning frown-smile. "But apparently he likes the columns."

"He ought to," Alice said, stepping into the living room, drying her hands and looking down at Annie, who looked up at her with a barely contained glee. "Annie has some big news."

"What's that?" Craig said, looking from one to the other.

"I'm in the play!" Annie said.

"That's great," Craig said. A moment went by as he felt Alice watching him. "What kind of play is it?"

"It's a padgin . . . ?" she looked at Alice.

"Pageant . . ." Alice said, looking back at her.

"Padgint about Thanksgiving."

"Wow. And . . . you're going to be in it."

His daughter nodded, exaggeratedly, jumping up and down again.

"Annie's going to have lines to remember and everything," Alice said, looking down at her.

"Who wrote the play?" Craig said.

Alice narrowed her eyes at Craig, slightly, as if to say, Is that the most appropriate thing you could think of? "Mr. Bourne."

Mr. Bourne, Annie's third-grade teacher, was a gentle man with sandy brown hair, who wore ties with Bugs Bunny on them. Craig found him irritating, and had told Alice after parents' night three weeks earlier that he thought Mr. Bourne was "professionally un-threatening." She had looked at him as if he were crazy and said, "It's a problem that her third-grade teacher is unthreatening?" What he had meant was that he found something suspect about the man's warm fuzziness, but it was undeniable that every student at the school loved him, including Annie.

Craig nodded, and said "Wow" again. "That is really great." Alice was staring at him. "I am so proud of you. When is the play going to be?"

"Just before Thanksgiving," Alice said. "Right around when you'd expect them to have a Thanksgiving pageant."

Dinner was strained. Malcolm ran a toy Ninja Turtle along the edge of the table even after Alice had told him, twice, to put it away, and Craig took it from him and set it on top of the refrigerator. This started Malcolm crying.

"Stop crying, Malcolm," Craig said.

His son kept crying, saying "I want Leonardo" through his tears.

"That's what happens when a grown-up tells you to do something and you don't do it. You have to listen."

"I want Leonardo," the boy wailed.

Alice began clearing the dishes. Annie sat at her spot, looking down into her plate. "Finish your peas," Alice said.

"I'm not hungry," the girl said.

"You were hungry before, Annie. Finish the peas you took."

Craig glared at Alice, but her attention was focused on Annie. One more pointless battle of wills, he thought.

"I have a stomach ache," Annie said.

Alice took a deep breath, then another, then said "Fine" and picked up Annie's plate, adding, "You may be excused from the table if you're not feeling well."

Annie got out of her chair and went to her bedroom.

They sat across from each other. What had begun as an after-dinner exchange about what his problem had been earlier, why he hadn't been more enthusiastic for his daughter's sake, had turned into a speech by Craig, about New Orleans, and how the city deserved their support, and Alice had gotten quiet, smolderingly quiet, as he went on.

"All I'm saying," Craig said, lying, because it was not all he was saying, "is that I don't know how great it is for her to get so attached to her new friends and to 'Mr. Bourne' when we may not even be staying here."

Through the whole conversation he had felt at a disadvantage, since he was covering up his own doubts; he didn't even really believe what he was saying anymore. He didn't know what he really felt or believed, so he tried twice as hard to pump up the idea that he knew what he felt and believed, and he knew it was unfair, but he was afraid. He didn't yet have a name for what it was he was really afraid of, but it was apparently painful enough for him to keep yattering away despite the fact that something was off-kilter in the way he was handling it, and maybe, if he just kept talking, whatever it was would just . . . stay away.

"Are you out of your fucking mind?" Alice said.

The question, delivered in a loud voice, startled Craig. He tried to quiet her, afraid that the kids would hear. She had never spoken in exactly that tone to him.

"I will not be quiet. What do you want? You want Annie to live in a . . . a . . . an oxygen tent? You want her to just stop living because you can't be in New Orleans? We have to find some way of having a life. Your own daughter has been through a horrible upset, and now she has a chance to make a few friends and have some fun, and some validation, and you don't know if that's a good thing? *Oh my God . . .*" She put both hands over her face.

Craig sat and watched Alice sob. He was left behind, with his own idiotic voice being played back to him. He gazed down, in shame, at the fake wood-grain veneer of the table on which his arm sat. Sand dunes, whirlpools, caverns. He pressed his hand against it. He heard Alice push her chair back from the table.

"Please wait," he said. He tried to press his slightly cupped palm flat, against the table. It wasn't as if there were a lot of places left to hide.

"Please wait," he said, again. "I am so sorry."

He stared at the table. Alice's words had made him hear himself as Alice had heard him, and as Annie had heard him. In that flash, a different angle had revealed something in the shadows that he had guessed at before but never been forced to acknowledge. He had been using Annie. He needed to sit with it for a moment. Alice was still there.

"I am so sorry," he said. It wasn't just Annie he was using. He knew that. But using for what? Don't you know, Craig? What was he turning into?

Alice said, "I don't know what to do, Craig. I don't know what to do. I don't know what we are supposed to do. We can't stop living."

Craig nodded his head, still unable to look at her. Living . . . living meant change—he remembered that much, he had read it someplace. Alice had been changing. Annie was changing. Now something was being asked of him—*him*—that New Orleans could not answer for him. None of what he had assembled around himself, none of the icons or heroes, the music, the cultural exoskeleton, none of it could answer this. He was going to have to answer, himself.

"I'm so sorry," he said, again. "Please give me a chance. I'm going to try. Just . . . give me a chance."

Palm trees, blue sky, then the woman waving frantically to the circling rescue helicopter . . .

"This is no time to be rescued," says the familiar voice, and then she is pulled down and James Bond pulls the orange and white parachute over himself and Pussy Galore, stranded on some Caribbean island as the CIA men in their gray suits circle in the helicopter and Craig felt around the bottom of the big green plastic bowl with his fingertips for any remaining popcorn. Alice was curled up at the other end of the couch, reading. The *Goldfinger* theme music came up with its foreboding yet sensual rising and falling ostinato, then the striptease trumpet with the plunger mute and Shirley Bassey's brassy vocal as Craig reached for the remote on the low coffee table.

"Can you turn it down a little?" Alice asked, looking up from over the top of her copy of *Middlemarch*.

"That's just what I was about to do," Craig said. It was the night after their argument. He hit the volume button and rode the closing theme music down to a tolerable level. Annie and Malcolm were long since asleep, and Alice seemed happy enough—warm, protected, immersed, pillows behind her back and legs covered with the hemp throw her brother had sent them for Christmas two years ago. Craig wondered if there were time enough for another movie before they would have to cash it in for the night. Sometimes you could reach a point of diminishing returns, though; you could wake up in the middle of the dream, as if awakening from anesthesia in the middle of an operation, and ask yourself, what the hell am I doing?

He looked around the warm, nicely furnished living room that Alice had found for them and which had been the center of their life for the past month and a half in Elkton, Illinois. The gray slate backing behind the fireplace with its chain mail curtain and tools. Craig had been boycotting the fireplace, even though it was fireplace weather. He resisted making a fire, with its overtones of staking a claim to Home, to shelter; it felt too much like ratifying their presence there. He would not sign off on the implied contract. Alice seemed to understand this intuitively; twice in the preceding weeks she had suggested making a fire, but at Craig's mumbling about not being sure whether the flue was open, or it being too late and he didn't want to let it smolder after they were asleep, she let it drop. Deflecting Annie had been a little harder—a fireplace was an absolute and compelling novelty for her—but the fact remained: the fireplace had not yet been used.

The television sat up against the wall that ran at an oblique angle to the fireplace, and the sectioned, angled couch had been set up nicely so that you could enjoy either the electronic or the actual hearth. At the other end of the room the dining table, near the kitchen, was smallish but offered everything necessary, including a window that looked out across the banked-up ground with its well-groomed lawn to the leafy and pleasant street. A bedroom for them and one for the kids, and even a small storage room that he had dragooned into use as the World's Smallest Study, as he called it in e-mails to friends, some of whom were exiled like himself, some of whom were back in New Orleans, and some of whom were old friends from another time with whom Craig, suddenly, had a renewed appetite for contact.

It was not a permanent arrangement, but it was as comfortable as anything could be for the time being, while the roulette wheel spun and the ball of their future bounced around and Craig hung suspended in an agony of ambivalence. Somewhere down in New Orleans, his life was on hold, a red light blinking on a phone in a darkened office, waiting for someone to pick up.

He glanced at Alice and, to his surprise, found that she was watching him.

"Hey," he said, for lack of anything better, out of embarrassment, as if she had been reading his thoughts.

"Hey," she said, with a serious expression on her face. She kept her eyes on him. Craig tried to imagine what this look was, what conversation they were headed for.

Finally, he said, "What are we doing?"

Alice didn't answer immediately. She held his gaze, then she said, "I think we are trying to do the right thing, and there is no right thing." Quiet again for a moment, and then, "Every choice we have ends up with some kind of huge . . . loss. It ends up with something getting lost that is really just . . . irreplaceable. And I'm sorry, Craig. I am really sorry about that. I want you to know that I am really sorry about that."

"Yeah," he said. He was holding his breath, and he decided to breathe. "I don't know what to do."

"I know."

"They offered me a job," he said.

"Peter did?"

Craig nodded. "I walked all around the Loop . . ."

He didn't finish the sentence, shook his head a little. "I feel so fucking torn. How are you supposed to make any kind of reasonable decision under these conditions?"

"I don't think you can," she said. "The whole thing is unreasonable."

"I was walking around, and I just felt like . . . I can be free. We could have a whole new life, and be here, and I felt so fucking ashamed of myself for thinking that."

Alice watched Craig say this, and she suddenly imagined birds, a lot of them all at once flying up into the air, as if they had been suddenly released from a cage, all in different directions. Where, she thought, did these weird images come from? She used to write down her dreams; that was something else she needed to start doing again. After a moment she said, "Do you remember when you bought me the journal?"

He tried to locate the memory.

"Just after we moved to New Orleans," she said.

"Yeah," he said. "The leather one. The black one." He smiled.

"I was thinking about that the other day."

Craig waited for her to go on, but that seemed to be it. He made a mental note to buy her another journal, someplace.

"I miss it, too, Craig."

He nodded his head, closed his eyes. Silently, in his mind, he said *Thank you.*

"I know," he said.

"But it's like something has to . . ." she searched for a word . . .

"Readjust," he said.

"Yeah," she said.

Craig let out a long sigh.

"I don't want to lose it," he said.

"You can kill it if you hold on to it too tight," she said. "Maybe it has to change."

"I . . ." he shook his head, didn't go on. It was going to take a while to shake out.

The next morning, Craig sat at his desk with the coffee he had carried in from the kitchen. He did not open his laptop but sat drinking the coffee and feeling the hot liquid make its way down inside him. He looked out the window into the yard under the low branches of the rhododendron hedge.

He picked up the wallet that sat on the bookcase to his right, retrieved the card he wanted, righted it, looked at it for a long moment. He checked the time. Then he picked up the phone and punched in the number and after two rings heard the oddly familiar voice say "Chuck Bridges . . ."

24

Wesley had driven under the expressway, twice, as the directions had indicated, and he still couldn't find Alhambra, which was supposed to run north-south just on the other side of the overpass. He pulled the truck over to the curb by a hurricane fence topped with coils of brand-new razor wire that glinted in the sun, and he studied the wire-bound Houston metro map book. Just behind him cars echoed under the expressway . . . He pointed with his finger at the page: Baedy, Seville, Freeman, Alhambra . . . There's the expressway . . . and there's Alhambra . . .

He looked up and around. He would try it one more time and then he would phone in to the office and ask what he was supposed to do. Put the truck into gear and made a left at the corner to go back under the expressway. He had had Tupac pumping out all over as he drove earlier, but now he kept the system off to see if he could concentrate a little better. He used to idolize Tupac, had a big picture in his room on Tennessee Street. He still listened to him now, as he drove the streets, in the moment, not sure what he was feeling. It was a familiar sound, like Kanye, 50 Cent, Mystikal . . . But more and more he focused on the work. He was trying to feel his way along, and not make any mistakes. New Orleans had been a recognizable landscape, a game where he knew the rules. There was a whole world in Houston, obviously, but he didn't know what it was. He was getting to know the city schematically, at least, although the outlying areas, so spread out, were confusing and illogical, slippery, compared to New Orleans. It all felt virtual to him, like a giant video game.

He passed under the expressway, barely stopped at the stop sign, and as he crossed the next street out of the corner of his eye he saw the sign: Alhambra Boulevard. How many times had he crossed over it without seeing it? Somehow he had gotten turned around and thought he was heading east when he was heading west.

Two more blocks and he found Buckler Avenue easily now, made the right turn onto a treeless street paved with sand-colored cement studded with grape-sized pebbles and stones, burned-out cars at the side of the road and up on what might at one time have been grass. It was six blocks of yellow cinder-block abandoned housing projects, then blocks of two-story apartment buildings, more like hotel units, watching the numbers now, cross Iberia and here was 3124–28.

Wesley pulled the truck over and slid it into park. After double-checking the address and scanning the street carefully before getting out—an old New Orleans habit that would never leave him—he turned off the engine, locked up, walked to unit 1-D, and knocked.

From inside, a man's voice hollered what sounded like "Carol."

Wesley waited. At the end of the building a three-year-old boy looked at him. Inside, the voice hollered the name again.

The door opened and there was a tall, light-skinned black guy, about his age, wearing no shirt, his chest barely dusted with small curly black hair, and over his left breast the word *JAUNE* tattooed in dark blue script. He wore black jeans and was barefoot.

"Allright," the young man said. "You from the cable?"

"Yeah," Wesley said, looking past the young man inside the room, checking to see who else might be there. "You need a primary hookup?"

"I don't know," the young man said. "My sister know what's happening." Turning away, he hollered the name Carol again.

Behind the young man Wesley saw an older man approaching, tentatively, wearing a plaid shirt open to his bare chest, and with his arm in a sling. His curly gray hair seemed untended. As he came closer, he appeared to have a slight tremor in his head.

"It allright, Pop," the young man said. "He from the cable."

Wesley wondered if they were from New Orleans. The way he greeted him by saying "allright," and also something about the way he addressed the old man. He didn't know enough about Houston yet to know the characteristic mannerisms, but he definitely got a whiff of New Orleans here.

"Why he got to stand outside?" A woman's voice.

"I been hollerin' at you," the young man said.

The voice belonged to a young woman whose appearance made every word slide out of Wesley's mind. Struck dumb would be the phrase. Plaid slacks like the Catholic-school girls wore, and an over-sized blue sweatshirt that did not disguise her lithe body. She was slightly darker-skinned than the two men, but not by much, and her hair had been done in the lacquered, curly waves that were in fashion and which Wesley had never cared for. But somehow they looked correct on her. Her face was thin and smooth and her eyes were quick and intelligent and looked right into his. He felt like one of the butterflies he used to catch with his Uncle J, pinned to the board. Wesley stepped into the room at her apparent invitation, looking around.

"You *are* here to do the cable hookup, aren't you?" she said.

Wesley looked at her and thought to himself, You better wake up Wesley . . . "Yeah," he managed to say. "Where you wanted me to run it?" He looked at the papers in his hand.

"We want one line in here and another one into the bedroom in back. You can do that today?"

The old man made some croaking sounds, which the young woman seemed to understand.

"We don't know if he has a name, yet, Daddy. He been kind of quiet."

Wesley began to get a handle on himself enough to tell her his name, and then point to where it was sewn onto his Westco shirt, right there above the breast pocket, as if to say, It was apparent enough, wasn't it? He said, "You're Carol."

"Coral," she said. "Louis pronounce it like that when he wants to bother me. You thinking about putting a shirt on any time today, brother?"

The tall young man laughed, but he walked out of the room and came back a minute later wearing a shirt.

The installation was straightforward enough, and in the course of it, and after it, over some sweet tea in the kitchen, Wesley learned that the family was indeed from New Orleans, from Gentilly, and that they had lost everything, too. They had been in the Super-dome, then the Astrodome, and then they had gotten this apart-ment through FEMA. It was just the three of them; her mother had died years before. Before he left the house she had given him her cell phone number, and three nights later they went out to the movies.

Wesley was very guarded the first couple of times they went out, try-ing to make an impression, but his charm didn't seem to particularly impress her. He did notice that when he would tell her something about his uncle or mama her expression softened and she got warmer toward him.

She was different from Chantrell. Coral liked to ask questions, asked him about where he went to school, what he did before the hurricane. Chantrell liked to flirt and tease all the time, always playing

some kind of a game. Chantrell never asked questions; she just reacted. Her whole thing was based on how you reacted to her. That was
what was important to her about you. It wasn't as if Coral didn't like to
tease, she did. But she also, apparently, wanted to know who he was. It
tripped him out a little bit. But he liked it. Initially he liked it because
it flattered him. She obviously saw something in him she liked, and
when they started getting close physically there was a lot she liked.

At one point he said, "It kind of hard to know what you thinking a lot of the time."

"I'm trying to figure out what's important to you," she said,
looking at him with her eyebrows slightly raised.

It put him off balance. He had never bothered to ask himself
that question.

They had been going out for three weeks when something happened that changed things between them. They were driving to the
Galleria to shop on a Saturday afternoon; he had picked her up in
the three year-old Camry he had bought from Aaron's cousin with no
down payment, and they had come up to a traffic light and stopped.
In the lane to their right, a car with two young men in the front
seat. They were looking over at Coral and saying things, laughing. It
lasted no more than ten long seconds, but when the light changed
the other car turned left in front of them, cutting Wesley off and
heading down a side street.

Wesley immediately turned after them and sped down the street,
throwing his hands around as if he were in a video, cursing, saying,
"I'm going fire these motherfuckers up." Coral sat frozen, eyes wide,
and after a block and a half she shouted, "Stop the car." Wesley did
not stop. One more time, with a note of something final creeping
into her voice, "You stop the car."

Wesley braked hard and swerved to the side of the street, the
other car disappearing off down the block. "Why you stop me for,"
he shouted at her, gesturing with his hands.

"Don't you talk to me like that. Take me home," she said.

"I'm a man," he said. "You understand? I don't let nobody fuck over me. They were disrespecting you."

She stared at him. "Take me home," she said.

He threw the car into gear and did a U-turn and they drove back to her house without speaking. As they pulled up, he said, "What I'm supposed to do when somebody disrespect you?"

She got out of the car and started up the walk toward her door. He got out of his own side and shouted at her over the car roof, "What you want me to do?"

She turned around; he remembered the look on her face scaring him because she was so beautiful and he felt as if she was slipping away like a rope going through his hands too quickly for him to grab on to. "You figure out a different way of talking around me. Start with that. I don't care what some bustas in a car saying about me. I don't want to be with somebody don't know how to control themself."

Then she disappeared inside the apartment where she lived, and he stood there, stunned.

Later that night, unable to sleep, he called her cell phone. Lucy was long since asleep, and he was in his room, in the darkness. To his surprise she answered, sleepy, saying "Hello" more as a statement than as a question, which was how she did it. He liked the sound. But, hearing it, he was not sure what to say, the way he had been the first day he had met her. "It's me," he said. She didn't respond, but she didn't hang up either.

Okay, Wesley, what will you say now? What have you learned?

After a few moments, her voice: "You wake me up for that?"

"No," he said. "I just wanted to say you right."

She was quiet. Then she made a light grunting sound and said, "I know that."

He stifled the laugh her remark triggered. No use giving her all that much satisfaction. He couldn't help being impressed by her self-possession. "All right," he said. "So I know it, too."

"That's good," she said. They were both quiet for another few moments. "You gonna let me go back to sleep?"

"If I was there I wouldn't."

"But you not," she said. "Call me tomorrow."

Lucy brought her plate to the table in the dining alcove just off the pocket kitchen—stewed chicken and greens and sweet potatoes. Television going across the room, a procession of flashing, disconnected images. Wesley watched as he ate, still in his uniform from his day at Westco Cable. Lucy sat down and started eating her food. Once in a while she looked at her son, there, across the table from her in this strange city, Houston, in which they had made a provisional and—it had to be—temporary home.

His hair had been cut back into a neat arrangement and he wore a well-trimmed, super-thin, razor-cut mustache. When Lucy looked at him she still saw a boy, many years a boy, but becoming a man, no doubt. He put money into the house fund, did most of the shopping, had him a girlfriend, a New Orleans girl, who he met somewhere. Lucy liked her. Seemed like they were taking it slowly, which was good. He had not gotten another bike, for which she was grateful. He had one of the company trucks parked outside with all the equipment they used, cords and wires . . . but he was always handy. Didn't have to worry about it wasn't going to be there in the morning like back in the Nine. Went off to work in the morning just like a man. She thought about how strange it was that it had taken all this upset and dislocation to pull Wesley into focus. He was even finding time to coach a little football team of some displaced New Orleans boys. He was turning into a man. Sitting there watching the TV. She had apparently done something right with her life, somehow. She had made him. What she was supposed to do now, she wasn't exactly sure. She had been thinking about getting a high school equivalency diploma and trying to find something more interesting to do with her time than braid people's hair.

"You want some more Barq's, Wes?" she said, watching him.

"Nah, I'm all right, Mama," he said, watching the sports recap on the news.

She wouldn't have minded that, take some classes. SJ liked to read, and he had given her the book about da Vinci that everybody was reading, which Leeshawn had given him, but she gave up on it after a few pages, too hard to focus. She was trying not to drink and had been successful for several weeks.

A commercial came on and Wesley busied himself catching up on the cooling food on his plate.

"You want me to warm that for you?" Lucy said, watching her son.

"No Mama; I'm allright." He chewed, his leg jiggling, thinking about something, looking to see where any more meat was on the chicken. Then his leg stopped jiggling, as if something had occurred to him. She loved watching her boy, could watch him all day. To her surprise he looked right at her and said, "What's wrong, Mama?"

"Nothing wrong," she said, smiling slightly, looking at him. "Baby boy."

He examined the chicken again and she could see him go away again in his mind, the leg starting up. She didn't want him to go away again quite so soon, not quite so soon, and she said, "I was thinking to get a equivalency diploma. Get a high school diploma."

"You serious?" he said, eating, setting the bone back on his plate and smiling a little.

"Serious as a heart attack," she said, one of Wesley's favorite expressions.

"Where they got the course?"

"I don't know but I'm-a find out."

"You tell Unca J about that?"

"Not yet; it's something I'm thinking about is all." She got some sweet potato on her fork and put it in her mouth, slightly self-conscious, now, and it was Wesley's turn to watch his mother, his own mother, who had survived so much, and here they were together. After being almost sure they had lost each other. A pang in his chest, Mama, all those years of longing for her when she wasn't there, off on a long line someplace; how was it he never hated her, never stopped wanting her to see him, and be proud of him, and somehow knowing that she was, even nights when he had to put her to bed because she was too drunk to walk, a lot to ask of an eleven-year-old boy . . .

"I'll pay for it, Mama," he said, watching her.

"I don't even know where they have it yet," she said. She was quiet then, looking off across the room, somewhere in her mind, and Wesley watched her, sadness and love flooding in, and where did they come from, these emotions that he had kept at bay for so long? He was about to tell her that he loved her, but she spoke first.

"I'm proud of you, Wesley," she said, looking down at the table. "I'm so proud of you, and I know you going to be all right."

"I am all right, Mama," he said.

"I'm glad we together," she said. "I always wanted that, and . . ." she left off in mid-sentence. Wesley thought his mother might start crying. "I know I didn't do right," she said. "As a mother I'm talking about. I'm just glad I lived long enough to see you be a man."

Wesley looked down in his plate and pushed his fork under his greens; he did not know exactly what to do with what she had said. He ate the greens. For years he had heard his mother tell him, drunk, that she loved him, that she was sorry she was not a good mother, ask for his forgiveness. She had never used him as the brunt of her own demons. But hearing her, sober and present, express a deep feeling like what she had just expressed was nothing he was prepared for, and he didn't know where to put it, so he ate. Perhaps it triggered some buried and long-standing need he had had for her to be more present in his life, a need he had made some kind of peace with, pushed down, paved over . . . Was he a man, he wondered to himself? Like his Unca J? He was on some road of becoming, he was all stirred up and heading for something. He didn't know what his mother saw when she looked at him. He couldn't know. He knew she wasn't talking about just age.

Lucy looked across the table and found herself, or so it seemed, able to read this in Wesley's face, the body attitude; it cut her deeply, the awareness of all those years during which they could have been building to something more than this, although this was not nothing. But she looked at him across the table, as if he stood across a river on the opposite bank, and she wanted to tell him something that words alone can never give; she wanted to reach over to him and touch her boy again, make some kind of bridge backward across all the wasted, chaotic time. There in his shirt from work, watching the television. But, instead, she stood up and brought her plate to the sink and washed it, put it in the drainer, and prayed in her mind that they would find a place where they could live and she could see him become the man he needed to be, maybe grandchildren, but maybe be happy and find some love and stability; she knew she wanted to go back to New Orleans, it was all she knew, but she was not sure it was the right place for Wesley anymore. They would figure it out.

Then Wesley was wide awake in the dark, suddenly, with his heart racing, he thought it was a storm dream; he had had those. Rolled to his side and saw the glowing red numbers—3:48—the free fall of wondering where, or not even wondering, but an emptiness, a removal of the customary envelope. The dream, if it was a dream, slithering away, draining, seeping into the ground before he could catch any of it . . .

He sat up in bed. He had had the same sensation in Elba, at the Myerses's house, but now he knew where he was and he stood up, walked out of the room quietly so as not to wake Lucy—could it have been an intruder?—no lights on, just the barest film of silver gray in the less-than-total darkness through the drawn drapes as he made his way down the short hall past the bathroom and out into the living room, leaving aside to his right the end table he knew to be there, and then the coffee table and then his stride interrupted by something that made him stumble and twist to break his fall, and he knew even before he knew, reached out and touched what he knew to be her hip and he hollered out the word "Mama!" in the dark.

He scrambled forward to touch, feel if she was breathing, talking quickly to her, are you all right, felt for her hand, which was cold, so cold, and he had the presence of mind to stand up and run to the kitchen and call 911 immediately, shaking, and the light from the kitchen finding her misarranged legs on the living room floor as he told the dispatcher that his mother was dead, or dying, he couldn't tell, and gave the address, twice, and the phone number, said hurry, my mama going to die, hurry . . . and then hung up the phone as quickly as he could and went in to kneel on the floor beside her and feel to see if she was breathing, which she wasn't, and to put his arms around her and press himself against her as if it were possible to get back in the person who had given him a lifetime of such precious and imperfect love, to inhabit her as if such a thing were ever possible, and say, Oh no, Mama . . . Mama . . . Oh no . . . Mama, sobbing, there, on the floor, praying to bring her back just long enough to tell her just this, this thing he had no words for except I love you, and that would have been enough.

At the medical examiner's office, the pathologist, Dr. Gupta, told them—SJ, Wesley, Lucshawn, Aaron and Dot—that the autopsy showed evidence of a massive heart attack, quite possibly precipitated by the intense stress of the past weeks.

"We see this all the time," he said, as if to be reassuring, and with what SJ told himself was not a faint smile, and which, in fact was not, but rather a slight embarrassment. "So many from New Orleans. Stress is a killer."

"Were there preexisting conditions that could have had anything to do with it?" Leeshawn asked.

"Yes, yes; certainly," the doctor said, closing his eyes and nodding, slightly smiling. "There were clear signs of congestive heart failure. We could not retrieve the records from the hospital in New Orleans, of course, but I would assume she was on medications, perhaps that she was not taking regularly?"

SJ nodded, looked at the floor. Wesley looked as if he was in shock, which he was. There was not a lot more to say. The coroner asked where to send the body and Aaron gave them the name of their local funeral home. There, they asked Wesley if he had a strong feeling about whether Lucy should be embalmed or cremated, and he shrugged, his eyes dead, far off someplace. "I don't see why it makes a difference," he said. "She dead." Then as if remembering a question he wanted to ask, he said, "Did she say anything to you?"

"She said she didn't want to be buried here," SJ said. "She in fact said she didn't care which way, but that she wanted to go back to New Orleans."

In the end, they decided to have her cremated—the difference in cost was eight thousand dollars by the most conservative estimate— and SJ and Wesley agreed that they would take her ashes back to New Orleans, together, and put them someplace where she would have wanted them. Back somewhere in the Lower Nine.

25

It was still dark when SJ awoke in his apartment, alone, washed his face and pulled on the clothes he had laid out the night before. He opened a small duffel bag and threw in an extra shirt and some work gloves and walked downstairs and outside in the chill, dark air, across the parking lot of his apartment building and got into his car's cold driver's seat and headed out. It was November 10.

He was ready for this, he told himself. In fact, he did not know if he was ready, but he was going anyway. Before he could go with Wesley to bury Lucy, he needed to face it alone. He had told nobody about the trip, because he knew that Leeshawn, Aaron and Wesley would each want to go with him, each one for his or her own reasons, and this was a trip he needed to make on his own.

A half hour out of Houston the sky began to lighten, and he drove through the long reaches of east Texas with the sun coming up ahead of him. It was a bright morning by the time he crossed the border into Louisiana. The traffic slowed when he approached Baton Rouge, thickened and stayed thick until New Orleans.

SJ took the Franklin Street exit off the I-10, planning to drive down Franklin a few blocks and turn left on Claiborne heading for the bridge over the Industrial Canal, which divided the Upper Ninth Ward from the Lower Ninth Ward. But descending into the Upper

Nine from the interstate was a shock. From the I-10 he had passed the blue tarps on the roofs, the evidence, at a distance, of the cleanup and wreckage, but now it was as if he were riding a submarine into a shipwreck. The garbage everywhere lining the deserted streets, the grimy houses with the obscene brown waterlines on the shingles, the open doors like idiots' mouths, tongues lolling, vacant broken windows, the spray-painted signs on every façade indicating who had searched, and when, and how many bodies had been found. He had prepared himself as well as he could, but actually seeing it knocked you off whatever horse you happened to be on. He drove slowly down Franklin.

They were still not officially letting people back into the Lower Nine. Cleanup was being done on a large scale, and bodies were still being found. But he had planned to feel his way in. As he topped the Claiborne Bridge he could see the temporary repairs where the levee had burst, and just inside, a barge sitting at an angle. Beyond it, the Nine looked like a giant junk yard, spare parts or salvage, and the view folded up on itself as SJ drove down the other side of the bridge.

There was a checkpoint at the bottom, and a serviceman in camo approached his car as he rolled to a stop. SJ lowered his window; there were crews working, bulldozers, cats . . . SJ checked the stripes on the soldier's arm as he walked up to the car, gave a very small salute and said, "Good morning, Sergeant."

The young man bent down slightly to look in the window at SJ. Before the soldier could have a chance to tell him he couldn't come in, SJ spoke first.

"My house is on North Derbigny Street, and I'd like to do a short recon of it if I might, and secure some valuables I had to leave behind. I know it isn't procedure, but I drove in from Houston." SJ said, producing his driver's license with his address on it.

The young man looked at it cursorily, looked around him outside the car, looked back in at SJ. "You lived here?"

"Yes, sir. My house was still standing when I left."

"Veteran?"

"101st Airborne."

The young man nodded, straightened again and signaled to another soldier a block away, leaned back to SJ again and said, "You can proceed. I'd advise you to drive as little as possible because of the amount of debris still in some of the streets. If you pop a flat it's gonna be pretty difficult to get it repaired." Hint of a smile.

"I'll watch myself, Sergeant. Thank you."

The young sergeant tapped the sill of the open driver's window as SJ drove past and turned into what had been Reynes Street, waving at the other soldier stationed there.

Half a block in from Claiborne it was already too much to absorb.

This landscape could have been on the moon, or in some battle zone about which he had only read. The horizon was lower by exactly the angle of the houses that were no longer standing. The streets had been bulldozed to make way for the cleanup teams, and the division into blocks was still intelligible, although almost every trace of individual property lines had been effaced. Perhaps four houses still standing—somehow—between his car and the canal, and the very occasional tree. The rest of it reduced to shards, sticks, rags. A car upside down, tires in the air. A roof on top of a pile of rubble, a smashed floor fan . . .

Everything in the Lower Ninth Ward had been defiled. Mud, rust, dirt, and grit coated everything. If there was a hurricane fence it had been twisted, tortured into rusty chicken wire. If a roof had landed on rubble, it had been cracked at the peak like a wishbone. Sleeveless LP records, warped, cracked, perhaps the labels still readable as the Spinners, the O'Jays, Frankie Beverly. Door frames, cinder blocks, sheets and towels fouled with mud, the odd stuffed animal. The water had pushed one house halfway into the street at an angle, and its front wall had been torn out; inside it, the jumble of furniture and clothes, and a mud-coated chandelier, still improbably hanging above the sodden mess. Across the street, the cab of a semi, on its side, grill and windshield visible through the smashed window frames and weatherboards. Here and there a cement slab that had been a driveway, and nothing else. Three cement steps up into a nonexistent house. Exquisite ironwork, wrought into filigree for a gate or a railing, rusting now. Once in a while, like an ambush, he drove through an invisible cloud with a smell that made him want to be anywhere but there, an intolerable smell that spoke of a body not yet discovered, a smell that SJ remembered from the army, one you did not forget, ever.

He turned right, slowly, on what he knew to be North Derbigny. With each block heading away from the canal, the destruction was slightly less absolute. Certain blocks had as many as two or three houses, or structures still identifiable as houses, although these, too, had been defiled, windows smashed, car still in the driveway covered with debris, tree leaning into the smashed roof. In between the standing structures, avalanches of junk, parts of houses, everything that had been at the bottom of the lake he had paddled on two and a half months before. And over it all, the sky, lilting blue, treacherously tranquil.

SJ crossed what had been Forstall Street onto their block, and halfway down, standing exposed instead of nestled among other houses, was his house. Across the street, Bootsy's house presented a lobotomized face, a smudgy, greasy high-water line two feet below the peak of the roof, and smashed windows that revealed only a dark, unconscious interior. Next door to SJ's own house was the collapsed skeleton of Mrs. Gray's.

He pulled up in front; his house was missing most of its façade, and he could almost see into the wrecked interior over the small mountain of garbage that covered the driveway area. Above the roof of the front part of the house, set back, the front of the camelback with its open window, which he had last seen from the police boat, at eye level, and the greasy brown high-water line along the side of the house and, surprisingly, the sheets he had tied together to let himself down and get back out of the water still hanging down, browned and shredded but still knotted to the gutter pipe.

SJ turned his motor off and sat quietly behind the wheel for some moments.

The silence of the Lower Nine came flooding into his car, carrying with it the fact of where he was, as if the weight of the waters themselves were pushing him down into his seat. SJ decided to look at his dashboard for a bit, to collect himself. The steering column had a light film of dust on it, and SJ wiped off a line with his finger, then another.

This was right on the edge, he thought, of being too much. He struggled with the impulse to turn the key in the ignition and put the car in gear, drive off, don't look back. This was right on the edge, and he did not know if he could handle it. Right on the edge. But one thing that he did realize was that if he left at this point he would not be able to come back. He saw that quickly. It would be a burned bridge. Things were not settled here. Things were not settled inside himself. If he left without confronting it, he was defeated, and along with him his family, and the life he knew. He would be handing over the keys. That was clear.

He looked out the passenger window at his broken house. This was what he had left of a past. Leave without reaching back into it to see what was there, whether there was anything left to build on, and he might as well cash it in. He might be able to go on living in his brand-new apartment in Houston, but he would never know what the point was, or if there was one.

SJ closed his eyes and took a few deep breaths sitting there, behind the wheel. The air smelled bad, bad. Another breath, then, forcing himself, he opened his car door and put one foot out onto North Derbigny Street, stepped out and stood up in the fouled air under the brilliant sky. He shut the driver's door and walked around the front bumper, toward his house.

He needed to find a way over or around the unstable garbage that blocked his driveway. George's house, next door, was gone, nothing left of it. Mrs. Gray's house was a mountain of junk leaning on itself next to his house, barely distinguishable from all the debris piled next to it. Slats and weatherboard and wood and a box fan and someone's couch, upside down. Carefully, SJ picked his way over the wood, threaded together like pick-up sticks, testing each step before putting his full weight on it, holding on to some larger piece or, at one point, a Volkswagen that had lodged nose-down in the mess. It had all been pushed by the water, and then pushed by the bulldozers that were clearing the streets.

Because SJ had set his house back seven feet, all this junk sat where his curved driveway had been instead of being up against his house. He saw no evidence of his truck. Either it was buried under the garbage, he thought, or maybe the water had pushed it blocks away. After several minutes of painstaking climbing, testing, balancing, stepping, miraculously SJ found the cement steps leading up to his porch. At the foot of the steps, he knew, was the horseshoe he had laid into the cement when he put in the walk, but that was buried. The top two steps were not, however, and he stepped onto his porch—slippery, watch out—for the first time since the storm.

He stepped over some debris and through the torn-off front of his house into what had been the living room, which was no longer really a room but an annex of a garbage dump, a landfill with a ceiling. This was his first impression, before the individual elements began to make themselves visible. A place that had expressed life, turned now into its opposite, a place where time meant not growth but decay. All these objects that had once been endowed with life, now mocked. That was certainly the couch, which he had seen floating upside-down from the upstairs landing, come to rest against the side wall at the foot of the stairs. Plaster, curtains, smashed weatherboard, ceiling fan. On a built-in shelf across the room—two little vases, relics of Rosetta. How in God's name were they still there? He would retrieve those before he left.

A broom, plastic bottles, smashed blinds, curtains, bricks, pieces of plaster and more plaster, shards of Sheetrock, all mixed up together, on top of each other. Not a lot of floor exposed to walk on. Along the tops of the walls, mold spreading like camouflage, green, brown and gray and black kaleidoscopic tiny spots and large spots and clusters of spots. SJ climbed toward the stairs, stepped, almost slipped, stepped with small steps and one or two long ones, holding on. Near the bottom of the stairs, unmistakably, an ornate picture frame, a picture facedown. He reached for it and turned it over, and he recognized it as the photo of his parents taken at their twenty-fifth wedding anniversary party that he had kept on the television. The glass had been broken out; his mother was visible, if slightly obscured by water damage, standing sideways and looking at the camera with her hands out in front of her, holding hands with an invisible partner, his father; the paper had curled back from the frame, soaked, and his father was a grainy explosion of white and green mold. He set the picture back down on a pile of junk.

Carefully, SJ climbed the stairs, which were slick with scum until near the top, and then he was on the landing. He stepped into his bedroom, to the left, where he and Lucy had rode out the storm, light now, with the windows open as he had left them. Mold all over the rear wall, but not the other two. There on the floor was the duffel bag he had packed and never taken. The room was more or less just as he had left it. He had been worried about looting, but maybe prospective looters had decided to concentrate on areas that hadn't been so manifestly trashed. The area was pretty well patrolled by military and marshals, although nobody had yet challenged his presence there.

On the dresser, his father's watch and gold piece, wrapped in the handkerchief, just as he had left them. He picked up the duffel and was about to set it on the bed, which he had left bare after stripping it for the sheets that he had used to haul himself in and out of the water. He set the bag down on the floor, pulled up the blanket which had been bunched at the foot of the bed, pulled it even and folded it down at the top, grabbed the pillow from the floor and set it at the head. Then he set the duffel on the bed. Into it he placed the watch and gold piece, along with a few other things from his dresser, a tie clasp, a few linen handkerchiefs. He went into the drawer and retrieved the photo he had found on the morning of the storm, of himself and Rosetta at the nightclub in Texas. Then he sat down on the bed and looked around at his bedroom, the room he had shared with Rosetta, the room where he had slept for so many years. All his energy had deserted him suddenly, as if the power steering had gone out on him. He sat on his bed. He sat there for a long time.

After a while he was all right again. Across from him was the dresser, the framed photo of Rosetta. On the wall, the framed print of the man and the woman praying in the field at sunset. The rear window, which used to look out on the back of a house, now offered a view across Claiborne all the way to Holy Cross. The landscape had changed utterly, so ruined, so violated, so brutalized. And yet— this was an undeniable and strange music—sitting there on his bed in his room he felt a sense of comfort that he had not felt since the storm. Not in his new apartment in Houston with all the new things in it, not at familiar Aaron and Dot's, not at Leeshawn's. This was his place. Wounded so profoundly, but still there, somehow. The wound would bleed forever, perhaps, and when he thought of what was outside, and what it meant, it was too much to take in. And yet if he started from where he was at that moment, from where he was

. . . He could not quite get his hands around what he was feeling. But for the first time since the storm, except for that first time with Leeshawn (that was a good thing to remember), he felt that he was, somehow, in the present, instead of in a synthetic substitute for the present . . . That in itself was worth something, and maybe it was worth everything.

On the floor, his sneakers. And the floor lamp with the shade with the owls on it. Here was a center; here was his heart. He had no idea whether it was transplantable into another setting, nor of what he would do about it. But at least he had found it again. That it was still there at all was, undeniably, a miracle. He sat there and let himself be in that damaged heart, that bitter miracle.

Two hours later, with his duffel bag and some clothes and other items stashed in his car, SJ set off down North Derbigny and made the right turn at the end of the block, heading for Claiborne. Before he got to Claiborne, he stopped the car, threw it into park and put his head forward on the steering wheel. If you are there, he thought, let me know what to do. I will not question your motives, but let me see what to do, let me know it, and then I can go on, at least. He sat like that for a while. Then he opened his eyes again and headed out for the road back to Houston.

Dark. He reached for his watch on the nightstand, pressed the button for the blue glow. 5:12. He knew from experience that he would not fall back asleep, and he swung his legs over the side of the bed as quietly as he could and left her sleeping and closed the door behind him as he went down the hall to her kitchen.

SJ looked at all of Leeshawn's photos on her refrigerator under the bright fluorescent overhead light, including two different pictures of them together. The golden starburst clock on the wall and the jade plant on the windowsill.

He carried a glass of chocolate milk into her living room and sat on the sofa and closed his eyes. After a while he opened them again. The room was familiar enough—the glass coffee table on the white rug in front of the couch, the wooden hutch next to the television with her exercise tapes.

He needed his life back. He knew it sitting there, with all of Houston stretching off for miles in the dark, still asleep. He was in someone else's life, and a balance needed to be restored. Even a broken life of his own was better than a comfortable life that wasn't his own. Maybe later they could make a life together, a new thing. But first he needed to put his own life back together. He did not know what kind of future, if any, was possible in the Lower Nine, but if he didn't find out it would not be because he hadn't tried.

Once he knew this, he felt better. He drank the chocolate milk and sat there thinking until the sky got light outside.

26

Craig and Alice arrived at Gus and Jean's around two in the afternoon on Thanksgiving Day, after watching some of the Macy's parade on television. Peter Morehead had also invited them, as had their landlady, but Gus and Jean's was an obligation. The older couple had taken care of them when they needed it, and now they would spend the holiday with them. Craig and Alice took turns getting Annie and Malcolm dressed, which was not easy; Gus and Jean's was a landscape of recent pain, and Annie didn't feel well and Malcolm wanted to keep watching something on TV. But finally they got everyone corralled and into the car for the fifteen-minute drive.

Jean had bought little foil-wrapped chocolate turkeys for the kids, and had decorated the house with cut-outs of turkeys and pilgrims. ("I haven't had so much fun in years," she said.) She set the dining room table with their good china and water glasses and silver, and toward either end, facing out, she placed antique-looking candles in the shape of turkeys, which Jean said they had bought for their first Thanksgiving dinner after they were married.

There was all the usual flurry of activity on their arrival, the carrying of coats into the bedroom, the pouring of soft drinks for the kids, Gus saying, "Craig, you want something a little stronger than that? It's Thanksgiving . . . ?" Alice told Annie to get her little backpack and show "Mama Jean" her pictures from the Thanksgiving pageant. Gus made an abortive effort to box with Malcolm, who offered, instead, a Ninja Turtle from his pocket. "Now, what is that?" Gus said, squatting down and pulling his reading glasses out of the breast pocket of his flannel shirt.

Thousands of people from New Orleans had awakened that morning in hotel rooms in Pittsburgh, or Salt Lake City, or Phoenix, or in a cousin's house in Atlanta, or Chicago, or in an unfurnished apartment in Dallas on a rented bed, or Baltimore, St. Louis, Hot Springs, Nashville, Minneapolis, Seattle, Birmingham, Boston, Miami. They were the echo in the room, amid all that warmth, for Craig. He knew it was true for Alice, too, but she was better able to put on a game face. And yet, at the same time, he was glad to be there, embedded in this continuity. Their house had gone on the market and they had had one or two offers already, but Chuck Bridges had encouraged them to hold out for the asking price. Although he had made the decision, Craig still experienced attacks of grief, and even panic, at unpredictable times. But at least now he and Alice shared their feelings; they both expressed their doubts, they both expressed their ambivalence.

The kids played and colored while dinner was readying, and Alice helped Jean in the kitchen, and Gus and Craig sat on the couch in the living room, watching television. Craig had trouble knowing what to talk about with Gus, and so they sat there without talking except for occasional remarks on the football game. Craig had had to remind himself regularly how good the man had been to them, even though Gus was a Bobby Wise fan.

During dinner, Jean and Alice carried most of the conversation cheerfully, talking about the great job Annie did in the Thanksgiving pageant. Mr. Bourne had cooked up what Craig had initially thought of as a mishmash of more or less banal sentiments, delivered by the members of the carefully balanced multiracial cast, who stepped forward one by one to recite their words of thanksgiving. To his surprise, though, Craig found himself won over by the undeniable sincerity involved, and by Mr. Bourne's spoken introduction about Hurricane Katrina. And, more than that, Annie looked . . . radiant; it was the only word he could summon. She stood in the line in an orange velvet dress Alice had bought for her, and white tights, her eyes searching the audience. Craig gave her a surreptitious wave, which he saw her notice but not acknowledge, except with a smile. Then it was her turn, and she stepped out to center stage.

> *To say thanks for what we have is not enough;*
> *To give to others is the other part.*
> *Thanks go from hand to hand,*
> *But giving goes from heart to heart.*

She stepped back into the line of her classmates, grinning more broadly now that her lines had been delivered successfully. After the play, Annie was uncontainable, running and talking to the other kids backstage as Craig and Alice stood among the other proud parents, congratulating the children, and Mr. Bourne. Craig watched Annie. His daughter was happy—she was happy—and it brought a most bittersweet pride and happiness for Craig.

Now, at the Thanksgiving table, Annie recited her brief lines, again, to the applause of everyone. She looked up at Craig to check on his response, and he smiled back at her and gave her the thumbs-up, which she returned.

At one point, Jean suggested that they go around the table and that everyone talk about one thing they were thankful for. Alice started, saying she was thankful that they were all there together, and that they were all allright. Jean said, "Allie, I think you stole my answer, but I'd also say I am grateful that we have had a chance to spend time with all four of you, even though it's under such hurtful circumstances."

As he listened, Craig tried to figure out what he would say. He kept coming back to the question of what right did he have to be grateful, when so many other people had lost everything? Blessings seemed so arbitrary, and if you didn't deserve your blessing, how could you be grateful for it? Why had God been good to them and not to others? It didn't make sense . . .

Gus was up next. "I spent Thanksgiving of 19 and 52 in Korea," he began. "We had been there for maybe eight months I guess, at that point. And, you know, so many of your friends die when you are in a situation like that, or get injured, disappear, and you can wonder why you are still alive and they aren't."

Craig listened with a poker face, but his first impression was that the old man had somehow been able to read his mind. That was a little strange.

"We had a chaplain there with us, named Father Bill Joseph. He gave a blessing over dinner—it was so cold, and we were in a big Quonset hut—and there wasn't any kind of phone communication available, there was no cell phone back then, no e-mail; everybody was thinking about home and our families, and thinking about our pals who would never see their families again, and wondering whether we would make it home. Holidays are hard in the service; things you ordinarily train yourself not to think about, they're harder not to think about it during the holidays. Anyway Bill Joseph said, like he was reading our minds—but he was going through it, too, you see—he said, 'We don't know why we are here, and others are not. It's not just that we don't know; we can't know. People go away for reasons that make no sense, and we are left here. All we know is that's how it works; we can't know why. So the question for those of us who are left, is not why, but how—how do you use your time you have left, which you don't know how much it is. How do you want to live that time? Because that is the only thing you have any control over.' And I'll tell you, that made so much of a difference to every man there at those tables in that big hall. It was like he gave us back to ourselves, or . . . put us back where we needed to be. I don't know how to say it better than that." Gus stopped speaking for a moment. "So I'm thankful to Bill Joseph for that talk, and I am grateful to him every year, on Thanksgiving."

Craig sat looking at Gus, and in his mind he could almost feel the egg falling off of his own face. But you are not too old to learn something are you, Craig? It was as if one light on Gus had been switched off, and another, from another side, switched on. He would have stared at Gus for half an hour, pondering this, had it not been his turn to speak next.

He said, trying to keep his voice steady, that he was grateful to Gus for that story. And he was grateful for his beautiful family, and that they had come through the storm together, and that they would make it through this together.

"That's what I'm happy for, too!" Annie broke in, and everyone smiled, chuckled, and Jean began to get dessert ready.

Craig took the pause to step outside onto the porch in the smoky twilight and call Bobby's cell phone in New Orleans. Bobby and Jen were having Thanksgiving in the upstairs of their house-in-progress as Bobby called it. They had invited everyone from their circle of friends who was able to get back to New Orleans for the holiday, many of whom were living in Baton Rouge or Hammond and waiting to move back until school reopened in January—Doug and Connie, half a dozen of the families from Boucher, Derek was there (Gina was still in Memphis with the kids) and the drummer from the Combustibles, whose own father had drowned in the flood.

Bobby and Jen had in fact accomplished prodigies of work in the previous three weeks, although it would be months before they would be able to reclaim the first floor. In the meantime they had rigged up a makeshift kitchen upstairs, with a double hot plate and a rented mini-fridge; they used the bathtub to wash dishes. One lucky thing was that power had finally been restored in their area—their block, actually, since houses only three blocks away were still not hooked up to the grid; all over the city these kinds of inconsistencies drove the residents slightly mad even as they found ways of negotiating them and making the best of things.

For Thanksgiving, Bobby had told Craig that he was renting folding tables and using blue tarpaulins for tablecloths, in homage to the ubiquitous tarps people all over the city had used to cover as-yet unrepaired holes in their roofs. All the posters from downstairs, and any books that had been left on high shelves that could be salvaged, they brought upstairs and put in a special area, under a cheap print of Noah's Ark, pulled from a children's Bible they found at a flea market in Hammond on an afternoon escape from the city. To keep the dust from the gutting downstairs from seeping upstairs and coating everything, they had sealed off the first floor with hanging plastic secured with duct tape, leaving one hanging flap under which they would duck to ascend the stairs to their temporary quarters.

Out on the porch Craig punched in Bobby's number and stood looking up the street at the deepening blue sky behind the silhouetted houses and trees, lit here and there by a streetlight, the same time of evening that they had arrived at the same house not quite three months earlier. It smelled like fall; in the windows of houses he felt the warmth of light and the light of warmth, light from televisions pulsing against partly drawn curtains, all the familiar harmonies and rhythms of family life, of continuity, of reaffirmation. Craig heard the phone pick up.

"Thank you," Bobby's voice said, in the tones of a master of ceremonies. "Why? Because it's *Thanksgiving*." In the background, Craig heard a riot of voices, and some New Orleans R&B cranked up loud, yet distorted so that he couldn't recognize it. He instantly

felt a hint of vertigo on the contemplation of the bottomless distance separating that voice, those people, from him, on that porch, at that moment.

"Hey," Craig said. "Glad to hear you're in the spirit of the holiday." He hoped this sounded spry or ironic.

"Oh yeah," Bobby said. Then, his mouth away from the receiver, "Tell Jen the pie's gotta come out . . . Derek . . . Tell Jen to get the pie out." Then, back with Craig, "Microwave pie. Totally dubious experiment. How's Thanksgiving in the city of the big shoulders?"

"Quiet, man," Craig said. "It's quiet. But it's real nice. Alice's Aunt Jean and Uncle Gus made a real nice dinner, the kids are coloring on the living room floor . . ."

"Hey," Bobby said, "you gotta get them some coloring books. You can't just let them color on the floor . . ."

Craig recognized the music in the background—Big Boy Myles, singing, *"Well come on everybody take a trip with me . . ."*

"Hold on," Bobby said. "Here . . ."

"Hey," Jen said. "Where the fuck are you? This pie is a total disaster. Bobby made me make a pie in the microwave, and we were about to hit the button and Connie starts screaming, 'Take it out of the pie plate! Take it out of the pie plate!', like it was going to blow up the neighborhood . . ."

"Yeah—you can't put metal in there," Craig offered.

"I know that, goofball. But she scared me. You having fun watching Lawrence Welk?"

"I wish I was down there with you guys."

"No you don't," Jen said. "Bobby is singing along with the boom box. He can't sing; he sounds like a dog taking it up the ass."

"Thanks for that image," Craig said.

"Nothing you haven't seen before," she said. "I have to deal with this pie. When the fuck are you coming back home?"

"As soon as I can," he said. Then a wave of screaming, laughter, children screaming . . . Trying to keep Jen on the line for another minute, he asked, "How's Gertrude coming along?"

Her attention was elsewhere, though. "Oh shit," she said. "Bobby . . ." Craig heard a welter of voices, laughing . . .

Then Bobby's voice, laughing, mouth to the phone, "That pie was doomed from the start," he said. "I better go. You wanna say hi to Doug or anybody else?" Then, away from the phone, "Chloe . . . Chloe . . . Go help your mommy with the towels, okay?"

"Hey man," Craig said, "go deal with it, okay? Tell everybody I said hi. I'll give you a call tomorrow."

"Okay, man. It'll be a little calmer then."

After he hung up Craig stood in the brisk Midwestern autumn evening chill in his shirtsleeves, not yet ready to go inside. The life he heard over the phone was his life. But Alice, and Annie, and Malcolm were his life, too. He stood there for a minute, and then another, trying to get himself together, until he heard Annie's voice saying "Daddy?" and he turned to go back inside. Say thank you, he thought. Say it and keep saying it until you believe it.

At that moment, in Houston, SJ and Leeshawn were taking an after-dinner walk around the streets of Aaron's neighborhood. Music, the sounds of televisions and voices, were audible as they walked through the evening, along with voices and music from the backyards. A sadness had hung over the day that was exactly the size and weight of Lucy's absence. Camille and Melvin had flown in from North Carolina, and Wesley was there, and Jaynell and her two daughters had come over, too, along with Dot's widowed father. Aaron had cooked a fried turkey in the backyard, and Dot had made stuffing with sausage and sage in it, and yams with caramelized sugar and marshmallows, and cranberry sauce and mashed potatoes with garlic and cayenne, along with two pecan pies and a pumpkin pie, and this last made a postdinner walk of some sort absolutely necessary, unless you were Aaron, in which case you would sit on the couch with Dot's father and watch television while the women made noise cleaning up.

They had had fun early in the day, talking about SJ's parents, and times they had all had as children, and remembering Lucy, which added a heaviness to the edge of the mood, but they all knew how to give grief a place at the table without letting it run the show, although Wesley did have to leave the room twice, wordlessly, to return ten minutes later, silent but wanting to be there, in the middle of it, with his family.

After dinner, as they repaired to the living room and let dinner settle before dessert, Aaron said, "Wait a minute. I found these the other day," and left the room, thumping up the stairs to the bedrooms; he returned a minute or two later with a brown paper bag cradled carefully in his arms. "Look at this, J," he said. "I found this in the closet; I had forgot we had these. Your Daddy gave them to my Daddy."

On the kitchen table Aaron unrolled the heavy brown paper, reached into the bag and slid out a stack of old, heavy 78-rpm records. Everyone gathered around a little closer to see these artifacts of another era. SJ's father had been a great music fan; he loved the singers especially. He was a Billy Eckstine man, and SJ could remember that deep baritone from way back in his childhood, and the words *"I a-pol-o-gize . . ."* with that patented catch in Mr. B's voice between the syllables, coming out of their old record player. His Daddy loved Frank Sinatra, too, and a few blues singers. He wasn't much for instrumentals, unless it was something romantic like Gene Ammons playing "Canadian Sunset." Or he'd put a nickel in the slot to hear "The Masquerade Is Over" by Lou Donaldson if he was in a certain type of mood. But mostly it was the singers—Herb Jeffries doing "Flamingo," Al Hibbler singing "Ebb Tide" . . . that whole lost continent of smoky romance . . .

"Mahalia Jackson," he heard Camille's voice saying. "Daddy look at this."

SJ picked up the record his daughter had seen, a green label, Apollo Records, Mahalia Jackson singing "Didn't It Rain." SJ looked through the discs—the Famous Ward Singers, Dorothy Love Coates and the Gospel Harmonettes, the Pilgrim Travelers, the Caravans . . . He had never thought of his father as much of a gospel fan.

They brought the discs carefully into the den, where there was a forty-year-old wooden stereo console that could play records and still had the 78 speed, and Aaron took one of the records off the stack and looked at it before he put it on the turntable. "Mahalia Jackson," he said, to himself, but also as if he were seeing a photo in an album of a friend long gone.

They stood around as Aaron set the mechanism to 78 rpm and fit the disc over the spindle, and the automatic mechanism dropped the disc onto the turntable and after a moment a high hissing noise materialized, and some low organ notes. Aaron turned the volume up, and then the voice came out of the speakers:

Precious Lord,
take my hand.
Lead me on,
let me stand.
I am tired,
I am weak,
I am worn . . .

They stood silently, listening. SJ thought about his father, and his mother, and Rosetta, and Lucy. In that room with the people he loved around him, he also felt the presence of the others he loved, who were not there. Bury the dead, he thought, so they can live. It isn't enough just to survive; the ones who have gone have to survive, too.

• • •

SJ and Leeshawn strolled the evening streets of Aaron's neighborhood. SJ recognized that he wasn't ready to have a full-blown relationship with her. Leeshawn had been a source of strength for him after Lucy's death, she took care of details, brought food to the house, was a good and strong companion. And they had had fun, she had brought him back to life. But too many things had happened too quickly, and it was all going to take sorting out. He struggled to find the right words.

"SJ," Leeshawn said, looking at the ground as they walked, "I knew, in front, what you were dealing with. I went into it with my eyes open. I don't know how you managed the last couple of months."

"I managed because of you," he offered, quickly.

"Well," she said, "I know I helped out in different ways, but you been dealing with a lot of things that I couldn't help out with. And I seen you dealing with them. And I want you to know that you are the man that I thought you were." She fished a tissue out of her purse. "You even more. You a lot more, J . . ."

"I feel like I need to do this. It's not even that—I know I have to do this."

"I don't need convincing. And you going to do it. I know you need to deal with Rosetta's memory." She looked at him as they walked along. "Oh yes," she said. "I know that."

They hadn't talked much about Rosetta, and he was surprised that she had located that fact with such clarity. But more was involved than that, too. He had told her about the odd feeling of—peace wasn't the word; maybe comfort—that he had had sitting in his bedroom on his visit back, and she seemed to understand. "I need to prove to myself," he said, now, "that I can stand again."

"You will," she said.

"Allright, and it means a lot to me you saying that," he said. "I'm telling you . . . but I need to prove it to myself. I need to do that before I can move on."

She nodded, they walked. SJ remarked to himself, again, how she always surprised him by being stronger than he thought she would be. There was nothing she was saying that wasn't right. One of these days, after he had done at least some of what he needed to do, maybe if they could get through the next time period, maybe he would ask her to marry him. But he was getting ahead of himself . . . And he didn't want to say anything about the future that would make her hope for something that he wasn't a hundred percent sure of, himself, yet.

"Can we take it a step at a time is what I'm saying. Just see, see how time goes and what it does. Can you do that?"

She fished in her purse for another tissue. "Of course I can do it, J," she said. "If that's what you need. What else I'm going to do? I'm in love with you. What else I'm going to do?"

Craig and Alice drove back home along Wabash Avenue, with Annie and Malcolm asleep in the backseat, through the iron and steel heart of the country as it slowly readied itself for bed. All around them, off the side streets that led up from Wabash, and in the second-floor apartments along the avenue, where they saw people moving in the windows while they waited for the traffic light to change on the corner and the heater breathed warmth around their feet. Had they been in an airplane they would have seen, spreading around them across the suburban landscape and out into the countryside, twinkling diamond lights on the black velvet of the rolling land, and in the distance the glowing hive of the city, Chicago, and perhaps running lights from one or two adventuresome boats out on the lake. The traffic light changed, and they went on as the commercial strip dissolved into houses up on shoulders of land behind the sidewalks of Elkton, lights glowing warm in the windows they saw as they made their way home. Alice put her hand on Craig's leg and he took his right hand off the wheel to hold hers.

"Thank you for being so sweet today," she said. "I think it meant a lot to them that we were there."

"It was a nice day," he said.

Back home, they found a basket sitting by the front door, containing muffins and fruit, and a card from their landlady wishing them a happy Thanksgiving. Inside, in their warm apartment, they got Malcolm into bed, and got Annie into her pajamas, and they prepared coffee for the morning. Annie, not yet ready for bed, got out one of her books and curled up on the couch, so like her mom, Craig thought. They stashed the leftovers Jean had sent home with them, and then when things were put away and stable they made a movement in the direction of their customary evening television tableau. Alice brought a cup of tea into their living area, and Craig watched her walk to the couch and sit down next to their daughter and stroke Annie's hair, and Annie didn't stop reading. He looked at them there, his life.

Standing behind the couch, he quietly set down the TV remote and said, "How about if I build a fire?"

III

27

Some version of Mardi Gras has been held in New Orleans on the Tuesday preceding Ash Wednesday for almost two hundred years, the most famous expression of a tradition that goes back deep into pagan celebrations; a carnival, a farewell to the flesh. It kicks off the season of renunciation that precedes springtime.

There are many different Mardi Gras in New Orleans. There is the Mardi Gras of the large parades put on by krewes with hundreds of members, and there is the Mardi Gras of the small marching clubs with a couple dozen members, who parade around the quiet streets of their own neighborhoods. There is the day of families who stake out a spot along a parade route, and the day of individuals and couples who strike out for the unknown early in the morning and have no idea where they will finish the day. There is the day of the Mardi Gras Indians, and the day of the tourists and sybarites, gay and straight, who flood into the French Quarter. For some, it is a day of tightly scripted ritual, culminating in a masked ball, but for most, the day represents the spirit of improvisation itself. On Mardi Gras, you go where the day takes you.

In the months after Hurricane Katrina, New Orleans was deeply split over whether to hold Mardi Gras that February. Bodies were still being found in attics and under rubble. Many asked whether it wouldn't send the wrong message to people outside the city. Would it say that things were now okay, when everyone knew how far things were from okay? Or, worse, would it send the message that New Orleanians didn't know the difference between okay and not-okay?

For tens of thousands who couldn't make it back home, the question was, How could they have Mardi Gras without us? For the hundreds who had seen loved ones die in front of their eyes and seen their communities destroyed, the response was not linear at all. The sound of celebration assaults a grieving heart. The city had already said farewell to enough flesh for one year. The timing was wrong.

Others, just as passionate and often grieving just as much, felt differently. For longer than anyone alive remembered, New Orleanians had danced at funerals. It was an obligation on those who were still alive to restate the resilience of the human spirit with wit and style, to be present, to answer when called, even with tears running down your face. If you lost your ability to dance in the face of death or trouble, then you lost everything. The point of holding Mardi Gras, they argued, was not to show the world that the city was okay. Mardi Gras was for the people of New Orleans, to prove to themselves that the spirit was not dead.

And there was another factor: the city was broke. The tourist dollars on which New Orleans depended had slowed to less than a trickle in the preceding months. The images that had gone out around the world needed to be replaced with the familiar good-time images that drew tourists. Or so thought many of the city's business leaders, who were the engine behind the large-scale city-wide Mardi Gras in the first place. In any case, for reasons high and low, the city went ahead with plans to hold Mardi Gras.

There were changes designed to adapt the celebration to the city's reduced resources. The season, which usually lasts three weeks, would last one week. Parade routes would be altered and shortened to allow an overextended police department and emergency response teams to cover the routes. Endymion, one of the largest parades, which usually ran through still-devastated Mid-City, would run instead along St. Charles Avenue. Zulu, the city's great black parade, which rolled on Mardi Gras morning, would be shortened drastically, and would end, in supreme irony, near the Superdome, where many of its members had spent the longest week of their lives six months earlier. Every group had to adapt to something, and the city had to play it by ear. Nobody knew what would happen, or whether people would come. But Mardi Gras was on.

And New Orleanians came, from all over the country, by plane and by car, by minivan and bus. From Houston and Atlanta, from Dallas and Chicago and Memphis and Pittsburgh and St. Louis. They made elaborate costumes in friends' and relatives' kitchens and brought them to town in the trunk of a rented car. They flew in from Albuquerque and Salt Lake City, Baltimore and D.C. and Detroit. They stayed in the hotel rooms that were available, they stayed in friends' guest rooms, on couches, on inflatable mattresses and futons. Or they camped out in their own houses, with the mold on the walls, or the blue tarpaulin covering the holes in the roof. They stayed on the second floor, they showered at a friend's house across town. They made do, they figured out a way. And when they ran into each other for the first time since the storm they embraced and heard as much of the other's story as they could stand, saying, you are still here. You are still alive, the old New Orleans funeral message. The insistence upon the life that is left, the reminder of how finite it all is, how bitter and precious.

How, Craig wondered, did the rooms get so big?

It was, improbably, Mardi Gras morning again. The next day, March 1, the nice young white family who had been forced out of their Lakeview home by the flooding would technically take possession of his house, although they were allowing him to remain there through that morning.

Craig had arrived in New Orleans the previous Thursday and had spent the weekend boxing up a few last things, cleaning, sweeping, and vacuuming up the final evidence of his life in New Orleans. In the evenings he went to parades, had dinner with Bobby and Jen and Doug and Connie and their kids.

He was there alone. Coming down would have meant missing a couple of days of school for Annie and Malcolm. More to the point, Annie was involved in the spring play, and there were rehearsals for it, and Alice needed to be there, and Malcolm didn't want to leave, and so Craig was back in New Orleans for Mardi Gras, alone, as he had been years long before. As it had been years before, there was no necessity in the day, only possibility. But possibility had meant fullness to him in years past; now possibility felt like emptiness.

It was amazing, for example, how long his living room seemed without the couch bisecting it, and without the art on the walls, and with no rugs on the hardwood floors. All of it was currently appearing at Spotlight Storage in Skokie, where the 12-x-15 storage room felt very cramped indeed. Boxes of toys on top of the couch, comforters piled on top of bicycles, boxes of books, boxes of records and CDs, boxes of photo albums and clothes.

The Big Ugly Lamp was up in Skokie, too, along with the television and the beds from upstairs and the folding-leaf hall table where the Big Ugly Lamp had sat, and the kids' toys (some of which, dormant for months, had been sold surreptitiously at their giant two-day-only tag sale). The picnic table and benches had been sold at the tag sale, along with the four high stools that had sat around the kitchen counter and the tiki lamps from the backyard. Craig had hung on to the strings of chili pepper Christmas tree lights that they used for cookouts; he planned to put them around the ceiling in his home office in Elkton, like a crown of thorns.

The framed ad for Hadacol, the 1940s patent medicine, was gone from the maroon wall in the downstairs bathroom. The keeper plates, glasses, and silverware were long gone, and a giant dark green garbage bag slumped in the kitchen, partly full of the take out Styrofoam plates and Chinese food containers and bags from the deli on Adams Street that had sustained Craig as he cleaned up the last of the house's detritus—the rolls of packing tape, ninety percent spent, here and there, lying abandoned in this or that room. Upstairs, the futon where he slept (earmarked for Bobby and Jen's future guest room, made up for the weekend with borrowed sheets), and the towel and washcloth.

Doug had come over on Saturday to help, as had Bobby. Craig was festooned with offers of bedrooms and hospitality for all subsequent return visits in perpetuity, but the knowledge that he would be returning only as a visitor, outside looking in, weighed him down. It was easier to accept the logic from a distance—the disappeared hospitals, the environmental concerns, the fractured community, the corrupt city leadership, an epidemic of suicides and the resurgence of crime, the dicey odds on future hurricanes and proper levee rebuilding . . . He had gone over all the reasons why they were doing what they were doing, a hundred thousand times in his brain. But it still made him sad, and he still struggled with it.

It was Mardi Gras now, though, and Craig planned to get into the spirit and act like a New Orleanian. He had already been out to grab a double latte at his coffee shop on Magazine Street—the PJ's on Maple Street hadn't yet reopened—and even though his heart wasn't in it he had cobbled together a cowboy outfit with a hat and arranged a holster out of a belt and one of Doug's kids' spare toy police revolvers. He had bought an eyebrow pencil at Walgreens, finally open again, and had given himself a desperado mustache. At least I can get out in it, he thought. Doug and the kids were hooking up with the Krewe of St. Anne, and Craig figured he would see them later in the afternoon in the Quarter. Bobby and Jen were supposed to meet him at Igor's on St. Charles Avenue just off Jackson Avenue for the Zulu parade, their standard place for Mardi Gras morning. It was Mardi Gras. He would make a good showing of it.

Before he left for the drive down to Washington Avenue, which was where he parked every year, except usually with Alice and Annie and Malcolm, walking the rest of the way down St. Charles to Jackson, he stopped into the upstairs bathroom to relieve himself. The bathroom counter was bare, the shower stall bare and the medicine cabinet empty. All the foliage of shampoo bottles and razors and soap and drying towels was gone. That was what was weird, the defoliation, like a body with no hair. On his way to the john, Craig saw himself in the mirror and stopped and regarded the person he saw in the glass. His costume, he thought, in so many words, looked like shit. The holster looked lousy, not like a holster at all but like just what it was—a belt—and the toy police revolver, instead of looking like an intentionally funny replacement for a cowboy's six-shooter, looked like just what it was, a dumb replacement, part of a last-minute costume. He looked his fake-mustached self in the eye, under the brim of the ridiculous cowboy hat.

"Fuck you," he said, out loud. His voice sounded inappropriate in the empty house. He was sorry he had spoken, but that didn't mean he hadn't meant it. After the months of hating Alice and hating Borofsky and hating the government, it came down to this: he hated himself for leaving. He knew he was in an impossible situation, he had been through it all a thousand times, and his family had to come first. It would take a long time to sort it all out. But in the meantime, Craig unbuckled the "holster" and threw it down in the hall, took off the hat and skimmed it to land

on top of the holster, and rubbed his hand along the sliver of soap
left in the small indentation to the right of the sink and worked
the mustache off as well as he could. He would attend Mardi Gras
as himself. Warts and all.

Mardi Gras day was starting. Costumed riders, getting ready all over
the city since before dawn, were mounting spectacularly decorated
floats for Zulu and for the Rex parade, the final official parade that
caps off the festivities. Canal Street was packed with people waiting
for the parades behind police barriers, the crowd slightly thinner
than in years past, but still vibrant, drums in the distance.

Along St. Charles Avenue, heading uptown from Lee Circle,
the morning light filtered through the giant oak trees that shaded
the street and the houses, and here and there the light caught the
smoke from hibachis and grills where people were cooking and
the sunlight made the smoke glow blue as it rose. The night before, people had dragged couches and beach chairs out to the
grassy neutral ground that divided the avenue and cradled the
streetcar tracks, and now they sat out there, or stood behind grills
cooking food, or on couches watching battery-powered televisions, drinking beer, under the canopy of giant oak trees with
strings of beads dripping from the branches, caught there, and on
power lines, like multicolored icicles, snagged from a wild throw
during a week's worth of parades. The people walking down the
middle of the downtown-bound side of the avenue—individuals, couples, groups of free-lance celebrants dressed as Hawaiian
dancers, or wrapped in blue tarpaulins in homage to the tarps
that covered so many roofs, or dressed as chefs or nurses or nuns
or as anything you could imagine—crunched strings of beads un-
derfoot, the castoffs of the weekend's parades, past the big houses
that lined the avenue.

Craig was one of them, having parked up on Prytania Street by the cemetery just beyond Washington Avenue. He made his way toward Igor's, just off the corner of St. Charles and Jackson, to meet Bobby and Jen for their traditional Mardi Gras morning Bloody Marys. As he approached Jackson, where the Zulu parade would make its big turn onto St. Charles for its run toward downtown, the crowds thickened, pressing up against the police barricades, and police sat on horseback in the middle of the intersection, but Craig was able to walk across Jackson Avenue to the corner with the grocery store, and squeeze through the crowd along the barricade and make his way to Igor's without much trouble. Off in the distance he could hear the sound of drums from some marching band.

Inside Igor's it was dark but not impossibly crowded. He looked around for Bobby and Jen and didn't see them, ordered himself a Bloody Mary and brought it outside and stood on the sidewalk watching the people walking back and forth in the middle of St. Charles Avenue, under the electric wires hung with beads, people looking out from balconies on the ugly apartment building across the avenue. It was a miracle that this was happening again, he thought. The insistence on reasserting the spirit in the face of such pain and destruction. On Mardi Gras morning the world always felt new again; you could imagine yourself setting foot in the new world one more time, when everything was up for grabs . . .

"What are you, a fucking zombie?"

The familiar voice; he turned and there was Jen and, behind her, Bobby.

"We've been standing right next to you for the last half hour," she went on. "Drink that Bloody and get another one."

Greetings, happiness, taking stock. Bobby and Jen had not bothered to go see Pete Fountain and had in fact heard that he hadn't even shown up this year. "Can't blame him," Bobby said. "His whole house got trashed. I'd be depressed, too."

"Your house did get trashed," Craig said.

"Yeah, but I have an upstairs."

"And also we're not, like, a hundred and fifty years old like Pete Fountain."

They looked around the corner, at all the familiar press and jostle of people, the trees above, the clopping of the police horses, the people squeezing by. None of it had been guaranteed. Craig had promised Annie that he'd get her a Zulu coconut. Every year, the most prized throw at Mardi Gras was one of the coconuts that the members of the Zulu Social Aid and Pleasure Club, the city's largest and most prestigious African-American social club, spent weeks painting with their colors, black and gold, sometimes with a face painted at one end, and always with a big letter *Z* or the word *ZULU*, often spelled out in glitter. In the old days the members of the club threw them from the floats but the projectiles became a public health hazard, and finally they were forced to hand them down from the floats, which always created a big crush. Craig always carried Annie on his shoulders up to the floats, and invariably she would be handed at least one coconut by a smiling Zulu member smoking a giant plastic cigar.

Zulu had lost more than a dozen members between drownings and health complications from being in hospital during evacuation, or going weeks without necessary medication or treatment. The decision to parade had been difficult, but ultimately those who saw it as necessary to their own part of the community, a reassertion of spirit, of defiance, won out, and Zulu was rolling again. As always in years past, the members—black doctors, businesspeople, lawyers, judges—donned big black Afro wigs and grass skirts, put on blackface, and hit the streets in a brazen caricature of the stereotypes projected on their community. It was a tradition going way back, a lampoon of the mask of primitivity assumed by the black doctors and lawyers and businessmen and merchants and skilled laborers of the city. Zulu was many New Orleanians' favorite parade, and almost all of black New Orleans turned out to see it. It came down Jackson Avenue though the heart of one of the main black neighborhoods.

The members, many of whom were now without a home, had come in from Houston, or Little Rock, or Atlanta, or Memphis, or any one of dozens of other places. It is one thing to celebrate when you have a house to go back to and a dinner waiting, when your world is in place, and you can look back to years before, and ahead to years to come, with something like a reasonable expectation of continuity. It is another thing to celebrate when you have lost everything—your house, your neighborhood, your possessions, your family members—and you are living in a strange place, cut off from everything familiar to you, amid the continuity of other people's lives. To comport yourself with a defiant grace when your life has been pushed to the edge, and then over the edge.

Craig, Jen and Bobby walked up Jackson on the uptown side. Several blocks from St. Charles the police barricades disappeared, and you could actually approach the floats when they came, which was necessary for getting a coconut. They ran into Ted from the bookstore, and Jason in the Zorro outfit that he wore every year. People, most of them black, lined the sidewalks, lined the curbs, stood on steps or porches of houses with roofs still covered with blue tarps. Police cars, the leading edge of the parade, inched their way toward St. Charles.

Then the parade came, accompanied by the din of marching bands not quite out of earshot of one another. The floats loomed over the crowds as they approached, spewing beads and trinkets into the air from both sides, and the Zulu members looked down from above the heads of the screaming supplicants who pressed close to reach out for beads, for coconuts, for spears and tambourines and stuffed animals. Many of the floats had two levels, and the Zulus on the upper level would be busy untangling strings of beads from the bags and tape in which they came packaged, and others, next to them, would be taking aim and throwing balled-up strings of beads to people waving on balconies and porches, or to children on their parents' shoulders. In between floats, marching bands passed, serious-faced, twirling their instruments or doing tricky choreo-graphed steps, and drum majorettes with batons, and people along the route bounced in place, or stood looking up and down the street, or drank from plastic cups up on steps with friends and neighbors and family who, in many cases, they had not seen for months. The sun shone down on them all, and once again, as improbable as it seemed, Zulu was rolling through the streets of New Orleans.

A contingent of actual Zulu tribesmen, from Africa, had been invited to march with the parade this year, and they passed, in tribal dress, dancing and leaping into the air barefoot.

"Some orthopedist is gonna make a lot of money off of this," Jen said.

"Look at those guys," Craig said.

As each float approached, Craig, along with much of the rest of the crowd, swarmed into the street to beg for a coconut. Finally, after half an hour of hollering "It's for my daughter," Craig was handed a coconut by an unsmiling black police officer who had been handed three himself. Craig thanked him abjectly and placed the prize in his backpack.

Around ten, Bobby, Jen and Craig left Jackson Avenue and walked a few blocks uptown on Dryades Street to see the Wild Mag-nolias, Mardi Gras Indians who always came out near the old H&R Bar, which had burned a few years earlier but still served as a meet-ing point for the Indians on Mardi Gras morning. As soon as they were off of Jackson Avenue the day became quieter, individuals and groups of two or three here and there, walking through the beautiful morning in the ruined streets.

Everyone who loved New Orleans street culture wondered about the fate of the Indians, and their elaborate costumes. The word had trickled back that members of the Wild Magnolias had been working on their costumes at Houston's Astrodome during the evacuation, a vote of confidence in the future if ever there was one, but it was hard to confirm.

The Wild Magnolias always appeared from inside the H&R, hollering Indian patois, showing their feathers and plumes, and the beadwork on the suits that they had spent most of the year creating. Little by little, their Big Chief, Bo Dollis, would marshal them all together and they would start off down Dryades, with Chief Bo chanting one of the Indian songs accompanied by drums and tambourines, and the whole gang shouting back the antiphonal response. But since the H&R was a burned-out shell, and most of the nearby houses were presumed to be unlivable at the moment, how would they make their entrance onto the street?

They had their answer not long afterward. Near the corner of Dryades and Second Street was a pretty good crowd of the faithful. The bar on the corner, which had taken over from the H&R, dispensed drinks and pork chop sandwiches and barbecued chicken, and there, parked along the curb, was a giant U-Haul truck, inside of which the Wild Magnolias were getting dressed. People black and white milled in the street, in and out of the bar, eating pork chop sandwiches and sausage sandwiches and drinking beer. Members of a brass band had gathered, and tambourines and drums kept up a background rhythm to it all, like a low flame under a chafing dish. Craig and Bobby and Jen stood with everyone else, greeting friends and enjoying the scene, when suddenly a cheer went up as the back of the U-Haul opened and Bo Dollis, Jr., son of Big Chief Bo, appeared in a bright pink suit, shrill feathers ballooning out the opening of the truck and catching the morning sunlight, hollering to the gathered crowd. Bo himself followed, in white, an explosion of white, feathers and plumes and beadwork and Mrs. Dollis came out in blue, carrying two large feathered fans with appliquéd letters reading WE ARE BACK! and I LOVE N.O. They greeted members of another gang, the Golden Comanche, who had appeared from way down Dryades Street.

Slowly, after greetings, and homage, and picture taking, the Indians began readying themselves to head out through the streets, like a cruise ship casting off and beginning to maneuver slowly backward out of the dock, and they sang to the rhythm of the drums and beer bottles and tambourines, a variation on the traditional Indian songs, the Chief, or sometimes a designated temporary replacement, making up rhyming lines, and the rest of the gang and the people following responding with a repeated answering line, new ones for this year after they had come back against the stiffest of odds . . .

An ace, a trey, a deuce and a jack
> *Shallow water, yo mama*

Well I been in Atlanta but I made it back.
> *Shallow water, yo mama . . .*

The hell with the wind, the hell with the rain,
> *Shallow water, yo mama*

Indians dance in a hurricane.
> *Shallow water, yo mama*

Jump up and down and run all around;
> *Shallow water, yo mama*

We bad motherfuckers from way uptown
> *Shallow water, yo mama*

Well I don't know, but I been told
> *Shallow water, yo mama*

Some like to rock, but I like to roll
> *Shallow water, yo mama . . .*

I said way out in Houston all back o'town,
> *Shallow water, yo mama*

The Wild Magnolias, they don't bow down
Shallow water, yo mama

And they went off down the street, into the heart of Mardi Gras Day.

SJ and his group had come in on Saturday in two rented minivans— SJ, Wesley, Leeshawn, Wesley's girlfriend Coral and her father and brother, Lucy's friend Jaynell and a couple other evacuees. They had spent Mardi Gras morning watching Zulu near the corner of Jackson and Dryades, in the yard of one of his crew members, Charles, who was back living in New Orleans. SJ had set up the big Weber grill he had brought from Houston (his oil drum was a casualty of the storm) and they had put out the call to everyone they knew; Lester and Ronald from his crew were coming, and Shawnetta, in from Atlanta, and SJ's friend Alfred, whom he had last seen at the cookout for Little T. Jaynell had her two pretty little daughters with her, and Charles rigged up a butterfly net for them on a long pole so they could catch beads from the parade. SJ had pork chops, sausage, and hamburgers ready to go once the fire started rolling, and hotdogs for the kids.

Around one in the afternoon, after Zulu had passed, they packed up and drove to Loyola Avenue and Poydras Street, like hundreds of others, to wait for Zulu to finish, dismount, and continue the parade on foot. SJ parked the van in a nearby lot. SJ, Wesley, Coral, Alfred, Lester, Jaynell, her two daughters and Leeshawn got out and quickly ran into people they knew, except for Leeshawn, who sipped her Crystal Mist and stayed close to SJ. With Wesley's help, SJ set up the coolers and some folding chairs on the neutral ground, and he handed out cans of soda to people. All around he saw people he knew either from the Lower Nine or from work, other contractors, people he had done work for, old crew members. Everyone wanted to know how everyone else had made it through, where they were staying, whether they were returning.

The first Zulu floats began to arrive near the Superdome not long afterward, and the riders dismounted and milled around near the corner of Loyola and Poydras. The area began to fill with the Zulu riders still in their makeup, and their families and friends and well-wishers. The plan was to continue the parade, on foot, across Basin Street and into the Treme neighborhood, the oldest black neighborhood in New Orleans, and one of the oldest in the United States. They would wait until the last float had arrived and the riders had disembarked, wearing black T-shirts and wigs and grass skirts. Many had the letter *Z* painted in gold or silver on their cheeks, in imitation of war paint, or tribal scars. Some wore leopard-print vests and top hats, and one rider wore a T-shirt that read KATRINA DIDN'T WASH AWAY OUR SPIRIT. Members of the various marching bands stuck around, as well, and the sound of drums and horns could be heard, nearby and at a distance.

One of the brass bands, Cool Bone, was warming up, and the trumpeter began playing something funky, a repeated riff over a second-line beat, the New Orleans beat, and people started dancing in place, on the sidewalk, on the neutral ground, in the middle of Loyola Avenue. A Zulu member wearing a sash, white tie, and tails hollered for things to get started and the word got relayed to the members. Dignitaries were climbing into a series of convertibles. It was approaching two o'clock.

SJ thought about his own father taking him to the Zulu parade when he was a boy, back when the parade route was utterly unpredictable. They didn't have to have a mapped-out route in advance in those days, and the parade could go anywhere it wanted to. It seemed as if they were getting ready to have a throwback to that, now—Zulu on foot, with no map. So many gone. So many not able to be there, alone somewhere, or dead . . . And yet, yes, so many still here, too.

He was still here. Next to him Leeshawn, Wesley, and the rest stood watching in respect, each thinking his or her own thoughts, as the band started playing in earnest, and the first of the red convertibles began moving slowly down Loyola in the direction of the Treme, and all the members slowly started walking in that direction, as well. The band was playing "L'il Liza Jane," and people were cutting great second-line steps as they passed by. *"Hey pretty baby, can we go strolling? / You got me rocking when I ought to be rolling . . ."* and wordlessly, with little more than a glance around, SJ and Wesley, Coral and Leeshawn and Albert and Jaynell and her daughters, all stepped off the curb and into the river as it moved, dancing, down the street, in the heartbreaking afternoon sun, some of them dancing and some of them just walking in time, shaking hands with a friend as they moved along, sometimes arm-in-arm with someone they found themselves next to, whether they had known them personally or not—hundreds of them, down Loyola toward Basin Street, concentrating on being alive, in that moment, while they could.

Craig had made his way alone down to the French Quarter, across Canal Street and the tail end of the Rex parade. Bobby and Jen had cashed it in after walking with Craig behind the Wild Magnolias for about half an hour. Finally they decided to head home and Jen had given Craig a surprisingly emotional hug. Beyond that, they had kept it pretty short, as goodbyes went, agreeing that they would all see each other again before they knew it. Craig would be back within a month for a follow-up article. Still, after they parted the bottom dropped out of Craig's mood, and he walked for blocks fighting back tears.

In the Quarter, he went to an address that Doug had given him on Royal Street, but he knew nobody there, and he left. He then headed for Jackson Square to see if he could find the Krewe of St.

Anne, one of the walking clubs. Along the way, he ran into half a dozen people he knew. Some were back in New Orleans, some were stuck someplace else but were rebuilding, some had left town but had made it back for Mardi Gras.

He found the Krewe of St. Anne in Jackson Square, a mob of life-sized walking African dolls, harlequins, people in bird masks, women in pink ballet skirts with home-made moth wings attached to their backs. Several members had wrought ingenious variations on the ubiquitous blue tarpaulin theme, and one man walked in a suit, his entire body, flesh and clothing alike, painted silver from head to foot. There were nuns, there were Catholic schoolgirls, there were nurses in fishnet stockings, there were cowboys, and men with curly green wigs on, and everyone was smiling and laughing. Two people had dressed themselves up like matching bottles of Tabasco Sauce, and three people calling themselves the Krewe of Pew had dressed as moldy refrigerators. Others wore hazmat suits and respirators in homage to the mold specialists and disaster relief personnel.

After a while, Craig cut through Jackson Square and down Decatur Street to Rosie's to see if any of his reporter buddies were there. As he walked in, he heard—astonishing—the voice, admonishing someone, hilarity, hollers; music outside, people crowding to get a drink, on line for the bathroom, and the voice, saying "This is the Tap Root. We inhabit a bottomless well of scotch that descends to the deepest precincts of creation . . ." Serge sat at the bar in a purple satin jester's outfit, complete with three-pointed cap and sparkles on his face, surrounded by three women in ballet skirts and a guy wearing a gas mask.

"Shit!" the gas mask guy said, pointing to Craig, "that's the scariest costume I've seen all day."

"Craik!" Serge said. "This isn't a come-as-you-are party!"

"It is this year," Craig said, smiling.

"You might scare some little kids with that mask you got on," Dave said, pulling off the gas mask.

"I got to tell you," Craig said, "I saw you guys on the news up in Chicago, sitting here."

"We never left Rosie's," Serge said. "I was going to run out and grab one of those mules so that I would have transportation but they put a lariat on me and made me sign a release form and so I was bereft of my steed."

"That wasn't a lariat," Dave said. "That reporter was grabbing for your nuts."

"Dave is still haffing a midlife crisis and his mind secretes these fantasies the way your auditory canal secretes ear wax."

"That's disgusting," one of the ballet skirts said.

"Not really," Serge said, looking at Craig. "She thinks she is in love with me."

Nobody asked him about his house or his plans, and that was just fine with Craig. Music was playing and everyone was drinking, and this had once been his life, too. He stood there, warmed by it all, for perhaps twenty minutes, until he felt a sadness settling on him and he left as quietly as he could and started walking up Decatur Street again. He wanted to touch all of this and stay in it; he didn't want to leave town, these streets that had been his for all these years, all this life. The sand was running out of the hourglass.

He walked past the end of the French Market and up toward Café Du Monde in the distance and finally back into Jackson Square, feeling, stupidly, as if he were looking at it through a glass wall. Knowing that he was leaving was driving a wedge between him and experience. That, and not having Alice and Annie, and Malcolm . . .

In Jackson Square he checked the time—2:30—and thought he might try calling Alice; she ought to be picking Annie up at school right about then. He found a bench near the statue of Andrew Jackson, sat down and punched in the number.

"Hey," came Alice's voice. "How's it going?"

How's it going? Craig thought. How is it going?

"It's Mardi Gras time in Old New Orleans," he said.

"I know, I've been thinking about you all day."

That was nice to hear.

"Somebody wants to talk to you. Here, sweetie," she said, her mouth away from the phone, and then he heard the voice that he loved most in all the world.

"Daddy! I got an A on my painting!"

"That's great, sweetie," he said. He heard Alice saying something in the background.

"Mommy says How's Mardi Gras?"

"It's great. I wish you were down here."

"Did you see the Wild Magnolias?" She always pronounced every syllable in their name; it tore his heart out—Mag-no-lee-uhs . . .

"Yep, they were out there right by H&R Bar. They came out of a U-Haul truck." Annie was saying something to Alice. "I got you a Zulu coconut," he said.

"Yay," Annie said. "Are you coming home tomorrow?"

Craig took a deep breath from his stomach. "I'll head up tomorrow but it'll take me two days, so I'll see you on Thursday."

"I want you to see my painting."

"I can't wait," he said. "I'm proud of you."

"I miss you," Annie said. "What . . . ? Mommy wants to say bye."

"Bye, sweetie," Craig said. In front of him two men dressed as Laurel and Hardy passed.

"Are you okay?" Alice asked.

"It's really fucking sad being down here without you guys," he said.

"I know," Alice said. "I've been thinking about you all day. I didn't want to call because I didn't know if you wanted to be in it, if it would be an interruption . . ."

"Yeah," he said.

"Craig."

"Yeah."

"I wish we were down there, too. We'll do it next year."

"Okay."

"Promise."

"Okay," he said. Three people dressed up like bags of M&Ms walked past.

"We're going to work it out," she said. "In the meantime, can you just try and be there today? This day means so much to you. Don't waste it."

He looked around, at the Pontalba Apartments, at Andrew Jackson's horse rearing up, at the cathedral, and he nodded as if she could see. "I'm doing my best," he said.

"It's a promise, right? Remember 'Next year in Jerusalem, I mean the Ninth Ward . . .'?"

Craig remembered this, but, "Who said that, again?"

"Doug, that year he dressed like the Hassid and Connie dressed in the Arab robes?"

"Oh, God," Craig said, and even managed a laugh. "Yeah. 'Next year at the Saturn Bar.'"

"There you go," she said.

"Thank you, Alice," he said.

"Go on and eat a pork chop sandwich someplace," she said. "Call me later. Or earlier. Okay?"

"Okay."

After they hung up and Craig put the phone back in his pocket he sat on the bench for a while, and then he made his way up toward Rampart Street. When he got there he heard a band in the distance, and he kept walking across to Basin Street, where the last stragglers of the Zulu foot parade were following the procession toward the Treme. Craig noticed one man in the middle of a group of people, dancing wildly and waving what looked like sticks in the air. He moved closer and saw that it was a man in his thirties or forties, obviously missing one leg, dancing, balancing himself and thrusting a crutch up in the air in time to the distant music.

Craig watched him dance off along with the rest of them into the distance. What a spirit, he thought. What defiance. What human beauty. How can I leave this? What am I doing? And as soon as he thought this, an answering thought came—perhaps some spirit had passed into him from the dancer on the crutches—but Craig heard himself think, What are you talking about, man? Most of these people lost everything, and they are dancing.

The last few stragglers passed him, black and white, holding beer cans in the air, most of them doing steps in time to the barely audible music, while he stood there with his face hanging out.

What's wrong, man? The day won't last forever, so you don't want to play? He watched everyone heading off into the distance, dancing exactly because the day wouldn't last forever. Hadn't he learned anything during his time in New Orleans? You're supposed to dance while you have the chance. Because it won't last forever. Like them. Like you are supposed to be.

Run.

And with his heart leaping Craig took off, running, toward the sound of the band, to join in while it lasted.

2 8

The van turned onto what had been North Derbigny Street. Next to SJ in the front seat, Wesley carried the surprisingly small plastic box containing Lucy's ashes. He was very quiet; like everyone else who had made this trip, he was unprepared for what he saw.

It was the morning after Mardi Gras. Ten hours earlier, at midnight, the trucks had come out to clean the streets of the French Quarter, and police cars cruised the streets slowly, announcing that Mardi Gras was officially over. But no announcements had been necessary in the Lower Ninth Ward.

They spoke very little to each other. In front of a church, someone had put up a wooden sign, with black letters on a white background, reading LOWER 9TH WARD RESTORATION. CAN THESE BONES LIVE? O YE DRY BONES HEAR THE WORD OF THE LORD! EZEKIEL 37. 1-7. SJ noted all the cleanup that had gone on since his first visit three months earlier. Much garbage had been removed and quite a few properties bulldozed already. In the distance, one or two other cars crawled along the streets, like mourners searching for a gravesite in a cemetery.

SJ pulled up in front of his house, put the van in park and left it idling. Some of the garbage that had been piled in the driveway was gone. Now it would be easier to get inside, and that made him worry about whether looters had finally gotten to it.

"Do you want to go inside?" he asked his nephew.

Wesley sat in the passenger seat. He stared at the house for a long time without answering.

"I don't know," Wesley said, finally.

SJ shut the van off and they got out. He stood by the driver's door, looking around at the ruined landscape, and Wesley did the same on the passenger side. Neither of them made a move toward the house.

It would not be impossible to rebuild the house, SJ thought. All it would take was time. And energy, and willpower, and money. The entire front would have to be reframed. The whole first floor would have to be gutted back to the studs. That was carpentry; he knew how to do that. All the wood would have to be treated for mold. All the wiring would have to be replaced, and possibly the plumbing, too.

Above the porch overhang, a piece of the fascia that had finished the original roof hung down at an angle. SJ noticed it, and it bothered him. He wanted to nail that slat back up into position. With everything else so messed up, why would that one piece bother him? But before he left town he was going to fix that, at least. That would be his down payment.

"Look, Unca J."

"What?" SJ said.

"That your truck? The back of it over there."

Off to the left of the house, on what had been the yard next door, its rear sticking out from a hill of garbage, its maroon paint job still visible despite the striated lines of muck and silt that covered it. SJ hadn't seen it on his first trip. It had been hidden by the mountain of garbage.

He walked toward the truck.

SJ took his handkerchief out of his back pocket and used it to grab the handle of the rear double doors. A grayish brown dust came off on the kerchief as he tried to twist the handle down into the open position, but the handle would not budge. The rear window on the right-hand door had been broken out, and carefully, carefully, SJ reached in, and down, through the jagged-edged opening until he could grasp the interior latch. It grated and rotated slightly, and the bottom of the door popped out and SJ hopped down onto the ground and opened the door, grinding on its hinges, the rest of the way.

An overwhelming smell of mold rolled out of the truck. The carpeting on the truck floor was still sopping wet and covered with obscene fuzz, greenish in the light from the door. His tools were disrupted, scattered; the truck had been pushed by the water's surge, and the board along the right side on which he had secured wire cutters, cords and the like, had come loose and fallen over. The electrical cables would be useless, the fiberglass ropes more or less useless. Hacksaws rusted and useless, screwdrivers . . . His spare ladder lay along the left side, and that looked as if it might be usable.

Then, remembering something, he climbed in, pushing the collapsed hanging board out of the way, and he made his way closer to the rear of the driver's seat, looking for a line of jars that he had always kept in the truck, secured by two bungee cords. And they were there; he found them—three small mason jars containing nails. Their heavy, toggle-catch glass lids were secured over the rubber rings with the little tongues that stuck out, and he flipped the first one with some effort, the metal cap was corroded, but the latch finally opened, and he unhooked it and inside the jar the nails were completely dry. His father's nails, still in the jars where he had kept them. SJ had saved them and kept them in the truck as a reminder of his father, of the effort he had gone through, the ingenuity, the strength. There they were, still. He stood looking at the jar in the dim light in the back of his ruined truck.

The other two jars were in the same condition. Carefully, he removed them from the special shelf he had made for them and carried them, stepping down out of the back of the truck, over to the van.

"These were your grandfather's," he said to Wesley. "This is how he kept them."

Wesley knew about the nails, had heard it many times. But this time he looked; this time it meant something to him.

"They been in that jar for forty-five years. Probably longer." SJ stood up straight, looked around, holding the jars. After a few moments, he grabbed his windbreaker off one of the van's backseats and wrapped the jars in it and set them gently back on the seat. Then he and Wesley made their way to the front of the house, climbing carefully around piles of debris.

Inside, the house was as SJ had seen it in November, nothing changed except that the mold was heavier on the walls. They went upstairs, and then they came back down and walked back out by the van. They were as quiet as they might have been viewing a body at a wake.

"Should we go by Tennessee Street?" Wesley said. They had discussed earlier where to put Lucy's ashes. Wesley had asked SJ, and SJ had told him that he was a man, now. "You decide," SJ had said, "and we'll do it together."

"Is that where you want to do it?" SJ asked his nephew, now.

"I don't know. That might be good."

"You want to drive over?"

"I want to walk."

Wesley opened the passenger door and retrieved the small box, and the two of them set off walking up North Derbigny. The closer they got to Tennessee Street, the more the neighborhood resembled a huge, sprawling field that had been used to dump garbage. Here and there a house pushed off its piers and somehow more or less intact, although at an impossible angle. Cement steps leading nowhere, upside-down cars, computers with broken screens, pots and pans, all corroded, chairs with the fabric ripped off. They walked until they came to what had been Tennessee Street, and there they made a right until they came to the place where Lucy's house had stood. All that was left was a small section of hurricane fence on what had been the right side of the yard. Wesley looked at the lot for a long time.

"It's all right to cry, son," SJ said.

"I know," Wesley said. "What's gonna happen to this? They going to turn it into a park?"

"I don't know," SJ said. "The people still own their property."

Wesley looked around. "I don't want to leave her here," he said. "It feel like she just gonna blow away."

SJ nodded.

"What are you gonna do with your house, Unca J?"

SJ was quiet for a few moments. "Long term, I don't know," he said. "That land is ours. The house can be rebuilt, and I am going to rebuild it." He looked around in the morning light. "I know I'm not ready to move to Houston. Not yet. And I am not going to be run off my own property."

"I can help you with the house, Unca J."

SJ nodded, thoughtfully. "You have a lot of decisions to make. I don't see that this is necessarily the place where you want to be right now. You doing well, you got you a nice girl . . . You got life in front of you. I got some of my crew going to come back, you know; it's not like I'm not going to have help. There's going to be a lot of work in town. That would be something for you, I guess . . . But you would have to do it for you, not for me. You're not really tied here so much, as far as I can see."

Wesley nodded. "But you are going to fix the house?"

"Yes," SJ said.

"Can we put Mama down by you? We can bury the box by your house."

"All right," SJ said. "Let's do that."

They walked back to SJ's through what was left of the old neighborhood. It was a sorrow too large for words, just as their own presence there, or anywhere, was a mystery too large for comprehension. *There they were* was all you could say. What they did with that fact would make all the difference.

SJ had brought his toolbox from Houston, along with a shovel. When they got back to his house he got the shovel out of the van and they looked around to find a good place for Lucy's ashes, where they could be on the property but not get dug up when work was being done. They decided on a place by an oak tree in the backyard, if they could dig deeply enough between the tree's roots. When they had dug down about three feet they stopped, and Wesley got the black plastic box, brought it to the hole. SJ looked at him, noted the hesitation.

"What's wrong?" he asked his nephew.

"It weird putting her down in a box like this," he said. "It don't look like nothing. It look like it just come down to a plastic box," he said.

SJ closed his eyes, breathed. All the years that came down to that box, but did they? Wesley was doing something with the box. SJ watched his nephew open it, look into it. Tiny pieces of bone in a pound of ash . . . Wesley looked at his uncle.

"I'm-a pour it in, Unca J. Is that okay? Otherwise it like she just another piece of garbage or something, a plastic box. This way she here, she part of it. All right?"

"Go on," SJ said.

Go on home, Loot, SJ thought. We are here.

Wesley crouched down and looked into the hole in the ground. Then he took the black plastic box that contained all that remained of his mother in the material world and shook its contents in to mix with the earth in the only home she had ever known.

SJ watched, thinking but not saying the old words about ashes to ashes and dust to dust. His nephew finished pouring in the contents of the plastic box and then remained, squatting and looking down, weeping. He was proud of Wesley for being able to weep. After giving him a few moments, SJ stepped over to him and put his hand on his nephew's shoulder.

Wesley ran his forearm across his eyes, then stood up, nodding. They took turns shoveling the dirt back into the hole, mixing the ashes in with the soil. SJ nailed together a cross out of two pieces of weatherboard and drove it into the ground to mark the spot for a more permanent marker later. On the horizontal board he used a carpenter's pencil to write her name. They had done what there was to be done, and they carried the shovel around to the front of the house, climbing over and around the smashed wood and debris.

They stood together in front of the house, looking around wordlessly. It was late morning. SJ again noticed the fascia board hanging down. He could fix that at least.

Craig found himself stopping every half a block or so as his car crawled through the wreckage of the Lower Ninth Ward, stunned at some new angle of perception on what was inconceivable. He had decided before leaving to drive around town for an hour or so and take pictures of some of the worst-hit areas to show people in Chicago. People needed to see what had happened. He had locked the front door of his house, left the key in the mailbox for the new owners, then walked down the brick walk to the curb, to his car, and looked back at his house one last time. Then he had headed out, first to Lakeview and then to the Lower Nine.

The bastards, he thought as he drove and stared. The bastards who let this happen—who built the levees wrong, who didn't inspect them, who wouldn't listen to the reports of the problems all over the city, who didn't care enough, who didn't know that you had to take care of what was important, that it didn't just take care of itself. Who wouldn't fund the restoration because it could cost almost as much as a month of the war in Iraq. They were not going to sweep this under the rug. He would tell everyone he knew.

He took dozens of photos; he planned to do presentations and slide shows about this. People knew him in Chicago now; the *CHI EYE* could sponsor the lectures. If he wasn't going to live in New Orleans, he was at least not going to abandon it. This was not going to drop off the radar. He found himself almost choking with grief and fury as he drove down the wasted streets.

At one corner, Craig looked to his left and saw two men a block and a half away, in front of a ruined house, one on a ladder, one on the ground. He turned left onto the street and drove slowly in their direction, until he was at the next corner, half a block from them. If the men noticed him, they gave no sign. The man on the ladder was doing something to the façade of his house, which looked to Craig as if it had been wrecked, the front torn off. Still, it was one of the few left standing. The man on the ladder had hold of a piece of wood and was trying to lift it into position. The man on the ground was handing him something. Repairing a house, Craig thought. In the midst of this devastation.

What kind of person, Craig wondered? If you lived here, and lived through this, what kind of person did it take to come back and get on a ladder and start making repairs? To rebuild a life out of these ruins?

Craig put the car into park, rolled down his window, positioned his camera and zoomed in, framing the shot carefully, and took his last picture of the day. Later, he would put it above his work desk in Elkton, as a reminder of exactly what he needed to keep in focus for himself. Then, with a final look, he pulled the car around and headed out of the Lower Ninth Ward, to the northbound interstate and his new life.

• • •

The fascia board lifted easily into position, and SJ put his pocket level on it to make sure it was true. This was how you built something, he thought, as he had many times before. One step at a time. Touching the wood, even among the ruins, gave him an unreasoning happiness, the happiness from which all other happiness flowed. Maybe especially among the ruins. There was wood all around; he would build his house back from pieces of the wreckage. And on every piece of wood he would write the name of someone from the Nine until he ran out of names he could remember, and then he would start over again. Every piece of wood. As long as he had something to build, he thought, and a place to start.

SJ dug two nails out of his pocket and set them between his teeth. Then he looked down at Wesley. "It's straight?" he said.

Wesley nodded.

"Good," SJ said. "Hand me that hammer."